HE NEEDED TO KISS HER

Nathan saw the anticipation on Lydia's face, but instead of shying away as he knew he would if she'd been anyone else, he felt drawn by it. So many years had passed since he'd held a woman so close or been tempted by lips as soft and appealing as hers. He barely noticed the streaks of plaster dust on her cheeks and in her brows or the smudge of grime on her chin. He only took heed of her natural feminine scent, which mixed nicely with that of rose water still clinging to her skin from an earlier bath. For a moment he wondered if he ought to do this, if he would regret it, or if she would regret it, but when her eyes fluttered shut he knew she would take her chances the same as he would. With his hands around her shoulders, he drew her closer until his lips touched hers and her breath met his. He knew she could feel the heavy beating of his heart where her hands lay trapped against his chest, but it was too late to pretend he didn't care. So he gave in to the need that gripped him, the need to taste her, to feel her lips beneath his, searching, searching. . . .

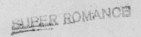

Abiding Hope

Melody Morgan

LEISURE BOOKS   NEW YORK CITY

To my sister Gerri,
A little laughter and some fun, a little more laughter
and a little more fun, a lotta laughter and a lotta fun!
That's the way life goes when you're around,
so don't ever stop laughing.
Love,
M.M.

A LEISURE BOOK®

March 1999

Published by

Dorchester Publishing Co., Inc.
276 Fifth Avenue
New York, NY 10001

ISBN 0-8439-4493-5

The name "Leisure Books" and the stylized "L" with design are trademarks of Dorchester Publishing Co., Inc.

Printed in the United States of America.

Abiding Hope

Chapter One

Peaceful Valley, Ohio, 1892

Lydia Jefferson rose to her feet, her heart thumping loudly in her chest as her hands gripped the edge of the square-backed chair in front of her. One would guess by a quick glance around the room that the entire town had congregated in the small schoolhouse. Every inch of space had been taken as concerned citizens squeezed into the seats between desks or stood two deep along the outside walls until there was almost no fresh air to breathe. The large windows had been raised, but little if any breeze circulated through the room.

"Do you want to say something, Miss Jefferson?" asked Mayor Butterfield.

"Yes," Lydia replied, then took a deep breath. She wasn't afraid, not really. It was just that her greatest dream was at her fingertips, finally within reach, and she realized

7

these people had the power to end that dream, or at least postpone it. For thirteen years she had hoped for a moment such as this, and now she was about to expose her deepest wish for everyone to see. If they refused her request or laughed at her . . . well, she didn't think she could possibly bear the disappointment.

"Yes," she repeated. "I'd like to purchase the house, to be used as a children's home." Her breath felt trapped in her chest, and she didn't dare look directly at the faces surrounding her that suddenly turned to stare. Instead, she focused her gaze on the mayor's waxed and curled moustache.

"You want to what?" Mayor Butterfield looked as though he was certain he hadn't heard her correctly. But he had.

"Purchase the house," she said, her voice returning to its normal steadiness. Now that she'd actually spoken her dream, she felt the familiar enthusiasm stir within her.

"But the council has already agreed that the house is an eyesore and needs to be torn down. This meeting is simply to decide what we should replace it with," said the mayor.

"And I'm suggesting a home for homeless children." She couldn't abide the word *orphanage* and all its negative connotations.

She could hear only part of the whispers going on around her as all heads bobbed with incredulity, including those of the rest of the town council seated beside Mayor Butterfield.

"And just where do you propose to get the money?" asked Mr. Davis, the town's only banker.

"I'm prepared to pay in cash," she replied, hoping that it wouldn't exceed her savings. She had worked and saved every possible penny since she'd started teaching.

"One doesn't just 'open' an orphanage, my dear," Mrs.

Butterfield said from the front row near the platform where her husband sat. "And I hardly think being a schoolteacher qualifies as a proper credential, especially when it's the *only* credential."

How wrong they were if everyone believed as Mrs. Butterfield, Lydia thought. She was qualified where it counted, in her life experiences and in her heart. Being a teacher had been part of her plan to learn everything she could about children. She was more than qualified, and she felt strong in her resolve to obtain this particular house.

"I mean," Mrs. Butterfield continued, enjoying the attention everyone paid to her words, "not that your goals aren't commendable, but reality is such that one needs only to see that you are alone. And how can one woman possibly look after all the needs of so many children?"

"I manage every day in the classroom, Mrs. Butterfield."

Conceding on that point, although Agnes Butterfield hated to do so since all her friends from the Monday Morning Coffee Club were watching, she went on to say, "Then I assume you'll be leaving the school?"

"Yes." And that was another problem. She needed funds in order to operate her home. Just buying the house would take everything she had. Charity would be hard to accept, but she saw no other way. She'd known that without a source of income her only possible chance of financially maintaining a home for children was through donations, as all privately owned orphanages were funded. But the opportunity of getting the house had come before the promise of money, and she was going to take that opportunity. She must abide in the hope that the money would soon follow.

There were children out there, somewhere and everywhere, who needed homes just as she and her brother, Jonathan, had needed a home, but not many of them would be fortunate enough to find a family like her foster mother and father. How many nights had she lain awake thinking about the children who lived in loveless orphanages, or just as bad, those who were "farmed out" to families who didn't really want them. And then there were those, like Jonathan and herself, who ran away and lived as best they could. No, she could not allow accepting charity to become a stumbling block. If need be, she would swallow her pride on behalf of those homeless children.

But first things first, and that meant purchasing the house.

Deacon Jones, who was actually an elder in the Baptist church, stood up. "A young woman can hardly expect to make repairs to that old house."

"Then perhaps some good citizens would contribute their talents," she replied.

All heads turned toward Nathan Stockwell, who sat silently with his arms crossed over his chest as his chair rested on its back two legs. Lydia saw the surprise that registered on his face, then one of firm refusal replaced it as his chair landed solidly on all fours.

"Sorry," he said with a shake of his head. "Too busy."

She knew it was probably true. He was by profession a wheelwright, but he also did any and all woodworking jobs that came his way, from mending porches to building coffins. She'd never seen a man who kept himself so busy. Still, he was the most logical choice and she knew she must approach him at a later time.

Then Hattie Arthur rose to her sturdy feet. "I believe you all have overlooked something here." She glanced around as though they were simple minded. "You want a bunch of undisciplined young'uns running through our streets? With nary a care for your flowerbeds and gardens? Or your white linens hangin' on the line to dry?"

Mrs. Butterfield, who at that moment almost considered

asking Hattie to join the M.M.C.C., added her agreement. "One must consider the consequences of such an undertaking. I, for one, do not wish to have *my* roses trampled."

"Nor I," added another member of the M.M.C.C.

"Me neither," said yet another member.

Lydia stared in disbelief at the group assembled before her. She had lived in this town for over three years and thought they were all compassionate people, but apparently she'd been wrong. They were selfish in not wanting to share their beautiful little town, or their talents. In her eyes, that made them worse than the undisciplined children they feared; after all, they were the adults! She never would have guessed that the townspeople would prevent her dream from becoming reality; she had always thought, *if only I could raise the money.* Shock and dismay brought words of reproach to her mind, and she didn't hold them back.

"How many of you know what it is like to wonder if you will have a place to sleep when nightfall comes? How many of you have wondered and worried if you'll eat today or tomorrow or even the next day? And how many of you have ever fallen asleep as a child wishing for your mother or father to hold you in their arms, only they can't because they are gone forever?" Her gaze roamed over the now silent room. The authority in her voice held them captive while the schoolteacher within her scolded the child within them.

"That's a very commendable speech, Miss Jefferson. I couldn't have said it better myself," said Preacher Ted, who led the flock at the Baptist church.

Always on the opposing side, Pastor Michaels, from the Presbyterian church at the opposite side of town spoke up. "I think we need to keep one foot logically placed on the ground. Exactly how do you propose to support this home for children?"

She had a plan, but that wasn't the issue in front of the council. The issue was whether they would sell her the house and for what price, but she could see that they were going to require some sort of an answer anyway. She glanced around the room at the pinched-faced frowns staring back at her, but she wasn't sure she was willing to have the rest of her dream treated so heartlessly. So Lydia relied once more on the answer she'd given to Deacon Jones. "Perhaps a few good citizens with a conscience would contribute anything in the way of food or clothing. . . ." But she could see she was asking too much. They did not want a children's home in their town. It was as simple as that.

"Well," Mayor Butterfield said, glancing quickly at his wife as he tugged his watch from the pocket on his vest. "I fear we've come to an impasse. I am of the mind that the council should discuss this latest development and then bring it before the town once more."

"I second that," replied Mr. Davis.

All heads of the council nodded in agreement.

"Therefore, we'll adjourn this meeting until further notice." He hammered his polished gavel on the table, announcing the end of the town meeting.

Everyone stood up to depart, while Lydia sat down in defeat.

The crush of people soon passed down the aisle and out of the building as Lydia sat staring at her hands. How had this happened, she wondered? She had planned so long for this moment, dreamed about it, worked hard for it, and when the opportunity finally arrived, the response was an overwhelming "no."

Disheartened, she left the nearly empty schoolhouse and walked home alone. No, not home. She hadn't been home since last summer and with spring fast approaching that meant nearly a year had gone by. How she needed her family right then with their cheerful faces and positive attitudes, instead of these dour-faced old hypocrites.

With the sun slipping past the horizon, she walked along the street where the house in question stood waiting for either its demise or its renovation. She gazed with longing at the weatherbeaten house that stood like a poorly dressed, unwanted orphan against the beautiful meadow behind it. The two-story frame construction, nearly bare of paint, had long, arched windows on the second floor and shorter rectangular ones on the first, giving it a haphazard appearance. It was boxy yet L-shaped, and had an addition on the back that looked like an afterthought, being single-storied with an almost flat roof. The one saving grace was the wide porch that extended across the front and nestled into the corner of the L-shape. Not by any stretch of the imagination would anyone call it a lovely house.

But Lydia envisioned a porch with posts that stood upright and the entire house painted pristine white. She imagined homemade curtains that fluttered behind unbroken windowpanes and children leaning out, calling to friends who passed by. But the real truth of the matter was that it was simply a dream. In reality, the porch had nearly collapsed on one end with most of the supports missing, the paint had long since peeled off, and most of the windows had broken glass.

Nevertheless, she wanted the house. The cost should be minimal under the circumstances and that was an important factor. She was willing to roll up her sleeves and set to work whether it be with hammer, paintbrush or broom. This was her house. How could they tell her no? Nobody wanted it, nobody but her. And where would she ever find another house she could afford?

Feeling as though she'd failed, she continued on toward the Graylings' house, where she now lived.

If only one person had stood up for her, had seen the good that could come of this, had offered their help, she might still have a chance. But other than Preacher Ted, not one had taken her side.

She let herself in the back door, where a single lamp glowed warmly on the kitchen table. Removing her hat and gloves, she listened for the sound of voices, but the house was unusually quiet since the inhabitants, all but herself and Sarah, had gone to visit family in the country. Lydia peeked inside the pie safe and finding half of a custard pie, she cut a small wedge. Then after pouring herself a glass of milk from the icebox, she sat at the table and pondered her situation.

"Back so soon?" Sarah asked, coming into the kitchen. She, too, cut a small piece of pie and joined Lydia at the table.

"I'm afraid so." She picked at a flake of crust, pushing it around the plate.

"Didn't go well, I take it." Sarah took a sip of milk from Lydia's glass.

Lydia set aside her fork and pushed the milk toward Sarah. "Not at all."

"Let me guess . . ." Sarah began, her elbow propped on the table and her fork pointed upward. "Mrs. Butterfield and the M.M.C.C. just couldn't abide the thought of so many uncivilized children on the loose." She scooped a chunk of custard and popped it to her mouth.

"In so many words, yes."

"You mean, using many, many words, don't you?"

A small smile teased Lydia's lips. "I guess you're right about that." Sarah had an honest approach to everything and Lydia loved her for it. They were kindred spirits in more ways than one.

"Oh, don't let her get you down. She only acts like that

because she's never had any children of her own to love."
She popped the last of her pie into her mouth then washed
it down with the rest of Lydia's milk. "And imagine the
poor things if she had."

Lydia laughed. "You're right. The poor things."

"Didn't anybody like your idea?"

"Preacher Ted said it was commendable."

Sarah waved her hand in the air. "That's because Pastor
Michaels was there I'll bet."

"He was."

"They never see eye to eye on anything, including the
best way to get into heaven," Sarah said with a devilish
grin. "Why, I heard that Preacher Ted secretly kisses the
young girls in his church."

"Sarah!" There wasn't much that shocked Lydia, but
this was truly an exception.

"That's what I heard," she insisted, then shrugged her
shoulders. "Of course, he isn't married so I suppose he
would kiss young girls, since all the old ones are taken."

Lydia leaned back in her chair, listening to Sarah's idle
gossip. Since the younger girl was only seventeen and
Lydia was twenty four, it was a wonder that Sarah hadn't
considered her one of the "old ones." But she hadn't—
mostly because she admired Lydia's goals and hoped to
have such fine goals herself someday. Getting married
wasn't the only thing in life, Sarah had told her many times,
and it certainly wasn't the best thing.

Whether it was the best thing or not, marriage had never
entered Lydia's mind either. She'd seldom considered that
path, so focused was her determination to have a children's
home. And that hadn't changed in spite of the setback she'd
endured that evening.

Sarah reached for Lydia's unfinished pie. "So what will
you do now?"

"I'm not sure. But I'm not giving up until they actually tear the house down."

"Why don't you talk to Papa about this?"

Lydia hadn't said a word to anyone but Sarah until tonight, and surprisingly enough, Sarah hadn't spread the news to a soul.

"What could your father do?"

"Maybe he could talk to Mr. Davis. They're friends, you know. Sort of. And maybe he could convince Mr. Davis to give you a loan or something. I'm sure if Papa had known what you were going to do at the meeting tonight, he would have been there and put in a good word for you. But since he wasn't, I can ask him to talk to Mr. Davis if you'd like."

"I don't think that's the main issue. Although, it certainly is part of it." Lydia sighed, unable to keep a little bit of her depression from seeping in. "I need funds to keep it going, too."

"Mmm. I see." Sarah leaned back in her chair, crossing her arms, thinking.

The room grew silent while the two young women considered numerous possibilities, none of which seemed like real solutions.

"If they would just let me buy the house . . ."

"Then we could have socials and benefits to raise money to fix it up."

"Sarah! That's an excellent idea!" Lydia nearly came off her chair. "A little competition would add some spice, too."

Sarah's eyes shone. "The Baptist church against the Presbyterian church. The M.M.C.C. against the Peaceful Valley Garden Club."

"Everyone could donate something that they're good at. Like Hattie Arthur's apple butter," said Lydia. "Everyone has something that they're proud to show off."

Sarah chuckled. "Mr. Stockwell could donate a walnut coffin," she offered in jest. "Nobody makes 'em better than Stoney Stockwell."

"A walnut coffin?" Lydia asked in disbelief as a light shudder crossed her neck.

"Sure, why not? He makes all kinds of things out of wood and I hear his coffins are in demand clear down to Cincinnati. But *you'll* have to ask him." Sarah raised both hands, palms out. "I'd rather talk to the dead person in it than the one who made it."

"He can't be that bad." But Lydia remembered the hard expression on his face when he'd said, "Sorry. Too busy."

"Well, you'll just have to see for yourself," Sarah said, giving a knowing nod of her head. But Lydia decided that was one donation they could do without.

Chapter Two

Mayor Butterfield pounded his gavel three times before anyone paid him any heed.

"See here, now! This meeting is called to order!" He smacked his gavel once more then everybody quieted. "That's more like it." He cleared his throat.

"As you know, we're here tonight concerning the old Mercer place. And as you also know we've had an offer to purchase the property as it now stands. But I have recently been reminded that this property was left to the town by way of an unfortunate inheritance, that is, we being the unfortunate ones. It has also been brought to my attention that the cost of tearing it down is a burden this town doesn't need nor does it want."

He raised his eyebrows as he surveyed the crowd to see if anyone disagreed. None did.

"So," he went on, "this council is of the unanimous

opinion that it be sold to Miss Jefferson for . . ." He paused, holding everyone enthralled.

Lydia held her breath, not daring to believe her ears! They were going to sell it to her after all! The house would be hers and so her dream would come true, at long last. With a thudding heart, she closed her eyes and sent up a silent prayer of thanks.

". . . five hundred dollars," finished Mayor Butterfield.

A collective gasp went up from the crowd, including Lydia.

"That is what we agreed upon. There are taxes that have to be paid for the years that the town owned the house and, after all, it was supposed to be a benefit to the community, which it never was. Until now. Plus," he went on, raising his voice over the growing murmur of the crowd, "she has three months to make the necessary improvements. Otherwise, she forfeits it."

Lydia sat dumbstruck. Five hundred dollars! And only three months to make repairs. Never had she anticipated such a gamble.

Sarah reached over and squeezed her hand in reassurance that she could do it. When Lydia looked at her, she saw her own spirit reflected in Sarah's eyes. Then, rising to her feet, with her chin lifted, she said, "Thank you."

Around her, the townspeople sat immobilized in apparent turmoil. On one hand, they didn't want an orphanage in their midst with its wild children on the loose, on the other hand, the agreement was unfair. Who could possibly live up to those outrageous terms? And why would she want to?

Lydia sat back down, and the ebb and flow of voices slowly penetrated her stunned mind. Here and there she heard snatches of conversation above the hubbub of shuffling feet and chair legs scraping the wooden floor.

"Poor dear . . ." said one of Preacher Ted's flock.

"Imagine, five hundred . . ." said one from the Presbyterian church.

"Young'uns or no young'uns," said Hattie Arthur, "it's unfair to expect . . ."

A change of attitude had overcome nearly everybody.

"Well, I'd say we have our work cut out for us, wouldn't you?" Sarah asked.

Lydia could only nod. Their work was indeed cut out for them, and in no uncertain terms.

A few of the Ladies from the M.M.C.C. walked by with concern plainly visible on their usually bored faces. Some even reached out to pat her shoulder, although not all felt so inclined to offer support. Agnes Butterfield simply arched a brow at Lydia as she passed.

Then Mr. and Mrs. Grayling stopped to speak to Lydia.

"Congratulations are in order. I think," said Mr. Grayling. "It certainly is a mixed bag."

"I'll accept the congratulations, thank you," she replied. "I'm sure your influence had an effect on their change of mind. Thank you, again."

With a half-grimace, half-smile, he said, "I did what I could. I wish it had been more."

"We'll see the two of you at home later," added Mrs. Grayling. Then they blended into the crowd as it exited the double doors.

Lydia and Sarah gradually made their way through the thinning group into the cool night air. Around them budding lilacs added their delicate scent to the heavier one of turned soil.

"I'll organize the first benefit since you still have another week of school," offered Sarah. "I don't know why we couldn't use the schoolhouse for that. After all," she lowered her voice conspiratorially, "it's neutral territory."

"I'm glad someone still has a sense of humor," Lydia commented drily.

With a nonchalant shrug of her shoulders, Sarah said, "I think it will all be great fun."

"Fun? I would hardly call begging for funds 'great fun.' "

"Oh, I do. When do you suppose the M.M.C.C. would ever have a better opportunity to out-do the Peaceful Valley Garden Club?"

"Or vice-versa," Lydia countered, showing her obvious support for the latter.

"Aha!" Sarah chortled. "Do I detect a note of interest in the competition here?"

"Just barely. I'm more interested in what I need to do to get those repairs completed within three months. Three months, for heaven's sake! And me with almost no money."

"Well, there's still Stoney Stockwell to be considered. But as I said before, that will have to be up to you." She shook her head. "*I* wouldn't approach him without a sack of sugar to dust him with first."

"Sarah, you're exaggerating. I'll admit he seems a little . . . foreboding, but I'm sure that's because he concentrates so hard on his work. And he's always working."

Lydia had never had the occasion to speak to Nathan Stockwell other than passing him on the street, and even that was unusual. More often than not, he could be glimpsed in the dim interior of his shop as he worked, like a shadow that appeared and was gone again. The smell of fresh-cut lumber seeped out into the street, a clean, pungent reminder to passers-by of the nature of his work. There were very few houses in town that didn't display his work-manship in one form or another.

"You could be right, but I've heard he hates children."

Lydia halted dead in her tracks. "Now why would he hate children? And why would anybody say such an awful thing?"

"I don't know . . . to both of those questions. I only know the stories that I've heard the younger ones tell each other."

"Well, I don't believe it for a moment," Lydia responded, resuming her pace. "I'm sure there's no basis for them."

They walked on in silence, the boardwalk hard beneath their heels.

Snatching a leaf from an overhanging bush, Sarah looked sideways at Lydia. "Are you going to ask him?"

"I suppose I'll have to. He's the only logical answer to my problem." But to herself she admitted she would as soon ask to become a lifetime member of the M.M.C.C.

Lydia stood outside the double doors to the woodworking shop. There was no sign to advertise the sort of business within, but then no sign was needed since everybody within fifty miles knew of Nathan Stockwell's quality work. No matter what he did, he did it to perfection, and everyone had come to count on that.

The coolness inside was a blessed change from the unusual warmth of the day and Lydia welcomed it as she pulled at her damp cotton shirtwaist below the neckline.

"Mr. Stockwell?" she called as she looked around at the heavy harness, hammers, saws and assorted metal tools that hung on the walls. Through another door of an attached lean-to came the sound of a saw rasping against wood, sending a pleasant sappy smell into the air. Stepping around an unfinished cabinet, she made her way toward the doorway of the lean-to and stood hesitantly on the threshold.

"Excuse me," Lydia said when she found him.

He glanced up from his work with a frown, then resumed cutting the board beneath his knee. She swallowed hard, but refused to be put off, reminding herself that the stories Sarah had heard were most likely untrue and he was, after all, just a man.

She waited patiently for the saw to eat through the pine board and fall to the floor while she studied him. He was of moderate height, sturdily built and cleanly dressed. A lock of thick dark hair fell across his forehead, defiant, unmanageable and stubborn. Somehow this seemed indicative of his nature, even though she really didn't know him at all.

The clatter of the board upon the pine floor signaled an opportunity to approach him, but she couldn't quite bring herself actually to step closer, so she began again from where she stood.

"Mr. Stockwell, if you have a moment—"

"I told you," he interrupted without so much as a glance in her direction, "I'm too busy. That includes yesterday, today and tomorrow." He turned his back to her in dismissal as he selected another board for sawing.

Her mouth dropped open with astonishment at his blatant rudeness. Perhaps those stories were true after all. She set her teeth together, added more determination to the tilt of her shoulders and went on.

"As I was saying—"

"Look, Miss Jeffries—"

"Jefferson," she corrected.

"I don't have time to argue with you, so I'll make it as plain as I can. I'm too busy to donate work and I'm not in the business of building orphanages."

"How sad for you," she replied, emphasizing the word "you."

At last she had his full attention as his gold-flecked brown-eyed gaze settled on her. A note of warning was clearly communicated, but she refused to be intimidated. Obviously, she could not force him to help her but she intended to leave him with a piece of her mind, a very honest and straightforward piece of her mind.

"I can't imagine how a person such as yourself got the reputation for being such a reprehensible individual or why you would care to cultivate that reputation, but I will say that the shoe certainly fits." With that said, she turned and made her way back through the first room, around the cabinet and out into the sunshine, where she nearly ran over Mrs. Marting in her haste to get away.

"Excuse me!" exclaimed Carrie Marting as she daintily sidestepped Lydia.

"Oh, pardon me," said Lydia, reaching out to steady the other woman. Although recently widowed, Carrie hardly fit the standard for a mourning wife. Lydia couldn't help but notice, as did everyone, that she was dressed in the latest fashion and her hair was perfectly coiffed in the style of Dana Gibson's "Gibson Girl."

Smiling prettily, the young widow patted Lydia's hand where it rested on her arm, brushing it ever so slightly away. "You must be in quite a hurry." She tipped a little more forward at the waist than the bustle called for in her attempt to look inside the shop. "I hope there isn't a fire."

"No."

"Thank goodness. Nathan is working on a cabinet for me and I wouldn't want anything to happen to it. Or to him either, of course."

"Of course," Lydia replied, trying to keep her irritation with him from her voice.

She suspected Carrie was much more worried about Nathan Stockwell than her cabinet. Until Lydia's controversial

24

purchase of the house, nearly three quarters of the gossip at the M.M.C.C., according to Sarah, was over Carrie Marting's snaring the unsuspecting Mr. Stockwell as her next husband. In Lydia's opinion, they probably deserved each other.

"Well, I don't want to detain you," said Carrie as she continued on her way. "Good day, Miss Jefferson."

Lydia nodded, but her mind was onto a new idea. Carrie had managed to get his attention by paying for his services and while their objectives were quite different, the results would be the same. It was just that in Carrie's situation she wanted it to go farther than the building of a cabinet, but Lydia would be more than happy if she could simply get his attention.

Naturally, this would mean her cost of renovating the house would exceed the already exorbitant amount of five hundred dollars. It irritated her to think that he was such a skinflint he couldn't donate some of his talent for such a worthy cause. Obviously he had no feelings. But if it was business he wanted then it was business he'd get.

Turning around, she marched back inside, crossed the floor of the first room, circumvented the cabinet and stood behind Carrie, who occupied the doorway to the lean-to where Nathan Stockwell worked.

". . . but, Nathan, I have this wonderful recipe for chicken with an absolutely delicious sauce and it makes so much more than I can eat by myself—" Sensing another presence, she stopped and glanced over her shoulder. "Oh, hello again."

"I just wanted to speak to Mr. Stockwell about some business, but I can wait until you're finished."

"I've already told you—" he began, but Lydia interrupted him before he could finish.

"I'm willing to pay for your services," she said.

He stopped what he was doing and stared at her. "Where would you get the money?"

"As long as you get it, does it really matter?"

He shrugged.

"I'll admit I won't be able to pay much, so the work I have you do will have to be only the work that I can't do myself." She would learn to use a hammer and nail even if it meant developing the muscles of a blacksmith.

He raised a skeptical eyebrow at that.

"When would you be able to start?" she asked.

"I didn't say I'd do it, Miss Jeffries."

"Jefferson," she corrected. "And why not? I'm willing to pay."

"I'm too busy."

Lydia forced herself to remain civil even if she didn't want to be polite. She needed this man's help, she told herself. "Won't you at least think about it?"

"I don't need to think about it. I'm too busy."

"In that case, I'll return when you're less busy. Perhaps by then you will have had time to consider it. Surely, a children's home is worthy of some consideration, Mr. Stockwell."

"I said, I don't need to think about it."

His stare chilled her in spite of the heat and she realized she'd better look elsewhere.

"Well, thank you for your time," she replied, and gave him a saccharine smile before turning and making her way back through the building.

When she reached the bright sunshine outside the doors of his shop, she almost welcomed the warmth. He was the most unfeeling, cold-hearted man she'd ever met. Not a charitable bone existed in his body, she was sure. And if he couldn't be any more pleasant and civil than he'd just been, well then, she didn't want him working on her house.

She decided there was no use wasting another thought on the man. She would have to find a way to begin work on the house without Nathan Stockwell.

Carrie assessed the young schoolteacher while gauging the amount of interest Nathan gave the younger woman. Apparently, the two were at odds, so she relaxed and took as deep a breath as her stays would allow. She did not need the interference of someone so young or refreshingly attractive as Lydia Jefferson. Carrie's plans were simple, her mind focused and her goal was within reach, even if Nathan was unaware of it. She would be a good wife and he would not be sorry, she silently promised, smiling secretly as Lydia left in a huff.

"Interesting young woman, wouldn't you say, Nathan?" she asked, trying to ferret out some of his feelings.

He made a grimace then returned to selecting another board to be cut. Carrie smiled broadly and continued on with her current approach: chicken in herb sauce.

"Now, Nathan, I simply won't take 'no' for an answer. I shall have dinner ready at five o'clock sharp and if you aren't at my house by then, I will just have to bring it to you here." She had stepped daintily through the wood shavings until she stood opposite him with the saw rasping the board between them. "Nathan?"

He dropped the board onto the growing pile beside him. "I won't be able to make it."

She gave him the most seductive pout she'd ever practiced and was rewarded with an infinitesimal lift of his brow. "I'll be so disappointed. I enjoy cooking, but I especially enjoy cooking for a man who works as hard as you do." And she meant it with all her heart and soul.

Widowed at the age of thirty, Carrie Marting was husband hunting, again. And it was not a task she relished, since she preferred to get on with the business of life while being well situated and secure, but it was a necessary task.

Less than a year had passed since Samuel had died of a heart attack while splitting wood in their backyard. Being a frugal man, he never paid for what he could do himself, and that principle carried over into the two mercantile establishments he had owned, one in Peaceful Valley and one in a neighboring community. Carrie was the second Mrs. Marting and had found it difficult to live as the second wife in the older home of her husband. So she had pressured Samuel to move to Peaceful Valley and build a new home, which he did. It, too, was modest but at least it was new, and it was *hers*. The moderate-sized two-story house consisted of a front parlor, followed in a line by the dining room and the kitchen. The design of the house called for a side porch that opened into the parlor and dining room, but the turned spindles were a special addition that Carrie had pouted over until she'd gotten her way. Upstairs were two bedrooms. One was for the two of them and the other for guests. Carrie had no intention of having children and marring her figure or her social life. Samuel had been very considerate of her delicate nature and had not bothered her too often.

But living alone was another matter. She missed him. He was not only a source of companionship, and money, but the work she now had to do was more than she could handle. Since he'd died, she'd had to empty ashes from the two stoves, carry in firewood—thank goodness Samuel had cut all that wood!—haul her own buckets of water for cooking, dishes, baths and laundry, since there wasn't a laundry in town she would trust with her clothing.

She needed a husband.

Carrie had chosen Samuel in part because of the great distance in their ages, and in part because of his wealth.

28

But this time she would choose a younger man, one closer to her own age so that she would be less likely to need to husband-hunt again. And since he would be younger, and would likely want more attention in the bedroom area, she preferred a good-looking one. He must be stable, hard-working, and have money, as well as own some type of business, as prestige was very important to Carrie. So, after keeping a watchful eye on the eligible bachelors of Peaceful Valley and those of neighboring communities, she'd decided on Nathan Stockwell. He was the perfect man for her needs.

"I will gladly bring dinner here," she said. "But it would be much easier for me if you came to my dining room. And you needn't worry about dropping wood shavings on my carpet, if that's what's bothering you. Just come as you are." She gave him her prettiest smile and hoped that a sparkle showed in her clear blue eyes.

"Sounds nice, but I can't." He picked up the stack of lumber he'd just cut and, with his back turned toward her, deposited them in a neat pile near his workbench.

Carrie blinked twice in surprise. She was unaccustomed to being refused, and wasn't sure if he was declining dinner only or her subtle invitation to be courted. Suddenly she needed to check her reflection for verification that all was in place, but there wasn't a mirror in sight. She resisted the urge to touch her hair, since a lady never primped in public, and make sure that the rat hadn't slipped or that some of her blond curls hadn't come down. So she allowed herself to smooth a small wrinkle from her broad-striped silk skirt and that calmed her.

"Now, I simply won't take no for an answer, Nathan. You can't skip dinner so you might as well be my guest. I'll look for you at five o'clock." Then, before he could reply, she hurried from the building.

Melody Morgan

Her mind was made up. Nathan Stockwell would eat her dinner if she had to bring it to his shop and feed it to him. And once Carrie Marting made up her mind, she seldom changed it.

Chapter Three

There was little doubt, according to Agnes Butterfield's way of thinking, as to how this whole episode of an orphanage in Peaceful Valley ought to turn out, but things weren't going as smoothly as she'd expected. As president of the M.M.C.C., not to mention wife of the mayor, it was her duty to build as well as preserve the aesthetic and cultural aspects of Peaceful Valley, and a band of delinquent, unmanageable orphans of all ages would be detrimental to that goal. She had spoken to her husband loud and clear on the subject, and he had appeared to have listened, but when she discovered that Mr. Grayling, the superintendent, had spoken to Cora Davis's husband, who also sat on the council, and the two men had actually considered *giving* the old house to Miss Jefferson, she'd almost called for her smelling salts!

The very idea! She had scolded the mayor while he had hung his head. Then she proceeded to list all the reasons

Melody Morgan

Miss Jefferson should *not* be allowed to have an orphanage in their town. He had listened dutifully through two plates of fried chicken, whipped potatoes, gravy, spinach wilted in bacon seasoning, and a large helping of apple strudel with fresh cream. Then, when she had finished her speech and he had finished his dinner, he'd replied, ''Very well, my dear,'' nodding in agreement.

Was it any wonder then that she had lost her breath and nearly all her composure when he'd sold Miss Jefferson the house? Even now, she had to set aside the cherries she had marinating in a sweet syrup so that she could sit down and fan herself. An orphanage in their town, why it was preposterous, to use one of her husband's favorite words. So preposterous in fact, that she had called an emergency meeting of the Monday Morning Coffee Club, and it was only Wednesday. But some things simply could not wait. One of the main strengths of their organization was the influence it wielded over those holding a political position or who were proprietors, and the M.M.C.C. members made no pretense about it.

Agnes mentally pulled herself together and dusted her apron. The ladies would be arriving in less than two hours and she needed to finish the cherry cobbler that would be served with their coffee after their business meeting was over, if indeed it could be over and settled with only one meeting. But for now she had to put aside that problem and concentrate on her baking.

As she moved about the large kitchen with its latest conveniences, tall cupboards and polished wooden floor, she felt some of the tension leave her shoulders. All her friends spoke highly, and enviously, of her culinary talents as well as her beautiful kitchen. Her baking cupboard was well stocked and everything she needed was close at hand: the flour bin with sifter attached beneath it, drawers under the pullout counter that held every imaginable utensil, and a sugar bin that defied insect invasion. Her cooking range was not only huge but lavish with its enameled, intricately detailed exterior, and she kept it spotlessly clean. Agnes kept everything in her kitchen spotlessly clean because that was the one place in which she had complete control. Whenever she felt life robbing her of being in charge, she turned to her cooking and cleaning.

At three o'clock sharp, the members began arriving. Everyone knew that Agnes didn't tolerate latecomers and that it was almost better not to show up at all than to be late.

All eight of the ladies sat in the oversized parlor on the various settees and high-backed chairs, talking among themselves while they waited for Agnes to take charge of the meeting. She glanced around at each of them, much the way a general would assess his troops before battle. Cora Davis was practically a newlywed, having been married less than a year, but that would be to her advantage before all of this was said and done. Carrie Marting, being a widow, would have little impact on the decisions of the council unless she could attract the attention of Mr. Stockwell, which was unlikely to be a benefit given their short amount of time for strategy. In the future Carrie would be a fearless ally, but for now . . . well, Agnes couldn't count on much. Myrtle Grange, whose husband was the postmaster, could be relied upon to furnish whatever information crossed her dinner table and that was usually a valuable source. Penelope Chase had the distinction of being the wife of Jeffrey Chase, local blacksmith, whose brother was a state congressman. Agnes had considered it a personal blessing to have such a prestigious family in their group. The remaining ladies, Lucinda Murtz, Jenny Poole and Laura Brown, all had husbands who were councilmen. Agnes surveyed the group once more and concluded, as she always did, that these women could impact the community in a powerful way. The final judgments of the council might come from the mouths of men, but were in fact decided by the women who spent Monday mornings discussing important matters over coffee and cake.

"Ladies." Agnes waited one minute while they all quieted before she proceeded. "I have called this emergency meeting to discuss what we can do to turn around the decision of the council concerning the orphanage."

"But, Agnes," Penelope said, "that has already been determined. I don't see that we can do anything."

"Well, I for one do not believe that is the case. There were stipulations given and until those are met, the orphanage cannot come into being."

"Are you suggesting that we sabotage Miss Jefferson's efforts?" Myrtle asked, somewhat appalled.

"Of course not. We are ladies. And it would not benefit our community in any way to act otherwise," Agnes said. "But we can and must campaign against this ridiculous notion of an orphanage in our town."

An undercurrent of unrest rippled through the air as visible as a sheet in the wind. A few of them squirmed noticeably in their seats, but nobody brought forth a difference of opinion. Nobody dared. Still, Agnes was aware of it and knew she might as well confront the opposition before it had a chance to fester into something she could not handle.

"You disagree?" she asked to no one in particular and to everyone in general.

"Well," began Myrtle, "perhaps we shouldn't be so quick to assume that Miss Jefferson's idea is so wrong. After all, orphans do need a place to live. You have to admit that her idea is a charitable one."

"Charitable? And who do you think will be donating to

this charity?'' Agnes asked, furrowing her brow. ''Besides that, do you want your children to be forced into daily contact with those who come from questionable backgrounds? I hardly think that there are many orphans in *this* town. I suspect they will be shipped in from the cities and there is no telling what sort of riffraff they will be.''

''I hadn't thought of that,'' Myrtle said, but she didn't look convinced.

''I have,'' said Cora. ''And as heartless as it may sound, I do not want the children I plan to bring into this world either playing or going to school with city orphans.''

Agnes looked at Carrie. ''Is there anything you would like to say, Carrie?''

''Hmm? Oh! No, not really.'' Carrie had been noticing the new draperies and the lovely matching pillows on the settee and had hardly heard any of the conversation. Truthfully, she cared little if there was an orphanage in town or not. Her problems centered around getting Nathan Stockwell to sit up and take notice of her. Coming to the M.M.C.C. was strictly a social event in her life, and she always loved looking at the furnishings in Agnes's house, so she always attended.

''I've heard that the Peaceful Valley Garden Club is considering participating in a benefit to collect money for the orphanage.'' Penelope offered.

''A benefit?'' chimed Lucinda and Jenny.

''A benefit?'' repeated Agnes. This was news to her.

''It's only a rumor,'' Penelope went on. ''But I think it's most likely to be true.''

''Oh, I'm certain that it's true,'' Myrtle said. ''Hattie was in the post office the other day and Sarah Grayling asked her if the Garden Club would be interested in donating some of their prized canned goods to benefit the children's home.''

"Hattie Arthur couldn't cook her way out of a pantry if her life depended on it," Agnes replied in a huff. "Let alone claim that her canned goods are 'prized.' "

"We could donate some baked goods," Myrtle said tentatively. "And we all know who makes the best pies in town." Myrtle had several children of her own and while she didn't like the idea of bringing in hooligan children, she couldn't stop thinking about what would happen to her children if she were not around to care for them.

Agnes accepted the flattering comment about her pies, but there was absolutely no way she would contribute one flake of a crust to build an orphanage. She narrowed her gaze on Myrtle as though finding a traitor in their ranks. "Are you suggesting that we shirk our commitment to this town? I am shocked and disappointed."

Myrtle wasn't one to cause a division in the group, but on the other hand she had to follow her heart. "But Agnes, the decision has already been made by the council."

"And we can see to it that the council rescind that decision. We've done it before." Agnes raised her chin with self assurance.

"But that was different," Lucinda said. "Getting the council to change their meeting days because of a conflict with our Social Supper had nothing to do with the lives of children."

"But it set a precedent," Agnes argued. "And that wasn't the only time. Remember the issue of a curfew?"

Yes, indeed, they all remembered the curfew.

Carrie tore her gaze away from the lovely oak side table that she just knew had to be a recent purchase, and brought her attention to the new subject. The curfew. What a bone of contention that had been between the women of Peaceful Valley and the men, with the result being the demise of the town's one and only saloon. Samuel had never been a drinking man but he took the side for the men at the council meetings, just for the sake of principle. Carrie, on the other hand, stood with the women, and couldn't understand Samuel's stubbornness on the issue. All the women of the M.M.C.C. had elected to give their husbands a choice: abstain willingly from the saloon by imposing a curfew or the wives would see to it that they abstained in the bedroom. Samuel's determination to stand on principle had given Carrie two weeks of blissful, uninterrupted sleep alone in her bed. She had more than enjoyed those two weeks, but if they imposed such a reign on amorous attentions at this time, how would that affect her flirtation with Nathan?

Myrtle remembered exactly when the confrontation had ended, just nine-and-a-half months before little David was born. She didn't think she cared to commit to abstention this time around.

Cora's face turned pink when she thought about giving up those conjugal privileges that she'd discovered she enjoyed as much as her husband did. And she wasn't sure if abstaining from them wouldn't be more painful for her than for him. But Agnes had some worthwhile points to consider. The idea of their streets being overrun with city orphans whose habits would most likely include thievery, with only Miss Jefferson to control them, wasn't at all appealing.

"I agree with Agnes," Cora said. "If we can influence the council in any way, then I believe it is our duty to do so. We have no way of controlling the types of children who will come into the orphanage and if we wait it will be too late."

"And to be perfectly honest," added Jenny, "Miss Jefferson is only one person. Do you really think she could control a ruffian boy of thirteen or fourteen whose ways are set on devilment?'' Her friend Laura nodded in agreement.

Everyone turned to stare at Penelope and Lucinda.

But Lucinda returned their stares. ''I intend to give it more thought, although I'm not convinced.''

''Neither am I,'' said Penelope. ''And where is Opal Grayling?''

Agnes didn't flinch at the accusation in Penelope's voice. ''I would say it is obvious that she has chosen which side she intends to take up with. I saw no need to invite her to this emergency meeting.''

''I hardly think that's fair, Agnes,'' Penelope replied. ''She could have possibly offered some insight.''

''Be realistic, Penelope. She has taken sides against us,'' Agnes said, waving her hand in dismissal of Opal's opinions. ''Division is not what we need here today. Although, I dare say we seem to have enough of it anyway.''

''Exactly what do you expect us to do, Agnes?'' Penelope asked.

''Simply to prevent Miss Jefferson from running an orphanage in our town. And I don't see that it should be so difficult to accomplish.''

''Are we to vote on it?'' asked Lucinda. ''Now?''

Agnes surveyed the faces of the members as they sat around her. She was certain that it would not be a unanimous decision in favor of her idea, so she thought perhaps she should take a little more time to bring together proof of how other towns had dealt with similar situations. And she felt convinced that she would be able to swing them to her side.

''No. I can see that we need some time to consider the negative effects so I will do my best to obtain some facts on the subject and present them to all of you before we vote. But we haven't any time to waste. We will have another meeting and vote then.''

The women all nodded in agreement.

Agnes rose, signaling the end of the discussion. "Ladies, I have refreshments in the kitchen if you would care to follow me.''

With the business part of the meeting behind them, they all relaxed, at least for the time being. Now came the enjoyable aspect of the M.M.C.C.: gossip, good food and coffee, and in that order.

The sound of eight pairs of shoes walking across the wooden kitchen floor was quickly accompanied by the sound of eight cups and saucers with spoons tinkling as cream was stirred into each cup. Lucinda asked Myrtle how her youngest was doing, and she said fine. Then someone exclaimed over the cherry dessert and everyone had to take a moment from talking to taste theirs. Feminine sighs of delight and envy filled the room and someone else demanded to have the recipe. Agnes replied that she would give it to them all at the next meeting.

As the meeting wound down, Myrtle pulled Carrie aside. "And how is Mr. Nathan Stockwell?'' She added a mischievous smile then sipped her coffee.

"He seemed quite . . . busy the last time I saw him.'' Carrie didn't even want to think about the fiasco of a meal she'd prepared for him. "The man hardly takes time out to eat.''

"So I've heard.''

"I can't imagine how he manages to stay so strong and healthy,'' Carrie went on.

"I'd say he certainly needs a woman to look after him.''

"I'd say so, too. But he isn't listening to me.''

"Well, don't give up, my dear.''

When it was finally time to go, Carrie gave one last look

of longing at Agnes's house, then sighed, thinking, *That is what comes of having a husband.* As she walked home, she concluded that she needed to do something more if she was ever to land Nathan Stockwell. And enticing him with her cooking was definitely not enough. The only other avenue that came to mind was not appealing nor did it fit in with Agnes's plan of abstention, but a woman alone had few choices. By the time Carrie reached her small house, where the ashes needed dumping and the firewood waited on the back steps to be taken inside, she knew that Agnes would have to rely on the other members for support in this matter of an orphanage. Carrie had a campaign of her own to conduct and she couldn't allow herself to be sidetracked by a houseful of orphans.

The last day of school had come and gone, leaving Lydia with a sadness she had not anticipated. Somehow, she'd allowed the challenge of opening a children's home to minimize the feelings that now overwhelmed her as she resigned from her teaching position. For years she had planned to teach in order that she might understand children better than most of those who were overseers of orphanages. She had set her path when she attended the normal school for teachers in Bowling Green, then with that knowledge she taught two years in Grand Rapids at the same school where she and Jonathan had shared a classroom as children and where her foster mother had also taught. From there she'd followed her heart and took the position in the Peaceful Valley School near Cincinnati, spending three more years in the classroom. And now it was time to say good-bye to the profession she had discovered she loved so much. But her goals had not changed and she had to keep her face forward, so she'd written the letter of resignation and given it to Mr. Grayling. That was yesterday.

ABIDING HOPE

Today is the beginning, not the end, she told herself as she stood on the wide front porch of the old Mercer house. Stepping carefully, she walked to the far side and studied the surrounding area. Around the corner was a view of the meadow that lay behind the house, stretching across the hilly expanse of open country with a carpet of wildflowers that bloomed in late spring. There would be no need for the children to "run the streets" as Hattie Arthur had suggested, not when they had such a beautiful playground so close. Lydia knew she would not replace the picket fence along the back. She had no intention of allowing a lovely fence to function as a barrier. Instead it would serve only as an attractive border on the street side.

After taking in the view from the front porch, she turned her attention to the interior of the house. She hadn't even peeked in the windows yet and her curiosity brimmed to overflowing. With one palm she rubbed the dirt and grime off the nearest window, then, cupping her hands to her face, peered inside. The room was larger than she'd expected and would be more than suitable for a parlor once the walls and floor were mended. Surprisingly, most of the plaster was intact even though a large wet stain showed on the interior wall, a stain she suspected a chimney had caused.

Well, that was just the first thing on her list of things that would need repaired. She wiped her hands against the plain work dress she wore and decided there was no sense in putting off finishing the list. Today she was just going to give the house an inspection, then she would tally up all the projects later. Pushing open the door with concentrated effort, she mentally noted the hinges would need oiling but if that was all it needed she counted herself lucky. She worked the door back and forth, and saw the scrape marks on the wooden floor. Perhaps the door only needed to be removed and the bottom shaved off, which immediately brought to mind Nathan Stockwell and the woodworking tools that covered his walls. Undoubtedly, this would be a small job for him, one that he would make short work of, while she would most likely spend a good day or two as she struggled with it. Well, she wouldn't worry over that now. She had to stick to her inspection and go over the details later.

Footsteps on the porch behind her drew her attention and she turned to see Sarah coming toward her.

"So, how does it measure up?" Sarah asked as she glanced around the room littered with fallen debris, broken chairs and broken glass.

"It is a little overwhelming," Lydia replied. Then she smiled and added, "But it's mine. Well, almost."

Sarah waved her hand to discredit those last words. "A lot of elbow grease is all this place needs."

"You sound like my Grandma Winnie," Lydia said with a small laugh. "She believes in hard work and always made sure I was never short on elbow grease. But what I really need is money. Hard work is only going to go so far."

"You might be right." Sarah tried to set up a three-legged chair. "You're going to need furniture, too."

Neither of them mentioned the obvious person to build the furniture. Lydia had earlier recounted the conversation she'd had with Nathan, which made Sarah grimace and roll her eyes. Both agreed that they would have to find other ways of getting the carpentry work done.

"Did you bring your hammer?" Lydia teased.

"I told you I don't have a hammer, but I plan to get one." Sarah let the chair fall. "But I do have some good news."

"I'll take it. What is it?"

"Hattie Arthur said she would talk to Preacher Ted and some of the ladies at the Baptist church to see if they would be interested in having an ice cream social with all proceeds going to benefit the new children's home. So how about that for good news?'' she asked, smiling broadly.

"Sarah, you are a dear friend." And Lydia meant it. In spite of the difference in their ages she found herself confiding many of her dreams and doubts to the young woman.

"There's more," Sarah went on, her eyes sparkling with wicked delight. "I spoke to Myrtle Grange and she said she'd heard about the Baptist church wanting to sponsor a benefit, and wondered if the Presbyterian church could do something, too."

Lydia laughed. "Sarah! You are truly a wonder."

Sarah shrugged. "I knew a little friendly competition would be good for their souls. And maybe even a little entertaining for the rest of us."

Lydia let out a big sigh as relief poured over her. It was a start, maybe not the whole answer, but it was definitely a good start.

Sarah looked around the room again. "It's been a long time since I've been in here. Maybe three or four years. Not that it's changed all that much."

"You mean you were trespassing?" Lydia said, with pretended wide-eyed surprise. There wasn't much that Sarah could say or do that would really surprise her.

"Certainly. All the kids in town have been in here at one time or another. Midnight dares and such." She smiled. "We loved to scare each other as well as ourselves. And we always believed the house had to be haunted. Of course, nobody saw anything even close to resembling a ghost."

Lydia looked around, trying to see the abandoned old house as a child would see it, but she couldn't. She saw only finished walls, curtains lifting in the breeze that came through the open windows, and bouquets of roses sitting on tables beside new wooden chairs. Maybe a few rugs would cover the painted floors, giving the house the warm feel of a real home.

"Lydia?" Sarah called softly to her.

"Hmm?" Lydia came back to the present with a blink of her eyes.

"You seem to have drifted off somewhere."

"Not really. I'm right here with you, but I'm seeing everything in a different light than when I first came in here."

"Well, before you get too dreamy maybe we ought to get you back to solid ground by taking a tour. Back here is the kitchen . . ." Sarah led the way, talking as she went.

Lydia followed, but she kept seeing each room the way it ought to be. And contrary to Sarah's belief, her feet were definitely on solid ground. This was no longer a dream, it had become a reality and she didn't even have to pinch herself. It had been a long time coming, but finally it had happened.

Chapter Four

Nathan pounded the four-penny nail home as he nearly finished building Carrie Marting's cabinets. He'd worked longer hours than usual, burning up the lamp oil until well after midnight in his determination to get the job done before the woman drove him to complete distraction. She'd been underfoot since the first moment he'd agreed to take on the work, but worse than that, she'd talked incessantly. He did not harbor bad feelings for the opposite sex, but he did prefer to be left alone while he worked, and while he ate, too, for that matter.

He had not taken her up on the invitation to come to her house for dinner, so she had brought it to him in a basket, a complete dinner with china and silver, too. The aroma had been so enticing that he'd called upon every bit of willpower that he'd possessed to turn it down. As he stared at it, he couldn't remember the last time he'd eaten chicken, that looked as though it would melt in his mouth before he could swallow it, or potatoes covered with dark gravy and carrots all around them. But he knew if he so much as looked as though he wanted it, she would misconstrue that to mean more than just her dinner that he wanted. And that would be a lie.

Now, he lifted the cabinet onto the workbench and slid the shelf into place on the last bracket he'd just nailed along the inside. The fit was perfect, just as he expected it to be. There was no room for shabby workmanship to his way of thinking. He couldn't abide a sloppy fit, a poor grade of wood, or even a bent nail. Good carpentry was only as good as the carpenter himself, and Nathan made a practice of making sure that the carpentry was better than the carpenter.

This piece of furniture was built in two sections in order that he could work in his shop where his tools were handy. When it came time to move it, he would enlist the help of the blacksmith, Jeff Chase, whose shop almost adjoined Nathan's. The two men often lent each other a helping hand, as well as a strong back. And he hoped that this time, Jeff's presence would deter the widow Marting from trying to tempt him again.

Nathan wasn't blind, neither was he immune, which he freely admitted even to himself. She was an attractive woman with all the attributes most men stared at and even ogled, but he wasn't most men and he was smart enough to know that beyond the ogling lay the danger of getting a wedding band jammed onto his finger. So he avoided that pitfall altogether. Flirtation was not a game he intended to play. Ever.

Running his hand along the smooth exterior finish, he checked for hammer indentations. There were none. Just a little more work of sanding and he could begin rubbing in the wax. Then he would be finished, and he didn't think he wanted to take on any more of Mrs. Marting's jobs.

There were too many hazards and they cluttered up his mind just trying to be careful of all of them. He preferred keeping his thoughts focused on his work.

For the rest of the day he managed to do that, with only a few distractions. At noon, a man came to ask about getting a wheel repaired and later another man wanted to put in an order for a new wagon. Those were the kinds of jobs that he especially enjoyed, where he could put his muscle into it and let his mind get completely absorbed in the precision work of being a wheelwright. But for now, he had to get the cabinet done and into Mrs. Marting's house.

Around six o'clock he decided to see Jeff and ask for a hand in moving the cabinet in the next day or so, depending on when he could spare the time to help, but before he could get out of the door, Carrie was coming in it.

"Hello, Nathan," she said, smiling, and he caught a whiff of a soft sweet scent coming from her direction. "I hope I'm not too late." She carried a container of some sort covered with a towel. "I brought you a little something to eat. You know a man like you has to keep up his strength. You work far too hard, Nathan."

In spite of his resolve to resist her cooking, his stomach growled and his nose twitched in appreciation of what lay beneath the towel. But he thought about the danger in accepting a flirtation, and he said, "No, thanks. I don't have time right now."

"But, Nathan, I made this special for you. Surely, lemon cake is one of your favorites." She pulled the towel away and sure enough a creamy yellow cake lay nestled in a hat box. He frowned, but she persisted. "I'll just set it over here and you can take it home with you."

And that's when she saw the cabinet.

"Oh, it's so lovely! Is it ready to be delivered?" She walked around it, or rather glided around it. Nathan was amazed at how she was able to take steps like everyone else but appeared not to even touch the ground.

"Almost," he replied.

"Why, I can't imagine another thing that needs doing. It's perfect." She reached out a gloved hand to touch it.

"Don't."

She jumped as he practically barked at her.

"I've been waxing it."

"I see," she said, stepping back to admire it.

"You'll dirty your gloves," he added, then wished he hadn't since she would think he was concerned about her.

She made a small pout and smiled. "Is that all? I thought you meant I would mess it up and I wouldn't want to do that." And now he was certain he'd made a mistake since she was smiling broadly at him, looking more bold, too.

"So tell me, when will you be bringing it over? I want to be sure to be home and not off visiting somewhere."

"I was just on my way to ask Jeff when he could help me move it. I'll let you know." He was being abrupt, but that was how he treated everyone.

"Well then, I'll be on my way," she said, brushing past him and letting her arm graze his. At the door she stopped and turned toward him. "I'm looking forward to it." And then she glided out into the evening light.

He had the uneasy feeling that she hadn't been talking about the cabinet, but he refused to let his mind linger on that line of thinking as he headed for the smithy.

Jeff greeted him with a nod of his head, signaling that he'd be right with him as soon as he finished. Two of his sons worked alongside him, either operating the bellows or giving alternating swings of their sledge hammers on the current piece of iron. There was little opportunity for giving directions, but they seemed not to need any as the rhythm of their swing-*strike*, swing-*strike* filled the air with the ringing of metal as it impacted metal. The smell of smoke and ash was strong, converging with the oily one of harness leather, and overlaid with sweat.

Jeff had once said, in his good-natured way, that if he ever caught his own building on fire, Nathan's would most likely supply the fuel to burn them both down, maybe the whole town. It was a sobering thought. But Jeff had laughed at his own joke and whacked Nathan on the back to pound some of the seriousness out of him. He'd often said that Nathan ought to quit taking everything so dang serious because it would only shorten his life. Of all the people in Peaceful Valley, Jeff was the only man he considered his friend, even though they had nothing in common but their work. When he needed to tire a wheel he went to Jeff's forge, and when Jeff needed an extra man to swing a sledge Nathan was ready to lend his hand. But outside of work they seldom talked about their personal life, and when they did it was always Jeff who did the talking and Nathan who did the listening.

As soon as the boys set down their hammers, a deafening silence settled around them until their ears adjusted to hearing the background noises of everyday life. Red-faced and smiling, Jeff approached Nathan.

"I'll tell you, these boys of mine are something else." He clapped the nearest boy on the back in outward appreciation for his work. "Yessir."

Nathan nodded in agreement. They were hardworking boys and well mannered, too.

"So what can I do for you? Got a wheel you need tired?"

"No, I've got a cabinet to move over to Mrs. Marting's house but it isn't ready yet. I just wanted to see if I could get some help loading it and carrying it in."

"Sure," he replied. "As long as I'm not working at the

forge, I can drop what I'm doing anytime you say. And now that school's out, the boys will be here to pitch in." Then he leaned over to where the pump spouted into a horse trough and gave two great pushes on the handle, sending out a gush of water. He stuck his head under the flow and scrubbed his face then came up shaking it off. "Blessed cool water," he said with a groan of pleasure.

"Been mighty busy keeping Carrie Marting in furniture, haven't you?" he said, as though nothing had interrupted the conversation.

"Seems that way."

"That little house of hers ought to be about filled up by now. Be nary a bit of space left for a man to put up his feet, I'd say." Jeff gave him a knowing grin.

"I hadn't noticed." And he hadn't. His intention had been to deliver the furniture and leave immediately.

"Well, it's plain to see she's set her cap for you." Jeff leaned conspiratorially toward him. "You have noticed that, I take it."

Nathan didn't want to discuss Carrie but he nodded in agreement, acknowledging the obvious.

"Well, anytime you need some advice on the fairer sex," Jeff said, smiling broadly, "don't come to me. I couldn't help myself, so I don't know how I could help someone else."

Nathan couldn't help grinning. "Thanks a lot."

Jeff laughed loud and long then thumped him on the back. "Good to see you smile, Nathan." He turned to go back to his work but he caught a glimpse of Lydia Jefferson on the other side of the street.

"There goes the schoolteacher," he said. "At least she used to be the schoolteacher. Sure has caused a heck of rumpus with that orphanage of hers, hasn't she?"

Nathan didn't comment. Miss Jefferson affected him the

way a horsefly would a skittish horse. Every time she came around he felt like bolting and running as far as he could to get away from her. He didn't have to puzzle over it for long to figure out what it was about her that irritated him, but that was something he wasn't going to share with anyone, not even his one and only friend. So he grumbled an excuse about needing to get back to work and turned his back on Lydia Jefferson before she entered the hardware store across the street.

"Hello, young lady," said Harvey Mertz. "What can I do for you?"

"I apologize for coming in so late, but I was hoping to get some estimates of the supplies I will be needing before long."

"For your orphanage?" he asked.

Lydia overlooked the distasteful word, and replied, "Yes. I made a list of everything I could think of, but I'm sure there are plenty of things I have left out. Perhaps you could help me with this. If you wouldn't mind."

"Let me see your paper." He pulled his spectacles lower on his nose and studied her list then read it out loud. "Hmm. Nails, windowpanes, hinges, hammer, pry bar, lye soap, plaster, wood—" He glanced up at her. "Wood?"

"Boards. For the floors and the porch and the picket fence. Can't I get them here?" She hoped he would not tell her to go see Mr. Stockwell.

"You'll have to get them from Nathan. As a matter of fact, he would be much better at giving you an estimate on your project than I would. I only sell these things, but he works with them everyday." He looked past her toward the shop across the street. "I think he's still working. He seldom goes home this early." He handed her list back to her. "I'd be more than happy to deliver all this to the old Mercer house just as soon as you find out from Nathan how much you'll need.''

Lydia thanked him and left the store. Once she was back on the boardwalk, she wondered why that particular name had to keep cropping up. She slowed her steps as she stood parallel to the wide-open doors of his shop, and wondered if she had enough courage to approach the man again. Being turned down twice was two times too many, but then she wasn't asking for more than an estimate of the supplies she would need so she could plan a budget of sorts. Surely, that couldn't take him very long, especially if he was the expert everyone claimed him to be. And she would pay him for his time, if that was the way he wanted it, although she still thought he was a skinflint for his unwillingness to give anything for the well-being of homeless children.

She took a tentative step off the walk then realized that long shadows were creeping around the edges of all the buildings and it appeared to be dark inside the carpenter shop. Perhaps he was preparing to go home, she thought. Then again, she might do better talking to him this time of the day. At least she wouldn't be disrupting his work. Yes, she would try again. After all, what harm could he really do to her?

As she stepped through the wide double doors, a lamp suddenly glowed to life somewhere toward the rear section, and it surprised her to find a sense of warmth and friendliness radiating from the shop, in spite of the man who worked there. The same feeling had hit her when she'd come calling a week earlier. It must be the smell of the fresh-cut wood and the shavings that lay everywhere, she decided. Certainly, that friendly feeling couldn't have anything to do with Nathan Stockwell himself.

She followed the lampshine to its source and found him working on a cabinet that sat on a bench in front of him.

Knowing that he hadn't heard her approach, she was reluctant to startle him and incur an undeserved bout of anger, so she watched as he wiped a stained cloth across the surface. Back and forth, back and forth. He appeared to have more patience than she would ever have given him credit for having. Unfortunately, it seemed to be reserved for woodworking only.

Clearing her throat, she braced herself for the scathing look he was bound to send her way.

"Ahem. Excuse me."

Sure enough, when he turned to stare at her, a frown settled between his brows and she nearly changed her mind.

"What is it, Miss Jeffries?"

She let the misnomer pass this time. "I wondered if I might have a minute to speak with you."

"About that house? No." He returned his concentration to his work, and for once she was almost glad to be ignored. Almost, but not quite.

"If you will only listen, you will find that I am not trying to hire your services as a carpenter. I mean, in a sense I am, but—" She stopped, feeling angry with herself for allowing him to steal her composure. Just how bad did she need *his* opinion or his estimate? Not that bad, she told herself.

"I've changed my mind." She felt the tightness in her jaw as she held back the words she really wanted to say. "Good evening, Mr. Stockwell." With that said, she turned and practically ran out of the shop. The quicker she was away from him the better off she would be.

Outside, the heat of the day had quickly cooled with the lowering sun, but she barely noticed it since her face was hot with anger and even embarrassment, if she was to admit the truth. How could one man cause such a roiling of emotion? She amended that to: one rude, tactless, discourteous man. He reminded her of an ill-tempered horse who deserved to be bitten by a particularly vicious horsefly. She wished she could smile at the justice that would serve up, but she couldn't.

By the time she'd reached the Graylings' house it was nearly dark. A lamp in the parlor cast a glow onto the front porch where Opal Grayling sat waiting for her.

"Hello, dear," she said, her voice full of concern. "You're back late tonight. Were you at the old house?"

"No." She couldn't tell her that she had foolishly asked for help and been turned down for the third time. "I've been walking. It's a nice night, isn't it?"

"Why don't you sit with me awhile? The children have all gone to bed and Mr. Grayling is visiting down the street. I would enjoy your company." She patted the empty chair beside her. "Sit here."

Lydia accepted the seat, slipping her hands beneath her and rocking forward then back, forward then back.

"You know," Mrs. Grayling began, "this is the kind of night that reminds me of when I was a child and chased after fireflies. Did you ever do that when you were a child?"

Lydia nodded. "Yes. Although, it seems like such a long time ago."

"Well, for me it has been a long time." She laughed lightly, then sat quiet for a bit. "But then sometimes childhood seems like only yesterday. I wonder if my children will feel that way, too, after they're grown and have families of their own. I wonder if they will cherish the memories of the times we've spent together as much as I cherish those of my own growing up years. Those were precious moments. And like all precious things we hold them close to our hearts."

Lydia remembered well the times that her mother had

54

held her in her arms those few years before she'd died. Those were indeed precious.

"I believe we give those moments, in part, to our own children when we rock them and sing to them and even when we hug them."

Lydia stopped her back-and-forth motion and pulled her hands from beneath her. "I haven't had any children, but I know what you mean. That's how love grows."

"That's right," Mrs. Grayling said, smiling at her. "That's how love grows. And that's why your idea of a children's home is such a wonderful thing."

Irene Barrett Hollister suddenly came to mind. Even though she'd never had any children of her own, she'd opened her heart to two frightened young orphans and given them the gift of her love and eventually became their foster mother. Lydia had blossomed in that love. She'd felt nurtured and she'd grown into a woman who wanted to give to other orphans that same gift of love.

She turned to Opal Grayling. "Thank you," she said, then kissed the older woman's cheek. "For reminding me of what I'm really doing."

Opal reached out and patted Lydia's hand. "Why, I was only reminiscing, my dear. But I'm glad you found something worthwhile in our talk."

They sat quietly enjoying the night sounds for a few more minutes before they heard footsteps coming down the street. Mr. Grayling had returned home. The three of them exchanged a few pleasantries before the older couple excused themselves, saying it was past their bedtime.

After they'd gone, Lydia continued to sit, staring out into the summer night. She wrapped her arms around herself to ward off the cool night air, snuggling back into her chair as best she could. In a little bit she would go in, but for the moment she wanted to savor those memories that had just come to mind, to reflect on what it meant to grow up in not one, but two homes full of love, and to ponder the idea of how she could pass that love on to other children. It was more than a goal; it was an all-consuming need. And she would not allow a group of people or a single man to get in the way of that need.

Nathan poured hot water from a kettle into a basin, feeling almost too tired to wash up before falling into bed. He had nearly finished with the first coat of wax when he realized it was well after midnight. After extinguishing the lamp and locking up, he walked home through a dark town. Nobody had been up except him and a few stray dogs who probably followed him because he carried the hatbox with Carrie's cake in it. When he reached his house, he quickly built a fire using cottonwood so that it would burn hot and fast, then turn to ash without heating up the house too much. Instead of a regular meal with bread, beans and coffee, he settled for cake and coffee before stripping down for a basin bath. Then he crawled into bed, too exhausted to do much more than groan with the pleasure of lying flat on cool sheets.

For a moment, only a moment, he thought about Carrie Marting's silk dress gliding above the floor over the wood shavings as she walked toward him and around the cabinet. No, he told himself and pulled the pillow over his head. He must have eaten too much cake and it had affected his head instead of his stomach.

Then he pictured Lydia Jefferson asking him politely, the first time, to help her, then asking him the second time with a stern determination. And finally, asking a third time in anger and frustration. Well, he had enough anger and frustration of his own; he didn't need hers, too.

And he damn well didn't need any more cake.

Chapter Five

Rising early the next morning, Lydia selected a simple cotton work dress to wear for a day of cleaning, prying and pounding. She intended to start in the attic, checking for holes in the roof and possible chimney damage. Even though she was far from being an expert on such matters, she ought to be able to judge whether the roof was sound or needed repairing. It only made sense to start at the top and work her way down through the house.

When she arrived at the kitchen table, Opal had already set out a platter of hotcakes with a small crock of butter. The Grayling children, including Sarah, were seated and filling their plates.

"What a surprise to see so many bright shining faces this morning," Lydia said, tousling the blond hair of ten-year-old Alexander. "I was certain that we wouldn't be seeing you this early once school let out."

"We're going to help you at the old house," said his

look-alike brother, Aaron. The twins were identical right
down to the cowlick on their foreheads. When she'd first
met them, she'd found it impossible to put the right name
to the right boy and they had enjoyed confusing her. But
after spending a whole day in school with them and then
living in the same house, too, she'd clearly noticed a difference in their voices, their mannerisms and even their
loping walk. Now they had a more difficult time confusing
her, much to their dismay.

"Do you have tools?" she asked, teasing them. "I would
certainly appreciate any workmen who brought their own
tools."

"Papa said we could bring his hammer and prybar, but
only if you said it was all right," said Alexander.

"He doesn't want us breaking up anything that you say
we shouldn't," Aaron added. "But that old house looks to
us like a lot of breaking up might be necessary."

Lydia filled a coffee cup and took it to her seat at the
table. "It does look that way, doesn't it? But I'm hoping
we won't have to tear out very much."

The boys nodded but looked a little disappointed.

"Of course, I can't think of any two boys I'd rather have
working with me than you two," she said. "And I'm certain there will be some tearing out that will have to be
done."

They brightened at that and gave each other an enthusi-
astic grin.

"How about you, Sarah? Can we count on you today?"
Lydia asked, as she reached for a hotcake.

"Absolutely. But sometime today, maybe this afternoon,
I think I'll visit Mrs. Arthur and find out the latest news
on the ice cream social, then drop by Myrtle Grange's
house to see if the Presbyterians are truly planning something."

Lydia was grateful that Sarah had taken on the job of getting sponsors. She didn't think she could take any more rejections at this stage and preferred to spend her time working at the house. She knew that getting funds to build the house was extremely important, but she felt that it was just as important to get started with the cleaning out. Time was not her friend in this situation, and she had to make every minute count. If Sarah could prod the townspeople into helping, then Lydia could spend that same time cleaning, hauling and pitching. The work would be hard, but she was ready for it.

After breakfast, Mrs. Grayling shooed the girls from the kitchen, denying them the chance to help with the breakfast dishes. They had enough work to do, she told them. Then she promised that Mr. Grayling would lend a hand that evening when he came home.

So they loaded themselves down with buckets and lye soap, a hammer, a prybar, a broom and a tin pail of cookies for nourishment and headed toward the last street along the meadow where the old Mercer house stood. When they reached the broken gate all four of them stopped and stared at the overwhelming project ahead. For the first time Lydia saw the house as it really looked instead of the vision she carried in her heart.

Aaron broke the silence first. "It looks bigger than the last time we were here."

"You mean the mess looks bigger or the house looks bigger?" asked Alexander.

"Both."

"We can do this," Lydia said. "We'll take one room at a time, then move on to the next." She led the way through an opening in the picket fence, her bucket and broom catching on the wooden spire so that she had to tug them free.

They trampled across the tall, rangy grass, making a path to the front porch.

"I don't suppose the pump is in working order anymore," she said wistfully.

"Well, it hasn't been used in a long time," Sarah replied.

"It doesn't work," Aaron informed them.

"Nope, it doesn't," Alexander agreed. "We've tried it before and it never did."

Sarah raised an eyebrow at the twins, then smiled at Lydia. "See? Midnight dares."

"Then we will have to beg some water from a neighbor, unless someone wants to haul it all the way from home," Lydia said

"I'll ask at the Petersons' place." Sarah headed for the neighbor to the right of the property, with the twins behind her.

Lydia studied the paraphernalia they had brought, then realized they'd forgotten a very important item. "Wait!" she called to Sarah. "We forgot to bring a ladder. Do you suppose we could borrow one?" Her answer was a nod and a wave.

She would need one if she was going to climb into the attic, and that was first thing on the list that she and Sarah had made. So she prepared to confront the cobwebs by pulling the dust cap that Mrs. Grayling had given her over her hair for protection. She glanced at her reflection in a window darkened by dirt and the mirrored result made her smile. She looked a little bit like Grandma Winnie except for the tendrils of light brown hair at the front of the cap, which were nearly hidden by the broad ruffle that rimmed it.

Well, she told herself, it was time to start acting like Grandma Winnie and attack this old house and not stop until it was finished. So she grabbed her broom and headed for the upstairs.

In the hallway at the top of the stairs was a trap door on the ceiling. She had to stand precariously close to the edge of the first step in order to raise her broom handle and push the door up and finally over. A cloud of dust motes rose, then drifted downward toward her. Thick old dust settled over her and she sneezed.

"So that's where you are," she heard someone say from the bottom of the stairs and looked down to find Preacher Ted smiling up at her. "Mind if I come up?"

"Be my guest, but be careful, too. You never know when a loose board will give way."

When he reached her, she realized he was dressed in work clothes. He wore a blue chambray shirt with the sleeves rolled up and the tails tucked neatly into the waist of paint-stained trousers. Either he'd just left a painting job or he'd come to help, and she prayed for the latter.

"What would you like me to do?" he said smiling at her, his blue eyes crinkling with friendliness.

"You've really come to help?" She felt like throwing her arms around his neck and hugging him. The urge was almost overpowering. His was the first friendly face she'd seen, outside of the Grayling house, since she'd gotten up and spoken at the town meeting, exposing her dreams for all to scoff at. But then she remembered that Preacher Ted had not scoffed at her during that meeting; he had openly commended her.

"I put on my special clothes just for the occasion," he teased.

"Me, too," she replied, touching her dust cap.

He leaned forward a little and said, "It looks like you're hiding in there."

Lydia laughed. "I think it's going to get hot wearing it, but I've already discovered it's value when I raised that door," she said, pointing upward with her broom.

"Are you planning to go up there?" he asked in surprise.

"As soon as Sarah brings the ladder. I have to know how bad the roof is and the chimney, too."

"I'll be the first to admit that I'm not a carpenter by any stretch of the imagination. As you can see, painting is my strong point," he smiled, indicating the dried paint that dotted his pants. "Although, I usually get more on myself than what I'm painting, but I'm willing to give anything a try. And that includes roofs and chimneys."

A clatter of feet tripping over junk, followed by a thud and then a howl of laughter, brought their attention to the twins, who suddenly came into view at the bottom of the stairs.

"Aaron got clumsy with his end," giggled Alexander, holding the front end of a long ladder. "He stepped into a pail." A seizure of giggling overtook him and he had to cover his mouth to stop it.

"Yeah, well, I didn't see it," replied Aaron, looking less amused than his brother.

Sarah walked past each of them, smoothing her hand along the tops of their heads, saying, "Boys," as she started up the steps and motioned them to follow.

"Sorry, Aaron, but you did look funny," Alexander whispered loudly, suppressing another giggle, but Aaron ignored him.

"Hello, Preacher Ted," Sarah said halfway to the top.

"Sarah." He nodded, smiling pleasantly. "Looks like there's plenty of help here today. We ought to get quite a lot accomplished." He rescued the boys from their burden, set the ladder securely in place and went up the rungs, then Lydia followed while Sarah held the bottom steady.

At the top, Lydia stepped awkwardly off the ladder and had to grab Preacher Ted's hand. Around them a floor of thick planks stretched unevenly across the dim attic. Only two small windows, one at each gabled end, were a source of light. But the poor light within the attic became a benefit when they searched for holes in the tin roofing. Bright sunlight showed through in more places than Lydia had expected to find, and the two chimneys needed re-chinking near the roof line. She could only guess what must be above the roof where the weather had likely taken its toll.

"It's a little disheartening," she told him. "But not impossible."

"I like your spirit," he replied. "Some mortar for the chimneys and a bucket of tar for patching those holes in the roof and you should be all set." He studied the rafters over head. "At least there isn't any major damage up here that I can see."

Lydia accepted that as good news, but the idea of hauling a bucket of heated tar onto the roof was a little daunting, not to mention mortar for the chimneys, but there would be no use working downstairs until this repair work was done, and that meant she had to do it herself or ask someone else to help her do it.

"You're going to need some building materials," he said, a small frown settling thoughtfully between his brows. "And that takes money."

She sighed. "I know." She had practically emptied her savings when she paid the five hundred dollars to the council, which left her hardly anything at all for supplies and her room and board at the Graylings'. "But I have enough to fix the roof."

"I think," he mused out loud, "I think someone at the church mentioned an ice cream social. And someone, I don't recall who, suggested that the proceeds go to the new children's home.''

With his blue eyes twinkling and dust motes settling in his sandy blond hair, Lydia thought he resembled a mischievous boy not unlike the twins downstairs. She felt sure she could guess who had suggested the money go to the children's home.

''I don't know how I can ever thank you,'' she replied, her voice lowered with emotion. ''It isn't easy to . . .''

''It isn't easy to start an admirable venture such as this with nothing more than a kind heart to see you through,'' he finished for her, putting words into her mouth that she hadn't even thought of saying. ''So another group of kind hearts is going to help you.''

She blinked hard against the tears that were threatening, and struggled to smile when what she really wanted was to give in and let them flow. She knew he understood, really understood, how she felt about the house, and the impact of the friendship that he'd just offered was almost more than she could bear.

''Thank you,'' she said. ''I promise you won't be sorry.''

He shook his head. ''You don't have to promise me anything. That's what friends are for. Right?''

''Right.'' Suddenly she felt like laughing, and brushed a fingertip past the corner of her eye.

''Hey!'' called Sarah. ''How does it look up there?''

''Not as bad as it could be,'' Ted called back, with a wink for Lydia. ''A little tar, a little mortar and we should have a fairly decent roof.''

''That sounds pretty good,'' Sarah said, as the two climbed down the ladder. ''At least I think it does. I guess it depends on whether I have to go up on the roof. I get kind of shaky up so high.''

64

"It wasn't always like that, but things have changed in some ways." And she proceeded to tell her about the resistance she'd met when she first presented her idea. Winnie listened carefully and made no comment when the subject of funds came up, but a deep frown creased her brow. Then as Lydia spoke of Nathan's unwillingness to help at first, Winnie's frown deepened and Lydia wished she hadn't mentioned that part of the story.

"I hardly know what to say about your home, dear. It's such a vast undertaking. Especially for one woman. Are you sure you're up to it?"

She couldn't let any doubts slip in now, and she didn't dare admit them if they did. But, truthfully, with Grandma Winnie's arrival, she'd begun to see everything through different eyes and all their progress seemed so insignificant. So she knew she had to keep up the good front, for herself if not for her grandmother, and concentrate on one thing only, her dream of a children's home.

"Yes, Grandma Winnie, I am definitely up to it."

"Then tell me again about your plans."

So Lydia went over them again and found her enthusiasm was still there. She still believed that she could accomplish what she'd set out to do, because she simply would not give up.

When they had finished with their breakfast and the dishes, Lydia went to work on the house and Winnie put on her jacket to walk into town.

"I'll just be a little while, dear," she said, pinning on her hat. "I only want to get a better look around today than I had yesterday when that nice young man brought me in his wagon. I had no idea you were so far from a train station. That is certainly a handicap, you realize, don't you?"

"I hadn't thought of it that way, actually. It's rather nice

273

not hearing a whistle blow the way they do at home."

"That's a good point. I hadn't thought of that." She patted her hair beneath the hat. "Well, I'm off."

After Winnie had gone, Lydia found she couldn't get her mind on her work, so she took a second cup of coffee out to the back step where she could watch the flowers in the meadow and think. She kept remembering Nathan's tender touches and how wonderful he'd made her feel. And afterward she'd felt so close to him, as though they could never be separated again. It seemed he was a part of her and she a part of him. The only dull spot in her shining moment of remembering was when she thought of how unfair she'd been not to give Ted her answer. Suddenly, she knew she couldn't put it off anymore. She could not continue thinking only of her own discomfort in telling him, but had to consider that the quicker she did this the sooner it would be over, for both of them.

With her mind made up, she hurried to change her dress, all the while trying to come up with the right words. She didn't want to lose his friendship, but it was a risk she had to take. There was no choice in the matter and she had been thoughtless to let it go so long. The need to have it done made her feet hurry through town, avoiding the main street so she didn't run into Winnie. The last thing she needed was having to explain where she was going and why.

When she arrived at Ted's door, she was pleasantly surprised to find him on both feet and with no cane to help him get about.

"Well, hello, Lydia. How have you been?" He opened the door wide in welcome. "Please, come in."

"I'd rather hear how you're doing. It's wonderful to see you up and about like this."

"I've been doing quite well for over a week now." Then he dropped his gaze from her face. "I haven't been out to help like I should have, but, well . . . it's been busy at the church.''

She felt a dagger of sorrow go through her. He hadn't wanted to face her, and she couldn't blame him. She had ignored his request and it was no wonder he'd stayed away.

"Could we sit down and talk?" she asked. Her heart thumped as she led the way to the parlor chairs were she chose one opposite from his. "First, I want to apologize."

He frowned and said, "You're not going to bring up the fall I took, are you? Because—"

"No," she interrupted. "This is something I should have told you before now. It's about not answering your proposal of marriage." Then she rushed on before she could turn coward again. "I value your friendship more than I can say. And I mean that from the bottom of my heart. And I wouldn't want to lose it no matter what, but I'll certainly understand if you withdraw it." She paused for a breath.

"You have my friendship no matter what, dear Lydia. Please, go on."

She almost couldn't. His words made her feel unworthy of such a friendship, especially when she was about to reject his proposal.

"Wait," he said. "It isn't fair to put you through this." He leaned forward and took her hand in his. "You are going to tell me no, aren't you?"

All she could do was nod, and continue holding her breath.

"It's all right. I understand."

"But you've been so good to me. Helping on the house and all."

"I never wanted you to feel obligated to me. I helped because I admire you. And I admire what you're doing. I still do."

"But I feel awful, Ted. You've been so kind and here I

am refusing the only proposal I've ever gotten. And I've taken so long to come to you." She was nearly in tears.

He shook his head. "Don't feel that way. I've got a confession of my own." He studied her hand then looked up at her. "I've fallen in love with someone and it happened after I proposed. If you want to talk about feeling bad, I've never felt worse."

She could hardly believe what she was hearing. Ted was in love, but not with her, and he'd been feeling just as guilty as she had. Her first reaction was that they could still be friends. She squeezed his hand and smiled.

"I'm so happy for you." And the sincerity came though in her voice. "May I ask who? Or am I being too personal? Does she know?"

"I don't think she does," he said and blushed.

"Well, she is a very lucky woman," she replied with a smile. "Does this mean we can still be friends?"

"I hope so. I'd like that very much."

"So would I." And they sat looking at each other, enjoying a new kind of companionship which was very much like the one they'd had in the beginning. "I'm glad you're not angry with me," she said.

"Me, angry? I was afraid you would be angry with me."

Then they laughed together, each of them relieved to have everything out in the open. Now that they had it all settled and straightened out between them, they shared what had been going on their lives since last they'd met. He told her he was sure he'd gained twenty pounds since most of his clothes didn't fit, and he was thankful the food had stopped arriving in large dishes. She told him about her grandmother and he laughed, saying she sounded like a delightful woman. Then Lydia said she had to be going or that 'delightful woman' would have the law out looking for her with guns and hounds. He made her promise to come back again and he promised to check on the progress of the house soon.

They stood at the door for a moment before she said good-bye. Then she went down the steps, turning once to wave at him, and feeling light enough to float all the way home. A burden had been lifted and a friendship renewed. She just couldn't ask for anything more.

Ted watched her go, feeling a new freedom and a sudden burst of energy that had been missing from his step, which had nothing to do with having been laid up for the past several weeks. He had felt troubled over how to handle his proposal, worrying whether it was really fair to Lydia to continue with a relationship that his heart was not truly committed to, yet he still could not bring himself to retract his offer of marriage. Until she came to him today, he'd had no answers. But all that was changed. Now he felt a lightness in his heart and he could not contain it. He wanted to share it. So, without wasting any time, he quickly shaved, changed his shirt, grabbed his good hat and headed down the street toward Carrie's house.

He knocked on her front door, removed his hat then smoothed the brim while he waited. No speech came to mind, not even a good reason for being there had occurred to him on his way over. He knocked again and waited. Perhaps something would come to him before she answered the door, but nothing did. And then she was standing in the open doorway, looking like an angel from heaven with wisps of her blond hair haloing her head and her sky-blue eyes round with surprise.

"Ted! My goodness." She stared through the screen door at him and then she gave him the friendliest smile he had ever seen.

"I hope I'm not bothering you."

"Not at all." Then remembering her manners, she asked, "Please, won't you come in?"

He glanced around, then said, "I wouldn't want to cause any problems for you. Maybe I should just stay out here."

"I won't hear of it." She pushed the door wide open. "If the neighbors want to gossip, then they'll do it no matter what. Please, do come in."

"Thank you." He suddenly felt clumsy and wondered what he could say now that he was there. Without a doubt, he couldn't tell her about Lydia's visit, nor the sudden freedom he felt with her releasing him from his offer. So he guessed he would just enjoy Carrie's company and not worry about what he would say next, hoping she'd fill in the silent moments.

"I have some fresh squeezed lemonade," she said, leading the way to the parlor. "Would you care for a glass?"

"Yes. Thank you. It's still quite warm outside so that would be nice." He turned his hat round and round by the brim in his nervousness.

"I'll be right back," she said as she left the room, heading toward the back of the house. "Go ahead and sit down."

He glanced over her parlor, noticing the beautiful wooden furniture, expensive rugs, fancy doilies and bouquets of flowers in tall vases as well as short ones. A mantel clock over the fireplace delicately chimed the hour of eleven o'clock while beside it a matching pair of figurines flanked it. A new realization came over him and he nearly decided to just accept the lemonade, drink it and leave. She was used to having so much more than he could offer her. Why would she want to give up her comfortable life to live as a preacher's wife in less than fashionable surroundings? But he couldn't bring himself to go, not until he'd told her about his deep feelings for her. If she said no, then he would leave and he would simply have to get over it. He hoped.

Looking down the length of the house, he could see her moving about in the narrow kitchen beyond the dining room. He heard the clink of glasses, the close of cupboard doors, and then she was walking toward him carrying two lemonades.

"Thank you," he said, standing when she entered the parlor.

She chose the chair nearest him, and he noticed that she sat with the grace of an angel, too.

"I'm so surprised to see you out and about," she said. "I'm glad you're feeling better."

"It's good to get outside," he said, then sipped his drink, watching her every move.

"That was quite a ways for you to walk. It isn't hurting, is it?"

"No. Not at all. It seems just fine."

A lull fell between them, but neither felt compelled to fill it with conversation. He smiled at her and she smiled back, then he relaxed against his chair. An attractive pink tinge of color climbed up her neck from beneath the collar of her blue-striped dress to her cheeks; then she quickly looked down toward the glass in her hands. His earlier fading resolve suddenly strengthened, and he decided to ask her to go for a walk with him.

"Would you care to—"

"Would you like to—"

They laughed at having spoken at the same moment. Then he said, "Please. You first."

"I was just going to ask if you'd like to go on a picnic. That is, if your ankle is up to it."

"A picnic?" Why hadn't he thought of that, he wondered? "I think it sounds perfect. And my ankle is fine."

He extended his foot and waggled it to prove his words. "When would you like to go?"

"I'm not doing anything tomorrow. Is that too soon for you?" she asked.

"Not at all." And his mind raced ahead, taking his heart along with it, as he considered if then would be the appropriate time to ask her. He didn't think he could wait for several more weeks to pass, and he wasn't sure that he ought to. A woman as lovely as Carrie would certainly have many callers.

"The weather is lovely and I think it should last another day."

"Where would you like to go?" he asked.

She blushed again and he wondered if she was thinking the same thing he was about the willow trees along the river. "I'm not sure. What about you? Do you have a preference?"

"I like the riverbank farther down beyond town where it's quiet. There are a few willows for shade but it's more a part of the meadow."

"Sounds nice." And her blush deepened to a light rose. "I've seldom gone that far from town so it will be an adventure for me."

The last thing he wanted was for her to feel unprotected or unchaperoned or that her reputation would be compromised. They would choose another spot if she preferred. "If you'd rather not go there . . ."

"Oh, but I would. Really."

"If you're sure." And he hoped she was.

"I am. Truly I am."

He nodded, believing her. He would hold his proposal until the perfect moment during their picnic. Somehow that seemed more fitting than here in her parlor.

"What would you like me to bring along?" she asked. "Or would you prefer it to be a surprise?"

He smiled. "Anything at all will be fine with me. Having your company is all I really care about."

This time she didn't look away, but met his gaze straight on with a smile of her own. "That is the nicest thing anybody has ever said to me."

The soft timbre of her voice raised the hairs on the back of his neck. He shifted uncomfortably in his seat as he ran his hand around the back of his collar to smooth them into place. He never would have guessed that just the sound of a woman's voice could do that to a man, but he supposed not any woman's voice would have. Carrie's alone had that power over him.

"Would you like another glass?" she asked, indicating his empty one.

Not wanting to leave just then, he replied, "Yes. Thank you."

When she took the glass from him, their fingers grazed and immediately they glanced at each other. The hairs raised on the back of his neck again as she smiled at him. Then as she walked through the length of the dining room once more, he unabashedly watched the natural sway of her hips. Back in the kitchen, he could see her moving about and humming a tune. Before long he heard her call his name, and he hesitated thinking he must be wrong.

"Ted? Could you help me with this?"

"Certainly," he replied, and followed her steps through the house. Once more he was taken aback by the expensive furniture and lavish rugs that seemed to be scattered everywhere over the warm wooden floors. She had a special touch for turning a house into a home and the kitchen seemed especially so. He knew he could sit at her small kitchen table and watch her bustle about without ever getting tired of being there.

"I don't know why I put that canister up so high, but I do that every time and then I usually have to get a chair to get it down. Would you mind saving me the trouble?" She pulled out a chair for him. "But please, be careful. I'd feel terrible if you fell or something and hurt yourself all over again."

She steadied the chair for him while he climbed up to retrieve the tin with "sugar" printed on the outside. When he was on the floor once more, she breathed a loud sigh of relief.

"I really do appreciate it," she replied. "The next time I will have to find some other place for it." She took the tin from him and set it on the counter of her baking cabinet beside them.

"I don't like the idea of you climbing on chairs when you're here all alone. What if you fell?" He could hardly bear thinking about it.

"I always try to be careful," she said as she dipped in a measuring cup then transferred it to the pitcher of lemonade and stirred. The small confines of the room kept her close to him.

"Now I'm going to worry about you," he said softly, and she turned to look up at him.

"You will?"

"Of course, I will." And the overpowering need to take her in his arms was too much to resist. She came to him willingly, setting aside the spoon as if she didn't care whether it landed on the counter or the floor. "I suppose it isn't exactly proper for me to do this while we're alone, unchaperoned and all." He leaned down close to her lips, grasping her by the waist and pulling her to him.

"I think it's all right," she said, and that soft voice was

back. "I'd rather we were alone if we're going to kiss than have someone watching us."

He grinned. "I have to agree." Then he touched his lips to hers and she leaned into him with her hands trapped between them, clutching lightly at his shirt front.

She tasted sweeter than the sweetest nectar and he couldn't seem to get his fill. Then her arms came up to circle his neck while her soft breasts pressed into his chest. Needing more, his arms went around her back to pull her closer and a soft sound in her throat vibrated to him, intensifying his need until he knew he had to put a stop to it. He raised his head, then laid his cheek against her fevered one while her breath blew erratically against his ear.

"Maybe this isn't such a good idea after all," he said, his eyes closed tight as he tried to regain his control.

"I think it's a wonderful idea," she replied, and he heard the smile in her voice. "But it certainly is warm in here, isn't it?"

"A little bit."

"A lot, actually."

He smiled and agreed. "A lot."

She lowered her arms from his neck and nestled her head beneath his chin. He cuddled her close, enjoying the feel of her in his arms and hoping it would always be that way. For a moment he considered asking her right then, but changed his mind. He liked the idea of proposing on a picnic on the meadow along the river and he found himself wishing she would wear the same dress she'd worn on Independence Day.

"I suppose I ought to be going," he said, but he didn't move.

"You could stay if you like."

A bolt of electricity went through him as he wondered what she was offering.

"It's nearly time for the noon meal," she said. "I could make us something simple."

He smiled and hugged her tight for a second before loosening his grip on her.

"No. I think it would be best if I go. I've probably stayed too long as it is."

"You're worrying about my reputation, aren't you?" She smiled and reached up to kiss his cheek. "It isn't necessary."

"It is to me." He stepped back and took both of her hands then brought them to his lips.

"I liked it better like this," she said, and put his hands around her waist. Pulling his head down to hers, she gave him a lingering kiss that nearly curled his toes inside his shoes. "I never knew that preachers could kiss like that," she said, when they parted at last.

"Me neither," he replied, and she laughed softly with him.

"I really think I'd better go now."

"Maybe you should," she said. "But I will be counting the hours till tomorrow's picnic."

"Me, too. What time should I come by?"

"Around eleven?"

"Eleven it is." Then he stepped back from her once more, holding both of her hands in his.

"Tomorrow," she said, letting him go and walking him to the door.

He smiled at her, then pushed the screen door aside and went out. "Good-bye."

"Good-bye," she said, watching him walk toward the street.

He raised his hand in farewell, then turned and headed back home with a lighter step than he'd had before he'd reached her house, which he wouldn't have thought was possible.

Chapter Twenty

Carrie watched until he was out of sight, then she stepped quickly to her desk where she grabbed the handiest paper and fanned herself. My word, she thought, but he certainly did raise her temperature. All the men she'd kissed had never done that to her, and poor Samuel hadn't even been able to make her blush. But Ted, well, he positively made her feel like her body was on fire from the inside out. Although she'd been married for a few years, she hadn't realized what could happen between a man and woman, that is, *really happen*. Why, just the thought of being with Ted the way Samuel had been with her made her whip the paper a little faster. Somehow, knowing exactly what did happen seemed to make her want to kiss him all the more, and that thought made her aim the fanned air down the front of her bodice, which she held open at the collar.

When she'd finally cooled off, she hurried to the kitchen to check her pantry before making a list of items she would need. This was not going to be a simple picnic lunch. She wanted it to be special so she spent a good share of the afternoon thumbing through her recipes and making a list of groceries. The bread would have to be as fresh as possible even if she had to stay up half the night to do it. Thank goodness she had put up strawberry preserves this year, and sweet pickles, too. When she was done with the list she had to go over it again and cross half of it off since she had more than two people could possibly eat in one sitting. So she whittled it down until she was satisfied that it would still be a good sampling of her cooking, not that he didn't already know what it was like. Then the shopping itself took almost as long as making the list, but at last she was ready to begin.

By nine o'clock she had nearly everything cooked except the bread, which she'd just set out for the first rising. Hardly able to keep her eyes open, she decided a short nap was in order until it was time to knead the dough before the second rising. So she climbed the steps with her feet dragging and let herself fall across the bed. In no time, she was dreaming wonderful dreams of Ted beside her, kissing her and loving her the way she never thought a man could.

When she awoke with a start, she felt disoriented and couldn't understand why she hadn't undressed for bed. Then remembering her bread, she let out a cry and hurried through the dark house taking just long enough to light a lamp in the diningroom and one in the kitchen. The bread had expanded to more than twice its normal size and she almost cried at the sight of it. She feared she'd ruined it, but punched it down anyway and spent several minutes kneading, rolling, turning, and kneading it again. Satisfied that she'd done the best she could, she let it rise again, only this time she had to stay awake. So she lit a lamp in the parlor and took out some mending and sat where she could see into the kitchen, and then she noticed Ted's hat. He'd left it beside his chair. She walked over to pick it up and held it, turning it by the brim the way he had. She wondered if he realized yet that he'd left it. Keeping it beside her on the settee, she picked up her mending once more and thought about the morning, his boyish smiles, and his not-so-boyish kisses.

Before long it was time to knead the bread again, and put it into the pans for baking. The extra warmth in the kitchen added more tiredness to her bones, and she found herself yawning so much she feared she would surely fall asleep and then the bread would bake to a black crisp. The hour had nearly reached midnight when she finally pulled the hot brown loaves from the oven. They were beautiful and well worth the time and effort she'd to put into them.

Yawning again, she shook down the grates and closed the dampers, then listening carefully she thought she heard a noise from . . . outside? Surely, she must have been mistaken, or perhaps it was just some hungry stray dog that had smelled her baking. But there it was again. On her porch? Cautiously, she slipped into the other room and with a lamp in her hand, peered out through the screen door.

"Is someone out there?" she called softly, not wanting to wake the entire neighborhood.

Then a small voice said with a whimper, "It's just me, ma'am." And he stepped into the ring of her lamplight. "I smelled your bread, and I'm powerful hungry."

"My goodness!" A young boy, not more than ten she was sure, stood on her porch. His face was grimy with streaks down his cheeks. Undoubtedly he'd been crying and the tears had made clean tracks in the dirt on his face. "Come in. Come in."

He shuffled tiredly through her doorway and stood off to the side. Then he politely pulled his hat from his head to reveal a thick thatch of unkempt brown hair. She had never seen him before, but decided that was unimportant since the child had said he was hungry.

"Would you like some bread and jam with some tea? I'm afraid I haven't any milk left." She'd used it all in her cooking.

"Yes, ma'am."

"Well, follow me." And she led him to the kitchen and pulled out a chair from her small table. "Sit here and I'll have it ready in a minute."

"Yes, ma'am."

She hurried to cut the bread and butter while the tea steeped in her teapot using the hot water from the kettle she kept on the stove. Occasionally, she turned to watch him. She was concerned he might fall off his chair with exhaustion since he looked that tired. She wanted to ask if he was all right, but knew he would resist telling her just as she knew it would do no good to ask who he was. There was an air about him that said he was not likely to impart any information to anybody, but there was also a look in his eyes that said he was frightened. What should she do? Take him to the police? Was he a runaway? Then she nearly caught her breath as she remembered the orphan trains Cora had warned everyone about. Could he have escaped from one of them?

Then she thought of Lydia and knew immediately what she ought to do. The hour was late, but this was an emergency and she was certain that Lydia would want to help. As soon as the boy finished eating his fill she would somehow get him to her house.

She gave him the dish with the pieces of bread and jam, then carried the pot of tea with two cups to the table.

"Mind if I join you?" she asked.

He shook his head while he chewed his food. "No,

ma'am.'' His wary eyes watched her carefully as she sat across from him and poured the tea.

"Do you prefer a little sugar in your tea?'' she asked.

"Doesn't matter to me.''

"Well, maybe a little sugar would be good for you tonight, although, I understand that children shouldn't make a habit of it.''

"I'm not a child.''

"Oh. I see. Well, please excuse my mistake.'' She sipped her tea then said, "It isn't very hot, I'm afraid. But it's still good. Try it.''

He sipped it carefully, then, finding it cool enough, drank it down without stopping. She poured another cup for him.

"May I ask if you are from around here?''

"No, ma'am. I'm not.''

"Are you just passing through then?''

"No, ma'am.''

He certainly didn't offer much information, she thought. But she wasn't going to give up.

"Oh, so you came to see somebody here in Peaceful Valley.''

"Yes, ma'am.'' He drank his tea but a little slower this time. "Might I have another piece of bread, but without jam this time?''

"Of course.'' She brought the sliced bread to the table along with the crock of butter and set it in front of him. "There. Help yourself.''

"Thank you.''

She let him eat in silence then asked, "Might I ask who you've come to see?''

He studied her carefully then drank the last of his tea, but he didn't respond.

"I would like to offer you a place to stay for the night, but I'm afraid I can't. But I do have a friend who would love take you in for the night, or for as long as you would like.'' At least she believed Lydia would do that, after all, wasn't that what an orphanage was? ''You look like you could use some sleep.''

''Yes, ma'am. I could.''

''Have you come a long way?''

''Farther than I ever thought I could. But I made it.''

''Yes, you made it.'' But his eyelids were beginning to droop and she knew she would have to hurry if she was going to get him to Lydia's. ''Will you come with me to my friend's house?''

He thought about it for a moment then nodded. ''Guess I am tired. My feet hurt, too. And I thank you for the bread.'' He propped his arm on the table with his elbow and set his chin in his hand.

''Well, why don't we go before you fall asleep on that chair? Do you feel well enough to walk a little farther?''

He nodded.

''It might help us to talk if we introduce ourselves. My name is Mrs. Marting. What's yours?''

''Daniel,'' he mumbled tiredly, and she knew she had to hurry or he would soon be sleeping on her kitchen floor.

''Well, Daniel. Let me get a lantern.''

She hurried about as fast she could, then stood before him, urging him to follow her, which he did willingly.

When they reached the front gate of Lydia's house, Daniel stopped suddenly and stared at the weathered old building.

''Does someone live here?'' he asked.

''Yes, and she's very nice. She'll do everything she can to help you.'' Carrie had long since gotten past her unkind feelings for Lydia, and in large part that was Ted's doing. He had nothing but good things to say about her and the children's home she was trying to start. Well, it looked as though this child would be her first needy child, Carrie thought, as she gently tugged Daniel along to the front door.

She hated to make a commotion so late at night, but there was simply no help for it, she decided as she pounded on the door. With the lantern held high so that Lydia would see who was there and not be frightened, they waited, then pounded again. At last, the door opened.

Lydia held her lamp in front of her while Grandma Winnie looked over her shoulder.

"Carrie," she said, surprised, but her eyes went immediately to the dirty, disheveled boy with her.

"We're sorry to bother you so late and all, but I'd like you to meet Daniel. He came to my door tonight and has no place to stay."

"Please, come in. Both of you." Lydia swung the door wide to allow them to enter then led the way to the kitchen.

"Well, I declare," Winnie said softly, and padded along behind the others.

Everyone sat around the table except Lydia, who crouched down in front of the boy. She smiled and said, "My name is Lydia and you are welcome to stay here."

"I came to see my pa."

The three women looked at each other but none of them had an answer to the obvious question, so Lydia asked, "What is his name, Daniel? Maybe we know him."

"Nathan Stockwell. He's my pa." And all three women gasped.

Lydia had to clutch at his chair to keep from falling over backwards as her mind reeled. She knew she had heard him correctly so there was no use asking again, but she desperately wanted to understand.

"Nathan is your father?" she asked.

"Do you know him?" His eyes brightened.

"Yes." Her heart suddenly felt very heavy but she ignored the slow thud. Right now, Daniel came first.

"I'll take you to him tomorrow," she replied.

He yawned and slouched in his chair. "Thank you, ma'am. I'd like that."

Winnie immediately went into action, saying, "I think a bath is in order." She pulled a large wash basin from beneath the stove and set it on the wash table then dipped warm water from the reservoir into it.

"A bath?" he said sleepily, but Lydia knew he was too tired to offer much resistance.

The three of them left him to his bathing in the kitchen while they followed Carrie back through the unfinished house. None of them said a word about the shock and surprise that Daniel had just given them.

"Thank you for bringing him here. I'll see to it that he's fed and taken care of." Her hand shook slightly and she had to steady the lamp with both hands. She couldn't let herself think about the ramifications of this revelation, not now.

"I've already fed him bread and jam with a little warm tea. I doubt if he'll need anything but sleep by the looks of him." And Lydia read her thoughts loud and clear: How could this child be Nathan's son?

Carrie said a solemn good-bye, then walked toward home as Lydia and Winnie watched her lantern light until it was out of sight.

"I declare," Winnie said for the second time and then she was speechless, but Lydia knew that was most likely a temporary thing. She was simply composing her thoughts into a lecture that Lydia did not want to hear.

Outside the kitchen door, Lydia called, "Daniel? Are you finished?"

"Yes, ma'am," he said, stepping into view. He had put his dirty clothes back on and Lydia wished she had something clean for him to at least sleep in, but she didn't.

When her grandmother started to object, Lydia interrupted, saying, "We'll make a pallet on the floor for you in the bedroom upstairs with us." She didn't want to let him out of her sight since she knew firsthand how a runaway child thought, if he was indeed a runaway.

Now, the questions started flying at her and she had to hold them off or at least dodge them until she could be alone to think everything through to a logical solution. There had to be a reason why Nathan hadn't told her he had a son just as there had to be a reason why this child had showed up here looking for his father. Where had he been and why wasn't he with his father in the first place? No, she couldn't think about it yet. Later, she promised herself, when the room was dark and she didn't have to talk. That's when she would try to sort it all out.

"A pallet sounds pretty nice. I slept in an old barn last night. It was kinda scary."

Lydia's heart nearly hurt for him, as her own memories were suddenly dredged up. She and her brother had made a similar trek and had ended up on Irene Barrett Hollister's doorstep, and lucky for them that they had.

"I declare," Winnie said, but Lydia quickly shushed her.

"This way," Lydia said, taking her lamp and gently steering Daniel to walk alongside her up the stairs. She wanted to ask him more questions, but her grandmother's presence prohibited that from happening.

After they got him settled on the pallet he looked up at her and said, "Ma'am. I don't want to go back."

Lydia hardly knew what to say. How many times had she said those words as a child? How many times had she cried into her pillow at night over the death of her parents, hating the rigid regime of the orphanage they'd been forced to live in? But Daniel's situation was different, he did have a father. Families stayed together no matter what, so there was no reason he shouldn't be with him, no reason at all. Somehow, she would get this all straightened out, but until then she had no answer for Daniel.

He yawned and said, "I just want to stay with Pa."

Then before she could turn down the lamp to blow it out, he'd fallen asleep. Winnie started to speak, but Lydia shook her head. She simply could not discuss any of this, not before she had some time to think it through.

But as they crawled into bed and pulled up the sheet, she heard her grandmother mutter, "I knew there was something about that man I didn't like." Then she rolled over and was silent.

The words cut straight to Lydia's heart as tears of hurt and disillusionment welled behind her closed lids. Nathan hadn't been completely honest with her. At the very least, he had kept an important part of his life hidden, and now she felt confused. Had everyone known he had a family, and simply failed to mention it to her? What about Daniel's mother? What had become of her? Had Nathan abandoned her as well? Were there other children? She didn't want to believe that he had abandoned anybody, but what else was she to think? The child plainly said he wanted to live with his father, and she could see no reason why that wasn't possible.

She felt a sudden kinship with Daniel and her first instinct was to look after him, even if his father wouldn't. There was so much that needed to be said to Nathan, so many questions to ask. Already the small hours of the morning had come and gone, but she still couldn't find any answers. Finally exhausted from thinking so much, she fell asleep.

When Lydia awoke it was to the sound of pots and pans coming from the kitchen. One hasty look confirmed that both Daniel and Grandma Winnie were out of bed and most likely downstairs cooking breakfast. Without wasting a movement, she hurriedly dressed and pinned up her hair then dashed down the stairs. She found Daniel sitting at the table eating hotcakes smothered in the butter her grandmother had bought the day before, among other things which made her small cabinet doors bulge.

"Good morning," she said to them, relieved that Daniel was still there. Her first waking thought was that he'd run away, but she knew her grandmother would have told her immediately if that had been the case.

"I thought you were going to sleep the day away," Grandma Winnie said. "So I decided to give this boy a hearty breakfast."

"Is that bacon I smell? And maple syrup, too?"

"I simply can't abide a kitchen without a proper pantry so don't give me any disrespect. Now, sit down and eat. He's a growing boy, but he won't be able to eat all of that by himself."

Lydia sat at the table and gave him a wink in hopes of letting him know that he had nothing to be afraid of, that she was on his side and would stick by him. But as far as eating anything, she couldn't. The talk she intended to have with Nathan loomed like a confrontation and her stomach repelled the idea of food.

"Did you sleep well?" she asked Daniel.

"Yes, ma'am," he said between bites. "I guess being clean helped." She could tell he was trying to be appreciative of her help, and had to smile.

Winnie set another dish of hotcakes on the table. "Clean clothes would be even nicer."

"Yes, ma'am. But I didn't have time—" He stopped

abruptly, his eyes wide as he stared across at Lydia.

"It's all right," she said, reaching her hand over to touch his sleeve. "I'm sure your father will take care of that as soon as he can." She let it pass that he'd just told her he was a runaway. Her only concern at the moment was for him to know she understood.

Daniel nodded, but said nothing else while he studiously finished his breakfast. After he swallowed the last bite, he said, "Can we go now?"

"Yes. We'll go." Then she turned to her grandmother, saying, "I don't know how long I'll be."

"I have plenty to keep me busy," she replied. "I'll be waiting."

The two of them walked side by side through town while Daniel stared at everything with great interest.

"I've never been here before," he said. "Is this a nice place to live?"

Her heart went out to him as she realized that he had come in search of his father with the intention of staying. How long had it been since Nathan had seen his son? An angry knot formed in her stomach, and she knew that whatever the reason for abandoning this child, it had better be good. At first she'd wondered if it was wise to go to his shop where others might overhear their conversation and draw attention to Daniel's predicament, but her only other choice was to go to his house after he closed up. Somehow, she didn't think the boy could wait that long and frankly, neither could she. So she prayed Nathan would be alone.

She stopped outside the open front doors where the sappy scent of pine floated out to greet them. Holding Daniel back, she peered inside to see if Nathan was alone. When she didn't hear any voices, she took a fortifying deep breath and stepped forward as she held Daniel's hand. Inside the cool interior, she walked past piles of lumber, odd pieces of wagons and assorted other things that she paid little attention to as she made her way toward the man at the bench. He hadn't heard them approach from behind and Lydia suddenly stopped, watching his shoulders move as he worked with some sort of device she couldn't see. At just the sight of him she realized once again how dear he had become to her. But now her feelings felt bruised while these new emotions roiled and conflicted with those lovely ones she'd been holding close to her heart since the night of the storm. Then a tug from the warm little hand in hers reminded her why she was there.

"Nathan." Her heart pounded, but not from fear or worry what he might say to her. It pounded with deep regret for what was about to happen.

He turned to look at her and smiled with pleasant surprise, then his eye caught sight of Daniel. He stood as if frozen to the spot, but the young boy, ecstatic at seeing his father, bounded across the open area and threw himself into Nathan's arms. Then grasping him by the shoulders, Nathan held him away.

"Son, what are you doing here?"

Lydia tried to read the emotions behind his expression, but the barrier had come up. She couldn't tell if he was glad to see his son or if he was angry or if he even felt anything at all. He was an expert at hiding his emotions.

"I came to stay with you, Pa. Don't make me go back." Tears filled his eyes as his voice thickened. "Please, Pa."

Nathan gave her a quick look before turning to his son. "We'll talk about it later." Then he rose to his feet and faced Lydia. "Where did you find him?"

She continued to stare at him, torn between wanting to understand and wanting to demand answers for his treatment of his son.

"Carrie Marting brought him to my house last night after she fed him." Her words sounded cold but she didn't care. And the barrier went up a little higher.

"I'll take care of him. Thank you for bringing him here."

He couldn't dismiss her like that. She wouldn't allow it. He had to offer some sort of explanation. She needed to know what was going to become of this child, and what was going to become of them? Had everything between them meant nothing at all?

"Will you let him stay?" she asked with her chin up and her stare unshakeable.

Silently, he returned her stare, but this time she saw a new fire in his gold-flecked eyes. His mind was made up and she knew he wouldn't allow her to change it. Still, she couldn't let this happen, not without knowing why he was being so heartless.

"A child needs his father," she said, and suddenly she knew that she had stepped beyond a boundary.

"This is my problem and I'll take care of it."

She would not be easily intimidated, not when a child's well being was at stake. Someone needed to take the boy's part, and if his father wasn't going to do it then she would!

"He doesn't want to go. Doesn't that matter to you?"

"I'll take care of this. It doesn't concern you." His voice was cold enough to make frost appear.

"All children concern me, especially the ones like Daniel." She knew the boy was listening to every word, as his head followed whichever one of them spoke. It wasn't fair to allow the boy to hear their conversation, but she couldn't walk away until she discovered Nathan's intentions. A child had the right to live with his father as long as that father was perfectly capable of taking care of him, and Nathan

298

was more than capable. Why did he want to abandon his son?

"You don't know. . . ." But he stopped there.

"Tell me, Nathan. I want to know."

Her gaze searched his face for answers, but all emotion was buried. There was nothing for her to read, nothing but stony silence as he retreated further behind his self-made barrier. She started to take a step forward in a plea, an offer to help, but he placed a hand on Daniel's shoulder and stood firm. There was nothing else she could say or do, although plenty of things came to mind.

"I'll go," she said to him. Then, turning her attention on the boy, she forced her face into a smile and said, "Good-bye, Daniel."

He looked up at his father then back at her. "Good-bye, ma'am. Thank you for keeping me."

She smiled again, but this time the tears of frustration blurred her vision and she had to turn and hurry from the shop. Out on the street in the bright morning sun, she made her way home letting the tears roll unheeded down her cheeks.

Chapter Twenty-one

Carrie hurried to answer Ted's knock, taking a quick peek in the mirror to make sure nothing had come loose. Slowing her steps before she reached the screen door, she smiled and pushed it open.

"I hope I'm not too early," he said.

"Not at all. Come in." And she retreated a little to allow him to enter. "I've got the basket all packed. Would you mind carrying it for me? It's a little heavy."

"Certainly," he replied, and looked around for it. She thought he looked especially handsome in his simple dark jacket, but she couldn't help but noticing that he seemed a little more nervous than usual. Somehow that didn't worry her. He had seemed uncomfortable in her house the last time, too. And his concern for her reputation only made him more dear to her.

"It's in the kitchen," she said, leading the way toward the back of the house.

"Smells really good in here," he said, following her.

"I made cinnamon custard. You do like it, don't you?" She stopped beside the table where the basket sat open, displaying the custard pie on top.

"Oh, yes. I do. One of my favorites."

"I guess we're ready then," she said, her anticipation for the day mounting. Just spending time with him, talking to him, was enjoyable, and yes, kissing him, too, she freely admitted to herself. No other man had ever made her feel so young or so wanted, neither had she ever wanted a man so much.

"I guess we are," he said.

"I'll just get my hat." But he put out his hand and gently stopped her.

"I wish you didn't have to wear it. Your hair is too beautiful to be covered and I don't get to look at it often enough." He looked suddenly more relaxed, more at ease, just the way she preferred him to be.

"Thank you. That's such a nice thing to say," she said. "Maybe I'll just take my parasol."

As they passed through the parlor, she lifted a blue one from the stand and looked at him for approval. When he nodded she smiled and opened the door, holding it for him to bring the awkward basket through. She popped open the parasol and stared up at the bright sky, loving the new lightness she felt in her heart. Her worries had simply faded over the past few weeks and she owed it all to the feelings that she shared with Ted. She no longer felt alone or worried about the simplest chore. Her frantic searching had come to an end that day beneath the willow trees, and she thought he felt the same about her.

After he loaded the basket into the back of the buggy, he asked, "Would you like the top up?"

"Oh, no. Leave it down so we can enjoy the breeze from

301

all directions. And if it musses my hair, well, I won't mind if you don't."

"Mind?" he said, surprised. "Not at all." She thought he looked as though he might say something else but quickly decided against it. Then he helped her climb in and walked around the buggy to climb in beside her.

"It is such a beautiful day." She laughed and added, "I might have already said that, but it bears repeating."

"Indeed it does." Then he gently slapped the reins and they moved along the street.

Outside of town they followed the river, passing the group of willows where their first kiss had taken place. She'd relived that moment many times over the weeks that followed right up until the second kiss he'd given her, and then she'd had two moments to remember. She slipped a sideways glance at him, hoping he wouldn't catch her, but he did and they shared a smile. A summer breeze floated by and, thankfully, cooled her heated skin. He just seemed to always have that effect on her, but she didn't mind it at all.

At last they arrived at the spot he had told her about, and it was even more beautiful than she'd expected. The river was deeper here with high banks and fewer trees to block the view of the meadow.

"I've never really been out on the meadow this far," she said. "I love those rolling hills beyond the edge. Over there . . ." she said, pointing in the distance. The only times she crossed the meadow were to follow the main road to the next town, and she seldom if ever noticed how lovely it was.

"I like to come here often. It's a good place to think."

"It's so quiet." And as if being asked, the wind settled down and the birds ceased their singing for a moment while they sat in the buggy, listening. Then suddenly it all came alive with the natural sounds of the meadow as the tall grasses sighed, the locusts churred, and the birds burst into individual song.

"Maybe it isn't so quiet after all," she said, laughing.

He watched her until she sensed his gaze and turned toward him. "What is it? My hair? She lifted a hand to touch the wisps that floated around her face.

Without saying anything he leaned over and kissed her, not long and lingering like she wished he would, but short and tender. "That's for thinking of having this picnic."

"I'll remember that in the future," she said, staring into his eyes, which seemed to reflect the blue of the parasol over them.

He smiled. "We might like to take a lot of picnics."

"Indeed we shall," she replied softly.

"If I kiss you again, I'm afraid I'll forget why we came here."

"And if you don't, I will be disappointed."

"I wouldn't like to have you disappointed."

"Then, I'm waiting. . . ." She leaned forward, closing her eyes, and he met her halfway.

The kiss was as tender as the previous one, but she felt the restraint in him as he kept his hands on her upper arms holding her close and yet far enough away to be safe. She almost sighed, wishing it could be more. Then he broke away from her.

"I think I'd better set up the picnic," he said. Then he turned her loose and climbed down from the buggy.

She watched while he walked a short distance to the river's bank and came back only to walk it again. He did this one more time and she had to laugh at how silly he looked.

"What are you doing?" she asked.

"I'm tromping down the grass so you won't snag your

dress,'' he replied as he flattened a circle at the base of a small tree where they would lay out a tablecloth. "I think that should do it.'' He came back to the buggy and lifted her down, hesitating with her in his arms long enough for a quick resounding kiss, then he hefted out the basket.

"I have to ask,'' he said as they walked his freshly-made and very fragrant path. "What is so heavy in here? I think you've put bricks in the bottom just to make me think it's loaded with food.''

She laughed again, thinking she hadn't ever laughed so often. "Oh, but it is loaded with food.''

When they reached the spot he'd trampled she opened the lid and pulled out a very large tablecloth and he spread it under her supervision. Then he helped her to sit on one corner while he knelt beside her.

"Would you mind taking everything out?'' she asked.

Ted lifted out the dishes and a couple of canning jars filled with colorful pickled things, and two more jars of lemonade. "These are why this thing is so heavy.'' Then he took out the bread, roasted chicken, glazed carrots, fried corn and two pieces of chocolate cake.

"I brought that in case you don't like cinnamon custard,'' she said.

He looked at the custard pie and then at her. "No, no. I like custard pie. But I like chocolate cake, too.''

Carrie set aside her parasol before they set the food around the cloth within easy reach. Ted crossed his legs Indian-style and balanced his overflowing plate in his lap. They talked about many things while they enjoyed their picnic lunch. They began with the progress of his ankle then went on to the ladies in his church who had cooked so much food for him, and next discussed the kinds of wildflowers that now surrounded them, and even mentioned

took time to enjoy a decent full-sized meal at the little restaurant beside the hotel, but that was a rarity.

He reached for the coffee mug on the shelf beside his
tools, dumped the wood shavings out of it and headed for
the blacksmith shop where Jeff kept a pot of coffee going
all day. Skipping a meal was one thing but foregoing coffee
was another. Even Jeff's overcooked black dregs was better
than none.

"Hey, Nathan," Jeff called. "How's it going?"

He poured enough coffee into the cup, then swirled it to
rinse out the sawdust before he pitched it out the back door.
"I've got just enough stock hoops for these hubs. Could
you make me up another bunch?" He filled his cup and
took a swig. It was hot and thick and rich, and it stuck to
his ribs.

"Sure thing. As long as you're not in a hurry for 'em."

Nathan shook his head. "I should have asked sooner, but
I was a little preoccupied with cabinets and cakes and
such."

"Hmpf. I know what you mean," he said. "Women.
They're the darnedest to understand. You're a smart man
to stay unhitched for so long."

Nathan took another drink and avoided joining the conversation.

Jeff grabbed his coffee mug and filled it while he leaned
against a workbench as though he needed to discuss what
was on his mind.

"You know," he began, "I always thought Penelope
was a woman with a mind of her own. She sure tells me
what she thinks often enough, and she tells it straight and
true. Most of the time, anyway. But lately, well, there's a
conspiracy going on and it all started with that orphanage
of the teacher's." He gulped down a swallow of coffee.

"No, I take that back. It all started with the mayor's wife. And now we're right back where we were during that saloon rumpus." He swigged another gulp. "And I'm damn tired of Agnes messing in my personal life."

Nathan wasn't sure what he meant by that last statement, but he remembered the bad temper his friend had been in just before the saloon closed up. Personally, he was glad that the temptation had left town. He'd spent enough money and wasted enough time in such places . . . but that was a long time ago.

Jeff leaned a little closer and whispered, "I hate chocolate cake."

Confused, Nathan sort of tipped his head in acknowledgment that he'd heard him, but he didn't reply.

"I've been eating chocolate cake for dessert for a week now. I'm fed up with it. And I'm fed up with the M.M.C.C. And I'm starting to get fed up with this seat on the council." He drained the coffee mug and set it down hard on the bench.

"Don't look at me," Nathan said.

"Why not? You'd be great for the council. You're not married." A devilish smile spread across his face. "Agnes wouldn't be able to control *your* life."

Nathan stepped back and raised his hand to stop that line of thinking. "I haven't got the time."

"Come on, Nathan. A little civic duty would do you good. And it would be good for Agnes, too."

He frowned. "What does she have to do with the council?"

Jeff lifted his eyebrows in surprise. "Why, she thinks she runs it! Her and that damn club of hers."

"That's impossible."

"She wanted the curfew. She got it."

"And you give her the credit for that?"

"Believe me, she gets the credit."

Nathan would never have thought that Agnes Butterfield was that powerful. He still didn't think she was. "So why does the council give in to her?"

Jeff clapped a hand onto his shoulder. "Nathan, my friend, I'm amazed at how green you really are." Then he shook his head as though he hated to dispel that kind of innocence, but he would anyway. "When a woman wants something that a man doesn't, the woman takes away something that the man wants. Are you following me?"

Nathan almost grinned since he definitely followed what Jeff was getting at. Penelope had kicked him out of their bed, and he blamed the mayor's wife and her club. Didn't sound logical to him, but then he guessed he didn't know much about the politics of the council.

"The result of all this is that I'm eating more chocolate cake and liking it less all the time. And now, it's turning into an issue of principle. Even if I was dead set against the orphanage being here, I damn well wouldn't change my mind." Jeff's frown deepened and he looked like he could flatten a ten-penny nail with one hit of his hammer. "Well, I've bent your ear long enough. I'm sure you've got work to do. Sorry, Nathan, but I haven't been in such a bad humor since the last time there was a rumpus."

Nathan refilled his cup and turned to go to his own shop where the only thing he had to think about was work. But he did feel sorry for his friend and said, "Hope things get better for you."

Jeff grumbled, "Thanks."

Nathan returned to his lunch, and once that was out of the way, and the last of his coffee gone, he went back to checking his measurements on the wheel hub. Soon the sound of the lathe filled the shop and the pile of shavings at his feet grew. His concentration was deep, his interruptions were few, and before long the afternoon had slipped away. The rumble in his stomach told him he ought to go home, and since his next step was to begin on another block of elm, he decided he'd call it a day. He spent some time putting his tools in order, then gathered up his empty knapsack and closed the wide doors behind him. After locking up, Nathan paused outside the shop while he considered the thought that had been hanging at the back of his mind while he'd been working. He couldn't help wondering what the preacher had done to the porch at the Mercer house, and so he decided to walk by and take a look even though it was out of his way.

Mayor Butterfield stared at the fried mush on his plate. How he missed the beautiful, delicious meals Agnes always prepared. He especially missed the baked ham swimming in sugared glaze with cloves stuck into the little squares all around it. And the sweet potato casserole. And the green beans. . . .

He hated mush. But mostly he hated what it stood for, which was a loss of control in his home. A steady diet of mush was demeaning and not to be tolerated. One afternoon he had slipped into the restaurant for a decent meal and had been questioned by Richard Davis as to why he wasn't at home eating steak. Too embarrassed to explain, he made up an excuse that Agnes had been busy with a meeting of the M.M.C.C., and that was the last time he attempted to eat away from home. Somehow he had to get a grip on this situation before he died of malnutrition.

Pushing aside the untouched plate, he faced Agnes across the table.

"This will not do," he said.

"You don't like it?"

"You know I don't like it."

"The choice is up to you," she said, looking very satisfied with herself.

"Yes. It most certainly is up to me. And I choose not to eat another bite."

"I think you might go hungry."

"I might." That idea didn't set any better than eating mush.

"Of course, you could change your mind about the orphanage."

"Agnes, that is extortion," he replied, angry enough that his moustache quivered.

"Call it what you like."

Giving in to her wishes over the saloon had been difficult, but the others on the council had seemed even more eager than he was to have it over and done with. Although they had not said as much, he'd decided that their wives had put pressure on them, too. But this time he hadn't heard one word from any of them, and he'd be darned if he would bring it up and give the appearance of being a henpecked husband.

He rose from his chair and strode to the kitchen.

"Where are you going?" she called quietly from her seat at the table.

"To look for something to eat."

"You won't find anything but bread."

Bread would do just fine. He'd lather it with butter and jelly, if he could find any. One way or another, he was going to win this battle.

Richard sat in the parlor waiting for Cora to join him, just as he'd waited for her to speak to him through dinner. He would have offered to help with the dishes, but her sharp glance warned him not even to consider getting that close.

So he had taken the coward's way out and gone to the parlor.

He was still mystified by her reasons to protest against the orphanage. She loved children, and he would never have thought that she would put a distinction on loving only some children. But whatever her thinking, he wasn't changing his mind. The council had made a good decision and he saw no reason to change it. Of course, sleeping in the small spare room alone was giving him pause on that notion, especially in the middle of the night when he turned to pull her into his arms and she wasn't there. He surely did miss her warm softness when she snuggled against his back and her arm would lie across his bare hip, and sometimes she would even reach for— That line of thinking would get him into trouble, he decided, and shifted to a more comfortable position in the chair. Until she stopped locking their bedroom door, with him on the outside and her on the inside, he might as well concentrate on something else. So he picked up the Cincinnati newspaper, gave it a shake and then angled it toward the light coming in the window. And that's when she came in and sat opposite him. Suddenly, the air in the room came alive with tension, just like the electric lights he'd seen in the city. He lowered the paper enough to get a view of her eyes, which were red and puffy, and he knew she'd been crying again. Exhaling loudly, he dropped the paper to his lap.

"Cora. This has gone too far. I don't like to see you so upset all the time."

She picked up her needlework and diligently wove the needle through the fabric. But her sniffle told him that she wasn't finished crying yet.

"Then change your mind," she said.

He sighed, feeling at a loss to explain the same thing he'd already said using different words. "I don't know why you are so dead set against this. She only wants to help children, for God's sake." Frustration was leading to anger, which was about to break out into words he'd wish later that he could take back, so he clamped his mouth shut and hid behind his newspaper once more. He hoped that would be the end of it for the evening.

Moments passed. Then she spoke. "I think you are being unfair to me."

He dropped the paper. "*I'm* being unfair? And what do you call being thrown out of one's own bedroom?"

"Justice." She sniffled again.

"For what? Having a different opinion?"

"No, for not caring . . . for not being concerned. . . ." Suddenly, she threw down her sewing and rushed from the room, and the next sound he heard was the bedroom door slamming with the turn of the key immediately following it.

He gave up. They hadn't had a coherent conversation since that blasted orphanage subject became the topic. Tossing the paper to the floor, he strode from the room, grabbed his hat off the hook by the door and left. Where he would go, he didn't know, but he had to escape before the sound of her crying drove him to distraction. If the saloon was still in town, he would have gone there. But the M.M.C.C. had taken care of that, too. He guessed he'd just have to wander the streets until bedtime.

Penelope stirred up a batch of dumplings and set it aside while the beans and ham simmered a little longer at the back of the stove and two pans of cornbread baked in the oven. She'd been ironing all day and figured that if the stove had to be kept going then she might as well have supper cooking, too. But the heat had made her irritable. Her back ached, her feet hurt and to tell the truth, she missed Jeff's easygoing, fun-loving presence. His teasing always made her worst days bearable and his playful pats on her bottom as he passed by made her smile. But lately neither of them was smiling. He'd taken the whole orphanage thing out of perspective and turned it into a battle between the men and the women, but she didn't see it that way at all. This was an area that men could not understand, she told herself, and yet they were in charge of making that decision. Of course, she was feeling a little guilty over refusing him the privileges of a husband, but she had accepted the pledge along with the other women and knew that they must all stand together if they were going to make a difference.

And that was another thing she kept wondering about. Were the others living up to the pledge? She hadn't talked to Jenny and Laura since the last M.M.C.C. meeting. As a matter of fact, she hadn't talked to any of the women since that meeting. Jeff had been very vocal in letting her know just what he thought of the goings-on at Agnes's, and she didn't like having to defend her friends. So rather than stir the pot any more, she'd stayed away. But now that she was feeling irritable, she decided she should pay a visit to some of the other women. After all, she didn't much like being told what she could and couldn't do.

Taking the bowl of dumpling dough, she dropped spoonfuls of it into the big pot of beans. The rising heat collected under her collar and formed more perspiration which then rolled down her back, making more irritation rise within her. When the top of the beans were covered with the expanding dough, she turned to the chocolate cake that had cooled on the table and cut a slice for herself before she even added the icing. It soothed her nerves like a cool hand on her hot body.

Tomorrow she would visit Laura or Jenny or Cora . . . or *somebody*. This was too much isolation for her; she needed to know how it was going with the others, and Jeff could like it or not.

By the time Nathan reached the broken gate the sun had slipped and now cast long shadows around the big house. The first thing he noticed was the rough work on the first post where Ted had fashioned a square support that couldn't be called a pillar by any stretch of the imagination. Lured by what else he might find, he went in for a closer look and discovered the sagging end was propped up by a heavy rock that, no doubt, had to have taken some doing to get it into place. He didn't want to be critical of the preacher's work, especially since he'd obviously put a lot of effort into the job, but the whole thing promised to turn into a very sad affair. In order for the porch to give any justice to the rest of the house, it would have to have pillared posts that had been turned on a lathe and then painted white. He judged the wooden floor to be mostly rotten and needing complete replacement with one-by-six pine boards, but even before doing that the joists beneath needed replacing since patching the floor would do no good if the two-by-sixes gave way under it. A railing would be nice, but not necessary since the porch was only two steps off the ground. Overhead, the rafters were surprisingly sound, which was an indication that the roof didn't need any work. A complete lack of maintenance had provided the undoing of the house.

He stepped off the porch and studied the broken second-story windows. They were arched across the top and gave the house an interesting look, but replacing the curved glass would take a lot of patience if the framing wasn't good. If the sashes were sound, then it would just be a matter of cutting and glazing. And most likely, the interior trim had been ruined by the weather. He walked to the back of the house, surveying the lines to judge if the building had settled, which would be an indication of an undermined foundation, but as far as he could tell in the shadowy light, everything looked plumb. He would have liked to look around inside, but figured he was already trespassing and didn't care to have a run-in with the owner, so he thought it best to leave. But when he reached the gate, he looked over his shoulder at the partial repair on the porch and had to force himself to shrug it off. Poor workmanship was a hard thing to overlook, even if it was done with the best of intentions.

Chapter Nine

Lydia sat on the front porch step with Sarah, their lunch between them, studying the boards that Ted had put in place to hold up the roof. They had such a long way to go.

"It isn't very pretty, is it?" Sarah asked as she squinted a wary eye at the support.

"Ted says it's purely functional at this point."

"Thank goodness."

And Lydia had to agree with her. The house she'd pictured in her mind had lovely white posts that were smooth to the touch, but she trusted Ted's judgement when he said they needed to keep it safe and looks didn't count right now. They would work on that later. But she wondered if it wouldn't be better to block off the entire porch from use since the floor was in such bad shape. At one point during the day before, one of the twins had stepped on a rotten board and almost gone through it. As a result, they had been temporarily banned from the area.

"Where did the boys go today?" Lydia asked as she unwrapped a sandwich from a napkin and gave half of it to Sarah.

"Fishing at the river with some of the other boys—but I'll bet they really went swimming. Mother will have a fit." Sarah accepted the sandwich.

"Hmm. I guess I ought to know about these things," Lydia said. "When I have any boys who want to go fishing then I'll know what they're most likely doing." She thought about that for a while and discovered a new warmth seeping in. Boys and girls of any and all ages would one day live here with her. She would look after them, nurture them, teach them, and guide them into the world so that they would do the same with their own children. The girls would learn to sew, to cook, and to care for others, and maybe even take up a career. The boys would learn skills through the local craftsmen by taking jobs as apprentices. And that was another thing. She needed to contact the businesses and find out which ones would be willing to hire her boys.

"What are you smiling about?" Sarah asked. "You look awfully happy."

"I am." And she almost laughed out loud. "I was just dreaming about how things are going to be. Sometimes lately, I have to pinch myself just to make sure this is all real. I've waited a long time for this, over ten years."

"I hope I don't have to wait that long for my dream to come true," Sarah said.

"Tell me your dream, Sarah, and I'll wish along with you."

Sarah waited a moment, tearing at the piece of crust on her bread. "I'd like to be a nurse."

"Why, that's a wonderful dream! And you'll be a good one, too." Lydia studied the young girl beside her. She had been an excellent student and it should come as no surprise that Sarah wanted to go on to further her education. The surprising fact was that she had graduated a year ago and was still at home.

"I wish Mama and Papa thought so." She bit into the sandwich and Lydia waited for her to go on. At last she said, "Mama thinks it's inappropriate for young girls to tend the physical ailments of others, but I know she means men." Sarah shrugged. "Nurses don't think like that. They think about healing, not about bodies."

"Are there any nursing schools in Ohio?"

"In Columbus, I think. But Mama would never allow me to go. And it isn't the money, because she already told me I should consider Bowling Green's Normal School, where you attended. So if I could change their minds, then I could go." She gave Lydia a pleading look. "Do you think you could talk to Mama for me? She would listen to you, I know she would. She admires you and, well, I just think you'd be the best person to speak for me since you know what it's like to have a dream."

"I don't know, Sarah. Not that I won't try—"

Sarah threw her arms around Lydia's neck, cutting off her words, and hugging her in gratitude. "Oh, thank you, Lydia! You are the best friend ever."

Lydia hugged her, patting her back and laughing. "I said I'll try. I can't promise anything more than that, all right?"

Sarah turned her loose, smiling. "That's all I'm asking. Honest." She let out a big sigh. "I'm so relieved. I've been wanting to ask you for a long time, but I just didn't have the nerve."

"You can ask me anything, anytime. What are friends for?"

After that, Sarah was practically giddy and full of enthusiasm, which bubbled over and affected Lydia. They set aside the last of their lunch, donned their old-fashioned dust caps and returned to the work in the kitchen. Lydia decided that with all the sawing, hammering and hauling of wood, the porch was best left to Ted since he was so willing to do it. So she and Sarah had spent the last two days in the kitchen knocking out plaster with a prybar and scooping it into buckets to be hauled away. The work was dusty but they made good progress and expected to have the walls bare to the wooden slats before long. Lydia looked forward to fresh new plaster, some cheery wallpaper and bright curtains, and that would bring her closer to the next stage of her dream, which she decided to share with Sarah.

"When we get this room finished, plaster and all, and the cookstove, too, I'm hoping to move in." She waited for Sarah's response.

"You want to live here before it's all done?" she asked in wide-eyed disbelief.

"Why not?"

"You are braver than I am. This house is still spooky at night."

"It won't be. You'll see. It will be cheery and homey, even if it's one room at a time."

Sarah looked suddenly apologetic. "Oh, I didn't mean to make light of your dream. Especially since you were so good to listen to mine. It's just that I get goose bumps in dark old houses."

"Well, it doesn't seem like a dark old house to me, I guess."

"If you do move in and you find out you're afraid, you can always come back to your old room. And if the new teacher arrives first, then you can stay with me in my room."

"Has your father located a new teacher already?" She knew it had to happen, but she hadn't expected it so soon.

The schoolhouse and her desk would belong to another woman, and she hadn't truly let go of it, not yet. A small stab of regret made her look backward to the years of teaching, and for a moment she had to face that feeling before she could remind herself to look forward again.

"He has two candidates, and he said both of them seem well-suited. I think he plans to have one of them hired within a month." Unaware of the effect the discussion had on Lydia, Sarah worked her broom over the dust pan, filling it with broken plaster. "Looks like we'll have this done in no time, don't you think?"

"Yes," she replied, bringing herself to the present. "Yes, I do."

After that, there was less talk and a lot more dust-making. They worked until nearly suppertime, taking occasional breaks and pumping glasses of fresh water from the new pump to ease their dry throats. Just when they were ready to call it quits, the twins showed up soaking wet from head to toe, including their shoes.

Sarah gaped open-mouthed at them.

"Aaron fell in," giggled Alexander.

"Did not. You pushed me."

"So I had to jump in and rescue him," he said with a shrug.

"Wait till Mama sees this. And I would not want to be in your shoes when she does." The boys started to bolt at the same time, but Sarah got hold of them by their shirts. "Oh, no, you don't." And even though they squirmed, she held tight, leading the way home. "See you later, Lydia," she called over her shoulder.

They were a sight, all three of them, with the twins in their dripping wet clothes and Sarah looking like she'd been dusted with plaster. Lydia stood at the front porch and watched them go. She smiled and shook her head, enjoying the sudden warm feeling she'd been having of late. It was a feeling of belonging and of home, and she wished it would never go away. Unwilling to dispel it, she sat on the steps and folded her arms in a sort of hug. If she missed supper, she didn't mind. She sat staring across the tall grass in the yard, past the gate and beyond the street. This view had become so familiar that it truly was home and she hated to leave it. The minutes slipped by and the air cooled, but still she sat. Then a passerby strolled into the background, catching her eye, and she followed his form until it dawned on her who he was. Sitting up straight, she felt a bolt of shock course through her as Nathan Stockwell stopped at her gate and stared at her house.

Even though she sat front and center, she felt invisible since he seemed not to have seen her yet. His gaze roamed over the porch then finally met hers. He appeared as surprised as she was, and being caught, he couldn't turn tail and run. But then he didn't really seem to be the kind that ran from anything.

He nodded at her then came down the weed-clogged walk until he stood within a few feet of her skirt. She didn't know what to say so she said nothing at all, and neither did he. With one hand he tested the rough support beside her that rose to the roof, seeming satisfied with its strength he walked to the end of the porch and studied the place where Ted had placed a rock to brace it up.

"I would suggest replacing all the joists. Actually, I'd suggest replacing the entire porch except the roof." He stared at the rafters as he talked, and she might have thought he was speaking to someone on the roof if she hadn't known there wasn't anybody up there. "It's surprising that it's held up this well," he said, but apparently not to her, because he hadn't made eye contact since he'd passed through her gate. "But that doesn't mean it couldn't stand a good tarring in places," he went on.

"We did that," she said, unable to keep silent any longer. An angry feeling rose within her toward this man who had rejected her pleas for help not once but three times, and she didn't appreciate his unwelcome criticism of her home-to-be.

"That's a beginning," he said, which was stating the obvious in her mind.

"I see some of the upstairs windows need to be replaced."

"I didn't know you lived at this end of town."

"I don't." But he didn't elaborate further, not that he needed to, since everyone knew where everyone else lived in Peaceful Valley. "I happened to be walking by last night and noticed a few things."

"And tonight?" She was being rude, but couldn't help herself. He'd been more than rude to her when she'd offered to pay for his workmanship.

Finally, he looked at her. "Tonight I just wanted to see if anything had changed, and when I saw you sitting here I thought I would offer some suggestions."

"I don't need suggestions, Mr. Stockwell." His direct stare nearly went through her, but her sense of protectiveness for the house gave her the motivation to stand up to him. As she slowly came to her feet, she found that the step on which she stood brought her almost to his eye level, and she liked that. Now he couldn't look down on her.

"Maybe you should take them," he said.

They stood so close she could see the gold flecks in his brown eyes, and something else, too. Was he baiting her on purpose? Was he looking for an argument?

"Maybe I don't want them."

"Do you want the house to last or to fall down?"

"Of course I want it to last."

"Then you'd better listen to a little advice."

"Ted is going to fix this porch, if you're referring to that."

"If he is, then he will want to know that the joists have to be replaced first and that means tearing out everything."

"It seems to me that you've already given me that advice."

"I just want to stress the importance of it."

Whatever had fired those flecks in his eyes to a deep golden suddenly disappeared and the gold seemed to lighten.

"I think I understand, but it really isn't your concern." She couldn't quite forget the stubborn refusal he'd given her those three times she'd asked for help. And now, here he was offering advice as though she had never approached him at all. She could not just step aside, invite him in and accept his sudden interest in the rebuilding of her house. Her pride wouldn't get out of the way.

"Those second-story windows," he said with a quick look in that direction, "will most likely need a lot of repair work or else you'll have to tear them out. It would be a shame to do that."

"I love those windows. They won't be torn out."

"Depends." He shrugged as though that remained to be seen.

Giving up the advantage of being near his height, she stepped down, turned to face the house, then backed up in order to look at the windows. They were in sad shape, even worse than she'd thought now that she studied them. Until this moment, she'd seen the house the way she wanted it to be in every respect, but his critical eye had brought it to her attention and she could not deny the truth. But her pride still wouldn't budge, and she swallowed her words before she asked for help again. After all, he only stopped to offer advice.

"Ted will fix them," she said.

He gave the porch a meaningful glance, and she didn't miss the look.

"This is only temporary," she said in defense. And it was. Ted had assured her of that, and she believed him.

"Is he planning on getting to it soon?" His question was very matter-of-fact, very businesslike.

"I don't know," she replied hesitantly. "He wasn't able to work today. He was needed at the church." She didn't expect Ted to spend every single day working on her house and had told him so. His help was very much appreciated but he was not to feel obligated when he had other things to do.

Nathan nodded. "This will to have to be first on the list since it affects the rest of the house at the roofline." He pointed to where the porch roof joined the siding on the house. "If it pulls away, then there will be more damage to the interior walls. And it's hard to say how much more this old house can take."

He sounded so certain and knew his work so well that she had to bite her tongue to keep from asking for his help one more time. She hated to risk losing the house, but then she reminded herself that he was only offering advice. If he'd wanted the job, he would certainly have said so. He wasn't the kind of man to beat around the bush; she'd found that out firsthand and had come away barely unscathed.

"I'll mention it to Ted when I see him." Ordinarily she would have said thank you, but in this instance she couldn't bring it forth. She resumed her position on the step, waiting for him to take his leave.

"Guess I'll get on home," he said.

She nodded politely, expecting him to walk toward the

gate. When he lingered, staring at the house, she felt her ire rise at his continued appraisal of their lack of knowledge and inability to get the job done quickly. She almost told him that they were doing the best they could, but held her tongue hoping he would just go. Then finally when she thought she would burst with the need to say what she'd been thinking, he turned and walked away.

Relieved at having him gone, she took one more walk through the house, then collected her lunch basket and walked home slowly. She refused to let the task overwhelm her and she refused to let Nathan Stockwell's so-called suggestions bother her. Whether he'd come out of curiosity or just to needle her, didn't matter. She had work to do, and she would take one day at a time.

When Nathan arrived at his home, he dropped the knapsack on the small kitchen table then emptied the contents into the dishpan to soak. He started a quick fire in the cookstove using cottonwood sticks to give just enough heat to boil coffee and cook a simple supper. After he'd eaten, he pushed aside his plate and took out a pencil to make a list of materials for the old Mercer house.

He hadn't wanted to have anything to do with it, but the house was bound to fall to ruin if left to the hands of Miss Jefferson and Ted. Having their hearts in the right place, as he'd overheard someone say at the council meeting, was not going to build a sturdy house or, in this case, rebuild one. A definite lack of understanding of the process would undoubtedly be their undoing, and even though he had to shut out of his mind the purpose of the house, he could not seem to ignore the poor craftsmanship. He knew he ought to stay away, but he couldn't. So he decided to make a list of materials for the porch only, materials he probably already had, and repair it himself. He would go after his own work was done and hoped there wouldn't be anybody at the house. Miss Jefferson had asked for his help, and he decided he would give it after all, but it was more a matter of workmanship than charity and he wanted her to understand that. He still wasn't in favor of an orphanage, and never would be.

The next morning Nathan worked on the remaining hubs, his thoughts going too often to the old Mercer house and the first order of business there. Several times he caught himself forgetting to take measurements, but each time he'd been lucky and everything was accurate. At noon, he decided to forego the coffee at Jeff's and continue working in order to make up for the time he'd spend at the house that night. Of course, he would only help out for a short time so he wouldn't get behind in his own work for very long; still, he preferred to keep ahead of schedule on the wagon. And since he allowed no room for mistakes, he had to keep his mind on what he was doing.

Then he heard Carrie Marting calling his name from the front doors of his shop, and he knew his concentration was in jeopardy. He debated about leaving the hub on the lathe until she left and taking up some other job that needed less precision work, but then again he had a wagon to build. So he continued working until she stood inside the backroom door, calling him again.

"Nathan," she said, raising her voice over the rasping whirr of the lathe. "Could I speak to you? Please?"

He slowed the pressure on the pedal until it came to a stop, then turned toward her.

"I'm afraid that the last time we talked we parted not in the best of tempers. I hope we can remedy that since I wouldn't like to have you angry with me." She looked as if she might cry and Nathan felt a quiver of guilt. "I've brought a peace offering. I hope you'll accept it."

She held a basket covered with a napkin and he knew there was some sort of delicious food in it.

"I thought perhaps we could take a picnic out on the meadow. You do realize it's nearly time for the evening meal, don't you?"

He hadn't noticed.

"Well, it is, and you should take time for nourishment. I simply don't know how a man who works as hard as you can keep up his strength without proper nourishment."

She stepped closer and pulled back a corner of the napkin, but he smelled her soft, perfumed hair before he noticed the aroma of what was in the basket. It had been a long time since he'd stood that close to a woman, and her fresh, clean scent affected him more than he wanted to admit, but admit it he did. Then he backed a few steps away.

"I've got a lovely dinner," she said, showing him the crisp chicken, brown biscuits and a jar each of red beets and pickles. "I do my own preserving. Not because I have to, but because I enjoy it."

The food was as much an enticement as she was, and he nearly forgot his resolve to stay away from both. He knew there were strings attached and he'd be wise to stick to his better judgment.

"After I lock up tonight, I'll be working at the old Mercer house. I won't be able to take time out for a picnic. Sorry."

She blinked at him in surprise. "The old Mercer house?" she repeated. "Whatever for?"

"Repairs on the porch," he replied simply and without explanation.

She blinked again, trying to grasp the implication of what he'd said. "Well" was all she could say.

"If you'll excuse me, I need to get back to work."

"Absolutely not. We will just have our picnic here," she said, moving his tools around on his workbench to make a place for the basket. "You have to eat sometime so you might as well eat now." She looked up at him when she had it all set out. "I'm serious, Nathan. No excuses this time."

He stared at the chicken, sniffed, then felt his stomach growl.

She produced two plates from the basket and set one before him, then opened the jars and dished out pickles and beets for each of them. Then she chose a piece of the crispy chicken and set it on his plate, pointing at it with one delicate finger and nodding for him to go ahead. So he did. After all, she was right: he did need to eat and his own cooking was nothing like this.

"Do you like it?" she asked, not touching her own food.

He knew he'd be in trouble for admitting it, but he said, "You're a good cook, Mrs. Marting."

"Why, thank you!" she said, and seemed to relax. "Samuel always said that my pickles were better than he'd eaten anywhere. Try them. It's my own recipe."

She sampled one of the tiny sweet pickles from the jar at the same time he sampled one from his plate.

"It's good." It was more than good, but he figured he ought not say so. He'd already said too much and gone too far.

"I have a lovely bottle of wine in the cabinet at home, but I didn't think it would be appropriate to bring it along."

"I don't drink," he said, and his tone was abrupt.

"Oh," she said thoughtfully and placed another piece of chicken on his plate. "Then it's just as well I left it there."

They ate in mutual silence; she tasted small bites of everything while he ate his fill.

"So, you're working at the Mercer house? I suppose that

119

means you won't have time for another project for me.''

He knew he'd be sorry about giving in to the temptation of her food, and now it was time to pay up. There was plenty of work for him to do without the Mercer house, but if she believed he had time for that, then she would expect him to work for her when he finished.

''I can't promise anything.''

''Well, I wouldn't expect a promise exactly, but maybe when you finish working for Miss Jefferson you'll have time for my table. It's really very small, just a bedside table.'' She showed him an approximate size with her hands. ''I can't imagine it would take you too long to make it.''

He knew where this was heading, straight to her bedroom. A table that size wouldn't require asking for Jeff's help, but it would be more than she could carry up the stairway by herself, which left him to carry the table. Perhaps he was being too suspicious, but he didn't think so.

''It's hard to tell how long the job will last at the Mercer house.'' He wiped the napkin across his mouth, feeling like a beggar for taking her food and giving nothing in return. But then she wanted more than he could give.

''I'm so disappointed.'' And she let her full bottom lip protrude slightly in a pretty pout. ''It wouldn't take long to make it, Nathan. You're so very good at what you do. I would even be satisfied if it were a little bit smaller if that would save you some time.''

He shook his head. ''I'll be working here during the day and at the house in the evening.'' He quickly made up his mind to take on the repair job for just as long as it took Carrie Marting to tire of chasing him. And he hoped that would be soon, very soon.

''Now I'm really disappointed.'' Her blue eyes suddenly lost their sparkle and his hopes rose. She gathered up her dishes, napkins, jars of pickles and beets as well as the couple of pieces of untouched chicken. "Do you want to keep these for later?" she offered, her voice as downcast as her expression.

But he couldn't accept them under the circumstances and so he said, "No, thanks."

"Well, I've taken enough of your time and kept you from your work long enough." She tucked the top napkin neatly around the contents and lifted the basket off the workbench.

A bit of remorse made him say, "Thanks. It was delicious."

Her smile brightened and she said, "So you really did like it."

He nodded, trying not to be too encouraging.

"I'm glad." She walked toward the door, gliding in that way he associated only with her. "I'll check with you later, when your work is caught up." She raised one hand and fluttered her fingers at him in a small wave. "Good-bye for now."

When she'd gone, he relaxed with his back against the workbench, thinking about the narrow escape he'd just had. Carrie Marting was a smart, attractive woman who knew how to find a man's weak points, and once she'd found them she would persistently prod those places until he caved in. Well he had no intention of caving in or even letting her believe that he might. The unfortunate part of it all was that in order to keep from committing to one woman, he was going to have to commit to another, but at least Miss Jefferson didn't have matrimony in mind.

Now, he had to quit mulling over the events of the past half hour or so and get his thoughts aimed toward some kind of work, which was where he felt the most comfortable. So he put away his tools for the day, loaded the wagon with supplies and locked up the shop, then headed for the house at the edge of the meadow.

Nathan maneuvered the wagon close to the front gate of the Mercer house then set the brake and climbed out. He brought tools for prying away old boards, a hammer and nails, and several two-by-fours to shore up the porch roof while he tore out everything else. As he unloaded the wagon, he stacked the materials within easy distance of the working area. Then he studied the project before him, planning where to start, and knew immediately that he had to prop up the corners and remove the old posts as well as the one Ted had roughed in.

He worked with efficiency, handling tools that were as familiar to him as his own hands and making the most of every movement whether it was prying up boards or tossing them out of the way. The creak and squeak of rusty nails being pulled loose along with the boards should have brought Miss Jefferson running to confront him, but when she didn't appear right away he knew she must have gone home, and that suited him fine. He'd already had enough disruption for one day.

After two hours had passed and the sun started settling on the horizon, he wiped his brow and went in search of a pump for a drink. Around the corner near the flat-roofed kitchen, he found a new cast iron pump and gave the long handle a couple of hard pushes until fresh water gushed forth. He drank from his hands, then scrubbed his face with water alone, cooling his skin to the neckline of his shirt. Now that he felt refreshed, he went back to study what his next move should be, but coming toward him alongside the house was Miss Jefferson, and she didn't look happy to see him. Her face was free of the plaster dust that had covered her the night before and the strange-looking cap was also gone, leaving her brown hair visible with its tendrils loosened haphazardly. But the frown she turned on him and the abruptness of each step she took told him she was either annoyed or angry, or possibly both. He stopped where he was and waited for her to approach, knowing that a confrontation was about to take place. But it would be entirely one-sided. He hadn't come to argue; he'd come only to work.

Chapter Ten

"Mr. Stockwell," she greeted him coolly.

"Miss Jefferson," he replied.

"May I ask what you are doing here?" she asked, and he noticed for the first time that her eyes were such a deep brown they appeared almost black.

"Repairing the porch." He kept his reply casual.

"I don't recall asking you to do that."

"I thought you did."

"I did not."

"You asked me to help," he quietly insisted.

"Yes, well . . . I asked you some time ago and you refused, more than once if I remember correctly. And I did not ask you again. This is a different matter."

"It's the same house."

She opened her mouth to contradict him, then changed her mind. With one eye squinted angrily at him, she accused, "Are you splitting hairs with me?"

He tried not to grin, but couldn't stop himself. She looked so angry and frustrated, and yet in complete control of the situation, that he found himself admiring her fortitude.

"Are you?" she insisted.

"No. I only came to fix the porch right."

He watched her struggle with deciding whether to turn him away or let him continue working. At first, she angled her head toward the front of the house, then back to him. Then she crossed her arms under her breasts and studied the toes of her shoes, and next she studied the side of the house, then her toes once again. Finally she looked him in the eye, seeming to have come to some sort of decision.

"I'll pay you, but I can't pay much."

"I'm not asking for wages."

"I don't like charity."

"I don't blame you. Neither would I."

Silence fell between them so that the only sounds he heard were those of crickets, frogs and whippoorwills coming from the meadow.

"Maybe," she said, "maybe we could make a trade of some kind. Later on, when I have something to trade . . ." Her voice faded away to nothing, but she kept her chin raised and stared up at the house.

"That's a possibility," he replied, but couldn't imagine what it might be.

"I do need help," she admitted, and he knew by the catch in her voice that it took a lot for her say that to him.

"Yes, I can see that."

"Ted tries. I mean, he really has been a lot of help, but he'll be the first to say he isn't a carpenter. And it isn't fair of me to take him away from his church so much of the time. . . ." Her voice faded again and he barely heard the last word she spoke.

"I can come in the evenings after I finish at the shop. Maybe not every night. It just depends on the work that comes in."

He waited for her response. Then she nodded. "All right." And with that said, they struck an agreement.

"I've still got enough daylight left to finish tearing out the rotten wood, but I'd rather wait until tomorrow to start rebuilding."

"Certainly."

They stood for a moment longer, each one waiting to see if the other had something more to say. When the silence grew awkward, Lydia realized she was probably blocking his way, so she stepped aside to let him pass. Without speaking again, he went directly to work, prying the few remaining boards free and tossing them onto the growing pile. She watched him from a distance as a new sense of relief washed over her. It started in her shoulders and moved down her back until the tension she'd been carrying in her body dissipated. He had the experience she needed and without his help she would fall short of the deadline that had been set for her. She wondered now how she could have believed that she could do this all alone. Already, weeks had passed and she'd barely made a dent in the work that had to be done. True, she and Ted had accomplished an important part of it all when they'd fixed the roof and chimneys, but there were so many rooms and so many windows still to be done that she'd had to close those thoughts from her mind and tackle one small job at a time. But as she watched Nathan Stockwell work, her doubts fell away and were replaced by a surge of renewed enthusiasm. Once again she believed that this house could become a children's home, and Spring Meadows would become a reality.

Dusk had come on quickly and a night breeze swirled

around the house, eddying in the corners before lifting the hem of her skirt. She glanced toward the sky where a few clouds were beginning to roll in from the southwest and hoped it would not rain again. As he tossed the last board onto the pile, she stepped forward to speak to him. He wiped his shirt sleeve across his forehead, then stopped when he caught a glance of her coming toward him.

"I'll have these burned tomorrow," she said. "We have a small burning pile so that we can clean up as we go."

He nodded. "Next time, I'll bring the lumber for the floor."

"Oh, we already have the boards for the porch. Ted put them inside the house where they'll be sure to stay dry so we can get them painted as soon as the porch is finished. Would you like to take a look at them?" she asked, leading the way to the side door before he could say no.

He followed her onto the small stoop made of concrete with an overhang for protection from the elements.

"We seldom use this door because it sticks so badly," she said, trying push against it.

"Here," he said, moving around her and putting his shoulder to the door. Two bumps and it scraped open. "Probably just settled." He tested the door again after she'd stepped inside. "Could be just the dampness. There's something about living in a house that makes everything work better."

"I certainly hope so," she replied. "Over there is the wood. It's getting kind of dark in here. I guess I should keep a lantern handy in case you need one. Sarah and I haven't spent much time here after dark so I hadn't thought about it."

He knelt beside it and sorted through the stack, looking

down the length of individual boards he seemed to choose at random.

"Looks like he took my suggestions."

Lydia wondered at his statement and asked, "Your suggestions?"

"I saw Ted at the mill the day he bought this."

"Oh." Ted hadn't mentioned anything about that to her.

"It doesn't look as though he bought anything to make the porch pillars. Unless he put them somewhere else," he said, glancing around the room.

She brightened immediately. "Pillars? I really had hoped to put white ones out there, and maybe a nice railing with spindles." Then she remembered to be practical. "Of course, a railing isn't necessary." It was just part of her dream, but it was the part she could easily live without.

He seemed not to be listening to her, but looked deep in thought.

"Would you like to see the rest of the house? Or maybe you've already seen it. Sarah tells me that half of the town has been through here at one time or another in their childhood just trying to scare up a ghost or two. Did you ever do that?" She smiled at him in the dim light, hoping to see a smile in return, but he remained as serious as usual.

"I didn't grow up in Peaceful Valley."

That surprised her. She had believed, for some odd reason, that he'd always been a part of this community in his own isolated way. His business was so well established and everyone seemed to accept him without questioning his reclusiveness.

"I'd better be going," he said, turning abruptly toward the door. He held it open for her until she passed by, then stepped outside, scraping it shut behind him. "I'll try to get that fixed." And she could almost see him making a mental note to remember to bring a hand plane the next night.

Without wasting a movement, he gathered up his tools and carried them to the wagon. Lydia wondered if she'd said something that hurried him along, but couldn't think of what it might have been. Surely, asking a simple question about being in the house when he was a child hadn't been the cause of his departure, especially when the answer had obviously been no. She stood beside the gate and watched him climb aboard.

"Good night," she called, and he gave her a salute before driving the horses away.

Perhaps she only imagined his rush to be gone since he always seemed to have no time to linger at all. She put the thought behind her and studied the change he'd made to the front of the house. Progress, she told herself. They would make some real progress now. It was a warm thought to hold close as she walked to the Graylings' in the cool night air.

When she arrived home she found Sarah waiting on the porch alone.

"So what do you think?" She sat on the edge of her chair hardly able to contain her excitement. "Tell me!"

"About what?" Lydia replied hesitantly, wondering if Sarah could possibly know about the agreement with Nathan Stockwell.

"Oh, you know! The house . . . the porch . . . Mr. Stockwell!" she sputtered.

"How could you know already?"

"With all that noise, how could I not know? He sure makes a powerful racket when he tears something up. So I went to investigate."

"I didn't see you."

"Well, I stayed out of the way. It didn't look like you

were getting along too well at first. And I think he's kind of frightening, don't you? No, I guess you don't. You sure stood up to him, though, Lydia.'' She smiled with admiration all over her face.

"Sarah! You were spying."

She waved a hand carelessly in front of her face. "Spying is what you do when you see something you're not supposed to, and since you weren't doing anything you weren't supposed to be doing, then I wasn't spying. Right?"

"Close enough."

"Don't be mad. I'm sorry, I won't do it again. But I wasn't spying." She smiled impishly. "So what did he say?"

"You mean you don't know?"

"I left when the two of you went in the house. See?" she said, pointing a finger mischievously at Lydia. "If I had been spying I would have stayed and watched through the window. But I wasn't and I didn't."

"All right, all right." Lydia laughed. "I give in." Sarah was so exuberant and high-spirited that it was impossible to be angry with her.

"So tell me!"

"He didn't actually say he would work on the entire house, or even some of it. We just sort of mutually came to the conclusion that he'd fix the porch. Oh, and the side door, too. After that, well, I guess we'll have to wait and see, I suppose." Lydia leaned back comfortably in her chair opposite Sarah's. "He's certainly a strange man. He doesn't talk much."

"Is that what you mean when you say that you 'sort of' agreed?"

Lydia nodded, murmuring, "Yes."

"He is different. But he's always been that way."

"Always? How long is that?"

"Um let's see." Sarah counted on her fingers, thinking carefully. "Well, I can remember when someone else had the wheelwright shop, a Mr. Taylor I believe, and that was about six years or so ago I think."

"What do you know about him?" Now she felt like a spy, but her curiosity was up and if anyone could tell her, most likely that person would be Sarah.

"Mr. Taylor?"

"No, silly. Mr. Stockwell." She knew Sarah was teasing her by the grin on her face.

"So. You're interested, are you?" Sarah leaned back in her chair, too, idly tapping her fingers together while she watched Lydia. "He is attractive. Scary, but attractive. Of course, Mrs. Marting doesn't think he's scary. Do you suppose he's spoken for her hand yet?"

"I wouldn't have a clue about that, but I am curious about him."

Sarah shrugged. "Believe it or not, nobody knows much about him. He just sort of showed up one day working in the wheelwright shop, at least that's how it seemed to me, but then I was only about twelve. And watching wagons being built didn't really hold my interest."

"What happened to Mr. Taylor?"

"He died. But he was terribly old, and crippled, too. I suppose he must have left his shop to Mr. Stockwell." She shrugged again. "I guess I never thought about it much."

"So he has no family?"

"If he does, nobody's ever seen them. I mean, I've never seen them."

They sat awhile longer, silently contemplating the person of Nathan Stockwell until the mosquitoes finally chased them inside. But even after she'd readied for bed and climbed between the cool sheets, she continued wondering about him and why he was so taciturn and sometimes downright discourteous. Perhaps not having a family had made him that way. Everyone needed to feel they were loved, which brought her thoughts back to her reason for starting a children's home. Every child needed to feel loved.

Another sunny morning greeted Lydia and Sarah as they approached the house. Only this time, there was the promise of excessive heat ahead, which was not exactly the kind of day to work on sooty stovepipes, but it had to be done. Lydia's hope of having at least one finished room depended on their work in the kitchen. So, she thought it best to get the dirty job out of the way before they plastered the walls to a lovely white.

"Are you sure this is worth it?" Sarah asked as she reached her arm into the fire box, scraping out the old damp ashes that seemed to have molded to the stove. "I mean, how much does a new stove cost anyway?" She pulled up a scoopful of ashes and made a face.

"Too much, and that's all I need to know. Would you rather trade jobs?" Lydia scoured the large reservoir on the side with a heavily bristled brush, flaking off the rust as well as the skin on the ends of her fingers.

"No, thanks."

"I've saved the best job for last." Lydia nodded toward the back of the range top where the castiron collar disappeared into a rusting stovepipe. "You can take that one, if you like."

"I think I'll stick with this. Disgusting ashes are better than soot and tar."

Lydia halted her work. "Really, Sarah, you don't have to do any of this."

Sarah smiled and scooped out another glob, then dumped

it into the bucket at her feet. "It does go beyond the pale of friendship, doesn't it? Just remember that when I ask for a favor in return." She stuck her arm back inside the opening and grimaced. "And I do plan on asking."

Lydia laughed and started scouring again. "Ask anything you like and I won't say no. That's a promise."

"I'm counting on it."

At noon they washed up at the pump, scrubbing from their knuckles right on up their grimy bare arms past their elbows. The cool water refreshed them as they raised handfuls to their faces, but Sarah, unable to resist, went a step further and splashed water on Lydia, who in turn splashed water back. Then Sarah took charge of the pump handle with one hand while keeping Lydia at bay with her splashing, which resulted in a water fight that left both of them more wet than dry. Laughing, they staggered under the weight of wet skirts that dragged through the dirt as they made their way toward the front steps that led up to the missing porch.

"You are unfair!" Lydia said, giving her friend a light shove, walking beside her.

"And you are a mess."

"Oh? And what's that sticking to your hair?" Lydia reached out and pulled a small chunk of wet stove ash from Sarah's golden-blond hair.

"Well, I think you've lost a good share of your hairpins in the back."

Lydia knew she must be right by the feel of her hair along her neckline, but she was too hungry to be concerned about it.

They sat on the steps in the partial shade so they could enjoy a little breeze and sorted through the basket they'd brought. Their appetites were heightened by the physical work they'd done and neither wasted any time biting into their sandwiches.

"Mmm. This is delicious," Lydia moaned. "I can't remember when I've been so hungry."

"I can. Yesterday, when I had all that plaster to knock down, then sweep up."

Lydia brushed a straggling wet strand of hair from her cheek and the movement brought down several strands over her eye. Laying aside her lunch, she tried to pin it back.

From the day they'd begun working on the house, they'd had few passersby, since it was off the main path and along the outside edge of town. But when Sarah and Lydia looked up they found Carrie Marting standing at the gate, staring at them.

"Miss Jefferson?" she asked, as if she couldn't be sure.

Faced with the perfectly coifed, perfectly dressed and perfectly spotless Mrs. Marting, Lydia nearly groaned aloud with embarrassment, and Sarah did.

"Yes?" Unable to stop herself, Lydia touched the hank of hair that refused to be pinned.

"I hope you don't mind," Carrie said, walking toward them with her perfect walk. "But I just wanted to stop by and see what sort of work Nathan is doing. He told me he would be here every evening."

"He did?" Lydia finally fastened the wet lock of hair by securing it close to her head. It felt terrible and had to look even worse, she was sure.

"Well, yes. We talk quite often." Carrie stopped a few feet away from them and Lydia started to rise to her feet, but Carrie put out a hand to stay her. "Please, don't bother to get up. You look so . . . comfortable. And I didn't mean to interrupt your picnic." Before either of them could reply to that, she went on. "So this is what Nathan was talking about." She indicated the propped up roof.

"He worked on it last night," Lydia said as a trickle of water, or perspiration, slid down her back, and she wondered if Carrie ever perspired.

"Yes, he told me," she repeated for the third time, and Lydia decided it must be important for them to know just how much Nathan told her.

"This project could take quite some time, couldn't it?" Carrie studied the big old house and bit her lip with concentration.

"I certainly hope not," was Lydia's heartfelt response.

"Oh, that's right," she replied, looking at Lydia once more. "They've given you only a few short months, haven't they?" She gave a small shake of her head that made Lydia wonder if she sympathized with the unfair deadline or pitied her for the way she looked.

Sarah quickly got to her feet, brushing crumbs from her lap and scattering mud from her hem, saying, "Excuse me, but I need to go to the privy."

Carrie backed out of harm's way and said, "Of course, dear."

Lydia squelched a smile and promised herself to discuss a few manners with Sarah later.

"Well, I don't want to keep you from your meal. I know you must be anxious to get the house finished, and I must be going. I told Nathan last night that I would bring him a dish for his supper so I need to get back home and start cooking. Now, don't you ladies overwork yourselves," she said as she turned and walked away, then when she passed through the gate she waved at Lydia with a flutter of her white-gloved fingers.

Lydia gave her a quick smile and a short wave then returned to her sandwich, glad to be alone for a moment. How could one woman make another feel so shabby and inconsequential in all of ten minutes, she wondered? She glanced over her worn old shoes that were now mud-caked, as was her dress, thanks to their silly game at the pump. Her hands had callouses, scrapes, cuts and bruises, and she didn't even want to dwell on what her face probably looked like.

"You look like you've just lost your one and only friend in the world," Sarah said, as she sat on the step beside Lydia again. "I didn't know you and Mrs. Marting were that close." Her eyes danced with mischief.

"Would you like to return to the pump, young lady?" Lydia threatened.

Sarah laughed. "I'm far too old to take a threat like that seriously. Besides, you'd be the one to get drenched."

"Well, I couldn't look much worse, I'm sure."

"Oh, poot," Sarah said, with a dismissing wave of her hand toward the street. "You aren't going to let that man-chaser make you feel bad, are you? She has nothing better to do with her time than to stand in front of a mirror most of the day. But you, why, you have goals, Lydia. Wonderful goals. Admirable goals. And don't forget that for a minute." She munched on her sandwich. "I'd take goals any day over looking nice." Her eyes twinkled merrily at the inverted compliment.

Lydia laughed and gave her a quick hug. "I suppose that was meant to be flattering, but then again, I'm not sure it was."

"I'm just teasing you. But I meant what I said about your goals. Don't make less of them just because they're hard work and take a temporary toll on your hands."

Lydia studied them once more. They certainly had never looked like this when she was teaching.

"Besides, Mama knows some wonderful garden remedies to repair damaged skin and, even, hair. Then before you know it, you'll be chasing after Mr. Stockwell, too!"

Sarah laughed and dodged Lydia's playful punch to her arm. "Stop! I'm only teasing!"

"I think you are the one who'd better stop," she threatened, giving Sarah a devilish grin.

"All right, I will. Promise." She handed Lydia a slice of brown-sugar cake from the basket. "Peace offering?"

She accepted the cake with a smile. "That's more like it."

They sat quietly for a while, enjoying the rest of their lunch. Lydia thought about Sarah's words, and felt glad to be reminded that she could live with broken nails, limp hair and mud-caked skirts as long as she was getting closer to having a home ready for unwanted children. Suddenly, the scrapes and bruises seemed to be nothing at all.

After they'd put away the basket, they returned to the old cookstove to finish cleaning up. By late afternoon they had even banged and scraped the soot from inside the old metal chimney pipe.

"I'd like to try it out," Lydia said. "After all, how will we really know if it works if we don't try it?"

"Sounds like a good idea to me, but . . ." Sarah said as she eyed the distance to the chimney hole in the wall behind the stove. "Is it close enough?"

"I think it is," Lydia replied, but not with complete confidence. "Let's try it."

They attached the stovepipe to the collar coming out of the back of the stove and angled it toward the wall where the chimney was located, which turned into a real struggle that took quite some time. But neither of them was willing to give up.

"If we could just budge this thing a few inches," Sarah said in exasperation, eyeing the monstrous cookstove.

"That would be impossible."

"Why can't the thing have wheels?"

"That would be ridiculous," Lydia said.

"Well, you're a lot of help."

"Give it one more try."

They twisted the elbow pipe in a different direction and it slipped into the chimney, barely.

"We did it!" Sarah collapsed against the wall. "I can't believe we did it."

Lydia studied the connections. "They look safe. Don't they?"

"What can happen? We'll just build a small fire. Just so we'll know if the firebox leaks out any smoke. It would be nice to know if all this work was for nothing." Sarah went in search of the matches and a little kindling.

Lydia tested the pipe gently at the stove and at the chimney hole. It seemed to be secure in both places even if it wasn't exactly as tight as it ought to be.

"This should do it." Sarah shook out her skirt, unloading the splinters of wood that had recently been part of the front porch. "These are so dry they won't burn for long so I brought some bigger chunks, too."

Lydia was a little skeptical of the bigger pieces but decided that Sarah was right; they were so dry they wouldn't take long to burn up. So she laid the kindling in the firebox in crisscross fashion until she had a nice-sized pile, and then she dropped the lit match near the bottom of the sticks. She checked the dampers to make sure they were partly open for a little draft and kept the firebox door open, too. Soon, a few licks of flames caught, then held and a tiny fire burned inside the cleaned-out stove. They added more kindling and even a couple of the larger pieces of wood.

"I don't see anything happening anywhere," Sarah said, as she inspected the end of the stove. "Let's put in a little more wood. Maybe there isn't enough smoke."

"We'll have to open the dampers more if we do that," Lydia said, unsure that it was a good idea.

"It'll be all right," Sarah said confidently. "See, there isn't anything coming out of the connections so these must be tight."

"I suppose you're right. I guess I'm just nervous."

Lydia added more wood, opened the dampers completely and the firebox door only slightly. Within seconds, the fire roared up the chimney pipe and into the chimney hole and both of them stepped back involuntarily. A new sound like the crackling of a brush fire filled the room, seeming to come from the wall where the chimney went to the roof. Lydia rushed to close the firebox door and turn down the dampers, but the crackling continued. Then in horror, they watched the pipe gradually slip from the chimney hole and the room instantly fill with choking smoke. It billowed around the ceiling and scudded out the doorway like a low cloud.

Lydia clutched at Sarah, who stood too close to the stovepipe but seemed to be riveted to the spot. They needed help and they needed it fast.

Chapter Eleven

Nathan smelled the smoke as he walked through the gate. And then he saw it flowing out of the broken window of the flat-roofed addition. He dropped his tools and took off at a dead run, colliding with Lydia at the corner.

"Fire!" she said. "In the chimney. I'll get water." She had a bucket in her hand and ran for the pump, but he stopped her and took the bucket.

"I'll find another one!" she shouted, and ran back to the kitchen.

Nathan pumped furiously, then hauled the bucket inside, following Lydia. Walls denuded of their plaster had left tinder-dry slats exposed to the possibility of fire, but there were no flames, only smoke. He tossed the water at the area surrounding the chimney pipe and a new smoulder rose to mingle with the smoke. Behind him, he felt Lydia tug on his arm, indicating the bucket she'd brought. He tossed it at the wall, and the two of them ran for the well again.

Nathan pumped both buckets full and grabbed them before she could pick hers up. Inside once more, he tossed the water at the wall. The smoke lessened and followed the current of air up the chimney and out the broken windows as well as the open door. Instinctively, the three of them backed away, listening for the sound of flames within the chimney. But apparently the source of the fire had been burned out since all was quiet except for the sound of Lydia's heavy breathing.

She tried to catch her breath between every couple of words, saying, "I think there must have been a nest or a buildup of leaves in there." Then she pointed at the stove. "We were trying it out."

He looked at the stove, frowned and said, "You started a fire in it?" It was a wonder they hadn't burned the whole house down and them along with it. "Don't you realize how dry the wood is in here?"

She blinked in surprise at his sharp words. "Just what do you think was our intention?" she replied, her breathing calmer now but her voice just as sharp as his. "We've been cleaning that stove all afternoon and we only wanted to find out if it was usable." Her dark eyes snapped, daring him to accuse her of trying to burn down her own house.

"Well," Sarah said, fidgeting as she sidled closer to Lydia, "I didn't notice if there were any leaks, did you?"

"No." But Lydia wouldn't take her eyes off Nathan. This man was impossible to understand, she decided. First, he refused to help her and was rude in the process, then he showed up unexpectedly one evening and tore out her porch without so much as a "please" or "I'm sorry that I behaved so rudely." And now, after she'd nearly had the wits scared out of her, he had the unbelievable gall to practically accuse her of being addlebrained enough to burn down the house.

Sarah shuffled her feet nervously. "I didn't notice either," she said once again softly, her eyes round with apprehension as she watched the two of them.

"Leaks?" Nathan asked, puzzled.

"Leaks," Lydia repeated. "In the firebox. We were looking for smoke."

"I think you found it," he said, and a corner of his mouth lifted in a half grin.

Lydia didn't see anything humorous about the situation, but it crossed her mind that she wasn't at all surprised that he did, and that frustrated her—so much so, that she was unable to return his grin.

Finally, he turned away to check inside the firebox and the confrontation ended, but not Lydia's exasperation with him. In addition to that, her knees were still weak from what almost had happened. If there had been a chair nearby she would have gladly collapsed into it.

"Doesn't seem to be any danger here," he said, peering carefully inside the ash-filled box. Then he straightened and walked around behind the stove. "As soon as that pipe cools I'll take it down and inspect the chimney. But I'd say that was a pretty good test and since it didn't catch everything else on fire, most likely it will be fine from here on out."

Sarah clasped Lydia's arm. "I don't know about you, but I'm feeling a little shaky all over."

Lydia didn't care to admit anything in front of Nathan. He was an intimidating man, and she wouldn't allow herself to show him even the smallest sign of weakness. So she locked her resolve, as well as her knees, and said, "I'm fine."

"Well, I'm not. I need to sit down," Sarah said, and escaped out the door toward the pump.

Nathan glanced down the length of the long, narrow

room. "Looks like you've cleaned this down to the bones. I'd say the only thing left to do is the plastering and painting." He walked across the floor, studying its sturdiness and watching for rotten boards. "Floor seems solid."

Lydia felt her pride well up like a bee sting. She had to remind herself not to let it get in the way of asking his opinions, even though she didn't want to, because she needed his help.

"What about the window framing?" she finally asked. "Will they need to be replaced?" She hoped they would be fine since her intention was to finish this room first and live in it.

He checked for softness around the sills, sashes and muttins. "I'm sure all the windows ought to be replaced. The house is old and a lot of moisture has collected even though these windows aren't broken, but I think you could get by for a while. Eventually, though, you'll need to consider it. Even one at a time would be all right."

"And how long would it take to plaster it?"

"Just this room or the whole house?"

"This room."

"Hard to say. But it isn't too large so maybe a week." He shrugged. "Depends on how many hours you put into it at one time. Could take longer, maybe even less."

She wondered if he knew how to plaster or if she'd have to rely on Ted, or possibly hire someone else. The job wouldn't have to be perfect since she planned to put wallpaper over it. Then she began visualizing how the cookstove would occupy one end of the room with a long table down the center and at the far end would be a bench for washing dishes as well as a dish cupboard. The floor would be painted and warm rugs scattered around for those cold winter days. In summer, she would hang thin white curtains at each of the three windows so the breezes would blow through easily and in winter she would put up heavier material to keep out the cold.

"I'm no hand at plastering," she heard him say, and decided that he must not want the job. She would discuss it with Ted or maybe Mr. Grayling. Perhaps one of them would know someone she could ask.

"Guess I'll get started on the porch," he said when the conversation lapsed into silence.

After he'd gone, Sarah hurried into the kitchen from the yard.

"Isn't he the most formidable man you've ever met?" Sarah whispered. "You have a lot more courage than I do." She stared at Lydia with great admiration.

"It has nothing to do with courage," Lydia responded. "I'm simply not going to let him get the best of me with his rude manners, that's all."

"I'll bet he doesn't talk to Mrs. Marting like that," Sarah said, with a cautious look over her shoulder to see if he might suddenly appear at the door. When she felt safe that he wouldn't, she stood back and stared at Lydia's dress, face and hair, smiling impishly. "But then you do have a lot of grit and grime on you."

"Oh? And I suppose that means I'm to be taken less seriously?"

"Uh-oh." Sarah stepped back out of Lydia's reach. "I was just teasing you. But I can see this is not a teasing matter. I apologize."

Lydia sighed, her eyes closed. "No, I'm the one who should apologize. I didn't mean to snap at you. And I should never have done anything so foolish as risking your well-being with that old stove. I should have known better." She berated herself for not cleaning the chimney out and for not having the proper pipe and for being in too much of a hurry to take precautions. Those are the thoughts she would have had immediately, if Nathan hadn't spoken them first.

"I was an accomplice, not a captive. Remember that," Sarah said. "I prefer to take some of the blame, thank you, since that makes me a responsible adult, too."

Lydia grinned for the first time and said, "Then why did you run like a scared deer?"

Sarah accepted the good-natured chastising, but in defense of her actions, she countered, "I didn't leave until he'd calmed down. Of course, I didn't speak up much either. But my heavens! That man is scary." She whispered the last sentence just loud enough for Lydia to hear.

"Oh, poot," Lydia said, using one of Sarah's favorite expressions.

"He is!"

"Exasperating, maybe. But scary? I don't think so."

"Well, he is to me. And I'd just as soon not be around when he's here."

"He only comes in the evening, so you won't have to worry about that."

"Good." Sarah looked through the doorway that led to the parlor and saw Nathan open the front door. "Shhh!" She stepped aside and pointed. "He's out there."

Lydia turned her head in time to see him take a giant step up and inside the house. He sorted through the pile of lumber until he found the boards he was looking for and shoved them toward the door. He hopped back outside and shouldered the lumber away out of her sight.

"He isn't an ogre, Sarah. He's just unpleasant sometimes," Lydia said. And she guessed she would simply have to overlook that part of his personality if she wanted her house finished in time.

"It's past supper time, so why don't we leave him to his work while we go home and clean up and eat," Sarah said.

"I think it's going to take quite a scrubbing to get rid of this soot."

"You're right. So let's go."

Lydia followed Sarah outside with one hopeful backward glance. Someday soon, she would be heating water on that range for a bathtub in her house. Just listening to the sound of the hammer made it seem even more real.

For the next week Nathan came every night and worked on the porch, but unlike Sarah, Lydia wanted to stay and watch him work. She chose one of the rocks he'd discarded from the old porch foundation and used that for a seat. It was out of his way but close enough for her to see everything he did. She enjoyed the smell of sawed wood and felt a thrill of excitement as each board was hammered into place, making the floor solid and safe. When he took measurements for the posts she held her breath and wondered if perhaps he would be able to put up the kind she'd been dreaming about since she'd first considered the old house for her children's home. At the same time, a nagging awareness kept gnawing at her that she wouldn't really be able to afford the smooth circular white pillars, but she pushed the unwanted thought aside. By the end of the week, the porch was done, except for the posts, and she could hardly wait to put on the first coat of paint.

After that, she didn't see him for several days. Then one evening he came by again, catching her just as she was leaving.

"Hello," she said, stopping in front of the gate where he stood ready to enter the yard.

"I just thought I'd see about those windows up there." He pointed toward the second floor over the porch. "Should still be plenty of daylight for a while to check them out."

She had begun to believe that he wouldn't return other than to set the posts in place and secure them. He hadn't said a word about not coming back or whether he might take on more of the work; he'd remained as distant as he'd been on the first day he'd shown up. During the time he'd been absent, the old tension that had served as a constant reminder of her approaching deadline reappeared with a vengeance. The muscles in her neck and shoulders were constantly taut and a headache was never far away. Now that he was back, the tension slowly disappeared while they talked of window framing and glass glazing. And as usual, she pushed aside the nagging worry of how she was going to pay him.

She led him through the house, up the stairs and into the bare front bedrooms. He hunkered down to study the sill and framing below the window, then scratched his jaw in contemplation.

"This is in worse shape than I'd expected." He pulled away the crumbling plaster around the bottom and revealed wood that even she could tell was well rotted. He moved to the next window and did the same with similar results. Without a word he left the room and headed for the next bedroom, and she followed. All the front windows were the unusual arched ones, and she hoped that the news wouldn't be bad with every one of them.

"Well?" she asked, watching him go through the same process again.

"Looks like only two of them won't need complete rebuilding. The other three will. It's going to take some time. A lot of time, actually."

"But it can be done, can't it?"

He nodded and rose to his feet, absently crumbling the plaster in his hand. "It can, but . . ."

But what! she wanted to shout. But . . . he didn't want to do it? But . . . it would cost too much? But . . . it would take

147

too much time and she was bound to lose the house?

She waited for him to go on until finally, she had to ask again, "Can it be done?"

He looked up at her, apparently lost so far in his thoughts that he seemed puzzled for a minute by her question.

"Yes," he said at last. "But they will have to be altered somewhat."

"You mean, the arched glass?"

"No. The original wood was butternut and that's pretty hard to come by anymore." He touched the window trim and she felt as though he'd forgotten she was there. "Butternut," he repeated. "We used to have a woods that was full of it."

He sounded so lost, so far away, that she didn't want to speak and bring him back suddenly, so she waited for him to realize he wasn't as alone as he thought he was. As his hand dropped to his side, he frowned, and she knew the moment had passed for him. Strangely, she felt as if she'd looked over a wall and seen past the barrier he always had raised, and which now was in place once more.

"Of course, we could use pine," he said. "You'll want to paint it, so pine will do just as well."

"I have no objection to that at all," she said.

Without moving a step, she suddenly felt as distanced as if she were on the other side of the wall. He made no other comments as he went from room to room studying the windows and woodwork, and she followed him, keeping just as silent. When at last they returned to the front gate, they said nothing more than good night before they took opposite paths home. On the walk to the Graylings', she wondered if he would come back, and when might that be. Time was not her friend. The fourth of July was already creeping closer, and that meant half the summer would be nearly gone. She quickened her footsteps as if that would hasten the work on the house, as if she could race against the calendar, as if she could make Nathan Stockwell communicate his thoughts with her, but she couldn't do any of those things. And time really wasn't her friend.

What Nathan lacked in conversation, Ted more than made up for. The two men were like night and day. Nathan was silent and almost moody, while Ted was full of talk and good humor, and he was never rude. Lydia seldom followed him from room to room the way she'd had to do with Nathan in order to find out what he was planning to do next. Instead, Ted followed Lydia. He courted her opinions and listened so attentively that she felt uncomfortable and almost feared to give any opinions at all. His thoughtfulness had begun to stretch the usual boundaries of friendship until she worried when it might slip over into something more serious, and she didn't want that to happen. Whenever she sensed that he was considering saying something of a private nature, she quickly changed the subject or made an excuse to leave, but she always felt awkward doing that and even a little dishonest. Then one morning when they were alone and before they had gotten into the dirty job of tearing out more plaster, Ted took her by the hand and led her to the backyard where the meadow had gone from a carpet of spring colors to the taller, deeper-hued colors of summer. Patches of long-stemmed black-eyed-Susans waved in the breeze, intermingling with other flowers whose names she did not know, but at the that moment she did not care. Her attention was riveted on Ted's hand holding hers so tenderly.

"It's an exceptional day, isn't it?" Then before she could answer he went on. "And it seems appropriate to choose such a day as this for asking an exceptional lady a very important question."

149

Lydia felt panic rising within her. She liked Ted. He was an admirable friend, a considerate man and enjoyable company to be around. But her heart was hurting already with the answer she would have to give him, and she hadn't even heard the question.

"I think you know how much I admire you, Lydia. You are a wonderfully dedicated woman."

She wanted to change the subject, to withdraw her hand so they would be less intimately connected, but she couldn't bring herself to make such an insensitive gesture. So she stood still and listened, knowing that she had to tell him the truth about her feelings, that it would be unfair to let him go on thinking she cared for him in the same way he cared for her. But she couldn't bring herself to speak out loud.

"But dedication alone isn't what a man looks for in a wife."

Her heart skipped a beat in apprehension.

"He looks for a woman who is that other part of himself, who sees life through the same window, who has the capacity for great love. And I have found all of that in you." For the first time since he started speaking to her, he glanced away from her face to study her hand as he smoothed the bruise on her knuckle.

Lydia closed her eyes momentarily, and held her breath. He was going to ask her to marry him, and she was going to say no. Her heart hurt worse than it ever had, and she was going to have to inflict that same hurt on him. She didn't know if she could do that. She opened her eyes, found him watching her, and forced a smile.

Then he captured both of her hands in his and said, "Lydia, will you marry me? I would be honored if you would say yes."

If only she could say yes, but the fluttering in her stomach wasn't a sign of love and she knew it. He had become a dear friend, but she did not love him enough to marry him. So she hesitated in giving him an answer and immediately sensed that he knew she was going to reject him.

He squeezed her hand lightly. "Don't give me an answer until you've had time to think about it. I know this seems sudden, but it isn't really." He studied her face and smiled. "Perhaps I shouldn't admit it but I've observed you with the children at the schoolhouse and, well, I've loved you for a long time from afar."

Lydia caught her breath. She never would have guessed, and now it would be even harder to say what she had to tell him, but she just couldn't bring herself to say it. Maybe with a little time she could find the right words, or maybe he would come to realize he didn't really love her after all.

"I will take your advice," she said, feeling more than a little guilty for putting him off. "I will give it consideration then give you an answer."

She couldn't judge his reaction to her response, but when he leaned forward and kissed her softly on the mouth, she knew he still hoped she would say yes.

"A man can't ask for more," he said. "I'll give you all the time you need."

Not knowing what else to say, she simply smiled and waited. Then he took her by the arm, tucking it protectively beneath his own, and they walked together toward the house. She allowed him that privilege but felt even more dishonest for doing so.

They entered the house through the kitchen, where the walls still waited to be plastered, then into the parlor, which had partially been taken down to the slats and readied for plastering. With the roof and chimneys leak-proof, the next phase of weather proofing consisted of repairing the windows, and Ted had taken on that job in the parlor.

He patted her hand, then reluctantly released it. "I suppose today I should finish these, since there isn't much more to do." The trim boards had been removed at Nathan's insistence and the glass painstakingly replaced and glazed.

"I'll work on the upstairs bedroom overlooking the back of the house," she said, needing to converse about anything, including the obvious, except what had just taken place. With forced enthusiasm, she smiled and said, "I guess I'll get up there." And she hurried up the stairs, wanting to be alone to think about the best way to handle this new situation.

When she entered the room, Sarah grabbed her by the arm, quickly closed the door and nearly flattened her against the wall in her rush. Lydia saw the twinkle in her round blue eyes and knew that she had seen what had transpired between herself and Ted.

"I told you that he kisses all the girls," Sarah whispered, then clapped a hand over her mouth to keep her laughter in.

"Sarah, you have become the worst kind of spy," she chided, but was glad she had someone to talk to about it.

"Spy! I'll bet everybody hanging out clothes in their backyards saw you two."

Lydia closed her eyes and buried her face in her hands. "I hope not. Poor Ted."

"Poor Ted? What about you?" Sarah's grin was wide. "Compromised in broad daylight." She clucked her tongue in disapproval. "Well, there is nothing for it but to wed," she said dramatically.

"Please, don't say that." Lydia saw nothing humorous in any of this.

Sarah frowned with concern. "Why? What's wrong? I thought it was very sweet."

"It was but . . ." She couldn't go on talking about it with Ted just down the stairs.

"But what?" Sarah tugged on Lydia's hand as though she could pull the information out of her.

"I wouldn't want him to hear us," she whispered back. "He probably doesn't know you're here any more than I did."

"Would you like me to go down and slip outside then come stomping in with a big 'hello'?"

"Be serious!"

"All right, I will." She made an attempt to control her smiles. "Let's move away from the door. Over here."

They walked across the room and stood near the back window, just above the place where Ted had proposed to her.

"Did he ask you to marry him? Is that what has you all upset?"

"Yes." Lydia didn't say more.

"But you have your goals and your dreams."

"Yes." She sighed. Sarah did understand and that was a help.

"Did you tell him no?"

"Not yet."

"Why not?"

"He was so sincere."

"Well, I should hope he would be."

"He was. But I just couldn't bruise his feelings and see the hurt in his eyes."

"So you're going to put it off and hurt him later." Sarah leveled her a very adult look and Lydia felt chastised to the core of her conscience.

"I'm such a coward, I know." She stared across the meadow where someday children from her home would run and play and laugh. She most definitely had a dream, and she couldn't let go of it. But more important, she didn't love him, although she didn't understand why. He would make a wonderful husband to someone and a good father, too. Perhaps he would be just the man to help foster all the children she hoped to bring into her home, but she didn't love him as a wife should.

"You're not a coward at all," Sarah said. "You are a woman with a dream."

"I don't want to hurt him."

"How can you avoid it?"

"I can't," Lydia said realistically.

They stood side by side quietly contemplating the flowers in the meadow as the wind swept over them. Bending and bowing, lifting their heads, then leaning down, then standing up straight.

"You're strong, Lydia. And you have a lot of compassion. It's going to be all right."

She nodded, wishing she felt strong and compassionate, but she didn't.

"You know," Sarah said, "the reason I came up here without you knowing about it, was because I wanted to surprise you with the news about the Peaceful Valley Garden Club."

Lydia looked at her. "What about them?"

"Some good news would be good, wouldn't it?"

"Don't tease me, Sarah. Good news would be wonderful."

"Well, they're holding a benefit on your behalf. Hattie Arthur stopped me this morning on my way to the post office. Then when I got to the post office, Myrtle Grange asked how you were doing and said she hoped things were going fine for you."

"Doesn't she belong to the M.M.C.C.?" Lydia asked,

surprised to hear that anyone in their group would have a kind word for her.

"Yes. But I've heard that they are having a bit of trouble within their ranks."

"Because of me?" She really hadn't intended to bring strife to Peaceful Valley, or pain to anyone.

"Well, I'm not sure about that," Sarah said, and the impish twinkle was back in her eyes. "I've heard that some of the husbands aren't very happy."

"Who told you that?"

"Nobody. I just heard it." She shrugged, and wouldn't tell.

"Sarah, you've been eavesdropping."

"For shame. Accusing me of such a thing." She grinned but kept silent.

Lydia knew it would do no good to ask further, so she said, "Tell me about the benefit."

"Hattie said it would be next week at the schoolhouse and all the ladies of the garden club are donating their very best cooking and some other things, too, I guess." Sarah smiled. "See? It's all going to be fine."

Lydia tried to smile, saying, "I hope so."

But she felt the tension in her neck return, and she knew it would likely stay until she gave Ted an answer. Instead of ending, her troubles seemed to have suddenly multiplied.

Chapter Twelve

Hattie Arthur was glad they had asked permission to use the schoolhouse since the sky had been threatening all day the day before the benefit sale. So now if the sky did fall out, they would be under a roof. Unfortunately, the air was even more oppressive indoors and she waved a folded newspaper in front of her face, although it did little good. On the table at her end of the room were the preserves and apple butters and other assorted canned goods that she and the other ladies of the garden club had put up, so the flies were not a problem for her. But on the other tables where the pies, cakes, breads, and puddings were arranged, they'd had to drape netting to make sure the food stayed insect-free.

She watched as Etta swatted a fly while trying to carry on a conversation with Opal Grayling. Then she selected one of the pies from under the netting and handed it to Opal, which was not at all surprising. Everyone knew that they didn't come more unbiased in their opinions than Opal. She might be a member of the M.M.C.C., but that wouldn't stop her from contributing to a worthy cause.

On the other side of the room was Caroline, who had the easiest of all jobs. She sat near a window with the small breeze blowing across her back, crocheting a table doily that matched several others in front of her. Without missing a stitch she visited with Lila Peterson, laughing and chatting about the latest gossip.

Later in the day, the other members would come and take their places so that they could go home and catch up with their work. But Hattie was in no hurry. She enjoyed the steady crowd and was glad their benefit sale was turning out to be such a success. Deep down, she hoped it would teach that stuffy Agnes Butterfield a thing or two about the real meaning of Peaceful Valley's name.

When Opal reached her table, she said, "Good mornin', Opal."

"Hattie, this is a wonderful turnout you're having. And with so many appetizing dishes to choose from I suspect everyone will buy more than they thought they would."

"We certainly been thinkin' the same thing, and hopin' so, too."

"Is that your apple butter?" Opal asked.

"Yes, ma'am. Fresh last fall and I don't use dropped apples neither. Them bruised ones just don't have the best flavor."

"I haven't had any of your apple butter for quite some time. I'll take two jars. One jar alone will be for the twins." She laughed. "Those boys will eat me out of house and home before too many years pass."

"That they will. My own boys did the same before they went off and got married. Now it's up to their wives to feed them, and they do a pretty good job of it. Leastways, I ain't heard no complaints.''

"How are your boys?''

"They're fine. I don't get to see 'em much since they went so far away.'' She shrugged. "And the house seems kinda empty sometimes. But I keep real busy with church doin's and garden work. Sometimes it's more work than I can handle. Speakin' of work, how is Miss Jefferson comin' along with the Old Mercer place? I just never get over to that end of town much.''

"Well, I'm afraid it's going rather slowly, but your generosity with this benefit will certainly be a big help to her.''

"Now, I ain't one for gossiping,'' Hattie said, "or passing along stories, but isn't that Mr. Stockwell helping her out some?'' Lila Peterson had given that information at one of their meetings, and since her house was right next door to the Old Mercer place, she supposed it must be true.

"Yes, he is. At least, when his own work will allow it. He's made quite an improvement to the front of the house. You ought to make a point of going over to see it. Lydia would love to have visitors.'' Opal paid for the jars of apple butter. "I think I'll just go over to Caroline's table and see what that is she's working on.''

"One of them fancy doilies of hers. Some folks take to 'em, and some don't. Me? Well, I prefer less washing and ironing. I just can't believe some of the frills that people put in their houses these days.'' Then she let the subject drop as she suddenly remembered that Opal was one of those who had quite a few frills in her house. So she accepted the money handed to her and said, "Thank you.''

After Opal had made her rounds, weaving through the crowd and buying several items, she smiled and waved at everyone before disappearing out the doors. No sooner had she left than Myrtle Grange walked in. Hattie couldn't believe her eyes. To have two members of the M.M.C.C. come to their benefit all in the same day was nearly miraculous. The fact that she'd always considered Myrtle a staunch supporter of Agnes's opinions made it that much more surprising.

"Hello, Myrtle," Hattie said. "I gotta say I didn't expect to see you here today."

"Hello, Hattie." Myrtle smiled pleasantly. "Well, when I heard that the garden club was giving a benefit in favor of the orphanage, I just had to come and buy something."

"I'm real glad you did."

"I haven't been able to quit thinking about all those poor little orphans who need homes. My goodness, do you realize that any child could become an orphan? A simple accident is all it would take. And I couldn't bear to think of my own children as homeless. Miss Jefferson is doing such a wonderful service for our community."

"Too bad Agnes doesn't feel that way," Hattie said with her usual honest approach.

"Yes, well, Agnes sees things differently."

"She usually does."

Myrtle looked uncomfortable with the direction of the conversation and Hattie took pity, saying, "Well, we're all real glad you came. We've got baked things and canned goods, and frills and such over there by Caroline."

"Oh, I'm sure I won't have any trouble finding something I like," Myrtle said as she looked over the canned goods on the table between them. She chose a jar of apple butter and one of chutney then reached for her money. "Your apple butter is always the best, Hattie. I wish you'd share that recipe with us."

Hattie laughed. "It's an old family secret that'll probably go to the grave with me."

"Now, Hattie, that isn't fair at all. Secrets aren't supposed to be kept forever, you know. Speaking of secrets, is it true that Mr. Stockwell is helping Miss Jefferson at the old house? Carrie hinted at the idea but won't part with any other information. And the only reason I'm asking is because he seemed so dead set against helping. At least that's what Carrie said.''

Hattie nodded. ''I hear he's helping out whenever he can. 'Course, he's a busy man in his own business so he can't spend full time on it, but he goes out there regularly. Guess he must have a soft spot for orphans, too.''

''Imagine that. You just never can tell about a bachelor, can you? Speaking of bachelors, isn't Preacher Ted helping also?''

''He certainly is. Land a livin', but that man admires Miss Jefferson. He's out there nearly every minute he can spare away from the church a-workin' on that house. Don't matter what the job is, he'll do it. Fixin' roof and chimneys or mendin' that old rundown porch or just plain cleaning up. An orphanage in this here community is something he's plain proud to help with.''

''Why, that is just wonderful! I'm relieved to know that she's getting some real help with all that work.'' Myrtle leaned forward and spoke low. ''Do you think she'll be able to make the deadline set by the council?''

''Mark my words, she'll make it.'' Hattie nodded as if punctuating her sentence. ''And if she don't, then somebody ought to do something about that council. I say, they got voted in and they can get voted out.'' She knew she was treading on enemy territory with those words, but if Myrtle was two-faced enough to report back to Agnes, then let her have something worthwhile to report. The subject had come up more than once at the Peaceful Valley Garden Club, and the truth was, more and more of the women were tired of being pushed around by the decisions of the

A Special Offer For Leisure Historical Romance Readers Only!

Get Four FREE* Romance Novels

A $21.96 Value!

Thrill to the most sensual, adventure-filled Historical Romances on the market today...

FROM  LEISURE BOOKS

As a home subscriber to the Leisure Historical Romance Book Club, you'll enjoy the best in today's BRAND-NEW Historical Romance fiction. For over twenty-five years, Leisure Books has brought you the award-winning, high-quality authors you know and love to read. Each Leisure Historical Romance will sweep you away to a world of high adventure...and intimate romance. Discover for yourself all the passion and excitement millions of readers thrill to each and every month.

SAVE AT LEAST $5.00 EACH TIME YOU BUY!

Each month, the Leisure Historical Romance Book Club brings you four brand new titles from Leisure Books, America's foremost publisher of Historical Romances. EACH PACKAGE WILL SAVE YOU AT LEAST $5.00 FROM THE BOOKSTORE PRICE! And you'll never miss a new title with our convenient home delivery service.

Here's how we do it. Each package will carry a 10-DAY EXAMINATION privilege. At the end of that time, if you decide to keep your books, simply pay the low invoice price of $16.96 ($19.98 CANADA), no shipping or handling charges added.* HOME DELIVERY IS ALWAYS FREE.* With today's top Historical Romance novels selling for $5.99 and higher, our price SAVES YOU AT LEAST $5.00 with each shipment.

AND YOUR FIRST FOUR-BOOK SHIPMENT IS TOTALLY FREE!

IT'S A BARGAIN YOU CAN'T BEAT! A Super $21.96 Value!

M.M.C.C. Everybody knew who really made the council's decisions and it wasn't Mayor Butterfield.

"Well," said Myrtle, collecting her jars, "I wish Miss Jefferson the very best. Now, I suppose I'd better see what the other tables have to offer. It's been nice chatting with you, Hattie."

"Likewise," Hattie said, smiling pleasantly.

Myrtle made her way around the room, stopping to talk and to buy. When she reached Caroline's table, Hattie noticed that she stayed to visit longer there than she had at other tables and all three women seemed very interested in what the other had to say. Hattie could hardly contain her curiosity as she remained at her appointed table. But she didn't have to wonder for long. As soon as Myrtle had gone, Lila hurried over to speak with Hattie.

"I suppose you heard about Carrie?"

Surprised, Hattie replied, "No. What?"

"It sounds like she has really set her cap for Mr. Stockwell, but she's concerned that Miss Jefferson has also set her cap for him. But, of course, that isn't going to stop Carrie. You know, that woman has the determination and persistence of a dog in heat."

"Lila!" Hattie was truly amazed at Lila's comparison. It was true that Carrie wasn't exactly someone she would seek as a friend, but neither would she cast such an insult at her.

"I know that wasn't kind, but we both know the truth of it. Why, poor Samuel hasn't been dead and buried a year and there she is chasing after another man already."

"Did Myrtle tell you that?" Hattie seldom dabbled in gossip, but when she did she liked to get her facts straight.

"Not in so many words. But I can read between the lines and I have eyes, too."

"Well, it isn't as though Mr. Stockwell is taken or even

promised, you know. And I would imagine that having a wife would be sorta good for him, what with how hard he works and all. He sure spends a lot of time at the old Mercer place working for Miss Jefferson.'' She pondered the thought for a minute. ''So you don't think Miss Jefferson has set her cap for him? I would have thought it might be a likely thing, what with how much time they spend together.''

Lila waved her hand in dismissal. ''No. Miss Jefferson seems to pay no attention at all to him. But now, Preacher Ted is another story.''

Hattie caught her breath in shock. ''What are you saying, Lila Peterson?''

''Just that I saw the preacher kissing Miss Jefferson out behind the house where they thought nobody could see them, but I was in the privy and I saw it all.''

''They were what?'' Hattie couldn't believe her ears.

''Oh, for heaven's sake, Hattie. You mean to tell me that you never would have suspected any hanky panky going on over there? One woman and two men?'' Lila shook her head. ''Something was bound to happen sooner or later. And truthfully, it's a wonder there wasn't something more than that going on.'' When she looked up at Hattie's face, she retraced her thoughts and quickly adjusted her words. ''I didn't mean that Preacher Ted would do anything ungentlemanly.''

''I should hope you wouldn't.''

''And I didn't mean that Miss Jefferson would act in a way unbecoming to a teacher.''

''Then just what did you mean?'' Hattie was angry. She had a lot of respect for Preacher Ted and Miss Jefferson, too. And she knew that respect wasn't misplaced.

''Well . . . I guess, I . . . it's just that Carrie Marting thinks she can buy herself any man she wants with the

162

money she got from her poor dead husband.'' Lila was jealous, and Hattie had never seen that side of her before. She had always thought that Lila was a happily married woman.

"I wouldn't trade places with her," Hattie said, and meant every word.

"Neither would I," Lila said, trying to look as if she meant it.

Hattie, being a widow without much money, had rich, fulfilling memories of her husband as well as loving children, and it was difficult for her to imagine wanting something that belonged to another, but apparently, Lila didn't feel that way. Well, considering the source and the reason for this gossip, she completely discounted all of it. If Hattie was going to dabble in gossip, she wanted it to be based on facts and so far she hadn't heard any, other than that Preacher Ted had kissed Miss Jefferson right in broad daylight. In her book, that wasn't a sin, it was a blessing. And she couldn't think of two people she would rather see married than those two. So Lila could just peddle her idle gossip elsewhere.

Before Hattie could give Lila a piece of her mind, Mayor Butterfield came through the door and the two women turned to stare. He carried a picnic basket under one arm and nervously pinched at his curled moustache. Hattie thought she could count on one hand the number of times that the mayor had come to one of their socials or benefits, and never did he bring a basket. Everyone knew that Agnes's cooking was considered the best in town, and the mayor had often made a point of mentioning it. So it was a real surprise to everyone, not only Hattie, to see him there.

"Good morning, Mrs. Arthur," he said, barely glancing at her but giving his entire attention to the jars of food spread before him. "These look absolutely delicious."

He selected one jar each of apple butter, pears and peaches then put them in his basket. After paying for them he didn't dally in conversation but moved on to the breads, pies and cakes. Hattie watched as he carefully stacked two pies in his basket, using the jars for supports, then a loaf of bread and a zucchini cake. Then he quickly surveyed the remaining table, but decided against what it had to offer. With a nod of his head, he left the building, and the members of the garden club shared looks of disbelief.

Hattie knew of a certainty that Agnes would skin him alive if she knew he'd been there buying goods that would benefit Miss Jefferson's children's home. She also knew of a certainty that word would eventually get back to Agnes, and there wasn't a woman in that room who wouldn't give a pretty penny to be a mouse under a chair when she found out. Something was afoot in the Butterfield house, and maybe all those rumors were true after all. Perhaps the power of the M.M.C.C. was about to come to an end, at long last.

When Mayor Butterfield wasn't acting as mayor of Peaceful Valley, he could be found in the small office at the back of the barber shop which he'd owned for a good many years. It was just one of several small businesses that kept him busy. It was also his only hideaway from Agnes, and today he was using it as a kitchen cupboard. He had started planning days ago for this moment when he'd first heard about the garden club benefit. Without Agnes knowing it, he had pilfered one of her older dishes as well as a cup and a few pieces of silverware and had taken all of it to his little office. His plan was to make the food last as long as possible. It wasn't right that a man couldn't eat properly in his own home, and he couldn't put up with the situation much longer. A steady diet of fried mush was going to drive him insane. Although, to be honest, she had bent her rules and added fresh vegetables, boiled only, but he considered it nothing more than a tease. So he had decided to take matters into his own hands.

He opened the cabinet where he kept his ledgers and pulled out several of the big books to stack on his desk. Then he placed the contents of the basket where the ledgers had been, except for one blueberry pie.

With the door locked against possible discovery, he set out the dish and fork, then cut a large section of the pie. The berries were big and plump—actually, he'd call them luscious. The flaky crust was barely able to contain them and he nearly salivated. When he had the piece on his plate, he sat down and simply stared at it, wanting to savor the sight and the smell before he tasted its texture. But he couldn't wait forever; he'd already waited too long. He dipped his fork into the ripe, creamy berries, then put them into his mouth and just held them there with his eyes closed. He ran his tongue around each individual one, feeling as though he had truly died and gone to heaven. It was so delectable to have them in his mouth that he hated to move on to the next stage, but he reminded himself that there was more where that had come from, at least for a while. When it was all gone, he would have to do something else; he would have to make some changes. A man shouldn't have to sneak around for food. He should be able to get it in his own home, whenever he wanted it.

He forced himself not to eat more than two pieces of the pie, although he was far from satisfied. But that was what happened when a man had been denied for so long. With the pie put away, he faced the problem of cleaning his dish. The little office didn't have even so much as a bucket of water for drinking purposes. He guessed he would have to pilfer that, too. In the meantime, he would take the dish home, wash it and bring it back.

Removing his clean handkerchief from his pocket, he wrapped the plate and fork in it, tucked the bundle inside his coat and headed for home. And the smug smile he wore was that of a man who had cheated on his wife, and gotten away with it.

Jeffrey had been in a foul mood for days, or had it been weeks? he wondered. Just how long a man could go without the attentions of a woman, he didn't know, nor did he want to find out. He hated to admit the number of times he'd almost called an emergency council meeting, privately of course, in order to get his life back to normal, which meant sleeping in his own bed with his wife. He sorely missed having her soft body next to his, always ready to come to him whenever he reached for her. Sometimes he'd wake up in the dark of night and feel her round bottom nestled into the bend of his stomach, and his need for her would be like a prairie fire, swift and consuming. They would struggle together trying to remove the yards of her nightgown, both of them frantic in their attempt to have her bare skin touch his bare skin. Even on the cold winter nights, they would kick the quilts to the foot of the bed as their passion heated beyond bearable.

But now, he tossed alone on the small bed in his daughter's room while his daughter slept in his big bed. All around him in the filtered moonlight, he could see her playthings lined up along the back of a bench, on the windowsill and on a dresser. He considered this the worst punishment a woman could inflict on a man. Not only was he banned from his wife's nightly presence but his thoughts were restricted just by being in his daughter's room.

There was no good excuse to put up with this, he

thought, as he tried to stretch, but his feet slipped between the spindles at the foot of the bed and the sheet was too short to boot. No, he concluded, the damn bed was too short. So he rolled onto his side, using his arm for a pillow.

Tomorrow he would have a talk with Richard, just to see if he was experiencing any difficulties in his home life. And if that was the case, then they were going to have to come up with something. But he'd be damned if he would give in to another of Agnes Butterfield's demands. Enough was enough.

He flopped to his back again, thunking his head against the spindles, then swore loud and long in spite of being in his daughter's room.

Penelope heard Jeff's tossing and turning in the bedroom over hers. She also heard him swear and couldn't help but smile. The bed was far too small for a man his size, but that was all part of the battle. She would have missed him dreadfully if she weren't so angry with him. Why he was being so pigheaded was beyond her. Couldn't he understand that men shouldn't have the only say-so where children were concerned? Cora had told her she was having no luck at all changing Richard's mind, but she couldn't give up, then she broke into tears. Laura had said that she was enjoying sleeping alone peacefully and could be counted on for the duration of the fight, but Jenny sheepishly admitted she'd given in before the week had ended.

Penelope wished it was all over, but she wasn't ready to change her mind about the orphanage just to get the issue behind them so they could go on with their normal lives. Still, it was lonely without Jeff beside her.

Richard stared at the ceiling in the spare bedroom, his hands stacked beneath his head. He had tried to make amends with Cora by suggesting a buggy ride out into the country and then dinner at the restaurant. Perhaps a little time away from her usual household duties would put her in better spirits. Finally, with some coaxing he'd been able to get her to agree that the sunshine and fresh air would do both of them more good than harm. So he'd rented a buggy and drove it to the house where she waited for him on the porch. She was lovely in the lavender pinstripe dress and a large straw hat, and he told her so. Her smile went straight to his heart, making him brave enough to kiss her cheek without asking first. He tried not to push his luck and linger too long, but she smelled so wonderful and her skin was so soft that he had to force himself to step back. The sparkle in her eye gave him hope as he helped her into the buggy, and he'd felt encouraged.

They drove away from town until it was just a brown-and-white dot on the landscape behind them and they were surrounded by all sorts of wildflowers. Rabbits darted out of hiding spots and Cora had even laughed out loud in her surprise, which was music to his ears. And that was when he'd stopped the buggy, set the brake and asked if she would like to go for a walk.

"It's lovely here," she said, letting him help her down.

"Not lovelier than you," he replied, still holding her suspended but close to his chest.

"Oh, Richard."

"I've missed you," he said, letting her feet touch the ground but not letting go of her.

She shook her head. "Not more than I have missed you."

With the sun warm on his back and the brim of her hat shading their faces, he took a chance and leaned down to press his lips against hers. He waited for her response while he enjoyed the tender touch between them. It had been so long, so very long since he'd held her like that, with her firm breasts pushed into his coat and his hands around her slim waist. When she kissed him back, he nearly groaned with anticipation but tried to keep himself under control for fear of frightening her away. Then she broke their contact long enough to whisper against his lips, "Richard, Richard . . ." before kissing him fervently again. After that, he could no more gain control of his surging emotions than he could have held back a team of wild horses.

He nipped lightly at her lips, her jaw, her ear and silently cursed the stays she wore and the bustle, too. Without a care for the expensive material of her dress, he tugged at her skirts, raising them higher and higher until he could almost touch bare skin, but beneath her skirt was a petticoat or some such contraption that clung to her body and was fastened by ties and tapes. He'd never had to deal with these before, and hadn't a clue as to what he should do to be rid of them. She'd always come to him in her nightgown or nothing at all. But surprisingly, these obstacles of clothing did not curb his ardor one bit. Instead his passion mounted until he thought he couldn't stand it another moment. Carefully, he knelt to the ground, taking her with him until they fell all at once with her on top of him. He rolled with her until they lay on their sides, and she arched her neck, giving him access to the tenderest of spots. With one hand, she removed her hat while he worked at the buttons at the top of her dress until her breasts were bare in the sunlight. His breath caught at the sight of them as though it was the first time he'd ever seen them or touched them.

"Cora," he whispered, and leaned down to kiss that sweet soft crevice between them that smelled better than any flower ever could. She arched against him like she always did, encouraging him to go on, teasing him lightly by pulling away when he dipped his head. With one hand he captured her firmness, then tasted it, with the other hand he raised her skirt. Reaching down, she untied the bindings on her petticoat as far as she could, then he slipped his hand inside and felt the cool skin of her thigh, sleek and smooth, and untouchable for so very long.

When he moved away from her to undo his own trappings, the buggy also moved as the horses fidgeted and whinnied nervously.

She lifted her head, slowly coming out of their lovemaking stupor. "What . . . what is it? Is someone coming?" She started to raise up, but he stayed her with his hand as a feeling of panic overwhelmed him that she might change her mind. He was too far gone to stop now.

He leaned over her, trying to spoil her with tiny kisses on her face, her neck and her breasts. It's nothing," he said, between kisses. "They're quieting now. See?"

And they were, but Cora blinked in the bright sunshine as her senses returned, sitting up and leaning on one hand for support. Her voluptuousness amid the bounty of nature was nearly his undoing and he pressed his body to hers in order to lay her· down again. But she blinked again and pushed him away. Then she gathered her dress together with both hands and then he did groan.

"Richard, we can't do this. Someone will surely find us." She wrestled with the ties and tapes on her petticoat and frowned at the twisted bustle that should have been behind her. "Help me up. Please."

He sat with one knee upraised and his elbow resting on it as he stared at her with regret. He'd lost the moment just when he'd almost . . . almost . . .

"Please, Richard."

With a heartfelt sigh, he got uncomfortably to his feet

and extended his hand to her. With a gentle tug, she was on her feet again.

"What a mess I am. Why, I do think this bustle is ruined."

He stood watching while she dressed and adjusted and buttoned and tied, until she felt presentable. Then he picked up her hat and placed it on her head. They stood motionless for a minute in the shade of her straw hat, each searching the other's eyes for a clue as to when this stand off would end.

"Cora, I can't take much more of this. I'm only a man."

And with that, large tears welled up in her eyes and her mouth drew down at the corners as she tried to control her need to cry.

"Then please, understand why it's so important that this orphanage not be allowed to come to Peaceful Valley."

He sighed in exasperation. "I have been trying to understand, and I'm at a complete loss as to why you are so against it."

"You really don't know, do you?"

"No, I don't."

"And you really don't care either."

He sighed again, baffled by the complexity of women.

"All right then, I will tell you."

He waited, hoping for enlightenment, wishing for an end to this confrontation going on between them.

"If you loved me, you would not allow this orphanage to come to this town."

He waited for her to go on, but she didn't. Was that the reason? It didn't make sense to him so he made no reply. He simply waited for her to say something more, something that would explain why he'd been banished to the spare room.

And now, as he lay staring at the ceiling, he still didn't

understand. She had cried all the way home without saying another word then immediately locked herself in their bedroom. So he had gone to bed without supper, feeling mystified and downright miserable.

Chapter Thirteen

Nathan had discovered to his surprise that working on the old Mercer house was like a balm to a wound and even more satisfying than the precision work of a wheelwright. Increasingly, he found himself looking forward to the end of the day so that he could begin work on repairing the arched window casings or the facing boards on the porch or the stair treads and railing going up to the second floor. Each project was created and each detail thought out as he worked in his shop. There were only a few jobs during the day that required his complete concentration, and setting the spokes for the wagon wheels was one them, but even then his mind would wander back to the old house.

So it was with determination that he faced the hub gripped tightly in the cradle. Carefully, he marked out the mortises for the spokes, taking his time and double-checking for accuracy. When he was satisfied, he reached for the brace and bit to drill out the marked areas. All wheel work was critical in his estimation, but getting the right depth and angle of the mortise for the spoke was crucial— just as the railings on the stairway needed to be mortised and set at the exact angle to be in perfect balance. He let his mind go over the details of how he would do that and which tools he would need to take along, then forced himself to focus once more on the hub in front of him.

The final dish or slant of the wheel would be created by the slight angle cut at the front and back of each mortise, and for that he used the spoke-set gauge to guide him. This was simply a batten of wood temporarily bolted by a peg to the exact center of the hub. In this way, he could determine the circumference to which the spokes should be angled. He momentarily considered how he could apply this idea to the railing, then once again he had to set his mind on the task before him and save his engineering ideas for later.

The entire day followed the same sequence, his thoughts going back and forth between the house and his work in the shop. When it was time to lock up, he was surprised at the amount of work he'd actually accomplished since it seemed as though he hadn't been able to focus in his usual way. He grabbed his tools and his knapsack, which had an extra meal in it so that he didn't have to go back home before heading to the old house.

When he arrived at the front gate, he didn't stop to survey the place since everyone generally went home for supper and only on occasion did Miss Jefferson return afterwards. So he knew he would be able to eat his meager fare in peace while he contemplated which part of the project to tackle that night. And while he seldom took time to admire the simple things in life, he preferred to go around back to the kitchen step to eat, where he had a view of the meadow. Somehow, watching the tall flowing grasses and wildflowers eased his mind and relieved the tension in his back.

He'd barely gotten seated when Miss Jefferson came around the side of the house carrying a basket and holding it out as an offering to him.

"I wondered if you might be out here," she said. "Here. I brought you something to eat. I feel guilty when you come straight from work."

He had a notion to resist her offer, then realized that unlike Carrie Marting, there were no strings attached to this food, so he accepted it. "Thanks." When he opened it, he found good old fashioned just-plain-food, not the sauces and such that Carrie always brought him.

"It isn't anything fancy, just some green beans with ham and potatoes. And the cornbread is already buttered for you. And if you like coffee, there's a jar in there and a cup, too. But be careful, it's still pretty hot to the touch."

"Thanks," he said again, and this time he smiled.

She picked up a nearby pail, turned it upside down and sat on it, clasping her hands around her knees.

He held out the dish of cornbread and said, "Would you like some?"

"Oh, no, thanks. I've already eaten, but I'll take some of that coffee. There's an extra cup in there somewhere." She started to rise to help him find it when he fished it out and handed it to her. Then he carefully poured it full from the jar and repeated the whole thing with the other cup for himself.

"I wonder why coffee tastes so much better outdoors." she said, smiling at him.

"I guess I never noticed."

"That's because you work too hard, which is the reason I brought you supper."

He took a swallow of the coffee and decided maybe she

was right. It was better than the stuff he usually drank. Then he took the plate of food from the basket and the aroma hit him square in the nose, making his stomach growl in anticipation. Without any chatter from her, he was able to eat his meal in quiet while she sipped her coffee and glanced across the meadow. When he'd taken the last bite, cleaning up the juice with his cornbread, she took a napkin from her apron pocket and handed it to him.

"Cookies. Want one?"

He accepted the napkin and unfolded it to find several small sugar cookies. These were his favorite, but he didn't tell her so. Instead, he only smiled his thanks and offered her some.

"I think I will," she said. "They make good coffee taste even better."

He agreed, then swigged his coffee.

"I remember when I first moved into my foster mother's house," she began, smiling as she spoke, "Grandma Winnie used to bribe my little brother with cookies whenever she wanted him to do some chore for her. And it usually worked."

Nathan stopped chewing when he heard her say she had a foster mother. For some reason he'd imagined that she had come from a home where her folks were really her folks. "Your grandmother raised you?" he asked, not looking at her but steadily watching the cookie crumbs float as he dunked it in his coffee.

"No. My foster mother is lovely woman who took me and my brother in when we were quite young. Grandma Winnie is her mother, and a sweeter grandma you will never find."

Part of him wanted to ask about her real mother. And what about her father? But his curiosity wasn't so great that he was willing to risk being questioned in return.

"Sometime," she said, "I'll tell you the story about our great adventure when we went up the canal alone." She fell silent then, and he sensed she was watching him. Somehow he knew the story had to do with losing her mother and father, and he didn't encourage her to go on.

"So what are your plans for tonight?" she asked, then munched on her cookie as though she hadn't abruptly changed the subject.

"I thought I'd check the stairway again. Most of the treads need replacing and the railing is too unstable to be safe. Somebody is bound to get hurt before long if I let it go."

"Oh," she said, looking disappointed. "I thought maybe . . ."

"What?" he asked, finally looking at her instead of the toe of his boots.

"Well, I'd really like to have the kitchen done first. I mean, completely finished." She nervously glanced away, then back to his face. "I haven't had much luck finding someone to do the plastering. Ted said he would give it a try, but he admitted he'd never done it before."

He didn't know what to say. Telling her no had been much easier when he hadn't really known her, not that he knew her so well now, but she was easy to work for and even easier to talk to, and he found himself not wanting to be disagreeable. He supposed he'd been comparing her to Carrie all along, and it was gradually sinking in that the two women were nothing alike. So he'd let down his guard without realizing it and now he was caught between being a carpenter and helping a friend.

"Miss Jefferson."

She smiled when he called her by name, and for a moment he wondered why, then he remembered how he'd called her Miss Jeffries. And he had enough conscience to grin shamefaced at the ground.

"Please, call me Lydia."

He nodded and looked up at her. "Lydia, I don't have much experience at plastering."

"But I have none," she said, smiling. "And if you don't do it, then I'm going to have to do it."

His grin widened at the prospect of her mixing the sand and hauling it up a ladder then working over her head.

"Are you making fun of me?" she said, smiling good-naturedly.

"No," he replied, shaking his head but still grinning.

"Yes, you are!" She sat straighter on the pail, the palms of her hands pushing against her knees. "I'll have you know that I helped mix the mortar for the chimneys and I helped carry it up in buckets and I helped chink them, too!"

He almost said, *you did?* No woman he'd ever known would have climbed on a roof, let alone chinked the chimneys, and he couldn't keep the surprise off his face.

"You don't believe me."

"Yes. Yes, I do." He nodded, then shrugged slightly as he picked up a stick and scuffed it through the dirt.

"But you don't think I can plaster a wall."

"I'm not going to say that." He could sense she was getting defensive. "More than likely it's the ceiling that would get to you."

She seemed to settle down again. "Well, I suppose you're right. And that's the reason I'm asking you."

He kept his attention on the stick as he drew lines in the dirt near his boot. Plastering wasn't anything like carpentry and he'd not particularly enjoyed doing it, although he had taken on some of those kinds of jobs in the past, before he'd come to Peaceful Valley.

"I can pay you," she said. "The garden club held a benefit and donated the proceeds to the building of the home."

He frowned. "I told you, I wasn't asking for wages. And you'd better save your money for the materials."

She grew still, sitting without making any movement while he stirred the dirt.

Finally she spoke, "And I already said I don't like charity."

After a few moments, he replied, "We'll work out a trade of some kind." Which is what she'd said to him the last time the subject came up, but he still didn't know what kind of trade it could be.

"Are you saying you'll do it?" she asked, and he heard the hopeful sound in her voice.

He knew he ought to say no, but he heard himself say, "Yes."

"You will? That's wonderful!" She folded her arms at her waist and leaned toward him. "Thank you."

He continued to make lines in the dirt, then crossed them with other lines. For some reason he couldn't look at her, but he spent no time figuring out why, instead he pushed on to the next topic.

"So, you'd rather let the stairway wait?" he asked.

"Yes, I really would."

Suddenly losing interest in the stick, he dropped it on the ground then dredged up all that he knew about plastering from somewhere in his memory. The tools were simple ones. Although he had no trowels that were specifically used for that purpose, they could be gotten at the hardware store. Actually, it was just a matter of mixing the plaster properly and applying it to the slats, which were already bare and needed no further work. He preferred to do the woodworking on the stairway, but if she wanted the kitchen plastered, then he guessed he could work on the stairway later.

"Well, I can't begin working on it tonight," he said. "I'm not exactly prepared for it."

"That's all right. Make a list of everything you'll need and I'll have Harvey deliver it here. He's been so good about not charging me a delivery fee and that way you won't have to make an extra trip with the wagon."

He nodded, still deep in thought. "I'll take the list to Harvey at noon tomorrow."

"I'll help carry buckets or whatever you need," she said. "I've gotten some pretty tough calluses now." She examined her hands and he noticed they were scraped and bruised.

"No, I'll carry my own buckets." Then he saw that defensive light in her eyes again, and added, "I'm not used to having a woman doing heavy work, so you'll just have to find something else to do."

"I'll do whatever it takes."

"But it won't be necessary to carry buckets of plaster."

"Then I'll help mix it."

"That won't be necessary either."

"I don't mind the work," she said, sitting up a little straighter. "I enjoy it."

He felt the confrontation building and he didn't back away from it. She was stubborn and not altogether sensible when it came to this old house, and he couldn't keep from asking, "Why?"

"Because I want this house to get finished on time. I don't want to lose it." Then her voice softened. "It's important to me." But she didn't go on, and he didn't ask why this time.

As the silence lengthened, each of them grew more uncomfortable until Nathan rose to his feet, saying, "Thanks for the supper." Then he smiled. "And the cookies."

She laughed and stood up, too. "I suppose you think I'm like my grandmother, trying to bribe you with cookies."

"You chose the right ones. Those are my favorite."

"I'll remember that." She bent and retrieved the basket with the empty dishes and he handed her the napkin he'd laid on the step.

He felt surprisingly relaxed and not at all like rushing into the job, and he blamed that on the good food she'd brought him. "I'll just look the kitchen over," he said. Yet he lingered for as long as she stayed, listening to her talk about her ideas for the house. He liked her approach of keeping the rebuilding of the house simple. Most women wanted to add all the fret work and beaded rails the frame of the house could support. At least it seemed that way, judging by the looks of the newer homes. It wasn't that he was opposed to the new style; he just couldn't see adding it onto this old house, and apparently neither could she. But when she hoped someday to put in a water closet and bathing room like the one at the Graylings' he had to disagree.

"Those things are nothing but a problem waiting to happen," he said.

"Why?"

"Think about how cold it gets before the fire is built and you'll have your answer."

"Oh, but you're wrong," she replied, smiling confidently. "The Graylings have this wonderful old monstrous furnace-thing in the cellar and the heat comes right up and into the water closet. It is absolutely the best invention I've heard of to date. Bathing children in a cold room isn't healthy, and using the kitchen isn't private enough. Not to mention all the work of hauling out the tub. Someday I will have a bathing room and water closet *with* a furnace-whatever in the cellar.''

''There is no cellar in this house,'' he reminded her with a confident grin of his own.

''Well, then, we'll just put one in . . . somewhere.''

He glanced around the small backyard. ''*Somewhere?*''

''We'll buy some of the meadow,'' she said without much conviction but a little bit of hope. ''Certainly, somebody must own the meadow, and maybe they would be willing to part with a little of it.''

The meadow. He glanced out across it, measuring with his mind's eye where the unmarked boundaries lay beneath the tall grasses. He had always believed that the land was the only valuable asset a man could own or leave behind, so he'd purchased small sections of the meadow with the money he'd earned as a wheelwright. His physical need for money was small, and once he'd met his obligations, the rest went into purchasing the meadow, bit by bit. And the biggest chunk of what he owned lay right behind the old Mercer house, the very part she wanted to buy.

''I doubt it's for sale,'' he said, still watching the movement of the grass. Nobody knew he owned it; that had been one part of the stipulations of the agreement he'd insisted on when he'd bought it from the mayor. The other part dealt with making sure it went where it was supposed to go when he was gone, and the mayor had agreed to that, too. So he would leave something behind, an endowment to make up for the past, if only he could make up for it.

''I suppose it is too beautiful to sell,'' she said. ''I guess I'll just have to be satisfied to have it for a playground for the children.''

He stiffened involuntarily as she reminded him that this house was to become an orphanage. Somehow, he'd allowed himself to forget that aspect and had simply seen it as a carpenter would see it, nothing more than wood, windows and roof. It was only a place that needed hammer and nails, glazing and framing, plaster and paint. He had not looked toward the end result of its being occupied as a house—rather, a house full of unwanted, orphaned children. *Unwanted children.* Over and over, the familiar refrain echoed in his head, pointing an accusing finger at his heart until he wanted to shout for it to stop, but he couldn't. So he took a deep breath and exhaled with a cough.

"I ought to be going," he said.

"Yes, and so should I." She shifted the basket she'd been holding. "Will you be here tomorrow night?"

He coughed again. "I can't be sure."

"I'll bring you some more cookies," she said with a smile, and he managed a lame grin with a nod to acknowledge he understood what she meant.

Then finally she said good night and he was left alone.

It wasn't often that he'd gone home before dark whether he was working at the house or in his shop, but tonight appeared to be one of those times. Unless he decided to finish setting the spokes on that last wagon wheel. He could work by lamplight, and he could work until his mind was free. . . . Grabbing up his knapsack and tools, he left the old Mercer house and walked back to his shop.

Lydia let herself in the back door of the Graylings' house and set the basket on the table to take out the dishes. The kitchen was quiet, but the sound of laughter came from the parlor where the family was playing one of their favorite board games. Being in a rather reclusive mood, she stayed in the kitchen and cleaned up her mess, then slipped unobserved up the stairs to her room. She hadn't written a letter home for several weeks so she took out pen and ink as well as her rose-scented stationery, then turned up the lamp on her desk. Until now, she hadn't said a word about quitting her job or purchasing the old house, or even talked about her dream of a children's home. But tonight she wanted to let them know a little, just a very little, of what was going on in her life.

Dear Mother and Ross,

I apologize for being so delinquent with my letters, but please know that you are in my thoughts daily. The summer is progressing very nicely here and I'm kept quite busy with one thing or another, although I do miss being home with all of you. Perhaps, I will take the train home for a visit before the fall arrives.

Lydia felt a pang of guilt for letting them think she would be teaching in the fall again, but it was for the best. She did not want to alarm them or to make them worry. She would get along somehow simply because she had to, but she would deal with that when the time came.

I have made better friends of those who formerly were only acquaintances and have thoroughly enjoyed the events so peculiar to summer in a small town. As a matter of fact, Independence Day celebrations will be upon us soon and I look forward to watching the children participate in the foot races and other such games. How well I remember that holiday in Grand Rapids and the wonderful times we shared boating on the Maumee above the rapids. It was always so lively and fun. I'm sure it will be different here, since the

*river is so much smaller here, but I'm looking forward
to the festivities just the same.*

She went on to ask about the rest of the family and to
pass her greetings along to them, too. Then she managed
to finish up the letter without giving away any of what
she'd undertaken, which made her feel both relieved at ac-
complishing it and guilty for leaving them out.

When she'd addressed and sealed the letter, she sat staring at it for a long time. Oh, how she missed them all, and
especially her mother with her quiet, thoughtful ways and
her wise advice that had so often saved the day. And most
likely would have saved many other days, too, if only Lydia
had heeded that advice. But she'd always been a headstrong
girl and that had obviously carried over into womanhood.
Her biggest hope now was that being a strong-willed
woman would keep her in good stead and see her through
the ambitious endeavor she had begun.

She set aside the letter to be mailed the next day, then
readied for bed. When her hair was plaited and she was
about to turn down the lamp, she heard Sarah's soft voice
call to her through the door.

"May I come in?"

"Yes, please do." She hadn't seen Sarah since earlier in
the day and was anxious to tell her that Nathan had agreed
to do the plastering. She also wanted to ask about the owner
of the meadow. If anybody knew, Sarah would.

"So tell me. Did Mr. Stockwell enjoy the supper you
took to him?" She climbed onto the bed and sat cross-
legged, tucking her nightdress around her bare feet.

"He seemed to enjoy it very much. I almost wondered
if he was used to eating home-cooked meals." Lydia

stretched out on her side with her head propped up by a hand.

"Are you joking? Carrie Marting has made it her personal mission to keep him well fed. You know the old saying: the way to a man's heart is through his stomach. She apparently believes that Mr. Stockwell has a heart. I'm afraid I can't agree."

"Why do you feel so strongly about him? I admit he can be a little intimidating, but we got along rather well tonight. I found out he really likes sugar cookies. Maybe I ought to pass that along to Carrie," she said, smiling.

"I told you, he doesn't like children. And isn't it peculiar that he keeps to himself so much? I mean, it almost seems as though he doesn't like people in general, not just children."

"He definitely keeps to himself, but maybe it isn't because he wants to. Maybe nobody has tried to be his friend." She didn't know if that sounded like a plausible reason or not, but he had seemed friendly to her when they shared coffee and cookies and talked about the meadow.

"Oh," Lydia went on, "before I forget, I was wondering if you might know who owns the meadow behind the old house."

"Sure. Mayor Butterfield. He owns a few of the businesses and rents out some of the houses in town, too. Why?"

Lydia laughed. "Sarah, you amaze me. Don't ask me why, but you do. I should think that by now I would be used to you having all the answers to my questions. But I'm not."

"Oh, poot. I don't know everything." Then she grinned. "But I'm working on it."

They laughed together before a friendly silence fell between them.

"So why are you curious about the meadow?" Sarah asked.

"I was just thinking about the future, and possibly making some changes to the old house, but that's just a dream. I can't see that it's based on reality right now. First I have to find a way to make some money to keep the home going."

She hadn't followed up on her search of the places that might help fund Spring Meadows because she knew if they took one look at her house they would only laugh, and then frown. So obtaining money was still a problem, although she hadn't quite given up hope that something might turn up so that she could run it as a private home.

"I love dreams and goals, so tell it to me," Sarah said.

"Well, it's pretty far-fetched. I'll sound silly if I put it into words." She hadn't felt silly when she'd told it to Nathan, but now that she thought about it, she was surprised he hadn't laughed at her.

"Oh, come on. I promise not to think it's silly."

"All right." She adjusted her position to sitting up with her back against the headboard. "I would like to have a water closet and bathing room like yours so that the children could have some privacy. And I'd also like one of those furnace things to keep at least part of the house warm. It seems like they would stay healthier if they weren't subjected to going out into the cold all the time."

Sarah shrugged. "I don't think any of that sounds impossible."

"It does if you don't have any money or a job."

"Well, there's always Preacher Ted," she said, her eyes twinkling with merriment. Then she quickly retreated with, "I'm sorry, Lydia. That was heartless of me. And you know I didn't mean it. Marriage isn't something I believe should be entered into for any reason other than profound love, which I personally intend to avoid. I have too many goals to be sidetracked by a man and marriage. So forgive me.''

''Forgiven.''

''Have you decided yet how you're going to tell him?''

Lydia sighed. ''No. I haven't let myself even think about it. I know I ought to, but I just can't.''

''He'll probably want to escort you to the festivities on Independence Day. What are you going to say?''

''If I say no, I'll feel guilty. It's as though I think he's only good enough to be my friend if he's working on my house, and that's not true. But if I say yes, then he'll think I'm seriously considering his proposal, and that's not true either.''

''You're right,'' Sarah said. ''His feelings will definitely be hurt. I think you're going to have to say yes and deal with the rest later.''

''I suppose so. But I'm going to have to keep it on a friendship level.'' She drew her knees up to her chest and circled them with her arms. ''And how am I going to manage to do that?''

''Don't ask me. I've never had a beau, at least not a serious one.''

''Well, neither have I.''

They sat quietly contemplating the problem, but no solution came to either of them.

''Try to get some rest,'' Sarah said, getting off the bed. ''You'll figure it out. The worst that can happen is that you'll become a preacher's wife, and that's not all bad.''

''Thanks. That's a big help.''

''You're welcome.'' She opened the bedroom door to let herself out. ''Good night. Sweet dreams.''

Lydia turned down the lamp and extinguished the flame

before she crawled into bed. Sweet dreams indeed, she thought, as she lay wide awake staring at the darkened ceiling. She'd be lucky if she could even fall asleep, let alone have sweet dreams.

Chapter Fourteen

Main Street on Independence Day boasted a long series of flags and banners that rippled red, white and blue in the brisk wind. Ladies held onto their brimmed hats even though they had been well pinned; occasionally a gentleman would have to retrieve one as it rolled away. The day promised to be blustery with intermittent sunshine and scudding dark clouds, but hardly anyone seemed to mind. A makeshift platform had been set up near the schoolhouse for a small band of musicians who filled the air with patriotic music as well as any other songs that they all knew well. And nearby was the important podium, streaming with banners, where the mayor would give his speech and introduce other dignitaries who were invited to speak.

Tables of food were traditionally found at each end of town, one group of tables at the First Presbyterian Church and the other at the Peaceful Valley Baptist Church, and in between were small wooden booths that dotted the street where any and all could quench their thirst with lemonade. At the edge of the meadow, close to the festivities, were the roped-off areas for games of sack racing, three-legged races, egg tossing, and even a greased pig contest, which most young boys had been warned away from by their mothers.

The yearly celebration brought out the ladies in their finest picnic fashions, and Carrie Marting chose this day to wear her newest ensemble. She had ordered it especially for this occasion while on a shopping spree in Cincinnati and was quite pleased with the way it had turned out. The material, a lovely lightweight lawn, had a soft white background covered in modestly sized blue and yellow florets. The skirt draped naturally from a small waistline while the bodice was fashionably full and lightly pleated. The sleeves were pleasantly full from the shoulder to the elbow, tapering to her wrists. She didn't think she'd ever felt quite so feminine, and it was the most comfortable dress she'd ever worn. With such a brisk wind likely to be a nuisance, she chose a hat that had the best chance of staying put. Her only concern was that Nathan might not join her during the day, not that she had asked him. She had embarrassed herself enough and refused even to suggest that he take some time for himself and at least buy a nice lunch, which was exactly what she intended to do. She would spend the day as she pleased, without searching the crowd for his dark head or looking over her shoulder to see if was behind her somewhere.

When she left her house she barely considered taking a parasol since she would probably have to fight the blessed thing in a sudden downdraft, and besides, the sun was more absent than present. So she glanced once more in the mirror by the door, patted her hair, adjusted her bodice and smiled. Oh, but she felt feminine indeed!

Being a woman without an escort on the streets was a very uncomfortable situation, even on a day when there were so many people milling about and hardly anyone actually paying attention to her. It was one of the many negative aspects of being unmarried, and she'd listed them all countless times. But today, she planned to enjoy herself and forget all of that. Instead, she would buy a lemonade and sit in the shade of a tree while she listened to the musicians. From there she would just let the day unfold on its own.

The walk to the schoolhouse was more pleasant than she'd anticipated as the breeze filtered through her dress, keeping her cool and comfortable. When she approached the platform she spotted an empty chair under one of the large maples and made her way toward it with her glass of lemonade in her hand. But before she had gotten halfway there, she was intercepted by Agnes, looking stiff and straight in one of her usual dark-colored dresses. She eyed Carrie with her sharp features, and for the first time Carrie had to wonder why she had admired this woman so much.

"Have you seen Mayor Butterfield?" Agnes asked. It was commonplace for her to refer to her husband by his title when she was in public, but everyone knew it was her way of reminding them who she was, not who he was.

"I'm sorry, but I haven't. I've only gotten here myself, although I'll be happy to let him know you're looking for him."

"Oh, no. Don't do that," she said. "He already suspects I've been watching him." She sighed heavily. "I suppose he has gone to one of the churches."

Carrie knew better than to ask how the battle over the orphanage was going. Not only was it supposed to be a secret war, not to be spoken of in public places, but she had heard from Lucinda Mertz and Laura Poole that all was not well. It seemed that most of the men were angry enough to spit nails and had no intention of giving in to the whims of the Monday Morning Coffee Club. Some of the women feared the demise of the club, but others weren't quite so ready to quit just yet.

"Thank you, anyway," Agnes said, already breaking away and heading for the Baptist Church.

She suddenly felt sorry for Agnes, a married woman who should have been happy but wasn't, a married woman who seemed to have everything, but really didn't. The thought gave her pause as she made her way toward the empty chair once again, but was stopped by Mayor Butterfield before she could sit down.

"Mrs. Marting," he said in greeting. "Did I happen to see you speaking with my wife a moment ago?" She noticed he held a dish filled with fried chicken, assorted vegetables and a piece of cake.

"Yes." But she did as Agnes had requested, and kept silent about her searching for him.

"Could you tell me where she was going?" He kept the plate low as though it wasn't his, so she thought perhaps was holding it for someone else.

"She was going to one of the churches," she replied, seeing no harm in telling the truth.

He smiled and absently pinched his waxed mustache as he rolled the curled ends. "Thank you." He gave her a slight nod and said, "I hope you enjoy the day."

"Oh, I intend to." As he walked away she sat carefully on her chair, minding the folds of her skirts.

She sipped her lemonade and listened to the lively music while her toe tapped in rhythm beneath her dress. Around her, there were friends and neighbors visiting with one another and sometimes they stopped to talk with her. Their conversations usually centered around the events lined up for the day and were filled with much laughter and fun.

Then one of them suggested they all go to the Baptist Church since the noon meal was being served and they could get the best fried chicken that could be had. But someone quickly intervened with an apology of, "No offense, Carrie," because she was known for her cooking ability. And she suddenly became aware of how much she'd been missing by overlooking these friendships and focusing so strongly on her search for a husband. At that moment her feelings of loneliness dissipated, and she eagerly joined them in their walk to the end of town where the Baptist Church had set up table after table of succulent dishes of vegetables, meats, breads, noodles and desserts.

Behind the church were more roped-off areas for games and beyond that was the small river where several willow trees lined the bank, draping across the water. Some children had managed to venture away from the crowd, crossing a section of meadow to swing on the limbs or throw stones into the water. When Carrie finished her lunch she followed several people to watch a three-legged race just getting started, and to her surprise she saw Lydia and Sarah tying a short length of material around their ankles so that they were hobbled together. Amid much laughter the two young women grasped each other around the waist for balance and support, then tested their ability to walk. As the gun singled the beginning of the race, everyone shouted and whistled encouragement to their favorites. Carrie had to laugh at the impossible way the women and girls stumped down the field, most of them tripping each other, some of them stumbling and a few even falling in a lump of skirts. The first to cross the line and be declared the winners were Penelope's daughter and a young friend. The runners up were Lydia and Sarah.

As the two came off the field and back to the church, they had to pass by Carrie, and she stopped them.

"Congratulations to both of you," she said, smiling. I don't know how you managed to stay on your feet so long, and you looked rather graceful, too."

Sarah gave a quick glance at Lydia, then said, "I sure didn't feel graceful."

Lydia laughed. "The only thing on my mind was staying upright. I've never missed an opportunity to participate in the three-legged race since I was a child, and nobody has ever said I looked graceful, but thank you." She accepted the compliment in the spirit it was given.

Before Carrie could say more she heard Preacher Ted's voice from behind her.

"Hello, ladies." He nodded and tipped his hat. "Was that you I saw out there, Lydia?" His smile was broad and teasing.

"Oh, yes, and Sarah, too. We didn't win but we were close."

Sarah held up a ribbon. "See? Second place."

"Well, congratulations," he said. "You seem a little breathless—could I get all of you something to drink?"

"That would be very nice," Lydia replied; then she glanced at Carrie.

"Oh, yes, that would be nice. Thank you." She had intended on taking a walk to the river, but suddenly decided she would save her walk until later.

"I'll help you carry them," Sarah said, and followed him to the table of refreshments.

Feeling a little uncomfortable to be left in the company of someone she hardly knew, Carrie said, "It's turned into a lovely day for the celebration this year, hasn't it?"

"Yes. Although I thought for sure we were going to get a storm with those dark clouds hanging about in the morning, but it looks like they've gone away."

"It wouldn't be surprising if they came back. We always

seem to get one shower on the festivities every year.'' Carrie smiled and Lydia smiled back.

A short silence fell between them as each wondered what to choose for a topic next, but the appearance of Ted and Sarah with the lemonades saved them from further discomfort. For several minutes they all chatted casually about the music, the food and the games, and Carrie listened to Ted as he teased and laughed with them. She had never had many occasions to be in his company so she was surprised to find that he wasn't at all stuffy like she had expected a minister to be. There was a softness in his smile that said he genuinely cared for the people he spoke to, and his blue eyes had a merry twinkle that promised an element of mischief. Saying very little, she studied him over the edge of her glass. He had removed his hat and the sun glinted off the streaks of lighter blond that highlighted his already blond head. For a man who spent his time behind a pulpit, he was built rather broadly, she thought, and he was half a head taller than she was. Immersed deeply in her study, she hadn't heard the switch in conversation nor had she heard the question posed to her, until she realized that all three of them were staring at her. But truthfully, she barely sensed that Lydia and Sarah were staring, because she was only truly aware of being caught up in Ted's steady blue gaze.

''Don't you agree?'' he asked. And she thought the crinkles at the corners of his eyes were extremely attractive.

''Yes,'' she responded, although she hadn't a clue as to what she'd just agreed to.

Then Sarah interrupted her thoughts. ''I can go but I'll have to come right back and look for the twins.''

''Me, too,'' Lydia said, and they all started walking toward the river. And Carrie followed willingly.

As they approached the willows and ducked under the

thick, draping branches, a coolness surrounded them and they all sighed.

"Isn't this lovely?" Carrie said in the dim, filtered light. "Why, it's like an oasis."

"Haven't you ever been down here before?" Ted asked.

"No, I guess I haven't." Nature walks were never part of her lifestyle. She cared little for perspiring whether it was caused by working or walking, but this was so wonderfully cool that it was worth the walk.

"I come here often," he said. "It's the best place for meditation. And not many others come out this far."

It was true; very few others were there with them as they stood at the base of the huge old tree.

"Most of the kids prefer the deeper water down that way," Sarah said. "This is too shallow for much more than wading—" She stopped abruptly when she saw the twins walking along the bottom of the bank, their clothing soaked to their waists. "Uh, oh," she said. "Come up here this instant," she called.

The boys hung their heads and climbed the bank.

"We are going home right now," she told them. "And don't even think about running off."

"Aw, Sarah!"

"Don't you 'aw Sarah' me. Wait till Mama sees the mess you've made of yourselves."

"Please don't tell. Please?" Aaron flapped his arms and without intentionally doing so, splattered mud across Sarah's dress and onto Lydia's shirtwaist as well as her hair. Both of them let out a yelp and jumped back too late.

Carrie had been wary from the moment she'd seen them approaching and had stepped out of harm's way, and luckily so.

"If you will excuse us," Sarah said, grabbing each boy by an arm. "We have to go home."

"Wait for me," Lydia said, brushing mud from her cheek. "I'll talk to you later, Ted. Good-bye, Mrs. Marting."

Carrie stood near the tree with Ted and watched as the four of them headed toward town while the twins' cries of resistance echoed back across the meadow.

"I suppose that's the way little boys are," Carrie said.

"Yes, I'm afraid so," Ted replied with a smile. "I'm sure I gave my mother nearly as much fuss and bother when I was young, too. Although it seemed more like just having fun to me."

She turned toward him. "I can't imagine that you would give one bit of trouble even as a child," she said honestly, and thinking he had the most interesting blue eyes she'd ever seen. Not blue-green like hers, but a deep blue that bordered on violet.

"Well, thank you, Mrs. Marting," he said, his smile warm. "But I wasn't born a preacher so I did have my share of orneriness, like most boys."

He was so polite and gentlemanly, why had she never noticed this man before? she wondered.

"Shall we go back to the celebration?" he asked.

"Well, I wouldn't mind another glass of lemonade," she said, offering the opportunity for them to spend more time together.

"It is refreshing, isn't it?" He led the way, parting the draping branches so that she could walk through without snagging her hair or her dress.

She ducked her head through the opening he made for her, and felt herself blushing. If there was one thing Carrie Marting had never done, it was blush. She had always had complete control over every situation between herself and the opposite sex, except perhaps where Nathan was concerned, but he was an unusual case. When she'd made up her mind that she intended to marry Samuel, she'd carefully managed him so that he would court her, and when the time was right, she'd known exactly how to get him to propose. And she had never blushed. But standing in the arch of the willow branch, with Ted's shoulder touching hers, she felt the color rise up her neck and stop somewhere around the tips of her ears.

"Thank you," she said, without looking up.

"My pleasure," he replied, his voice soft and near.

Once they had stepped out of the shade, they were surprised to find imminent dark clouds hovering low instead of the heat that had surrounded them earlier. A brisk wind swirled across the meadow and Carrie had to grab at her hat to keep it in place.

"Oh, my!"

Ted took her hand and began to run with her across the wide-open meadow. "Let's hurry! Before we get soaked."

Carrie held him back with her lagging steps in order to breathe inside her stays, but when they managed to get several yards away from the tree, the sky let loose with a skin-needling downpour. Instantly, her white lawn dress absorbed the rain, sticking to her arms, her back and shoulders. Suddenly, Ted whirled and headed back to the tree, pulling her along behind him. The wind snatched her hat from her head, tearing out the pins and leaving wet bunches of blond hair to hang in clumps around her face. Then somewhere along the way she felt the rat she'd so carefully rolled into her hair slip and fall away. At last when they were under the tree, protected from the worst of it, Ted struggled out of his wet jacket, holding it out for her.

"It's wet, but . . ." he began.

She felt her knees turn to butter as he lifted the coat to settle it around her head and shoulders. When she looked up at him, he was no longer smiling but studying her face intently. He had the most incredible blue eyes was all she could think. Then as the raindrops collected on the leaves and fell in plops around them and on the jacket that sheltered her head, he leaned down and kissed her full on the lips. His hands grasped her upper arms, supporting her and pulling her closer into an embrace such as she'd never experienced in her life. His searching kiss was not at all what she would have expected from a preacher. It warmed her from the inside out, gathering in places she didn't know could be heated. Her breasts tingled and her stomach quivered. Then she leaned into him as her arms reached up to circle his neck, while his lowered to tighten at her waist. He smelled of sunshine and rain, spice and sweetness and she wished the moment would never end. She wished the kiss would never end, but it did, just as softly as it began.

"Should I apologize, Mrs. Marting?" he said.

"I think you should call me Carrie. And please, don't apologize. It would ruin everything."

Each took a serious study of the other, no smiles, no coquettishness, no teasing. Neither knew what to say, yet both wanted to say something. She felt a surge of happiness unlike any she'd ever felt, but his was mixed with a niggling of guilt because he had asked for the hand of another. She wanted to revel in these emerging feelings with no thought of making plans, and she knew her days of plotting and planning were over. He wished he could tell her what was in his heart but he needed to explain, to make things right with someone else first. So he held her close. Carrie smiled as her face pressed into the front of his wet shirt.

"It's stopped," he said. "We'd better go."

She nodded, but didn't move. Then he held her away from him, and smiled.

"We're going to set some tongues to wagging if we stay here much longer," he said.

"I've made plenty of tongues wag over the years." She smiled up at him. "I just thought you ought to know that."

"Well, I don't want to be the cause of it happening again." He started to unwrap the coat from her shoulders, but her dress was so perfectly molded to her rounded contours that he put it back. "You'd probably better wear this home."

"Thank you, I will."

Once again they emerged from under the tree, its branches dripping and drooping from the weight of the rain. They walked a respectable distance from each other all the way back to the church and the water-logged festivities. When they approached the tables of food where dishes had filled with rainwater, they stopped momentarily to say good-bye. Then each went their separate ways home.

"Well, did you see that?" Lila Peterson whispered to Hattie as Carrie walked by wearing Preacher Ted's coat.

"I did. What a gentleman that man is to give a lady his coat."

"Is that what you saw?" Lila sniffed at Hattie's observation.

"Land a livin', Lila. Ain't you got nothin' better to do?"

Ignoring Hattie's question, she said, "I wonder what Miss Jefferson and Nathan Stockwell would have to say about that?"

"Why would they have anything to say? I'm sure nothing happened, and if it did, what business would it be of theirs? Just like it ain't any business of yours either."

"Well, just the other night Nathan was at the old Mercer house with Miss Jefferson."

"He's over there because he's helping out."

"They weren't working. They were in the backyard almost in the same spot that I saw her and Preacher Ted kissing.''

''I suppose you were in the outhouse again. Spying.''

''A woman has a right to use her own privy. And if I want to look out the window, I can.''

''Hmpf.''

''And just in case you're interested—''

''I'm not.''

''Well, they were out there for a very long time.''

''Seems like you woulda been kind of tired of sitting in the outhouse that long.'' Hattie had to grin at the picture Lila had just painted for her.

''I could hardly leave—they might have seen me.''

''Seems only fair since you was a-seein' them.''

Lila glared at her. ''You are not listening, Hattie Arthur. I'm trying to tell you that there is some hanky panky going on and it involves that man-hunting Carrie Marting. Now she's after our Preacher Ted.''

''I'd say he's a grown man and can take care of himself.''

''Maybe. But with Carrie chasing him, there's a good chance he won't know what hit him till it's too late.''

''I'd think you'd be glad about it. Leastways she ain't chasing after Mr. Stockwell, and we both know what store you set by him. Or maybe that's why you was a-spyin' on him and Miss Jefferson.'' She levered a look of warning at Lila.

''Well!'' Lila huffed indignantly. ''I can't believe you'd say something like that. You have just the same as accused me of wanting to commit adultery.''

''My mama always told me, if the shoe fits, wear it.''

Lila gathered up her dripping dishes, sloshing the rain water out of them in her haste to depart Hattie's company.

When she'd gone, Hattie shook her head and mumbled, "That shoe most certainly does fit."

Lydia waited her turn to use the bathing room while she sat at the kitchen table listening to the howls of anguish coming from the twins, who had been subjected to a complete bath. Sarah stood guard outside the door, occasionally peeking inside to make sure they were at least making an effort to get clean.

"Remind me never to have twin boys," she said to Lydia, who laughed in reply.

"I'm serious. These two are enough to make me join a convent."

"My brother used to make me feel that way sometimes, too."

"Then imagine two of him."

Lydia laughed and shook her head. "I can't. I don't even want to."

Silence from the bathing room made Sarah put a finger to her lips for quiet while she listened through the door. Then she opened it a crack and closed it again.

"They're done and getting dressed. And they had better be clean."

When the boys came out they were mostly dry and fully dressed in clean clothes. Sarah checked behind their ears, scrutinized the palms of their hands and sifted her hand through their hair before she pronounced them clean. Then she sent them off with a warning to stay that way for the rest of the day if they knew what was good for them. With an exasperated sigh, she went into the room to drain the water and clean up the mess they had left behind.

"Go ahead," Sarah said to Lydia. "You can take the next bath. I'm just about too tired to carry the hot water in there. Maybe by the time you're done I'll be ready."

"Are you sure?" she said, rising from her seat.

"Absolutely."

Lydia hauled several buckets of water from the stove into the room where the lovely large tub rested in one corner. Then she slipped out of her clothes and climbed over the side to sit in the warm depth. Leaning back as far as she could, she washed her hair, nearly submersing her face as the long strands flared around her. Taking a bath in the middle of the day was not a common occurrence but she enjoyed it immensely as she relaxed against the curve of the tub with her head angled back at the top edge. High up on the outside wall was an open window, which let in a breeze of rain-scented air.

She didn't think she would return to the celebration. Instead she would go to the old house and enjoy the quiet view from the back steps and wile away some time before supper. It hadn't occurred to her until that moment that she hadn't seen Nathan during the entire day. Certainly he wouldn't work on Independence Day, she thought. But perhaps without a family to share the day with, there would be little reason to wander around the town alone. The thought made her feel a little sad for him. It was true she'd been without family, too, but that was out of choice, not out of a lack of having one. Now that she'd gotten to know him a little better, she'd come to the conclusion that he wasn't a difficult man, not really. He was simply a man who put work ahead of all else. And that made her even more sad. The most she'd seen him relax was the evening she'd taken supper to him in a basket; he'd smiled and even teased her somewhat.

Well, it was time for Mr. Nathan Stockwell to start enjoying a few things and she intended to do what she could to make him smile more often. A basketful of supper was a good starting place as well as a napkin filled with his favorite cookies, but man should not live by bread alone. He needed to laugh as well as smile. He needed to spend more time with his neighbors and let others get to know him better and he needed to share a little more of himself instead of being so reclusive. Maybe all of that was asking too much, but she'd give it a try.

Chapter Fifteen

As usual, Lydia arrived at the old house shortly after breakfast. She enjoyed the leisurely walk, taking her time while
she collected her thoughts about the work ahead. Occasionally, Sarah accompanied her but many times, such as that
morning, she'd elected to stay at home to help her mother
with the household chores, and on those days Lydia focused
on the smaller jobs she could handle alone. Even Ted had
not helped at the house for several days, although she imagined that church business kept him busy. She missed having
his help, but she understood and even felt somewhat relieved. There were times when she preferred to work alone
and it appeared that this would be one of those times.

As she walked across the front porch, she smiled in appreciation at the clean white paint on the posts and railing
before pushing the door open. The front of the house still
needed a lot of work but the porch made such a remarkable
difference she hardly noticed the rest of the peeling paint.

Inside, the odor of damp plaster greeted her and the same old enthusiasm that urged her to go on to the next project gripped her once again. They were making progress and even though it was slow, it was still progress. Nathan had started arriving earlier in the evenings in order to get in a few hours of plastering, and Lydia was surprised. She wondered again and again at his determination to work on her house, and even had to question how she could have misjudged him in the first place.

During the evenings, while Nathan plastered, she helped as much as possible, but when he wasn't there she worked on the upstairs bedrooms, tackling the job of removing the crumbling plaster or the woodwork that wasn't salvageable. He had shown her how to glaze some of the windowpanes and that had become her favorite job. So she pulled on her dust cap, which had become limp and faded from so many washings, and set to work. The time passed quickly through the morning hours as she alternately hummed a happy tune and contemplated her handiwork and before she knew it, Sarah had arrived with a basket filled with the noon meal.

"Hungry?" she asked.

"Now that you've brought it, I guess I am."

"You've made quite a mess in here," Sarah said, studying the piles of plaster and rotted woodwork.

"And it's been fun, too," Lydia responded cheerily. "What's in the basket?"

"Just some leftovers that Mama sent. Let's sit on the steps." She looked around at the dirt and grime on the floor and Lydia nodded in agreement and followed her to the stairway where they both sat on the top step. "If we stay in the house to eat we won't be watched by Mrs. Peterson," she added.

"Watched?" Lydia asked before biting into a buttered slice of bread.

"She's told several people that she saw Preacher Ted kiss you."

Lydia's eyes rounded in shocked surprise. "She did what?"

"She saw you."

Lydia groaned.

"She was in the privy and watched the two of you kiss. And I don't think she approves, from what Mama says." Sarah smiled, her eyes alight with that familiar mischievousness that Lydia had come to associate with only her.

"Your mother knows?"

"And countless others, too, I'm sure." She sorted through the basket and selected a cookie.

Lydia's appetite quickly vanished and she set aside the bread. It was bad enough that everyone was talking about her. "Poor Ted," she said, voicing her concern for him.

"Oh, poot," Sarah replied, dismissing her worry with a wave of her hand with the half-eaten cookie still in it. "Everyone knows what a gossip Lila Peterson is. Most likely nobody will pay any attention to her."

"But still. Poor Ted. He doesn't deserve being the center of gossip."

"I agree. Would you like me to tell Mrs. Peterson to mind her own business like Hattie Arthur did?"

"No!" Lydia stared at her. "Hattie said that?"

"So I've been told." She finished the cookie and scrounged through the basket for more.

"I'm not even going to ask who told you. I don't want to know."

"Good. I can't give away my best source anyway," Sarah said with a grin. "Just be forewarned that you could be seen if you are in the proximity of the privy next door."

Suddenly the whole idea seemed absurd, or perhaps it was just Sarah's impishness that was contagious, because she felt an uncontrollable urge to laugh. "From the privy?" she said in astonishment.

Sarah nodded. "The privy."

And then both of them started laughing and couldn't quit. They hooted and howled until the tears rolled merrily down their cheeks and their sides hurt. Neither could say a word as they bent double in their mirth, trying to ease the ache in their muscles and get a breath, too. Finally, with their laughter spent, they sighed their way into silence.

Sarah handed her a cookie and she took it. So, she was now the object of a new source of gossip. Evidently, the topic of an unwanted children's home was taking second seat to a supposedly improper kiss. It wasn't fair to Ted, and she would have to do something about it. Soon.

Throughout the afternoon the two of them worked on what Lydia had begun until Sarah went home to help her mother with supper. Lydia waited in hopes that Nathan might come early and finish the plastering in the kitchen. She asked Sarah to leave the basket behind since there were still some cookies in it, as well as bread that she and Nathan could eat during a break. And sure enough, he arrived a little earlier than the night before, carrying his knapsack, which held his usual meager meal.

"Hello," she called from the kitchen as he entered the front door. "I'm back here." And she hastily pulled the dusty, ruffled cap from her hair, poking the loose strands back into place as best she could. Suddenly, she had felt self-conscious with it on, but she couldn't say why. He had certainly seen her wear it many times and had never commented on it.

His footsteps sounded solidly through the empty house, and she realized that she'd begun to listen for them. When he stood in the doorway, nearly filling it, he smiled at her, then set his knapsack on the floor.

"I thought you'd have this finished by the time I got here," he said, teasing her.

"I considered it," she replied, accepting his tease. "But then I changed my mind and decided to work upstairs on something I could really handle."

"What did you do up there?" He always seemed interested in each of her projects and asked questions or offered advice. Sometimes she agreed, and sometimes she didn't, but they always had a discussion about it.

"Nothing much. Just made a mess mostly." She shrugged one shoulder lightly. "But Sarah helped me clean it up and now it won't be long before we can start patching up that bedroom." She had chosen that room for herself since it was at the top of the stairs and had plenty of room for a desk and shelves; that way she could combine it with an office and leave the other bedrooms available.

"I guess we'd better get this done before we think about working on another one," he said.

This was one of the areas they couldn't agree on, since she liked to continue thinking ahead of the actual work in progress and he did not. When she carried buckets of plaster to pour onto the mortarboard, she thought about the windows upstairs and which ones she could glaze next or she thought about how she would paint the stairway railing when it was all replaced. Several times he'd told her she was getting too far ahead of herself and she told him she had to keep thinking about the next step because that was what kept her going. She didn't understand how he could be content to think and work on only the job at hand. His reply was, "Plenty of practice." Well, that was one thing she did not have when it came to this kind of work, so she tried to take his advice even though it wasn't easy.

Without wasting any more time talking, he got busy mixing the plaster while she pumped a bucket of water, which she slowly added to the pulpy mess when he directed her to do so. As soon as the mixture suited him he sliced a trowel through it, cutting and scraping to test the texture. Then he scooped it into a bucket and hauled it to the kitchen. The ceiling and one end wall were finished, so he started on the inside wall near the finished one. Lydia kept his mortarboard filled, pouring the mix from the heavy bucket. He had told her not to lift it, that he could pour it himself when he climbed down from the ladder, but she had ignored him and finally he'd stopped trying to tell her what to do. And that was something else they disagreed on. She was determined to do at least her fair share, and he seemed just as determined that she should do less.

"It's starting to look like a real room," she said, placing her hand against the ache in the small of her back. "I'm anxious to see how it's going to look around the windows when the slats no longer show. Of course, then I'll want to see how it will look with wallpaper on it and curtains at the windows." She was always thinking ahead.

"That will take a while so don't spend too much time planning it yet."

She made a face at him, and he turned his head just in time to see it. With his trowel poised in midair, he grinned at her, letting her know she'd been caught red-handed.

"Well, you deserved it," she said, smiling back. "I like planning ahead and you're always trying to squash my enthusiasm."

"I never would have thought a teacher would do something like that."

"I'm not a teacher anymore, and besides, teachers are not as immune to normal reactions as most people think they are. I've even been known to stick out my tongue."

He smoothed a glob of plaster on the wall and said without looking at her, "I don't believe you."

211

"If that's supposed to be a dare, I'll pass. You'll just have to take my word for it." She poured the last of the plaster onto the board, which sat on the cookstove so that it would be closer to his ladder. Just as she turned away, he leaned down to scoop more onto his trowel and a splatter of it landed in her hair.

"Did you do that on purpose?" she asked, reaching up to remove the wet glob as she sent him a searching look.

"It was an accident. Honest." But his eyes were dancing with humor so she couldn't be sure if he meant it. "You were in the wrong place at the wrong time, that's all. Why aren't you wearing your hat?"

She picked at the mess, pulling at the long strands of her hair in an attempt to get as much as she could. "I should have been, but it's a little late now."

"I am sorry. Really." But his eyes still didn't register whether he was being truthful or not.

"I accept your apology in the spirit that it's given," she returned, smiling up at him "But I have to warn you, it may not be safe to turn your back."

Surprised by her threat, Nathan couldn't help laughing out loud.

"Are you mocking me?" she asked, grinning as she reached for a stone-sized ball of the squishy plaster.

"No. Not at all. And I said I'm sorry." Somehow he didn't look sorry enough to suit her.

"Oh, so now you're afraid and want to apologize more genuinely." She was prodding him on and she knew she would soon be in a corner that she could not get out of gracefully, but a sudden mischievous bent kept her going.

"I'm not afraid." He kept eye contact with her as he laid down the trowel and started backing down the ladder.

She retreated in order to keep some distance between them so she could throw with a decent aim but had to dodge behind the stove to prevent backing into the corner. When he continued to advance, daring her with his stare, she flung the plaster ball and hit him square in the chest. He stopped a moment, looked at it, then advanced once more. Laughing, she ran around the opposite end of the stove, scooped a handful of the plaster and stepped behind the ladder, peeking through the rungs.

"I'm well armed," she threatened. "Don't take another step or I'll shoot."

Without hesitating, he lunged forward. She screamed as she flung the mess at him and darted away to stand with the cookstove between them once more. Laughter bubbled up from inside her when she saw she'd hit her target.

"Not bad," she said, complimenting herself. "Lucky for you it was only plaster." She pointed to the spot on his shirt just over his heart where she had splattered him.

Nathan stared at it and felt the sobering effects of the cool, wet plaster soaking through his shirt. As pieces of it dropped onto the floor at his feet, he realized that he had overstepped his self-appointment boundary. He hadn't intended to participate in any horseplay, and it had nearly gotten out of hand.

"Lucky for me," he said, and he resurrected his boundary once more.

Before Lydia could respond, she heard Sarah call out to them.

"Hello, everyone! Supper has arrived!" She came into the kitchen and sniffed. "Smells wet and moldy in here." Then she handed the basket to Lydia. "But this will make it smell better."

Lydia accepted it and looked inside. Bread, chicken, potatoes fried in onions, a jar of pickled cabbage, a dish of green beans, and sugar cookies.

"What happened to you two?" Sarah asked, nodding

213

toward Nathan's shirt and touching the wet spot in Lydia's hair. "Something break loose and fall?" She looked at the ceiling for telltale signs of missing plaster.

"Just an accident," Lydia said without glancing at Nathan.

"Oh." Sarah seemed to sense that something was amiss, and Lydia knew she wasn't fond of being in Nathan's presence since she still considered him unfriendly. "I guess I'll be on my way," Sarah said, backing out of the room. "I'm sure Mama needs help with the twins." Then she made a hasty departure.

"I suppose we ought to eat this while it's still hot, don't you?" she asked.

"Why not finish the rest of this first?" he said, scooping up part of what was left on the board. "It won't take long."

Lydia waited while he worked, watching him as he smoothed the plaster over the slatted wood and covering the holes so that one solid wall emerged. He worked quietly, with only the sound of the trowel scrapping back and forth to fill the room. When he finished she followed him to the pump to wash up his tools and their hands.

Standing across from him, she smiled and said, "I hope I didn't ruin your shirt."

"Doesn't matter. It's a work shirt anyway." Then he scrubbed his hands beneath the water while she pumped. "I hope that plaster comes out of your hair without too much trouble," he said, looking at her.

"I'm sure it will, but if it doesn't . . . well, then I'll just have to come looking for you."

He smiled and relaxed, enjoying her good humor, and keeping a respectable distance between them as they walked back inside the house. He picked up the basket, then headed for the back steps to eat their supper just like they usually did.

"Why don't we sit on the stairs in here?" she said, remembering Lila Peterson's vantage point for watching them. Lydia had no intention of giving the woman more fuel for gossiping. When he looked as though he might object, she said, "It's cooler in here." But he surprised her when he agreed and followed her to the stairs, where they climbed partway up and sat side by side.

"What have we got in here?" she asked.

"More cookies?" he asked with a crooked half smile.

"Actually, yes. But let's see . . ." She dug through the pile of napkins and offered him some of Opal's bread.

"Thanks." He accepted the fresh bread and took a bite.

She took her time setting up the food on the step below them and above them; then he reached down to set the basket on the floor. They sat quietly enjoying their food and talking occasionally about the room in front of them. When they finished eating and the dishes were off their laps, Lydia opened the napkinful of cookies between them.

"These are very good," she said. "But I only have room for one. Why don't you put the rest in your pack and take them home?"

"Thanks. I think I will."

"As soon as the kitchen is finished we can move the stove and hook it to the chimney, then I'll be able to make us some coffee." She waited for him to remind her of taking one step at a time.

"Shouldn't be too long," he said, after he wiped the last crumb from his face.

"Really?" she replied, surprised.

"If the rest goes as easily as tonight, I don't know why it should take much more than two days to finish it."

She turned sideways to face him as she finally came to the decision to tell him that she intended to move into the kitchen just as soon as it was finished, but when she leaned back against the rail in order to study his reaction better, one of the spindles gave way. Suddenly off-balance, she let out a yelp and ducked in an attempt to protect her head from the banister. But Nathan responded quickly, reaching for her, snatching her away from the edge and closer to him. Her heart pounded from her narrow escape.

"Thank you," she said, staring up at him, close enough to count the gold flecks in his eyes. When he didn't reply, her heart thudded, but this time it had nothing to do with the near fall. As her breath caught in her throat, she was reminded of the moment that Ted had kissed her, except this time she was hoping it would happen.

Nathan saw the anticipation on her face, but instead of shying away as he knew he would if she'd been anyone else, he felt drawn by it. So many years had passed since he'd held a woman so close or been tempted by lips as soft and appealing as hers. He barely noticed the streaks of plaster dust on her cheeks and in her brows or the smudge of grime on her chin. He only took heed of her natural feminine scent which mixed nicely with that of rosewater still clinging to her skin from an earlier bath. For a moment he wondered if he ought to do this, if he would regret it, or if she would regret it, but when her eyes fluttered shut he knew she would take her chances the same as he would. With his hands around her shoulders, he drew her closer until his lips touched hers and her breath met his. He knew she could feel the heavy beating of his heart where her hands lay trapped against his chest, but it was too late to pretend he didn't care. So he gave in to the need that gripped him, the need to taste her, to feel her lips beneath his, searching, searching. . . .

Lydia drowned in the bliss of the moment. Somehow she maintained a measure of sanity through touching his shirt, roughened by the plaster she'd thrown at him, but when she concentrated on his lips moving across hers, she nearly lost her one last hold on reality. He smelled of sweat and plaster and wood shavings, and it all smelled absolutely wonderful. His grip on her arms was strong, yet gentle just like the kiss. Although this was not her first, it was certainly the deepest, most soul-rending kiss she'd ever experienced and she had the melted bones to prove it.

When he raised his head, she held perfectly still, unsure if she'd be able to move even if she wanted to, and afraid to dispel the languorous feeling that hung over her like a fog on the meadow. She could still taste his breath, his lips, as she tried to imprint them in her mind to be savored and reviewed in private. Outside of her thoughts were questions waiting to be asked, bumping gently against her mind as though not wanting to disrupt her. Later, she would answer them if she could, but right now she wanted only to feel his lips on hers again. With purposeful intent she reached her hands up to touch his cheeks and draw him into another kiss. She needed to know if the first one could be repeated or if it was merely a serendipitous happening, but when they touched again, her breath caught and held, and then she knew. After that, she simply gave herself over to the feelings that longed to be set free, and the questions that bumped more urgently against her mind had to be pushed aside with a promise to answer them when she was alone.

At last, when they parted, he said, "I probably shouldn't have done that." Their foreheads touched and their eyes were closed.

"I'm glad you did." Truthfully, she was more than glad. Her heart was singing.

"But tomorrow you might feel different."

She shook her head without breaking contact with him. "I can say with confidence that I won't feel different tomorrow." Her breath hadn't yet returned to normal and her words came out in phrases.

He was silent a moment, then went on. "You don't really know me." He took her hands and let them rest between them.

"Somehow, that doesn't matter right now." She smiled. "Not one little bit."

Around them, the house darkened in the twilight, casting long shadows through the doorways that opened to the west. They sat quietly on the steps, still resting forehead to forehead, hardly aware of their surroundings, but very much aware of each other. Then finally, Nathan broke the spell.

"It's getting late," he said, but he didn't move.

"Yes."

"If I don't get here as early tomorrow, don't think . . . don't think I'm purposely staying away. I have a wagon to get finished and it's almost done."

She raised her head so she could see his face. "Why would I think that?"

"No reason," he replied, wishing he hadn't said anything. And now that common sense was returning, he felt some confusion come along with it. He needed to be alone to think it all through. He knew it was time to go.

She sensed his withdrawal and let him pull his hands away.

"I'll help you," he said, reaching for the basket. Then she arranged everything inside it as he handed her the jars, dishes, and napkins. He felt clumsy as he accidently dumped the remaining green beans onto the napkins she'd carefully folded, so he took his hands out of her way and let her finish alone. When she was done he got to his feet, took the basket and helped her away from the broken railing.

"I'd better fix that tomorrow," he said, and she nodded.

At the bottom of the stairs he picked up his knapsack and walked with her to the front door, where he handed her the basket. Before stepping out onto the porch, he turned to her and lifted a tendril of hair from her cheek. He said good night and hurried toward the gate without looking back.

By the time he reached his small house, darkness had settled around the town. Inside the kitchen, he fumbled for a match as though he were in someone else's house and finally swore before finding one. At last he lit the lamp, then stared at the starkly furnished room, and swore again. He quickly doused the light, not wanting to be faced with his self-inflicted isolation for the first time since he'd moved there. So he stripped off his clothes, tossed aside the shirt with the hardened plaster in the spot over his heart, and took his bath in the dark.

Later, when he stretched out on the cool but scratchy sheets, he tried to sleep, but his thoughts kept returning to that moment when he'd held Lydia in his arms. For him, there hadn't been a choice. He'd had to kiss her, or be tormented, but as it turned out he was tormented anyway. And now he was convinced he'd made a mistake. She didn't know him or anything about him. Nobody did. He had successfully kept to himself by building a barrier that had no niches. He hadn't allowed any prying eyes or curious questions to intrude beyond the safety of that wall, until now. And he'd been the one to provide the niche, the toehold that could eventually tear down that barrier.

A slow, familiar ache spread through him and he closed his eyes against it. Years had passed since he'd felt that ache turn into an all-consuming pain, and he didn't want it to return. Working hard had been the best means of keeping it at bay, that and simply ignoring it, until eventually, he had become immune. Long hours and strenuous work had helped him to stay numb, to not feel anything, and he had survived.

But now the scar was being probed.

He had willingly walked into a situation that he'd known better than to get involved with, and all the warning signals had been there. The orphanage was the first warning. If he'd stuck to his original gut instinct and repeated the word "no" just a few more times, he'd probably be all right. Nothing would have changed. And if he had remained indifferent to her instead of noticing how honest and straightforward and unassuming she was, he might still have been all right. But the loudest warning bell was when he reacted to her simple charm and allowed himself to be drawn into her fun and laughter, which was something he'd given up a long time ago. There should have been little doubt in his mind where it would end, and he should have been better prepared for it. He should have kept his distance so that he wouldn't have noticed her at all. If he had said no, if he had simply done the work and gone home, if he had not touched her, and especially if he hadn't kissed her.

But he had, and the damage was done.

The ache he'd hidden away for so long surfaced and he didn't know how to make it go away anymore. He could tell Lydia the truth about himself and sharpen the pain, or he could just let this new incident drop with no explanation by simply walking away before he got in any deeper.

But he already was in too deep.

With no moonlight to illuminate the room, he stared into the pitch darkness and wondered where it all would lead.

Chapter Sixteen

Having lain awake until the early hours of morning, Lydia found it nearly impossible to keep her eyes open during breakfast. She stirred the oatmeal in her bowl without eating until Opal asked if it was overcooked. Not wanting to offend her, Lydia managed to eat all of it down to the last bit. Then she filled her cup with coffee in hopes of reviving herself enough to at least walk to the house, but the effort cost her dearly. She made her way around to the back steps where she could enjoy the meadow, not caring if Lila Peterson spied on her or not. With her elbows propped up on her knees and chin in her hands, she stared out across the meadow where the heads on the flowers nodded lazily in the breeze.

Even though the scenery was beautiful, her mind could focus only on Nathan's kiss and her reaction to it. She hadn't been able to answer a single question like she'd promised herself she would. Instead she'd discovered even more questions and no answers at all. And the most burning question, right after "How do I really feel about him?" was "How will this affect my dream of a children's home?" She had tried to puzzle through it during the night, but had succeeded only in keeping herself awake by reliving the emotions she'd experienced in his arms. Sarah had sensed her aloofness and politely kept her distance, which Lydia appreciated. Somehow, she would get it figured out. In the meantime, she had to muster up a little energy in order to get something accomplished in the house, but for the first time, working on the house was a chore.

Throughout the morning she managed to sweep up part of the mess from the day before and glaze a few windowpanes, but not without taking a couple of thoughtful breaks, sitting and contemplating the meadow from the back steps. Unfortunately, the afternoon progressed in much the same way.

And that was where Ted found her later in the day.

"Here you are," he said. After she looked up at him, he went on, "You've been working too hard."

She almost laughed, but wasn't quite up to it. "Not even close," she replied.

"Well, I came through the kitchen and was surprised to find it plastered. At least most of it. Has Nathan been working here every night?"

"Yes." But she didn't explain further.

"Listen. Why don't you just stay put while I see what else needs doing."

As he started up the steps beside her, she quickly got to her feet. Feelings of guilt wouldn't allow her to sit idly while he worked on her house alone.

"I'm fine. Really," she said. "I just had a hard time falling asleep last night, that's all. What do you say we work on the room upstairs?" She'd had her mind set on getting that room finished right after the kitchen.

He stopped in the doorway when she spoke, and turned to study her. "I absolutely insist that you sit here for a while," he said. "I should have been here helping you."

It was the first time she'd seen him without a smile. Instead, a frown shadowed his eyes. She didn't like being the cause of his solemn expression, and yet she knew sooner or later she would be when she finally had the courage to say no to his proposal. Perhaps, this would be the moment and she ought to get it over with.

"Ted—"

"Lydia—" They spoke in unison, then stopped and waited for the other to finish.

"Go ahead," he said.

"No. You go first."

"I wasn't really going to say anything."

"Me either." She'd lost her nerve and felt dishonest not owning up to the truth, which he deserved to know. It wasn't fair to allow him to go on thinking there was a chance for a relationship, nor should she continue taking advantage of his good heart by letting him work on the house. But she couldn't bring herself to reject him.

He gave her a small sideways smile then leaned down to kiss her forehead lightly. "Sit here. I insist."

She glanced in the direction of Lila Peterson's privy. Then she nodded in agreement, because working alongside him would only add more stress to an already stressful day.

"Well, just for a little while," she said, taking the coward's way out.

"Good." Then he went into the kitchen and she was alone again.

Berating herself for being deceptive and misleading, she sank down on the steps but a loud commotion inside the house had her on her feet again and running.

"Ted!" she called as she hurried through the kitchen, unable to hold down her rising panic. Before she even reached him, she knew he'd fallen through the broken railing of the stairs. "Ted!" she called again, then turned the corner to find him lying in a heap with his hands clasped around one ankle. His face was a mottled red as he bit his lip to hold back any sound.

"Oh, it's all my fault," she said, kneeling beside him and believing in her heart that it was. "I should have told you about the railing." But she'd been so wrapped up in her own selfish concerns that it had slipped her mind. If she had kept him at the back door and told him the truth, told him that she could not marry him because she did not love him, he would have gone home feeling sad and rejected but at least not in this kind of pain.

"Is it broken?" But he wouldn't release it for her to check for broken bones.

"I don't think so," he managed to say. "But it hurts like . . . the devil."

She bent over him, saying, "Wait right here. I'll get some help. We'll get you to the doctor."

He tried to grin at her. "I'm not going anywhere. Believe me."

Rising to her feet, she backed away, gesturing for him to stay put. "Now don't move. Stay right there."

"I promise," he replied.

Guilt and worry made her feet fly as she ran toward the only person she knew who could help. She found Nathan working in his shop but she was so out of breath she could hardly speak, and had to lean against his workbench to rest. When he grabbed her by the arms she knew she'd frightened him.

"What is it?" he asked, his voice calm but low with his gaze intense and searching.

She scraped back a hank of hair that had fallen in front of her eyes while trying to get a good deep breath in her lungs. "It's Ted. He's fallen. The railing."

"Is he hurt bad?"

"I think he's broken something. He's in a lot of pain. Can you come?"

Within minutes, Nathan had borrowed the nearest hitched wagon and they were driving back to her place, where they found Ted in exactly the same spot he'd fallen. Nathan gently got him up on his good leg, then half-supported and half-carried him to the wagon. Lydia climbed into the back to sit beside him, ignoring his insistence that he would be just fine and she didn't have to come along. The ride was jolting in spite of Nathan's best attempt to take it easy. At last they reached the doctor's office and Lydia ran ahead to open the door as Nathan helped Ted inside.

Without more than the necessary questions and comments, Dr. James probed and tested until he finally said, "Well, Ted, count yourself lucky. The ankle is badly sprained but not broken, although you're going to think it is if you walk on it before several weeks pass. That muscle has been pulled."

"Not broken?" Lydia repeated in disbelief.

"Nope. But he's going to be propping it up just as though it was. And that means very little hobbling around, too," he replied sternly. "You'll be sorry if you don't listen to my advice. Understand?"

"I'm grateful it isn't broken," he said. "And I will take your advice."

"Good."

After hearing the simple method of treatment, which was rest and applying cool cloths, Nathan and Lydia took him home. Once they got him inside the little house that sat near the church, Lydia hurried around finding towels and pumped a basin half full of cool water. She cringed for him as she laid them across his badly swollen ankle, which already had started turning shades of blue. And most likely a good part of his leg would change color, too.

Nathan stood back while she worked. "I'm sorry about this, Ted. I should have fixed that railing. If there's anything you need, well, I'll be stopping by to check on you."

"So will I," Lydia said.

Ted shook his head. "You both have enough work to do. The last thing I want is to burden you with more." And before they could object, he quickly added, "I'm just going to sit here and do as the doctor suggested."

"Well, you have to eat," Lydia said. "And I insist on bringing you some meals."

"That won't be necessary," he insisted. "Hattie and the other ladies will probably keep me well fed. As a matter of fact, I'll probably have more than I can eat and end up as round as a barrel." He attempted to smile and she was glad to see his sense of humor return, although it didn't alleviate her feelings of guilt for the fall he'd taken or the rejection she would eventually give him.

They stayed for a while longer, then agreed to leave to give him a chance to rest quietly. On their ride back to her house they kept their conversation limited to Ted. But when they arrived at her gate and Nathan helped her down, both of them lingered, letting their touches rest longer than was necessary.

He was the first to let his hands drop away, saying, "As soon as I return the wagon to Jeff, I'll come back and fix that railing. I don't want anybody else getting hurt."

She nodded and her heart skipped a beat as he stared intently at her. "I'll see to it that nobody goes near the stairs, including me,'' she assured him. He appeared to relax with that and climbed onto the wagon.

As he drove away, she felt the effects of the last twenty-four hours take their toll. A lack of sleep on top of the panic she'd just been through made her knees weak, but thank goodness it had turned out better than she'd feared. Now, she had to find a way to gently speak with Ted, and she had to do it before the gossips suspected the feelings unfolding between herself and Nathan, if they didn't already know.

Carrie had heard just that morning about Ted's fall and wasted no time at all preparing her most flavorful chicken soup with fresh vegetables from the local gardeners. Hattie Arthur had told her that Dr. James ordered him to stay off his feet for several weeks and that he was unable to fend for himself. She'd said it was a real pity since he'd had his heart set on helping Miss Jefferson and now it would all be left to Mr. Stockwell. Not that he wasn't capable, but they would be shorthanded in getting the job completed on time. Carrie had listened politely as Hattie talked, but she could hardly wait to get home and start cooking. This was her chance to see him again.

For the entire week after Independence Day she had worried and fretted about what had transpired between them beneath the willow trees, and for once in her life she'd been at a loss to figure out how to handle it. She had thought of nothing else, not even Nathan Stockwell. And when Ted had not come calling or even approached her on the street, she experienced a new kind of disappointment. This strange awakening both baffled and excited her; it also brought a new timidity that kept her from being the one to approach him. But now, all that had changed since he was restricted to his house. If he could not come to her, she would go to him and then discover exactly how he'd been affected by their kiss.

She leaned away from the stove to fan herself, unsure if the memory of that kiss had brought the heat rising up her neck or if it came naturally from cooking. On second thought, she knew it had to be the memory and fanned herself more vigorously. Each night since he'd kissed her she'd gone over every move, every touch, every look that had passed between them that day, and just the remembering alone had brought on such a heat wave she'd had to kick off the sheets to cool herself. And she couldn't help wondering if he thought about it half as much as she did.

When the soup had simmered to just the right flavor, she set it on a trivet on the sideboard to cool while she freshened up and changed her clothes. It took longer than usual to select the right dress. Modesty was important, mostly because he made her feel like an innocent yet desirable young woman, and that was something new to her. Blue, she decided. It had to be blue to match her eyes because he had looked so deep into them, clear to the bottom of her soul. Even now as she thought about it, goose bumps raised on her arms and she had to smooth them down.

In the back of her wardrobe she found a simple dress that was as blue as an evening sky. The collar was high, edged with tiny white lace, and the bodice was yoked with an edging of lace also. She frowned at the wrinkles in the skirt and hurried down to the kitchen to heat the irons, then hurried back upstairs to pin and comb her hair carefully into place. When she felt sure the irons were hot, she carried the dress downstairs and took out the board and pressed out the wrinkles. Before going back upstairs she poured the soup into several jars and placed them in her basket. Upstairs once more, she hurried through her toilette, then pulled on the blue dress and struggled with the buttons down the back. At last she was ready, with her hat adjusted and pinned at just the right angle. She stared at her sober reflection for a moment longer as she contemplated what she would say to him. Just thinking about it made her heart give a solid thud against her breast. What *would* she say to him, she wondered? And suddenly, none of this seemed like a good idea at all. She almost removed her hat and changed her mind, but she couldn't quite bring herself to give up so easily. Seeing him again was too important. So she took a deep breath and gathered up her courage then made her way sedately downstairs to collect her basket. She simply had to go through with it.

When she arrived at his house, she raised her hand to knock but pulled it back at the last moment. Then making a small face and biting her lip, she quickly reached out and rapped on the door. Inside she heard some scuffling, then silence, and she wondered if he might try to answer the door. Just as she started to knock again, she heard him call, "Come in."

Pushing the door wide enough to allow her basket through, she peeked around the corner and said, "Hello, it's just me. Carrie." She blushed, feeling foolish for using her first name as though they were longtime friends when in fact they hardly knew each other.

"Oh, hello," he said, sounding surprised to see her and smiling as though she had just brightened his day. And that gave her heart courage to go on with the visit.

"I'm so sorry about your fall," she said, immediately sitting on the settee across from him so that he would not feel strange that she stood while he sat. "Does it hurt much?"

"Not as long as I don't breathe," he said, but his twinkling smile told her he was exaggerating.

It wasn't proper to stare at his bare foot, but it was so

229

plainly propped up between them that she could hardly not stare.

"It's almost purple," she told him. "That has to hurt."

"Now that you mention it, yes, it does. But at least nothing is broken. It's always good to look on the bright side of things." And he gave her a teasing smile.

"I suppose so." But she didn't see anything bright in this situation at all.

"I keep cool wet cloths on it and that helps a little."

Carrie saw that the basin was nearly empty and got up to fill it. "This will only take a minute," she said and headed for the back of the house before she realized she didn't know where the pump was, and stopped.

"It's in the kitchen. You can't miss it."

With a nod she followed his advice and pumped the basin half full. While she was there she took the opportunity to glance around, since a person could tell a lot about another just by looking at their kitchen. A table with one chair sat against the wall opposite the sink and that told her that he always ate alone. The end wall held a rack of pegs which had two hats on it. One was obviously his good hat and the other had to be his working hat. Near the door was a small cookstove, one of the smallest she'd ever seen, and the only thing on it was a coffeepot. She held her hand out to see if perhaps there was any heat radiating from it, and she was certain there was, which meant the coffee might still be hot. Pleased with everything she'd learned about him, she returned with the basin.

"Would you like some help with the cloths?" she asked, not sure if she really ought to, but knowing it was silly not to make him more comfortable.

"I can reach it fine," he replied, and she sighed with relief.

A moment of awkward silence hung between them until she remembered the basket she'd brought.

"I've brought you some chicken soup. It's quite hearty and will help you to mend faster." She held up the jar for him to see. "Have you eaten your noon meal yet?"

"Yes and no."

"Yes and no?"

"Well, you see, one of the ladies of the church brought me a dish, but she was so embarrassed by the sight of my bare foot that she quickly set it on the stove and hurried out again. And since I'd lit the stove for making coffee the food burned. I didn't realize that she'd put it there until I smelled it. So I hobbled as fast as I could and salvaged some of it." He shrugged and grinned. "Yes and no."

She couldn't help laughing at the expression on his face. He looked both sorry and guilty.

"You have an infectious laugh," he said, smiling. "And lovely, too."

That same familiar heat rose up her collar until she wanted to fan herself, and it was only with great restraint that she didn't. It was his voice, she decided, that did it to her.

"Why don't I warm this up and bring you a bowl?" she said, rising once more. "I'll find a pan without help. Just sit right there." Then she escaped to the kitchen where she ducked out of sight so she could fan the heat from her face and neck. Whatever was the matter with her? she wondered. Never had a man had this effect on her before, but then she'd never truly cared for a man like this either.

"Did you find everything all right?" he called to her.

She quickly opened a cupboard door and searched noisily for the right size pan. "Yes, I found what I need." Then she added a chunk of firewood to the stove, poured the soup into the pan and gave the coffee pot a shake to see how much was in it. While everything was heating, she searched for a bowl, then decided on two bowls so that he wouldn't feel uncomfortable eating alone while she watched. She also found a tray, and when the soup was hot she filled the bowls plus two cups of coffee and carried the tray to the little parlor and set it on the table between them.

"That smells delicious," he said, accepting the bowl and spoon.

Then she realized what she'd forgotten. "Bread. It's at home in the bread box."

"I believe Hattie brought some last night. If you don't mind looking around for it."

She returned to the kitchen and searched every cupboard and even the drawers before finding it so obviously placed on the table under a napkin. With her hand to her forehead and her eyes closed, she questioned her sanity and wondered if she would be able to make it through the meal without looking as foolish as she felt. Then she gripped the table with both hands, trying to gain composure, reminding herself that she'd served dinner to men before and flirting had always been second nature to her. *But not with Ted,* cried a small voice inside. All her experience had suddenly taken flight, and all because of a little old kiss beneath a wet willow tree. Then suddenly she needed to fan herself again.

When she felt composed, she sliced the bread, instantly deciding against hunting for the butter, then carried the pieces back to the parlor where she set them on the tray. Then once again she was faced with silence except for the occasional clinking of a spoon against a bowl, and for the life of her she couldn't think of a single thing to say, so she suffered through it.

Ted set the bowl down and watched her sip from the spoon until she looked up and caught him staring. With her blues eyes wide, she returned his gaze as she lowered her spoon.

"I'm glad you came today," he said.

She touched the corner of her mouth with her finger, absently wiping away a bit of broth. "I'm glad, too," she said.

"The soup is as good as it smells. Even better."

"Thank you." She put her bowl on the tray. "I should have realized that you would have plenty of cooks to help you out."

"Nothing so far has compared to this." Then he smiled at her. "But don't tell anyone or I might not get any supper."

"Thank you," she said again, and wondered what had happened to all her witty sayings.

A gentle silence fell again, but even so Carrie struggled under the weight of it.

"Would you like more?" she asked.

"I don't think I'd better. Sitting all day doesn't do much to encourage an active appetite, I'm afraid."

"Then I'll just take these to the kitchen and clean up." She carried the tray to the table, located the dishpan and filled it with water from the reservoir on the stove. In no time she had everything back where it belonged just as though she'd never been there.

Standing beside her chair in the parlor, she bent down and picked up her basket, which still held the other jar of soup. "Well, I guess I should be going. I know you need your rest."

"Did I say thank you for coming?"

For the first time since she'd arrived, she gave him a genuine smile that felt easy and full of friendship. "No need. It was my pleasure."

"I hope you'll come back again," he said, and her heart

skipped a beat. That was what she'd been hoping to hear.

"Of course. Do you like blackberry pie?"

His face lit up. "How did you know it's my favorite?"

"I'll bring some with me the next time." She edged toward the door. "Well, take care of that ankle."

"Oh, I will." And he shrugged like he had no other choice.

"Well, good-bye," she said, backing away until she could reach out and touch the doorknob.

"Good-bye, and thank you again."

Then she was out on the porch with the door closed behind her, thinking she'd never spent a more stressful, more intense hour in her life. In spite of that, she felt light and almost giddy, which made the long walk home very enjoyable indeed. By the time she reached her yard she'd planned an entire week of meals and desserts. And she hoped before long she would be less tongue-tied; there were so many things she wanted to discuss with him. But mostly she wanted to get to know him better, and she wanted him to know her better, too, because she was curious if the second kiss would be as good as the first. Then she stepped into the shade of the porch and fanned herself.

Ted leaned his head back against the chair and closed his eyes. He had no intention of sleeping, but hoped to recall every moment of her visit. She had seemed like an angel to him with her halo of blond hair and her dress of sky blue. When she walked past his chair she set adrift a scent of sweet flowers that he thought he could still smell, and he was sure his ankle had stopped hurting during the time she was there.

He wished he'd been better company and could have thought of charming things to say the way other men in her life undoubtedly had. But he was just a simple man, and most likely she wasn't interested in him anyway. More important, he had no right even to think of courting her, not when he'd already asked for Lydia's hand in marriage. It was a dilemma he could not solve because he would not take back a proposal. If nothing else, he was at least honorable. But then he remembered the way he'd kissed Carrie and had to retract that thought. And since he was trying to be honest with himself, he admitted there was no comparison between the feelings he'd felt when he'd kissed Lydia and later, Carrie. Lydia had been soft and gentle and sweet, whereas, Carrie had raised the hair on the back of his legs with her electrically charged kiss. He'd never been so thoroughly rejuvenated by the touch of a woman, nor had he ever felt so protective of a woman. Unlike Lydia, who was quite capable of taking care of herself and anyone else who needed taking care of. She was spirited and independent and determined, and he admired her. But he realized now that he didn't love her. Carrie was the one he loved; he knew it as soon as he looked deep into her blue eyes and found himself drowning there, but as much as he wanted to, he couldn't tell her. He had to be an honorable man, and he'd already asked for the hand of another.

Chapter Seventeen

Lydia heard the many locusts in the trees around her, uniting into a single *churring* sound as they started low, then climbed to a crescendo, then slowly climbed down again before stopping abruptly, only to repeat the process all over again. Everyone accepted the fact that locusts were the early harbingers of cooler weather. Some even said that a frost could be counted on within just six weeks after they had first been heard. Normally she enjoyed listening to their unusual communication, but today it only heightened her concern that fall would soon be approaching and she hadn't completed the renovation of her house.

And that wasn't her only worry. She still needed money, even though there had been another benefit given, this time by the Presbyterian church, and later the Peaceful Valley Garden Club had held a raffle. Every penny given to her had gone into the house, but she was still short of funds to finish it. Without thinking twice, she'd moved her few belongings into two of the rooms that were now completed in order to save a few more dollars. Opal and Sarah had tried talking her out of it, insisting she did not need to pay for room and board, but she wouldn't hear of it. She'd taken enough charity and couldn't be coerced into taking more when it wasn't necessary. Nearly offended, Opal puffed up with indignation and had two young men deliver all the bedroom furniture from Lydia's room to the old Mercer house. She said to consider it a loan and to return it later when she no longer needed it. Finally, Lydia agreed and kissed the older woman's cheek, then thanked her from the bottom of her heart.

Sitting at her desk she listened while the locusts beyond her window predicted only six more weeks of summer, and that meant her time was running out. With the arrival of August just two days ago and the council's fast-approaching deadline, she could not hold back the anxiety that was building in her breast.

Whenever she felt the panic rising she would count her blessings, which could be summed up in the amount of work they had accomplished. Sometimes it calmed her to mentally check off each project on her list, so she started with the interior, where the most work had been done.

The kitchen, her favorite room of all, was plastered but hadn't yet been papered, not that she minded. And the windows were glazed, washed and curtained with bright yellow gingham, making the room cheery throughout the day, not just in the mornings. She had worked especially hard on the floor, scrubbing and saturating it with linseed oil to protect as well as to bring out the natural glow of the wood. Even though her back had ached all that night, she'd been well satisfied with the end result and sometimes enjoyed going without her slippers in the mornings just to feel the clean floor beneath her bare feet.

With a little coaxing, Nathan had moved the stove and hooked it up properly to the chimney so that she could use it without fear of fire. Each evening that he came to work on the house she cooked him a simple meal and fresh coffee, too. He had built a small table for her and brought two chairs from his own home that he said he had no use for, and she'd put all three near one of the windows so she could enjoy a view of the meadow.

Usually there was no need to go on with her list when she thought about the kitchen and how nice it looked, but today that calming feeling didn't come as easily, so she went on.

They had repaired the stairway immediately after Ted's fall, but she hadn't painted it, because Nathan suggested she wait until the upstairs was finished. Otherwise, they would likely put dents and gouges in the paint and it would just have to be done all over again. And she knew she couldn't afford to do that, so she accepted his advice. Upstairs, only two of the rooms were finished except for the wallpapering and she chose one for her room. Right from the beginning she had taken a liking to it because the view faced across the meadow. That was where Opal's bedroom furniture now stood; a bed that could sleep two—just enough room for a child or two who might be frightened and need comforting during a storm, a wardrobe for her clothes, a desk and chair, and even a bedside table with a lamp.

They really had come a long way, she thought, consoling herself. The house was waterproof now that the windows had all been repaired, even though from the outside it still looked like a run-down old house, contrasting sharply with the startling white of the front porch. She hoped the council would be understanding and not hold the unpainted exterior against her. She knew it would be impossible to get it painted before next summer, even if she was lucky. Simply put, the council was expecting too much and she was willing to fight for an extension on the deadline for that alone. If only that was all there was left to do.

She tried to set aside her worries as she prepared to write another letter to her mother. Between keeping busy with the house and trying to deal with her feelings about Nathan, she had neglected to write as often as she should have. Although, truthfully, she found it hard to talk around the issues that were so important in her life and yet she couldn't bring herself to tell everyone at home what she'd done. If things had worked out smoothly she might have been able to share every last detail, but nothing had gone the way she'd planned, nothing was certain about making this old house into a home for children. She knew her mother would worry and she didn't want to bring that down on her, so her letters remained short and evasive. How long she would get away with avoiding telling the truth she didn't know, but she was determined to keep it from her family as long as she could.

Dear Mother and Ross,

The weather has been perfectly lovely, not a cloud in the sky for days. It reminds me of the times we took a picnic and walked along the river past the rapids. What wonderful days those were! Sometimes I wish I were a child again and we could all be together as we were then. I often think of how different my life would have been, how much we would have missed, if Jonathan and I had not found your doorstep. And it also makes me wonder if there are children out there somewhere who might feel the same about me someday.

It was as close as she could come to telling them what she was working toward without really revealing everything. She had to be satisfied with that for now, but someday she would explain it all. Throughout the rest of the letter she made vague references to what she'd been doing and mentioned some of the friends she'd made, without mentioning Nathan or Ted. She was sure if she did, a red flag would immediately go up and she would be receiving notice of an imminent visit. She had to avoid that at all costs, which meant not telling the whole truth.

When she finished the letter and sealed it, she decided to take it to the post office that morning since she'd put off writing it for far too long as it was. Then she went down to the kitchen and on her way out the back door picked up a napkinful of cookies to take to Ted. Before stepping down she checked to see if the usual delivery had been made, and it had. Occasionally, she found a basket-size pile of garden vegetables on her back steps, which she'd first believed had come from Opal, but her adamant refusal had convinced Lydia that someone else had secretly left them. She would have guessed Ted but he still wasn't able to go far from his house, although he was getting quite good at hobbling with a cane. So she couldn't be sure who might have brought them. Nevertheless, she was grateful for their generosity. And this morning she found a fresh new batch waiting for her. After scooping them up, she carried them inside to be cleaned and cooked later.

The morning walk was pleasant but she couldn't dawdle with all the work that still had to be done, so she hurried to post her letter, then made her way toward the end of town to Ted's little house. Her frequent visits were to salve her conscience, knowing she ought to give him an answer, but until he improved and was back on his feet she simply couldn't do it.

She knocked and listened for his shuffling gait on the other side of the door. When he opened it, he gave her a warm smile that lately seemed tinged with sadness, which only broke her heart more.

"Come in, Lydia. How nice of you to come by." He shuffled sideways to let her enter, and her conscience felt another dagger of guilt. Then he noticed the napkin she held in her hands. "And what have you brought me?" He shook his head and smiled broader. "You really don't need to do that. Not that I don't appreciate your offer, but if the ladies in town aren't careful I'll be needing a larger suit. Very soon."

He could always make her smile, and that was something she missed. They'd had fun working together with one or the other pulling small pranks, or teasing about silly things, but now those silly things weren't as fun. His proposal had changed so much between them and her imminent rejection only made everything more difficult.

"Well, I could bring you a head of cabbage instead of cookies," she replied. "Or maybe some fine carrots or even a pound or two of potatoes, if you'd like."

He laughed as he accepted the cookies. "And when did you find time to plant a garden?"

"I didn't." When he gave her a puzzled look, she went on. "Somebody is sharing their bounty with me, but I don't know who."

He hobbled to a chair and indicated the opposite one for her. "So, some mysterious person wants to give you vegetables anonymously. Hmm." He looked thoughtful for a moment. "I don't think Hattie would be secretive if she were the one, but I don't know of anyone else."

"I hadn't even considered Hattie. The next time I see her I'll just say thank you and see what she says. That should be a simple solution to this mystery, wouldn't you say?"

He nodded. "That would be simple."

They sat for a while trying to think of something to say to each other, when Ted finally broke the silence.

"Would you care for anything? Some pie?" He grinned. "Or cake? Or cookies? I've got plenty."

She laughed and was glad to release the tension that had begun to build inside of her.

"No, thank you." Once more she wished they could return to their easygoing friendship. Then she would have responded differently and even offered to make some coffee to go with the dessert.

"How is the house coming along?" he asked, just as he did every time she stopped by.

So she proceeded to tell of the improvements that had been made since her last visit with him. Then she knew it was time to go and he said he understood.

When she stepped out onto the porch, she turned to him and suddenly had the greatest desire to give him her answer in hopes of ending her misery and perhaps beginning a new kind of friendship. But he looked so pathetic with his one stockinged foot and his cane that she just couldn't do it.

The walk home was her opportunity to mull over her situation a little longer and to torture herself a little more.

Later that afternoon, she prepared a soup using many of the vegetables and adding dried beef for flavor. Potatoes had become the staple of every meal since her secret supplier always left plenty of them, so she doubled the usual amount in hopes that Nathan would stay for supper. Her meals were always simple and she served them using the few dishes that Opal had sent over with Sarah shortly after her move into the house. A few pans, a coffeepot, a couple of bowls, dishes and silverware were all she had, but it was all she needed for now.

Whenever Nathan accepted her invitation to stay, he always talked about what they should do next. She was somewhat puzzled by the fact that since he'd taken on the project of her house it was as though he had never said no in the beginning. Several times she'd had to stop and wonder at this, but it had all happened so gradually that they had just slipped into opposite roles. At first, she had explained her ideas to him and he listened, then offered suggestions, but as time passed he had started making the decisions about the best way to get each job done. And now, she was asking him what he was going to do next so that she knew what her part of the work would be. Somewhere along the line the tables had turned completely. Not that she minded, but his reasoning for doing so bothered her.

Her sole purpose in finishing the house was to have a home for orphaned and unwanted children, but his seemed to be simply that he enjoyed the work. When she talked about orphaned children he retreated behind an invisible barrier that she could not even get close to, let alone scale. Somehow he had blocked from his mind the reason for the house in the first place.

Outside of that, she had found him to be less silent and more prone to smiling, especially since that moment they'd kissed. And when he wasn't looking, she would steal a glance at him, studying the strength of his jaw now softened by thoughtful consideration instead of the hard determination she'd first seen. The change in their relationship had gone from hired man and desperate woman to simply a man and a woman, and that was when she realized she was falling in love for the first time in her life. He hadn't expressed to her that he had feelings as deep as that, but she felt the undercurrent just the same.

While the soup simmered, she hurried out to the meadow to pick a handful of wildflowers to put on the table. A strong breeze out of the southwest whipped her skirt and pulled at her hairpins, but she didn't mind at all. No sound could reach her and she enjoyed the solitude as she chose myriad colors for her bouquet. When she straightened she saw the storm clouds forming and even smelled the scent of rain on the wind, so she turned back and headed home. As she reached the edge of the yard Nathan rounded the corner and met her there.

"I've been picking flowers," she said, holding them up. It was a simple, needless thing to say but he smiled in appreciation. "I heard the locusts today so I decided to make the most of the meadow flowers while they're still here."

"Hmm. Locusts. Then I guess I ought to be storing up some wood for you."

"Well, I'm going to need a lot," she teased. "Because I'm planning on having one of those furnace things to heat the house."

"And I suppose you're going to have a hole dug under the parlor to put it in."

"I hadn't thought of that," she replied, her eyes rounding with interest. "But I like that idea."

"I'm sorry I mentioned it."

"I'm not." But they both knew she was teasing because she had no money to buy such a modern amenity.

As she headed for the kitchen, she said, "Come on in, I have some soup simmering. You haven't eaten, have you?"

He followed her inside, leaving the door open for the heat to escape, then said, "I was hoping you'd ask me. I could smell it clear out to the front gate."

"The vegetables are fresh," she said, giving him a pointed look.

"The mysterious gardener again?"

She nodded, stirring the pot. "Ted said it could be Hattie. And I suppose it could."

"You saw Ted today? So did I. He seems to be improving. I'd say it won't be long before he's back on both feet again."

They had slipped into a familiarity that most married people shared. At least it was similar to the way her mother and Ross talked about the normal, everyday happenings. And she liked that comfortable feeling.

"I carried in some wood for him, but I think he only needs it to make coffee." He grinned and shook his head. "He seems well stocked with food from the neighboring kitchens. And I'd say Mrs. Marting brings more than anyone else."

Lydia had never broached the subject of Carrie, but it had been on her mind since everyone knew how determined she was to land Nathan as a husband. Perhaps now was as good an opportunity as any to bring it up.

"Carrie Marting?" she said, hoping she didn't sound too interested. "I didn't know she'd been keeping company with Ted." She turned to see the reaction on his face.

He shrugged. "I don't know as I would call it keeping company, and I'm only guessing, but I'd recognize those dishes of sauced chicken and gravies anywhere."

She started to set a bowl filled with soup in front of him but stopped in the middle of her movements. "You would?"

"I've eaten them enough to know they're her recipes."

Lydia stared at the plain vegetable soup that didn't even have real beef in it and almost took it back to the pot on the stove. She wasn't a very good cook. As a matter of fact, she barely got by with the essentials of making bread, soup and biscuits. Fancy sauces and gravies would never be found on her stove.

He reached out his hand and took her gently by the wrist. "I don't like sauced chicken. I like vegetable soup." Then he lowered her hand with the bowl in it until the soup sat on the table in front of him.

Without thinking first, she leaned down and kissed the top of his dark head then hurried back to the stove to fill her own bowl. She had her answer, and it made her feel like singing. Carrie was not a contender for the attentions of Nathan, at least not in the cooking department.

When she sat across from him with the steam rising from their bowls between them, she wondered how it would be to sit like this every day for every meal, and the thought made her smile. She would not have a problem sharing her life with a man who was as honest and hardworking as Nathan Stockwell.

"I thought I'd work on the parlor tonight," he said.

She'd been looking forward to having that room finished since it would be the center of activity for the children in her home. They would play games there and share stories with one another and even practice their math drills or possibly learn to play a piano someday when she could afford one. Of course, she had to be realistic, but she still had her dreams. Until then, she would get by with minimum furniture, painted wooden floors without rugs and simple cotton curtains for privacy.

"You're going to need a heating stove for the parlor," he said.

"How could I have forgotten that?" But she had.

"You've been thinking too much about a furnace," he said, looking up and smiling at her.

She smiled back and, under the cover of the table, had to secretly smooth the goose bumps that suddenly raised on her arms. It wasn't the first time he'd set off such a reaction in her. Sometimes just being close was enough to do it, like the times they studied a problem with a window frame or a sticking door. She had come to regard the scent of wood shavings the way some women did bay rum shave lotion; it practically made her senses reel.

"I think I know where you can get a used parlor stove." He scraped the last of the soup from his bowl and she got up to fill it again.

"Where?"

"The mayor wants to put in one of those new furnaces." His eyes twinkled when she suddenly turned to stare at him.

"You're carrying this teasing just a little too far."

"No. I'm serious." But he was still smiling so she didn't know whether to believe him or not. She set his bowl down and returned to her chair.

"I'm afraid I can't afford to buy even a used stove."

"You probably could this one."

She looked up at him. "Why?"

"It's free."

Her heart skipped a beat. "What do you mean? The mayor would give me a stove . . . just give it? I don't believe it. He hasn't shown one ounce of support, so why would he be so generous now?"

"I didn't ask him that. Would you like me to?" He was teasing her again.

"Well, no, I wouldn't want you to tell him what I just said," she replied. "Why do you think I could get it for free?" she asked.

He shrugged. "Maybe it's his way of rebelling."

"Against his wife?" She could well imagine there would be some satisfaction in that, if all the stories she'd heard from Sarah were true.

"Could be."

She pushed aside her empty bowl and thought about the possibility of a free stove. A free anything would be welcome, but a stove to heat her parlor would be wonderful since she simply didn't have a way of getting money.

"Should I speak to him?" she asked.

He pushed aside his bowl. "I'll take care of it."

Relieved to have his help on this, she said, "Thank you." Then she got quiet and stared at him. "I don't think I've really told you how much I appreciate all that you've done. I truly could not have managed this on my own."

"I enjoy the work," he said quietly. "And it's a very nice old house. I'm glad it isn't going to be torn down."

"Well, it isn't over yet," she said, feeling that familiar panic rising again. "The mayor may be willing to give me a parlor stove but that's a long way from having the council change its mind on the deadline." Then she asked, even though she was afraid of the answer, "Do you think we can really meet that deadline?" She valued his opinion, more now than a few months ago, and her heart stepped up a beat as she leaned forward waiting for him to respond.

He stared at the empty bowl and didn't say anything for a while, and she knew he was going to tell her it was impossible. She didn't want to hear it. She didn't want to believe it. "No, wait, don't answer that," she said. "I have to believe we can do this or I might as well give up right now."

"I wouldn't say it's impossible—"

"Good. That's all I need to know." And she meant it. As long as he thought it wasn't impossible then she would cling to that and work harder than she had been. She rose from the table, picked up the dishes and took them to the empty dishpan to be washed later, when Nathan had gone home for the night.

"So," she said, wiping her hands on her apron. "What do you say we get busy? Tell me what you'd like me to do next." She headed for the parlor and he followed her.

They stood side by side in the middle of the room and surveyed the bare-bones walls with slats showing, the repaired windows with new sashes on some of them and the exposed bricks on the chimney. It was pretty obvious what the next job was going to be.

"Plaster," he said with resignation. He'd made it plain when they'd worked on the kitchen that plastering was his least favorite job.

"I wish I knew how to do it," she said, but if there was one thing she'd learned since beginning work on the house, it was knowing her limits. And the way things were turning out she had more limitations than she'd ever expected, which wasn't easy to admit.

"If you'll pump the water, I'll do the rest," he told her.

"You're making it too easy for me," she said, smiling. "I expect to do my fair share."

He smiled back. "I think we had this same conversation once before."

"We did. And if I remember right, I won."

For the next couple of hours they pumped water, mixed plaster, scooped it and troweled it until Lydia's back ached and even Nathan had to slow down. The ceiling was always the worst and the parlor room was one of the largest in the house.

Lydia stoked the fire and brewed a pot of coffee while he finished up the last batch. Then they took their cups to the back steps to rest and enjoy the fresh air. The storm that she'd seen earlier had swung past, keeping to the south of them, but another one had formed and a strong wind whipped across the meadow toward them.

"Rain for sure by morning," he said, and he raised his voice to be heard before the wind snatched it away.

She nodded. "I hope the storm won't be too bad." She'd never really been frightened, but then she'd never really been alone during one.

He turned to look at her as they shared the same step

with elbows touching and shoulders bumping. Occasionally a strand of her hair came unpinned and floated over to tickle his ear so that she brushed it back into place, only to have several others come loose.

"Are you going to be afraid?" he asked.

She felt his concern for her go straight to her heart where it warmed her like no sunny day could. With both hands she skimmed her hair away from her face and held it while she returned his thoughtful scrutiny until their gazes locked, and suddenly she felt unable to move. As if suspended in time, there was only wind and meadow, and there was him and her. Nothing else was needed; nothing else was important.

Then he turned his body and leaned toward her, putting one hand on her cheek to rub a strand of hair from her lips before he bent and kissed her.

Chapter Eighteen

Lydia closed her eyes and waited. This time she knew what to expect and she wasn't disappointed. While the wind tugged at her hair and wrapped the fine length of it around both of them in a protective embrace, she gave up all thought of trying to contain it. The kiss was at first tentative, even restrained, leaving plenty of room for her to place her hand on his chest as they tested unfamiliar ground, searching for a boundary. But the pounding of his heart beneath her hand told her that his emotions could not be bridled for long and her own heart echoed his. With the sensation of the rough pad of his thumb moving gently over the sensitive skin of her cheek, she began to weaken and move closer. Then his other hand came up to cradle the back of her of head, and he moved closer to her. The gesture was so intimate, so full of care that she forgot the notion of boundaries and other foolish things as she circled his neck with her arms. A small groan vibrated from him to her, but it might have been the thunder from the imminent storm, although she couldn't be sure, nor did she care. Her only thought now was the need to return the pressure of his lips, to respond to his silent supplication and to throw all caution to the turbulent wind that whipped and tugged at her skirts. All around them the sky had grown darker with the coming of evening, and the low-hanging clouds scudded in from the west, dimming the natural twilight even more.

His firm but gentle kiss now became urgent and seeking, and his hand no longer rested on her cheek but had moved to her breast, taking the breath from her body like nothing else could. Then cradling her carefully, he laid her back against the steps while protecting her from the blunt edges with his arm. At that moment she would have lain in a field of briars with him and never noticed. Then her sensibilities heightened when his lips left hers to draw a heated line along her jaw to her ear and down her neck to the high collar of her plain dress. These new sensations riveted her so that she could do little more than revel in them. They overtook her body, creating hot little butterflies in places she did not know could feel that way. The tips of her breasts tingled and ached for the pressure of his hands while the deepest part of her yearned for a release that she had not known existed until now.

"Lydia." Then he covered her mouth with his once more, teaching and coaxing until she opened to him, letting him taste her and she in turn tasting him. That intimate discovery opened a floodgate of passion so that the storm overhead went unnoticed until the rain fell in singular, great drops in warning of what was about to happen.

He rose up slightly and stared into her eyes, silently asking if they dared go further. And she knew that the need growing within her would not go away as quickly as the storm around them, and she nodded. He acknowledged her agreement with a searing kiss that nearly melted her bones, and then he scooped her up behind the knees, lifting her into his arms and carrying her inside just as the rain began to beat against the house. He kicked the door closed behind him and she laid her head against his chest, listening to the thundering of his heart.

Upstairs in her room, Nathan placed her on the bed, kicked off his boots and lay down beside her. With his head propped up on his elbow, he searched her deep brown eyes for an answer.

"Are you sure?" he asked softly, running his hand along her cheek, down her neck, her shoulder and along the length of her arm which lay close to her side. She looked unsure to him, and defenseless. Her usually strong determination seemed to desert her now, and he did not in any way want to rush her. He wanted to reassure her, to say she had become so dear to him, but the words wouldn't come although they were true. So he stroked her hand and kissed her gently, then waited for her reply.

"I want you to know that I love you, or I would not be able to do this." Her voice was soft, and the pounding rain against the window nearly drowned out her words, but he heard them. His eyes slid closed and he choked back the emotion that suddenly rolled over him.

He needed to tell her, but how could he explain? In his heart he ached to love her, to have no secrets between them, but he was afraid she would not understand.

Reaching up, she placed the palm of her hand on his cheek. "It's all right. I want this. I want you." Then she slipped her hand behind his head and pulled him down to her lips, and the sweetness of her giving broke the last remaining layer of the stony, hard shell he'd used as a shield for so long.

And he whispered in her ear the words that he thought he never would say again as he pulled her into his arms. "I love you." Then he rolled, keeping her beneath him, imprinting her body with his own. "I love you," he said again, feeling a rare sense of freedom. Releasing her slightly, he kissed her forehead, then her cheek and she smiled with her eyes closed.

"You're getting closer," she said drowsily. And the sound of her deeply soft voice aroused him so that he had to shift his body for comfort.

So he kissed her chin and traced her jaw with his tongue before asking, "Am I close enough?"

"Nope."

"How about here?" And he kissed her lips briefly with a series of tiny touches and nibbles until an urgency built within both of them.

She moved beneath him, striving to get closer and struggling to undo the many buttons on the front of her dress. In his effort to help her, a few were torn loose and rolled away unheeded. When she finally peeled the dress from her body, exposing her heated skin to the cool damp air, she sighed out loud, but it sounded more like a groan to her ears. Without help, he untied the strings on the bodice of her chemise, then pulled it back to finish undressing her, but he paused first to stare and to touch. She bit her lip and gripped the coverlet beneath her, but her eyes were open, studying his face. He didn't say anything and didn't move for a while; then he stripped the thin garment from her.

"My shoes," she whispered, because that was all the breath she had left.

He rose from the bed to sit at her feet, then unbuttoned them with a patience that nearly drove her wild. First one then finally the other dropped to the floor with a thud. Then, as he shed his own clothing down to his bare skin, she kept her gaze on his face and he returned her stare as he climbed onto the bed alongside her. To her surprise, his skin was much cooler than hers, and she welcomed the temporary relief as he pulled her closer than she'd ever been to a man.

"Are you all right?" he asked, when she closed her eyes. She nodded and smiled. "I've never been better."

With their arms in a tight embrace, their lips met as her breasts touched his chest and her stomach came up against his. Lydia held her breath waiting to see what he would do next and was pleasantly surprised by the most tender of kisses yet. She let out her breath and relaxed against him, knowing she could trust him to be gentle with her. And he was.

He stirred her emotions with heady little kisses, caressing her body in places that no one else had ever touched, and she responded by reaching a feverish pitch that even those touches could not assuage. She clutched at him, arched against him and rolled with him until he finally pulled her beneath him, their damp bodies clinging. He urged her to prepare for him by nudging his knee against hers, and instinctively she complied, ready to meet his need with her own. For a brief second he hovered over her, separated from her for only a moment. But their desire had climbed beyond endurance and neither could delay for any reason. She had no thought for the pain she might feel, because to stop would have been pure agony. So raised up eagerly to appease the fire within and he met her there, and for one blissful second she felt relief. But there was more and she knew it and strove hard to reach it—not just one pinnacle to climb but many small ones, each taking her higher than the last until finally . . . finally, she achieved the ultimate, most satisfying, gratifying moment of her life, and she clung to him as though she could never let go.

Nathan rested his head in the crook of her neck and

shoulder. His forearms kept his weight from bearing down on her, but he could hardly hold himself up as his arms shook slightly in the aftermath of their lovemaking. He couldn't speak; he didn't have the words to express how he felt, so he kissed her beneath her earlobe and was rewarded with a languorous moan as the toes on her right foot lifted to tickle the bottom of his left. He jumped and she grinned.

She heard a clap of thunder and hazily wondered if it had come from nearby. Then a streak of lightning suddenly brightened the room and she remembered the storm that had sent them indoors. He rolled to his back and she nestled against him, curling her body to fit his. Overhead above the attic, the rain pelted the roof as they lay in the darkened room enjoying the sound. Lydia didn't want to talk and dispel the way he made her feel cherished. They could talk later. So she traced her finger along his chest, circled his navel and back up his chest, then repeated the trail again, content just to have him there beside her, but knowing he would have to leave soon.

Nathan heard the beating rain on the tin roof and allowed it to coax him into staying a little longer. He knew he would have to go soon or he wouldn't want to go home at all. When the rain didn't let up, he relaxed with his hand tangled up in her hair, enjoying the soft scent of it. She was much more vulnerable than she let on and he didn't want to hurt her. There was no need to wallow in the mess he'd made of his life or to dredge up the guilt or think that what had just happened could change who he was. So he said nothing as the rain lulled his senses into forgetting the pain he'd caused in the past. He knew he could never go back and fix it, and he'd accepted a long time ago that sometimes it wasn't possible to go forward. The present was all that he had. It was all anyone had.

Nathan held Lydia close while the storm stayed just beyond the window. He wished it could always be that way.

During the days that followed, Lydia couldn't seem to keep her feet on the ground. She hummed as she worked and laughed at the silliest things until Sarah began giving her strange looks. And everything that had worried her before no longer held a threat to her now. She was in love with the most wonderful, caring man in the world. Somehow, she knew everything was going to work out just fine. There wasn't much that could dim her happiness now, if anything could at all.

Nathan continued to come for supper and work on the house, but they were forced to subdue their feelings with Sarah present every evening. Apparently, she'd overcome her fear and dislike of Nathan. So he made sure he left while it was still daylight, as he didn't want the neighbors to gossip. Lydia didn't tell him that it was probably too late, that most likely Lila Peterson had viewed them on the back steps before the storm that night, but even that couldn't dampen her spirits.

Then one afternoon she answered a knock on the kitchen door, half expecting to find Nathan standing there, but she was wrong. A small elderly woman dressed in a gray traveling suit stared back at her. It took Lydia less than a minute to recognize her grandmother.

"Grandma Winnie!" she exclaimed, her hand over her heart. "Why—what—how—?"

"Stop your sputtering, child, and ask me to come in." Her voice and face were stern, but her eyes twinkled merrily at having surprised Lydia.

Stepping aside, she allowed the starchy little woman she loved so well to enter. As she quickly breezed past, Lydia planted a quick kiss on her cheek. "Why didn't you tell me you were coming?'' But she knew making surprise visits were her grandmother's passion. The true surprise was that she hadn't done it sooner.

Ignoring her granddaughter, she stared open-mouthed at the rustic kitchen with its bare plastered walls, simple cotton curtains and meager furnishings. ''What in heaven's name do you call this?'' Lydia cringed under her inspection, since Opal Grayling's house was nothing compared to her grandmother's

''It's a kitchen, Grandma.'' Lydia's heart beat faster than she cared to admit. Having a confrontation with this member of her family was never a joy.

''Well, it might be *someday*,'' she replied with a sniff. ''But it would hardly pass for one now.'' Turning, she riveted her gaze on Lydia. ''So. Tell me. What are you doing living . . . here?''

''First, why don't you tell me about your trip and catch me up to date on everything at home,'' Lydia said, smiling. It was a diversionary tactic and she hoped it would work long enough to pull some answers together.

''Don't change the subject, dear.''

Lydia sighed. ''All right. But how did you know to find me here?''

''The young girl, Sarah, told me you had moved to this . . . this . . .'' She gestured with distaste at the room and Lydia's heart sank. ''Now don't change the subject again. I asked what you are doing living here.''

There was no point in trying to hide the truth anymore. If anyone could find her out, it would be Grandma Winnie. That was just the way it had always been. Even her smallest white fib hadn't been able to escape that penetrating look. In the end, she'd given in and told the truth, and that's what she did now.

''I bought it.''

The blood drained from her grandmother's already pale face. "You what?"

"I bought it." And she said it a little louder, feeling somewhat braver now that the truth was out.

"I heard you the first time." Then Winnie reached for a chair, checked it quickly for soundness and dropped onto the seat. "What in heaven's name possessed you to do such a thing?"

"I needed it."

"But you have a home." It was plain to see she wasn't at all pleased with Lydia's answers. "And with your teaching job, why, you might have to move on to a new school. You know how the teaching positions are, here one day and there another."

Lydia gritted her teeth, grimaced, and said, "I quit my job."

Winnie rose off her seat. "You what?"

"Just listen to me," Lydia pleaded, knowing that it was futile.

"I knew it. I knew it," Winnie said, nodding her head vigorously. "When you didn't come home for Independence Day, I told Irene, 'There is something wrong.' But she wouldn't listen to me. She simply said I should wait patiently for you to come to us."

Lydia smiled. Her mother was a wise woman; she should have known she couldn't fool Irene Hollister. How like her mother to want to give her the chance to work things out.

"Oh, I knew I should have taken a train right away instead of listening to Irene. You girls will be the death of me yet. Just watch and see." Winnie dropped back onto the chair and stared up at Lydia with a hopeless look on her tired face. "What am I to do with you?"

"Nothing." She leaned down and kissed the soft, wrinkled cheek. "How about some coffee?" The storm had passed and she still had all of her limbs in one piece, so there was little to fear from that point on. Actually, there was little to fear anyway. She only hated to see the disappointment in her grandmother's eyes and to feel her disapproval, but once she had "vented her spleen" as she sometimes said, then everything would be fine.

"You don't have tea?"

"I'm afraid not. But if I'd known you were coming—"

Winnie waved her hand through the air. "You sound like Irene."

"Coffee?" she asked again.

"Yes. I'll take coffee," she replied, resigning herself.

Lydia poured coffee and carried the cups to the small table, where she sat across from her grandmother. Winnie eyed the mismatched cups with disdain and frowned.

"How is everyone at home?" Lydia asked, then sipped her hot coffee. Perhaps now that her grandmother had discovered the truth she'd come searching for, Lydia could get some news about home.

"Ross is working too hard as usual and your mother is fussing over him. As usual. Jonathan came home for a short visit. Then he was off to who-knows-where again."

"And Dr. Stephens?"

Grandma Winnie had been a widow when Lydia and Jonathan had come into the family, but a year later she married Grand Rapids's only doctor. So she'd sold her home in Cincinnati and moved north, never failing to let everyone know that the winters up there were much worse. In spite of that, she'd been very happy since her move.

"He's doing well, but then he never complains, so how can I be sure?" She sighed. "Besides, I came here to talk about you."

Lydia wanted to ask how long she intended to stay, but lost her nerve before the words came out of her mouth.

"Well, I've told you everything there is to tell," she said, knowing it was one those little white fibs, and hoping that once, just once, she could get away with it if only for a little while.

Winnie leaned forward with a stern reproachful look.

Lydia laughed. "All right. I give up."

"That's better," she said, resting back in her chair to study her granddaughter thoughtfully. "You bought this house so you could start a home for children, didn't you?"

Caught completely off-guard, Lydia could only stare at her. How she had missed this dear woman who knew her so well, how she missed all of her family. Why had she thought they would not understand? They knew her past, and they knew her heart. The tears welled as she nodded.

"There, there," Winnie said, putting her arms around Lydia, consoling her the same as when she was a young girl.

In response, Lydia wrapped her arms around the older woman's waist and cried. For so many weeks, for months, she'd withstood the strain of meeting her deadline against the wishes of those who wanted to see her fail, and now it all washed away. She hadn't realized that the pressure had built to such proportions to bring her to tears, but the release felt wonderful.

"Here now. Take this." Winnie offered the ever-present handkerchief tucked in her sleeve. "Take it."

Lydia accepted the lavender-scented hankie and blew her nose. "Thank you," she said, her voiced muffled and wet. "I shouldn't be crying. I'm not at all unhappy. Really I'm not."

Winnie glanced around the pitiful room and replied, "Of course you're not. Who could be unhappy in this?" Then she returned to her chair, the coffee forgotten.

Lydia smiled at her grandmother's dry wit. "You really don't like it, do you?"

"Well," she began, sounding as though she might change her mind, "I suppose it has possibilities."

She blew her nose again. "You should have seen it three months ago."

"It was worse?"

Nodding, she replied, "Much worse."

"You poor dear."

Lydia blinked back a fresh onset of tears. "Don't do that, Grandma. I'm really not unhappy." She sniffed and wiped her eyes.

"I'm almost convinced." She pushed away the chipped cup without a saucer.

"This is exactly what I've dreamed about since I was a girl."

"I know, dear. I remember." Her voice softened.

"It needs some work, I will admit."

"*Some* work?"

"Grandmother, please."

"I'm sorry. Go on."

"But the worst is over. Well, sort of. At least I won't have to climb on the roof and fix it again. That last rain proved we have it well sealed" She blocked out the image of Nathan with her in the bed upstairs during the storm, fearing her grandmother would read her mind and see that, too.

"You climbed on the roof?" Winnie asked in disbelief, and her eyes went round with shock.

"Well, how else were we to fix it?"

"We?"

"Ted. He's the preacher at the Baptist church."

"Heaven help us! You were on the roof with a preacher!" She leaned her elbow on the table and rested her head on her palm. "Lydia, you will be the death of me yet."

"That's finished, Grandma. I won't be going up there anymore. Honest."

Winnie sighed with relief, but mostly it sounded like bare tolerance. "I'm afraid to ask you to tell me more."

"There isn't really anything else to tell." She lifted one hand limply. "This is my home."

"Well, then so be it. Let's take a look at the rest of it."

"Now?"

"Why not now? Are you hiding someone upstairs?"

"Someone?" She had the uncanny feeling that her grandmother had indeed read her mind after all.

"I wasn't serious, Lydia." She rose stiffly from her chair. "Take me on a tour. The walk will do me good."

Lydia tried to hurry through the tour, pointing out all the good points and the possibilities. She talked about the children she hoped to bring into her home, explaining where they would sleep, where they would study and where they would play. Her dreams always came to life for her when she had a willing ear to listen, and in spite of her disapproving words, Grandma Winnie turned out to be a better listener than she'd expected.

By the time they returned to the kitchen, Winnie had removed her hat and her jacket and Lydia hung them on the back of a chair.

"I hardly know what to say, dear," Winnie said, sitting at the table once more. "It's such a huge undertaking for only one girl." Then added, "And a preacher."

Lydia decided against telling her that Ted had gotten hurt and was unable to help. She would only worry more. But she knew she ought to say something about Nathan before he arrived for supper.

"And Nathan Stockwell," she said. "He's the local carpenter and wheelwright, and he's quite talented, too. He's the one who repaired the porch and made the posts. You did notice it, didn't you?''

"Oh, my. I left my valise on the step out front. I considered coming in that way, but it just looked like an empty old house so I set it down and came around back. When I saw the curtains in the window, I decided to knock and take a chance.''

"You stay right there and I'll get your bag.'' As she headed through the doorway into the parlor, she called over her shoulder, "How long will you be staying?'' She stopped, waiting for an answer and holding her breath.

"I haven't decided yet, dear. It all depends.''

Lydia knew that the visit would have to be more than a day or two since it was such a long trip back home, but she wasn't sure how she felt about a two-or three-week visit. After retrieving the valise, she carried it up to her room. The two of them would have to share her bed; it was all she had. And she knew her grandmother would never consent to staying in a hotel when the other option was being able to keep an eye on her granddaughter twenty-four hours a day.

When she arrived back downstairs she found Winnie searching for a pan in the small cabinet.

"I thought I would cook supper for us," she said to Lydia. "But I can't find anything I'll need.''

"That's all I have.''

"Oh.'' Winnie straightened up to look at her. "Well, I guess we'll just have to make do. How about a nice pot of beans with ham and dumplings?''

"Sounds wonderful, but I don't have any ham. I do have some dried beef, though.'' She tried to sound as if that would make a wonderful supper, too.

"Lydia, dear. I can't cook beans with dried beef. I need ham."

"Then why don't we make a vegetable soup? I have lots of vegetables, and the beef would be just fine." She uncovered the basket that held the vegetables that had continued to show up mysteriously at her back door. "We have everything we need right here."

"My goodness. Do you have a garden? Those are lovely." She picked through the basket, pulling out carrots, potatoes, and an onion and handed them to Lydia so she could get the green beans. "I haven't seen carrots this size since I left Cincinnati. Yes, I think soup will be just the thing."

Lydia pumped water and carried the bucket inside while Winnie peeled, chopped and quartered until the pot was filled. Then she made a batch of biscuits and Lydia added more wood to the stove. The hustle and bustle of grandmother and granddaughter working side by side created a new sound in the old kitchen, a sound Lydia enjoyed very much.

"How about a nice cobbler while we're at it?" Winnie suggested. "You wouldn't have any fruit in that basket, would you?"

"No, but I can pick some rhubarb. It's just outside around the corner." And she hurried out to get it as her mouth watered and puckered just thinking about the dessert her grandmother always made.

"Oh, that's a very nice bunch. I declare, I'd forgotten how wonderful things grow down here." She set to work cutting and pulling the long strings from the stalks and chopping them into smaller pieces to cook.

When the room was filled with the aromatic scent of soup, biscuits and cobbler fresh from the oven, Lydia set the table with three styles of dishes and silverware from three different sets. Then she hurried upstairs to bring down the chair from her desk.

"Are we to have company, Lydia, dear?" Winnie asked, pausing as she held a pan of biscuits with a towel.

"Um. Well, yes." She wasn't sure how this would be received, but she couldn't put it off until Nathan arrived and have him go through a series of uncomfortable questions. "You know the carpenter I told you about?"

"Yes. Mr. Stokewell?"

"Stockwell." She smiled, remembering how Nathan had mispronounced her name when she'd first met him. "Well, I usually invite him to stay for supper since he's been so kind to work on the house and all."

"You invite the hired help? I'm not so sure that's a good idea, dear. Do you know him well?"

"Um, yes, pretty well," she said, and had to look away. She adjusted the chairs so they were all evenly spaced from each other. "He's very nice. I'm sure you'll like him."

"I see." And Lydia was afraid she really did. "Well, if you say so." Then she set the pan on the table and stared at the dishes for the first time. "We really must do something about your dishes. Food tastes better on good china."

Lydia leaned over and kissed her grandmother's cheek. She suddenly felt very glad Winnie was there, and she wasn't at all concerned about her meeting Nathan. These were two people she loved, and she knew they were going to like each other right from the start.

When at last she heard Nathan's footsteps coming from the front door and through the parlor, her heart surged with happiness.

"Good evening, Nathan," she said, and Winnie gave her a sharp look at the use of his given name. "I'd like you to meet my Grandmother, Mrs. Stephens, who has just arrived from Defiance."

The two stared at each other in silence, neither offering a word or a hand in greeting while Winnie studied him carefully, measuring everything about him. For a moment Lydia wondered what her grandmother might say when she finished taking stock of him, but was saved the worry when Nathan spoke first. "Hello, Mrs. Stephens. It's nice to meet you."

"And you, too," she replied. "I'm sure." But Lydia didn't think she sounded at all sure.

"Let's have supper," she interrupted before her grandmother could take over the conversation. "Grandma Winnie made her special rhubarb cobbler. I know you're going to love it." She was prattling, but couldn't seem to stop. "The soup is really thick this time. I guess we must have added more vegetables than usual."

Nathan stood awkwardly behind a chair while he waited for the women to sit down, but Lydia couldn't sit.

"Oh, please. Both of you have a seat while I fill the bowls and bring them over." At the stove, she ladled the hot soup into a bowl while she tried to get a grip on herself. After three nervous trips to fill the bowls, she finally sat down with them.

Nobody talked.

Lydia tried to think of something, anything, that might be of interest to all of them. Nothing came to mind. So Winnie filled in the silence with questions.

"Mr. Stockwell, what do you do for a living? Besides work on old houses, that is."

"I'm a wheelwright."

"Oh? That's a very nice trade." She broke her biscuit, looked around the table for the butter, then gave up when she saw there wasn't any. "And how long have you been in business?"

Lydia gave her grandmother a sharp warning glance that

267

said not to embarrass her, but Winnie ignored it.

"Too many years to count, I guess." Then he turned to Lydia and said, "The soup is very good."

"Thank you."

"Too many years? Why, you hardly look old enough to have been in business so long you can't remember." She sipped her soup but didn't take her eyes off Nathan.

He smiled politely and shrugged. "I guess I meant I never took the time to count."

"I see."

"More soup, anyone?" Lydia asked, half-rising from her seat.

"No, dear. We haven't nearly finished what we have. Now sit down and enjoy your meal."

Lydia wished she could but a knot had formed and wouldn't allow anything past it.

"So. Have you always lived in Peaceful Valley, Mr. Stockwell?" Winnie went on.

"Just a few years."

"Grandma Winnie, could we continue this after supper? You aren't giving Nathan a chance to eat and I know he'd enjoy having some of your cobbler before we have to start working on the house."

Winnie looked at her in surprise. "My goodness, Lydia. I'm only trying to get to know your gentleman friend."

Lydia felt her cheeks turn crimson with embarrassment. "I'd rather we finished our meal first."

"Certainly, dear. If that's what you'd rather do." And her tone made it clear that she didn't approve of waiting, or of Nathan either.

They ate the rest of the meal in total silence, while Lydia plotted how she would get even with her grandmother when they were alone later. Then as soon as she served the cobbler, Winnie took it as a signal to continue with her questioning.

"So, you've only been here a few years? Where did you have your business before that?"

Lydia wanted to roll her eyes, to pull her hair, and to shout, but she didn't. She would save that for later, too.

"Cincinnati," he replied.

"What a coincidence," Winnie said. "I used to live in Cincinnati. Whereabouts are you from? We might have been neighbors. One can never tell."

Nathan adjusted his chair and Lydia sensed that his discomfort wasn't due entirely to his seat.

"Coffee, anyone?" Lydia said, purposely interrupting. "It will get too strong if we let it sit on the stove, so I absolutely insist that we have coffee." She chose the chipped cup for her grandmother, just to divert her attention, then poured the other cups, too. "And after coffee, you and I will do the dishes while Nathan works on the house." Enough was enough, and she wanted her grandmother to know it.

"Yes, dear."

Lydia guided the rest of the conversation toward the work on the house while they drank their coffee, but her grandmother kept silent and offered no comments. Remarkably, Nathan seemed only a little ill at ease as Winnie studied him throughout the rest of the meal, never taking her eyes off him even for a minute. Lydia could not understand her grandmother's behavior and intended to question her as thoroughly as she had Nathan. Turnabout was fair play.

Chapter Nineteen

Lydia waited until her grandmother had crawled into bed before climbing onto the foot of it so they could talk. She hadn't forgotten how upset she'd been, and meant to hear an explanation for the way she'd treated Nathan.

"I know what you're going to say," Winnie said, scooting up in bed with her back against the pillows. Her arms were crossed over her chest and she didn't look one bit sorry.

Lydia sighed, glad to dispense with the questions after all.

"I can't explain it," Winnie began, "but there is something about that man that doesn't sit right with me. And does he always just walk into your parlor without knocking?"

"It's not a finished parlor, Grandma."

"Hmpf. Well, I still have bad feelings."

"How can you say that? You don't even know him."

"I was trying to do just that, but you wouldn't let me."

"You were embarrassing him. And me." She sighed again. "And why did you call him my gentleman friend?"

"Oh? Are you saying he isn't?" She might as well have pointed her finger at Lydia because her accusation had the same effect anyway.

"He hasn't said he is my gentleman friend."

"But you want him to be, don't you?"

"Yes. I guess I do."

"Well, I'm not sure he's right for you, Lydia. How well do you know him? What about his family? Have you met them? Does he talk about them? Those are important things in a relationship and you ought be discussing them."

"I'm sure we will. In time. But it isn't as though we are betrothed."

"I should hope not!" Winnie looked horrified. "Your mother hasn't even met him." Lydia knew how dedicated her grandmother was to the proper way of doing things, especially marriage.

"Let's not talk about that just yet." She hadn't allowed herself to plan that far ahead, and she didn't want anyone else planning either.

"I agree. There is much to be learned before that happens." She picked at the lace on her gown. "I don't mean to be difficult, dear. Really I don't. But you are so important to me, and to your mother, that we couldn't bear it if you made a terrible mistake like this."

"Like this? Like Nathan? Why do you say that?"

"I can't explain it. It's just a feeling. Something keeps nagging at my memory, as though I should know him, which I'm sure I don't. Unless, of course, he did come from the same neighborhood I used to live in. Although, I don't think so." She sighed. "My memory just isn't what it used to be, I'm afraid."

271

"I don't think you know him. You just can't let me make my own decisions about this, but I have to, Grandma."

"I suppose you're right. It's very difficult to be a grandmother of such a grown-up young woman." She smiled. "I want to keep you safe from all harm. I only want the best for you."

Lydia returned the smile. "I know. But it isn't easy being the granddaughter either, you know. I have to do things for myself."

"I think we could probably go around in circles for quite some time on this subject." She stifled a yawn. "Perhaps we should just go to bed."

"You're right. I am tired." She kissed her grandmother's cheek. "Good night." Then she turned out the lamp and crawled under the sheet on the other side of the bed.

"But do be careful, dear. And that is all I'm going to say on the subject. Good night." And she turned over with her back to her granddaughter.

Lydia rolled her eyes but managed to keep herself from replying. This was going to be a very long visit, she just knew it.

The next morning, Grandma Winnie was true to her word and never mentioned Nathan's name let alone her opinion of him. They went down to fix breakfast together and discovered yet another batch of vegetables on the steps, which amazed Winnie to no end.

"Is this where your lovely carrots and things come from? And you don't have any idea who brings them?"

"I haven't asked, but I think I know."

"And they arrive every few days?"

"Just about."

"That's so charitable." She seemed genuinely pleased that someone cared enough to help Lydia.

"It wasn't always like that, but things have changed in some ways." And she proceeded to tell her about the resistance she'd met when she first presented her idea. Winnie listened carefully and made no comment when the subject of funds came up, but a deep frown creased her brow. Then as Lydia spoke of Nathan's unwillingness to help at first, Winnie's frown deepened and Lydia wished she hadn't mentioned that part of the story.

"I hardly know what to say about your home, dear. It's such a vast undertaking. Especially for one woman. Are you sure you're up to it?"

She couldn't let any doubts slip in now, and she didn't dare admit them if they did. But, truthfully, with Grandma Winnie's arrival, she'd begun to see everything through different eyes and all their progress seemed so insignificant. So she knew she had to keep up the good front, for herself if not for her grandmother, and concentrate on one thing only, her dream of a children's home.

"Yes, Grandma Winnie, I am definitely up to it."

"Then tell me again about your plans."

So Lydia went over them again and found her enthusiasm was still there. She still believed that she could accomplish what she'd set out to do, because she simply would not give up.

When they had finished with their breakfast and the dishes, Lydia went to work on the house and Winnie put on her jacket to walk into town.

"I'll just be a little while, dear," she said, pinning on her hat. "I only want to get a better look around today than I had yesterday when that nice young man brought me in his wagon. I had no idea you were so far from a train station. That is certainly a handicap, you realize, don't you?"

"I hadn't thought of it that way, actually. It's rather nice not hearing a whistle blow the way they do at home.''

''That's a good point. I hadn't thought of that.'' She patted her hair beneath the hat. ''Well, I'm off.''

After Winnie had gone, Lydia found she couldn't get her mind on her work, so she took a second cup of coffee out to the back step where she could watch the flowers in the meadow and think. She kept remembering Nathan's tender touches and how wonderful he'd made her feel. And afterward she'd felt so close to him, as though they could never be separated again. It seemed he was a part of her and she a part of him. The only dull spot in her shining moment of remembering was when she thought of how unfair she'd been not to give Ted her answer. Suddenly, she knew she couldn't put it off anymore. She could not continue thinking only of her own discomfort in telling him, but had to consider that the quicker she did this the sooner it would be over, for both of them.

With her mind made up, she hurried to change her dress, all the while trying to come up with the right words. She didn't want to lose his friendship, but it was a risk she had to take. There was no choice in the matter and she had been thoughtless to let it go so long. The need to have it done made her feet hurry through town, avoiding the main street so she didn't run into Winnie. The last thing she needed was having to explain where she was going and why.

When she arrived at Ted's door, she was pleasantly surprised to find him on both feet and with no cane to help him get about.

''Well, hello, Lydia. How have you been?'' He opened the door wide in welcome. ''Please, come in.''

''I'd rather hear how you're doing. It's wonderful to see you up and about like this.''

''I've been doing quite well for over a week now.'' Then he dropped his gaze from her face. ''I haven't been out to help like I should have, but, well . . . it's been busy at the church.''

She felt a dagger of sorrow go through her. He hadn't wanted to face her, and she couldn't blame him. She had ignored his request and it was no wonder he'd stayed away.

"Could we sit down and talk?" she asked. Her heart thumped as she led the way to the parlor chairs were she chose one opposite from his. "First, I want to apologize."

He frowned and said, "You're not going to bring up the fall I took, are you? Because—"

"No," she interrupted. "This is something I should have told you before now. It's about not answering your proposal of marriage." Then she rushed on before she could turn coward again. "I value your friendship more than I can say. And I mean that from the bottom of my heart. And I wouldn't want to lose it no matter what, but I'll certainly understand if you withdraw it." She paused for a breath.

"You have my friendship no matter what, dear Lydia. Please, go on."

She almost couldn't. His words made her feel unworthy of such a friendship, especially when she was about to reject his proposal.

"Wait," he said. "It isn't fair to put you through this." He leaned forward and took her hand in his. "You are going to tell me no, aren't you?"

All she could do was nod, and continue holding her breath.

"It's all right. I understand."

"But you've been so good to me. Helping on the house and all."

"I never wanted you to feel obligated to me. I helped because I admire you. And I admire what you're doing. I still do."

"But I feel awful, Ted. You've been so kind and here I

am refusing the only proposal I've ever gotten. And I've taken so long to come to you.'' She was nearly in tears.

He shook his head. ''Don't feel that way. I've got a confession of my own.'' He studied her hand then looked up at her. ''I've fallen in love with someone and it happened after I proposed. If you want to talk about feeling bad, I've never felt worse.''

She could hardly believe what she was hearing. Ted was in love, but not with her, and he'd been feeling just as guilty as she had. Her first reaction was that they could still be friends. She squeezed his hand and smiled.

''I'm so happy for you.'' And the sincerity came though in her voice. ''May I ask who? Or am I being too personal? Does she know?''

''I don't think she does,'' he said and blushed.

''Well, she is a very lucky woman,'' she replied with a smile. ''Does this mean we can still be friends?''

''I hope so. I'd like that very much.''

''So would I.'' And they sat looking at each other, enjoying a new kind of companionship which was very much like the one they'd had in the beginning. ''I'm glad you're not angry with me,'' she said.

''Me, angry? I was afraid you would be angry with me.''

Then they laughed together, each of them relieved to have everything out in the open. Now that they had it all settled and straightened out between them, they shared what had been going on their lives since last they'd met. He told her he was sure he'd gained twenty pounds since most of his clothes didn't fit, and he was thankful the food had stopped arriving in large dishes. She told him about her grandmother and he laughed, saying she sounded like a delightful woman. Then Lydia said she had to be going or that 'delightful woman' would have the law out looking for her with guns and hounds. He made her promise to come back again and he promised to check on the progress of the house soon.

They stood at the door for a moment before she said good-bye. Then she went down the steps, turning once to wave at him, and feeling light enough to float all the way home. A burden had been lifted and a friendship renewed. She just couldn't ask for anything more.

Ted watched her go, feeling a new freedom and a sudden burst of energy that had been missing from his step, which had nothing to do with having been laid up for the past several weeks. He had felt troubled over how to handle his proposal, worrying whether it was really fair to Lydia to continue with a relationship that his heart was not truly committed to, yet he still could not bring himself to retract his offer of marriage. Until she came to him today, he'd had no answers. But all that was changed. Now he felt a lightness in his heart and he could not contain it. He wanted to share it. So, without wasting any time, he quickly shaved, changed his shirt, grabbed his good hat and headed down the street toward Carrie's house.

He knocked on her front door, removed his hat then smoothed the brim while he waited. No speech came to mind, not even a good reason for being there had occurred to him on his way over. He knocked again and waited. Perhaps something would come to him before she answered the door, but nothing did. And then she was standing in the open doorway, looking like an angel from heaven with wisps of her blond hair haloing her head and her sky-blue eyes round with surprise.

"Ted! My goodness." She stared through the screen door at him and then she gave him the friendliest smile he had ever seen.

"I hope I'm not bothering you."

"Not at all." Then remembering her manners, she asked, "Please, won't you come in?"

He glanced around, then said, "I wouldn't want to cause any problems for you. Maybe I should just stay out here."

"I won't hear of it." She pushed the door wide open. "If the neighbors want to gossip, then they'll do it no matter what. Please, do come in."

"Thank you." He suddenly felt clumsy and wondered what he could say now that he was there. Without a doubt, he couldn't tell her about Lydia's visit, nor the sudden freedom he felt with her releasing him from his offer. So he guessed he would just enjoy Carrie's company and not worry about what he would say next, hoping she'd fill in the silent moments.

"I have some fresh squeezed lemonade," she said, leading the way to the parlor. "Would you care for a glass?"

"Yes. Thank you. It's still quite warm outside so that would be nice." He turned his hat round and round by the brim in his nervousness.

"I'll be right back," she said as she left the room, heading toward the back of the house. "Go ahead and sit down."

He glanced over her parlor, noticing the beautiful wooden furniture, expensive rugs, fancy doilies and bouquets of flowers in tall vases as well as short ones. A mantel clock over the fireplace delicately chimed the hour of eleven o'clock while beside it a matching pair of figurines flanked it. A new realization came over him and he nearly decided to just accept the lemonade, drink it and leave. She was used to having so much more than he could offer her. Why would she want to give up her comfortable life to live as a preacher's wife in less than fashionable surroundings? But he couldn't bring himself to go, not until he'd told her about his deep feelings for her. If she said no, then he would leave and he would simply have to get over it. He hoped.

Looking down the length of the house, he could see her moving about in the narrow kitchen beyond the dining room. He heard the clink of glasses, the close of cupboard doors, and then she was walking toward him carrying two lemonades.

"Thank you," he said, standing when she entered the parlor.

She chose the chair nearest him, and he noticed that she sat with the grace of an angel, too.

"I'm so surprised to see you out and about," she said. "I'm glad you're feeling better."

"It's good to get outside," he said, then sipped his drink, watching her every move.

"That was quite a ways for you to walk. It isn't hurting, is it?"

"No. Not at all. It seems just fine."

A lull fell between them, but neither felt compelled to fill it with conversation. He smiled at her and she smiled back, then he relaxed against his chair. An attractive pink tinge of color climbed up her neck from beneath the collar of her blue-striped dress to her cheeks; then she quickly looked down toward the glass in her hands. His earlier fading resolve suddenly strengthened, and he decided to ask her to go for a walk with him.

"Would you care to—"

"Would you like to—"

They laughed at having spoken at the same moment. Then he said, "Please. You first."

"I was just going to ask if you'd like to go on a picnic. That is, if your ankle is up to it."

"A picnic?" Why hadn't he thought of that, he wondered? "I think it sounds perfect. And my ankle is fine."

He extended his foot and waggled it to prove his words. "When would you like to go?"

"I'm not doing anything tomorrow. Is that too soon for you?" she asked.

"Not at all." And his mind raced ahead, taking his heart along with it, as he considered if then would be the appropriate time to ask her. He didn't think he could wait for several more weeks to pass, and he wasn't sure that he ought to. A woman as lovely as Carrie would certainly have many callers.

"The weather is lovely and I think it should last another day."

"Where would you like to go?" he asked.

She blushed again and he wondered if she was thinking the same thing he was about the willow trees along the river. "I'm not sure. What about you? Do you have a preference?"

"I like the riverbank farther down beyond town where it's quiet. There are a few willows for shade but it's more a part of the meadow."

"Sounds nice." And her blush deepened to a light rose. "I've seldom gone that far from town so it will be an adventure for me."

The last thing he wanted was for her to feel unprotected or unchaperoned or that her reputation would be compromised. They would choose another spot if she preferred. "If you'd rather not go there . . ."

"Oh, but I would. Really."

"If you're sure." And he hoped she was.

"I am. Truly I am."

He nodded, believing her. He would hold his proposal until the perfect moment during their picnic. Somehow that seemed more fitting than here in her parlor.

"What would you like me to bring along?" she asked. "Or would you prefer it to be a surprise?"

He smiled. "Anything at all will be fine with me. Having your company is all I really care about."

This time she didn't look away, but met his gaze straight on with a smile of her own. "That is the nicest thing anybody has ever said to me."

The soft timbre of her voice raised the hairs on the back of his neck. He shifted uncomfortably in his seat as he ran his hand around the back of his collar to smooth them into place. He never would have guessed that just the sound of a woman's voice could do that to a man, but he supposed not any woman's voice would have. Carrie's alone had that power over him.

"Would you like another glass?" she asked, indicating his empty one.

Not wanting to leave just then, he replied, "Yes. Thank you."

When she took the glass from him, their fingers grazed and immediately they glanced at each other. The hairs raised on the back of his neck again as she smiled at him. Then as she walked through the length of the dining room once more, he unabashedly watched the natural sway of her hips. Back in the kitchen, he could see her moving about and humming a tune. Before long he heard her call his name, and he hesitated thinking he must be wrong.

"Ted? Could you help me with this?"

"Certainly," he replied, and followed her steps through the house. Once more he was taken aback by the expensive furniture and lavish rugs that seemed to be scattered everywhere over the warm wooden floors. She had a special touch for turning a house into a home and the kitchen seemed especially so. He knew he could sit at her small kitchen table and watch her bustle about without ever getting tired of being there.

"I don't know why I put that canister up so high, but I do that every time and then I usually have to get a chair to get it down. Would you mind saving me the trouble?" She pulled out a chair for him. "But please, be careful. I'd feel terrible if you fell or something and hurt yourself all over again."

She steadied the chair for him while he climbed up to retrieve the tin with "sugar" printed on the outside. When he was on the floor once more, she breathed a loud sigh of relief.

"I really do appreciate it," she replied. "The next time I will have to find some other place for it." She took the tin from him and set it on the counter of her baking cabinet beside them.

"I don't like the idea of you climbing on chairs when you're here all alone. What if you fell?" He could hardly bear thinking about it.

"I always try to be careful," she said as she dipped in a measuring cup then transferred it to the pitcher of lemonade and stirred. The small confines of the room kept her close to him.

"Now I'm going to worry about you," he said softly, and she turned to look up at him.

"You will?"

"Of course, I will." And the overpowering need to take her in his arms was too much to resist. She came to him willingly, setting aside the spoon as if she didn't care whether it landed on the counter or the floor. "I suppose it isn't exactly proper for me to do this while we're alone, unchaperoned and all." He leaned down close to her lips, grasping her by the waist and pulling her to him.

"I think it's all right," she said, and that soft voice was

back. "I'd rather we were alone if we're going to kiss than have someone watching us."

He grinned. "I have to agree." Then he touched his lips to hers and she leaned into him with her hands trapped between them, clutching lightly at his shirt front.

She tasted sweeter than the sweetest nectar and he couldn't seem to get his fill. Then her arms came up to circle his neck while her soft breasts pressed into his chest. Needing more, his arms went around her back to pull her closer and a soft sound in her throat vibrated to him, intensifying his need until he knew he had to put a stop to it. He raised his head, then laid his cheek against her fevered one while her breath blew erratically against his ear.

"Maybe this isn't such a good idea after all," he said, his eyes closed tight as he tried to regain his control.

"I think it's a wonderful idea," she replied, and he heard the smile in her voice. "But it certainly is warm in here, isn't it?"

"A little bit."

"A lot, actually."

He smiled and agreed. "A lot."

She lowered her arms from his neck and nestled her head beneath his chin. He cuddled her close, enjoying the feel of her in his arms and hoping it would always be that way. For a moment he considered asking her right then, but changed his mind. He liked the idea of proposing on a picnic on the meadow along the river and he found himself wishing she would wear the same dress she'd worn on Independence Day.

"I suppose I ought to be going," he said, but he didn't move.

"You could stay if you like."

A bolt of electricity went through him as he wondered what she was offering.

"It's nearly time for the noon meal," she said. "I could make us something simple."

He smiled and hugged her tight for a second before loosening his grip on her.

"No. I think it would be best if I go. I've probably stayed too long as it is."

"You're worrying about my reputation, aren't you?" She smiled and reached up to kiss his cheek. "It isn't necessary."

"It is to me." He stepped back and took both of her hands then brought them to his lips.

"I liked it better like this," she said, and put his hands around her waist. Pulling his head down to hers, she gave him a lingering kiss that nearly curled his toes inside his shoes. "I never knew that preachers could kiss like that," she said, when they parted at last.

"Me neither," he replied, and she laughed softly with him.

"I really think I'd better go now."

"Maybe you should," she said. "But I will be counting the hours till tomorrow's picnic."

"Me, too. What time should I come by?"

"Around eleven?"

"Eleven it is." Then he stepped back from her once more, holding both of her hands in his.

"Tomorrow," she said, letting him go and walking him to the door.

He smiled at her, then pushed the screen door aside and went out. "Good-bye."

"Good-bye," she said, watching him walk toward the street.

He raised his hand in farewell, then turned and headed back home with a lighter step than he'd had before he'd reached her house, which he wouldn't have thought was possible.

Chapter Twenty

Carrie watched until he was out of sight, then she stepped quickly to her desk where she grabbed the handiest paper and fanned herself. My word, she thought, but he certainly did raise her temperature. All the men she'd kissed had never done that to her, and poor Samuel hadn't even been able to make her blush. But Ted, well, he positively made her feel like her body was on fire from the inside out. Although she'd been married for a few years, she hadn't realized what could happen between a man and woman, that is, *really happen*. Why, just the thought of being with Ted the way Samuel had been with her made her whip the paper a little faster. Somehow, knowing exactly what did happen seemed to make her want to kiss him all the more, and that thought made her aim the fanned air down the front of her bodice, which she held open at the collar.

When she'd finally cooled off, she hurried to the kitchen to check her pantry before making a list of items she would need. This was not going to be a simple picnic lunch. She wanted it to be special so she spent a good share of the afternoon thumbing through her recipes and making a list of groceries. The bread would have to be as fresh as possible even if she had to stay up half the night to do it. Thank goodness she had put up strawberry preserves this year, and sweet pickles, too. When she was done with the list she had to go over it again and cross half of it off since she had more than two people could possibly eat in one sitting. So she whittled it down until she was satisfied that it would still be a good sampling of her cooking, not that he didn't already know what it was like. Then the shopping itself took almost as long as making the list, but at last she was ready to begin.

By nine o'clock she had nearly everything cooked except the bread, which she'd just set out for the first rising. Hardly able to keep her eyes open, she decided a short nap was in order until it was time to knead the dough before the second rising. So she climbed the steps with her feet dragging and let herself fall across the bed. In no time, she was dreaming wonderful dreams of Ted beside her, kissing her and loving her the way she never thought a man could.

When she awoke with a start, she felt disoriented and couldn't understand why she hadn't undressed for bed. Then remembering her bread, she let out a cry and hurried through the dark house taking just long enough to light a lamp in the diningroom and one in the kitchen. The bread had expanded to more than twice its normal size and she almost cried at the sight of it. She feared she'd ruined it, but punched it down anyway and spent several minutes kneading, rolling, turning, and kneading it again. Satisfied that she'd done the best she could, she let it rise again, only this time she had to stay awake. So she lit a lamp in the parlor and took out some mending and sat where she could see into the kitchen, and then she noticed Ted's hat. He'd left it beside his chair. She walked over to pick it up and held it, turning it by the brim the way he had. She wondered if he realized yet that he'd left it. Keeping it beside her on the settee, she picked up her mending once more and thought about the morning, his boyish smiles, and his not-so-boyish kisses.

Before long it was time to knead the bread again, and put it into the pans for baking. The extra warmth in the kitchen added more tiredness to her bones, and she found herself yawning so much she feared she would surely fall asleep and then the bread would bake to a black crisp. The hour had nearly reached midnight when she finally pulled the hot brown loaves from the oven. They were beautiful and well worth the time and effort she'd to put into them.

Yawning again, she shook down the grates and closed the dampers, then listening carefully she thought she heard a noise from . . . outside? Surely, she must have been mistaken, or perhaps it was just some hungry stray dog that had smelled her baking. But there it was again. On her porch? Cautiously, she slipped into the other room and with a lamp in her hand, peered out through the screen door.

"Is someone out there?" she called softly, not wanting to wake the entire neighborhood.

Then a small voice said with a whimper, "It's just me, ma'am." And he stepped into the ring of her lamplight. "I smelled your bread, and I'm powerful hungry."

"My goodness!" A young boy, not more than ten she was sure, stood on her porch. His face was grimy with streaks down his cheeks. Undoubtedly he'd been crying and the tears had made clean tracks in the dirt on his face. "Come in. Come in."

He shuffled tiredly through her doorway and stood off to the side. Then he politely pulled his hat from his head to reveal a thick thatch of unkempt brown hair. She had never seen him before, but decided that was unimportant since the child had said he was hungry.

"Would you like some bread and jam with some tea? I'm afraid I haven't any milk left." She'd used it all in her cooking.

"Yes, ma'am."

"Well, follow me." And she led him to the kitchen and pulled out a chair from her small table. "Sit here and I'll have it ready in a minute."

"Yes, ma'am."

She hurried to cut the bread and butter while the tea steeped in her teapot using the hot water from the kettle she kept on the stove. Occasionally, she turned to watch him. She was concerned he might fall off his chair with exhaustion since he looked that tired. She wanted to ask if he was all right, but knew he would resist telling her just as she knew it would do no good to ask who he was. There was an air about him that said he was not likely to impart any information to anybody, but there was also a look in his eyes that said he was frightened. What should she do? Take him to the police? Was he a runaway? Then she nearly caught her breath as she remembered the orphan trains Cora had warned everyone about. Could he have escaped from one of them?

Then she thought of Lydia and knew immediately what she ought to do. The hour was late, but this was an emergency and she was certain that Lydia would want to help. As soon as the boy finished eating his fill she would somehow get him to her house.

She gave him the dish with the pieces of bread and jam, then carried the pot of tea with two cups to the table.

"Mind if I join you?" she asked.

He shook his head while he chewed his food. "No,

ma'am.'' His wary eyes watched her carefully as she sat across from him and poured the tea.

"Do you prefer a little sugar in your tea?" she asked.

"Doesn't matter to me."

"Well, maybe a little sugar would be good for you to-night, although, I understand that children shouldn't make a habit of it."

"I'm not a child."

"Oh. I see. Well, please excuse my mistake." She sipped her tea then said, "It isn't very hot, I'm afraid. But it's still good. Try it."

He sipped it carefully, then, finding it cool enough, drank it down without stopping. She poured another cup for him.

"May I ask if you are from around here?"

"No, ma'am. I'm not."

"Are you just passing through then?"

"No, ma'am."

He certainly didn't offer much information, she thought. But she wasn't going to give up.

"Oh, so you came to see somebody here in Peaceful Valley."

"Yes, ma'am." He drank his tea but a little slower this time. "Might I have another piece of bread, but without jam this time?"

"Of course." She brought the sliced bread to the table along with the crock of butter and set it in front of him. "There. Help yourself."

"Thank you."

She let him eat in silence then asked, "Might I ask who you've come to see?"

He studied her carefully then drank the last of his tea, but he didn't respond.

"I would like to offer you a place to stay for the night, but I'm afraid I can't. But I do have a friend who would love take you in for the night, or for as long as you would like.'' At least she believed Lydia would do that, after all, wasn't that what an orphanage was? ''You look like you could use some sleep.''

''Yes, ma'am. I could.''

''Have you come a long way?''

''Farther than I ever thought I could. But I made it.''

''Yes, you made it.'' But his eyelids were beginning to droop and she knew she would have to hurry if she was going to get him to Lydia's. ''Will you come with me to my friend's house?''

He thought about it for a moment then nodded. ''Guess I am tired. My feet hurt, too. And I thank you for the bread.'' He propped his arm on the table with his elbow and set his chin in his hand.

''Well, why don't we go before you fall asleep on that chair? Do you feel well enough to walk a little farther?''

He nodded.

''It might help us to talk if we introduce ourselves. My name is Mrs. Marting. What's yours?''

''Daniel,'' he mumbled tiredly, and she knew she had to hurry or he would soon be sleeping on her kitchen floor.

''Well, Daniel. Let me get a lantern.''

She hurried about as fast she could, then stood before him, urging him to follow her, which he did willingly.

When they reached the front gate of Lydia's house, Daniel stopped suddenly and stared at the weathered old building.

''Does someone live here?'' he asked.

''Yes, and she's very nice. She'll do everything she can to help you.'' Carrie had long since gotten past her unkind feelings for Lydia, and in large part that was Ted's doing. He had nothing but good things to say about her and the children's home she was trying to start. Well, it looked as though this child would be her first needy child, Carrie thought, as she gently tugged Daniel along to the front door.

She hated to make a commotion so late at night, but there was simply no help for it, she decided as she pounded on the door. With the lantern held high so that Lydia would see who was there and not be frightened, they waited, then pounded again. At last, the door opened.

Lydia held her lamp in front of her while Grandma Winnie looked over her shoulder.

"Carrie," she said, surprised, but her eyes went immediately to the dirty, disheveled boy with her.

"We're sorry to bother you so late and all, but I'd like you to meet Daniel. He came to my door tonight and has no place to stay."

"Please, come in. Both of you." Lydia swung the door wide to allow them to enter then led the way to the kitchen.

"Well, I declare," Winnie said softly, and padded along behind the others.

Everyone sat around the table except Lydia, who crouched down in front of the boy. She smiled and said, "My name is Lydia and you are welcome to stay here."

"I came to see my pa."

The three women looked at each other but none of them had an answer to the obvious question, so Lydia asked, "What is his name, Daniel? Maybe we know him."

"Nathan Stockwell. He's my pa." And all three women gasped.

Lydia had to clutch at his chair to keep from falling over backwards as her mind reeled. She knew she had heard him correctly so there was no use asking again, but she desperately wanted to understand.

"Nathan is your father?" she asked.

"Do you know him?" His eyes brightened.

"Yes." Her heart suddenly felt very heavy but she ignored the slow thud. Right now, Daniel came first.

"I'll take you to him tomorrow," she replied.

He yawned and slouched in his chair. "Thank you, ma'am. I'd like that."

Winnie immediately went into action, saying, "I think a bath is in order." She pulled a large wash basin from beneath the stove and set it on the wash table then dipped warm water from the reservoir into it.

"A bath?" he said sleepily, but Lydia knew he was too tired to offer much resistance.

The three of them left him to his bathing in the kitchen while they followed Carrie back through the unfinished house. None of them said a word about the shock and surprise that Daniel had just given them.

"Thank you for bringing him here. I'll see to it that he's fed and taken care of." Her hand shook slightly and she had to steady the lamp with both hands. She couldn't let herself think about the ramifications of this revelation, not now.

"I've already fed him bread and jam with a little warm tea. I doubt if he'll need anything but sleep by the looks of him." And Lydia read her thoughts loud and clear: How could this child be Nathan's son?

Carrie said a solemn good-bye, then walked toward home as Lydia and Winnie watched her lantern light until it was out of sight.

"I declare," Winnie said for the second time and then she was speechless, but Lydia knew that was most likely a temporary thing. She was simply composing her thoughts into a lecture that Lydia did not want to hear.

Outside the kitchen door, Lydia called, "Daniel? Are you finished?"

"Yes, ma'am," he said, stepping into view. He had put his dirty clothes back on and Lydia wished she had something clean for him to at least sleep in, but she didn't.

When her grandmother started to object, Lydia interrupted, saying, "We'll make a pallet on the floor for you in the bedroom upstairs with us." She didn't want to let him out of her sight since she knew firsthand how a runaway child thought, if he was indeed a runaway.

Now, the questions started flying at her and she had to hold them off or at least dodge them until she could be alone to think everything through to a logical solution. There had to be a reason why Nathan hadn't told her he had a son just as there had to be a reason why this child had showed up here looking for his father. Where had he been and why wasn't he with his father in the first place? No, she couldn't think about it yet. Later, she promised herself, when the room was dark and she didn't have to talk. That's when she would try to sort it all out.

"A pallet sounds pretty nice. I slept in an old barn last night. It was kinda scary."

Lydia's heart nearly hurt for him, as her own memories were suddenly dredged up. She and her brother had made a similar trek and had ended up on Irene Barrett Hollister's doorstep, and lucky for them that they had.

"I declare," Winnie said, but Lydia quickly shushed her.

"This way," Lydia said, taking her lamp and gently steering Daniel to walk alongside her up the stairs. She wanted to ask him more questions, but her grandmother's presence prohibited that from happening.

After they got him settled on the pallet he looked up at her and said, "Ma'am. I don't want to go back."

Lydia hardly knew what to say. How many times had she said those words as a child? How many times had she cried into her pillow at night over the death of her parents, hating the rigid regime of the orphanage they'd been forced to live in? But Daniel's situation was different, he did have a father. Families stayed together no matter what, so there was no reason he shouldn't be with him, no reason at all. Somehow, she would get this all straightened out, but until then she had no answer for Daniel.

He yawned and said, "I just want to stay with Pa."

Then before she could turn down the lamp to blow it out, he'd fallen asleep. Winnie started to speak, but Lydia shook her head. She simply could not discuss any of this, not before she had some time to think it through.

But as they crawled into bed and pulled up the sheet, she heard her grandmother mutter, "I knew there was something about that man I didn't like." Then she rolled over and was silent.

The words cut straight to Lydia's heart as tears of hurt and disillusionment welled behind her closed lids. Nathan hadn't been completely honest with her. At the very least, he had kept an important part of his life hidden, and now she felt confused. Had everyone known he had a family, and simply failed to mention it to her? What about Daniel's mother? What had become of her? Had Nathan abandoned her as well? Were there other children? She didn't want to believe that he had abandoned anybody, but what else was she to think? The child plainly said he wanted to live with his father, and she could see no reason why that wasn't possible.

She felt a sudden kinship with Daniel and her first instinct was to look after him, even if his father wouldn't. There was so much that needed to be said to Nathan, so many questions to ask. Already the small hours of the morning had come and gone, but she still couldn't find any answers. Finally exhausted from thinking so much, she fell asleep.

When Lydia awoke it was to the sound of pots and pans coming from the kitchen. One hasty look confirmed that both Daniel and Grandma Winnie were out of bed and most likely downstairs cooking breakfast. Without wasting a movement, she hurriedly dressed and pinned up her hair then dashed down the stairs. She found Daniel sitting at the table eating hotcakes smothered in the butter her grandmother had bought the day before, among other things which made her small cabinet doors bulge.

"Good morning," she said to them, relieved that Daniel was still there. Her first waking thought was that he'd run away, but she knew her grandmother would have told her immediately if that had been the case.

"I thought you were going to sleep the day away," Grandma Winnie said. "So I decided to give this boy a hearty breakfast."

"Is that bacon I smell? And maple syrup, too?"

"I simply can't abide a kitchen without a proper pantry so don't give me any disrespect. Now, sit down and eat. He's a growing boy, but he won't be able to eat all of that by himself."

Lydia sat at the table and gave him a wink in hopes of letting him know that he had nothing to be afraid of, that she was on his side and would stick by him. But as far as eating anything, she couldn't. The talk she intended to have with Nathan loomed like a confrontation and her stomach repelled the idea of food.

"Did you sleep well?" she asked Daniel.

"Yes, ma'am," he said between bites. "I guess being clean helped." She could tell he was trying to be appreciative of her help, and had to smile.

Winnie set another dish of hotcakes on the table. "Clean clothes would be even nicer."

"Yes, ma'am. But I didn't have time—" He stopped

abruptly, his eyes wide as he stared across at Lydia.

"It's all right," she said, reaching her hand over to touch his sleeve. "I'm sure your father will take care of that as soon as he can." She let it pass that he'd just told her he was a runaway. Her only concern at the moment was for him to know she understood.

Daniel nodded, but said nothing else while he studiously finished his breakfast. After he swallowed the last bite, he said, "Can we go now?"

"Yes. We'll go." Then she turned to her grandmother, saying, "I don't know how long I'll be."

"I have plenty to keep me busy," she replied. "I'll be waiting."

The two of them walked side by side through town while Daniel stared at everything with great interest.

"I've never been here before," he said. "Is this a nice place to live?"

Her heart went out to him as she realized that he had come in search of his father with the intention of staying. How long had it been since Nathan had seen his son? An angry knot formed in her stomach, and she knew that whatever the reason for abandoning this child, it had better be good. At first she'd wondered if it was wise to go to his shop where others might overhear their conversation and draw attention to Daniel's predicament, but her only other choice was to go to his house after he closed up. Somehow, she didn't think the boy could wait that long and frankly, neither could she. So she prayed Nathan would be alone.

She stopped outside the open front doors where the sappy scent of pine floated out to greet them. Holding Daniel back, she peered inside to see if Nathan was alone. When she didn't hear any voices, she took a fortifying deep breath and stepped forward as she held Daniel's hand. Inside the cool interior, she walked past piles of lumber, odd pieces of wagons and assorted other things that she paid little attention to as she made her way toward the man at the bench. He hadn't heard them approach from behind and Lydia suddenly stopped, watching his shoulders move as he worked with some sort of device she couldn't see. At just the sight of him she realized once again how dear he had become to her. But now her feelings felt bruised while these new emotions roiled and conflicted with those lovely ones she'd been holding close to her heart since the night of the storm. Then a tug from the warm little hand in hers reminded her why she was there.

"Nathan." Her heart pounded, but not from fear or worry what he might say to her. It pounded with deep regret for what was about to happen.

He turned to look at her and smiled with pleasant surprise, then his eye caught sight of Daniel. He stood as if frozen to the spot, but the young boy, ecstatic at seeing his father, bounded across the open area and threw himself into Nathan's arms. Then grasping him by the shoulders, Nathan held him away.

"Son, what are you doing here?"

Lydia tried to read the emotions behind his expression, but the barrier had come up. She couldn't tell if he was glad to see his son or if he was angry or if he even felt anything at all. He was an expert at hiding his emotions.

"I came to stay with you, Pa. Don't make me go back." Tears filled his eyes as his voice thickened. "Please, Pa."

Nathan gave her a quick look before turning to his son. "We'll talk about it later." Then he rose to his feet and faced Lydia. "Where did you find him?"

She continued to stare at him, torn between wanting to understand and wanting to demand answers for his treatment of his son.

"Carrie Marting brought him to my house last night after she fed him." Her words sounded cold but she didn't care. And the barrier went up a little higher.

"I'll take care of him. Thank you for bringing him here."

He couldn't dismiss her like that. She wouldn't allow it. He had to offer some sort of explanation. She needed to know what was going to become of this child, and what was going to become of them? Had everything between them meant nothing at all?

"Will you let him stay?" she asked with her chin up and her stare unshakeable.

Silently, he returned her stare, but this time she saw a new fire in his gold-flecked eyes. His mind was made up and she knew he wouldn't allow her to change it. Still, she couldn't let this happen, not without knowing why he was being so heartless.

"A child needs his father," she said, and suddenly she knew that she had stepped beyond a boundary.

"This is my problem and I'll take care of it."

She would not be easily intimidated, not when a child's well being was at stake. Someone needed to take the boy's part, and if his father wasn't going to do it then she would!

"He doesn't want to go. Doesn't that matter to you?"

"I'll take care of this. It doesn't concern you." His voice was cold enough to make frost appear.

"All children concern me, especially the ones like Daniel." She knew the boy was listening to every word, as his head followed whichever one of them spoke. It wasn't fair to allow the boy to hear their conversation, but she couldn't walk away until she discovered Nathan's intentions. A child had the right to live with his father as long as that father was perfectly capable of taking care of him, and Nathan was more than capable. Why did he want to abandon his son?

"You don't know. . . ." But he stopped there.

"Tell me, Nathan. I want to know."

Her gaze searched his face for answers, but all emotion was buried. There was nothing for her to read, nothing but stony silence as he retreated further behind his self-made barrier. She started to take a step forward in a plea, an offer to help, but he placed a hand on Daniel's shoulder and stood firm. There was nothing else she could say or do, although plenty of things came to mind.

"I'll go," she said to him. Then, turning her attention on the boy, she forced her face into a smile and said, "Good-bye, Daniel."

He looked up at his father then back at her. "Good-bye, ma'am. Thank you for keeping me."

She smiled again, but this time the tears of frustration blurred her vision and she had to turn and hurry from the shop. Out on the street in the bright morning sun, she made her way home letting the tears roll unheeded down her cheeks.

Chapter Twenty-one

Carrie hurried to answer Ted's knock, taking a quick peek in the mirror to make sure nothing had come loose. Slowing her steps before she reached the screen door, she smiled and pushed it open.

"I hope I'm not too early," he said.

"Not at all. Come in." And she retreated a little to allow him to enter. "I've got the basket all packed. Would you mind carrying it for me? It's a little heavy."

"Certainly," he replied, and looked around for it. She thought he looked especially handsome in his simple dark jacket, but she couldn't help but noticing that he seemed a little more nervous than usual. Somehow that didn't worry her. He had seemed uncomfortable in her house the last time, too. And his concern for her reputation only made him more dear to her.

"It's in the kitchen," she said, leading the way toward the back of the house.

"Smells really good in here," he said, following her.

"I made cinnamon custard. You do like it, don't you?" She stopped beside the table where the basket sat open, displaying the custard pie on top.

"Oh, yes. I do. One of my favorites."

"I guess we're ready then," she said, her anticipation for the day mounting. Just spending time with him, talking to him, was enjoyable, and yes, kissing him, too, she freely admitted to herself. No other man had ever made her feel so young or so wanted, neither had she ever wanted a man so much.

"I guess we are," he said.

"I'll just get my hat." But he put out his hand and gently stopped her.

"I wish you didn't have to wear it. Your hair is too beautiful to be covered and I don't get to look at it often enough." He looked suddenly more relaxed, more at ease, just the way she preferred him to be.

"Thank you. That's such a nice thing to say," she said. "Maybe I'll just take my parasol."

As they passed through the parlor, she lifted a blue one from the stand and looked at him for approval. When he nodded she smiled and opened the door, holding it for him to bring the awkward basket through. She popped open the parasol and stared up at the bright sky, loving the new lightness she felt in her heart. Her worries had simply faded over the past few weeks and she owed it all to the feelings that she shared with Ted. She no longer felt alone or worried about the simplest chore. Her frantic searching had come to an end that day beneath the willow trees, and she thought he felt the same about her.

After he loaded the basket into the back of the buggy, he asked, "Would you like the top up?"

"Oh, no. Leave it down so we can enjoy the breeze from

all directions. And if it musses my hair, well, I won't mind if you don't.''

''Mind?'' he said, surprised. ''Not at all.'' She thought he looked as though he might say something else but quickly decided against it. Then he helped her climb in and walked around the buggy to climb in beside her.

''It is such a beautiful day.'' She laughed and added, ''I might have already said that, but it bears repeating.''

''Indeed it does.'' Then he gently slapped the reins and they moved along the street.

Outside of town they followed the river, passing the group of willows where their first kiss had taken place. She'd relived that moment many times over the weeks that followed right up until the second kiss he'd given her, and then she'd had two moments to remember. She slipped a sideways glance at him, hoping he wouldn't catch her, but he did and they shared a smile. A summer breeze floated by and, thankfully, cooled her heated skin. He just seemed to always have that effect on her, but she didn't mind it at all.

At last they arrived at the spot he had told her about, and it was even more beautiful than she'd expected. The river was deeper here with high banks and fewer trees to block the view of the meadow.

''I've never really been out on the meadow this far,'' she said. ''I love those rolling hills beyond the edge. Over there . . .'' she said, pointing in the distance. The only times she crossed the meadow were to follow the main road to the next town, and she seldom if ever noticed how lovely it was.

''I like to come here often. It's a good place to think.''

''It's so quiet.'' And as if being asked, the wind settled down and the birds ceased their singing for a moment while they sat in the buggy, listening. Then suddenly it all came alive with the natural sounds of the meadow as the tall grasses sighed, the locusts churred, and the birds burst into individual song.

"Maybe it isn't so quiet after all," she said, laughing.

He watched her until she sensed his gaze and turned toward him. "What is it? My hair? She lifted a hand to touch the wisps that floated around her face.

Without saying anything he leaned over and kissed her, not long and lingering like she wished he would, but short and tender. "That's for thinking of having this picnic."

"I'll remember that in the future," she said, staring into his eyes, which seemed to reflect the blue of the parasol over them.

He smiled. "We might like to take a lot of picnics."

"Indeed we shall," she replied softly.

"If I kiss you again, I'm afraid I'll forget why we came here."

"And if you don't, I will be disappointed."

"I wouldn't like to have you disappointed."

"Then, I'm waiting. . . ." She leaned forward, closing her eyes, and he met her halfway.

The kiss was as tender as the previous one, but she felt the restraint in him as he kept his hands on her upper arms holding her close and yet far enough away to be safe. She almost sighed, wishing it could be more. Then he broke away from her.

"I think I'd better set up the picnic," he said. Then he turned her loose and climbed down from the buggy.

She watched while he walked a short distance to the river's bank and came back only to walk it again. He did this one more time and she had to laugh at how silly he looked.

"What are you doing?" she asked.

"I'm tromping down the grass so you won't snag your

dress,'' he replied as he flattened a circle at the base of a small tree where they would lay out a tablecloth. "I think that should do it." He came back to the buggy and lifted her down, hesitating with her in his arms long enough for a quick resounding kiss, then he hefted out the basket.

"I have to ask," he said as they walked his freshly-made and very fragrant path. "What is so heavy in here? I think you've put bricks in the bottom just to make me think it's loaded with food."

She laughed again, thinking she hadn't ever laughed so often. "Oh, but it is loaded with food."

When they reached the spot he'd trampled she opened the lid and pulled out a very large tablecloth and he spread it under her supervision. Then he helped her to sit on one corner while he knelt beside her.

"Would you mind taking everything out?" she asked.

Ted lifted out the dishes and a couple of canning jars filled with colorful pickled things, and two more jars of lemonade. "These are why this thing is so heavy." Then he took out the bread, roasted chicken, glazed carrots, fried corn and two pieces of chocolate cake.

"I brought that in case you don't like cinnamon custard," she said.

He looked at the custard pie and then at her. "No, no. I like custard pie. But I like chocolate cake, too."

Carrie set aside her parasol before they set the food around the cloth within easy reach. Ted crossed his legs Indian-style and balanced his overflowing plate in his lap. They talked about many things while they enjoyed their picnic lunch. They began with the progress of his ankle then went on to the ladies in his church who had cooked so much food for him, and next discussed the kinds of wildflowers that now surrounded them, and even mentioned the children's home. When they had exhausted every avenue of interest and the remains of the lunch lay off to the side, Ted stretched out with his head on her lap.

"I probably shouldn't bring this up. It's rather personal, but if one can't talk to the preacher about things like this, who can one talk to?" she asked thoughtfully, thinking about Nathan and his son.

"I'm very good at keeping confidences," he said. "It's a big share of what I do. You can tell me anything you like, if you want to, that is."

"Well, last night I had a visitor around midnight."

He looked up at her sharply, worry creasing his usually easygoing features. "Why didn't you tell me sooner?" he asked, starting to rise up, but she pushed him gently back until his head was lying in her lap again.

"Not that kind of a visitor, but it's sweet of you to be concerned for my welfare." She smoothed his brow with one finger. "This visitor was only ten years old, or around that age. I was quite safe."

"And I always want you to be." He took her finger and kissed it, sending shivers along her arm. "So tell me about this child. Was he lost? Or should I say she?"

"No, Daniel wasn't lost. At least, not completely. He had come a long way in search of his father, and Ted, the poor thing was so dirty and just worn out from traveling alone that it nearly broke my heart. How many children do you suppose there are like that? Just searching for someone, runaways who sometimes surely get lost."

"More than we realize." He looked thoughtful. "Lydia is doing a wonderful thing with her house."

"Yes, I'm coming to understand that. I took Daniel to her and it was the middle of the night, but you should have seen her. She has so much care and genuine concern for children like that."

305

"Did you say he was looking for his father? In Peaceful Valley? Who could it be?"

"Nathan."

Stark surprise registered on his face and this time he did rise up to sit beside her. "Dear Lord."

She nodded. "You should have seen the look on Lydia's face. Well, you could have knocked me over with a feather, too, for that matter. But with her . . . I don't know. Something went straight out of her. I could almost feel it. Do you suppose she and Nathan are attracted to each other?"

He studied the tablecloth as though intently interested in the design. "I suppose so. But honestly, I don't know."

"Anyway, I left the boy with her at her insistence and since I know she is better trained to handle such situations, well, I just thought it best."

"Don't think too lightly of your own abilities in that respect."

"I've never been one to consider children in my life, but my heart went to this child. He looked so lost and forlorn." She stared off into the distance, but not seeing the loveliness of the meadow. "And I haven't been able to quit thinking about Nathan either. Why wasn't that boy with his father?" She felt angry and frustrated with Nathan. "Children should be with their parents."

He took her hand in his. "I'm sure there is a logical reason for this. Nathan doesn't seem like the sort of man to abandon his own son."

She turned to look at him. "I know. And I'm sure that somehow Lydia will look further into this so that the boy is taken care of properly. But I can't quit thinking about other children who might not have fathers or mothers or even someone like Lydia to stand up for them."

He kissed her hand and smiled at her. "Carrie Marting, have I told you that I love you?"

She blinked, not sure she had heard him correctly. "No." She breathed the word more than spoke it.

"Then let me tell you now. I love you. With all my heart and soul." He reached out to touch a wisp of her hair and brush it back from her face. "I love your kindness, your sweet nature, your . . . well, just you."

"Oh, Ted." Tears filled her eyes so that she could hardly see him clearly. Crying had never been an art she'd practiced like pouting or flirting, and she was sure her features must look like the worst kind of grimace.

"Don't cry. Just tell me you feel the same."

Unable to talk, she nodded vigorously and sniffled.

"Then . . . will you marry me?"

"Oh, Ted," she said, trying not to wail. This was no way to act during the most cherished moment in her life, and she sniffled again. "Yes. I love you heart and soul, too. Really, I do. And yes, I will marry you."

She took a hankie from her sleeve and blew her nose, embarrassed to have to do such thing right after being proposed to by the man who meant more to her than anyone in the whole world.

"I'm sorry," she mumbled into the hankie. "I suppose my nose is all red, isn't it?" She tucked the hankie away.

He smiled and said, "Only a little, but it's still the cutest little nose I've ever seen."

She gave a small laugh, her embarrassment leaving her.

"Do you suppose we could seal that proposal with a kiss?" he asked, pulling her to him.

"I'd be ever so disappointed if you didn't," she replied as she slipped her arms around his neck and met his lips with her own.

The kiss was as sweet as the moment and she wouldn't have changed that for anything. She knew that, soon, they would be able to loose their passions and her body was telling her not to wait too long. For the first time in her life, she experienced the excitement that existed between a man and woman, and she looked forward to a lifetime of it.

Cora and Richard sat across from each other during the noon meal. Neither was speaking and the air was as ripe as a five-day-old skunk carcass. Having reached the final point of bursting, Richard suddenly stood up, letting his chair rake backwards across the wooden floor. Cora jumped.

"I have had enough of this, Cora Davis. A man cannot live like a hermit in own his house while his wife sits in judgment of everything he says and does. I demand that you talk to me!"

She stared open-mouthed at him.

"And don't you dare start crying again!" He marched back and forth behind her chair so that she had to turn to see him. "I do not think you realize that you can actually drive a man mad with silence, but you can. I have tried to be reasonable. I have tried to be understanding. And to put it bluntly, I have tried to stop thinking about the conjugal bliss I used to know. That *we* used to know. And I am simply at my wits end!" He continued to pace, staring alternately at the floor in front of him then at her.

"Richard, do not yell. Please."

Her subdued voice stopped him. Just listening to her speak was music to his ears. Then she slowly rose from her chair, facing him. He waited, almost holding his breath, wondering if she would at last end the unbearable rift in their relationship.

"I'm sorry," she said, keeping one hand on the back of her chair while her body leaned ever so slightly toward him, and his hopes rose. "Please don't be angry with me." She studied his face in earnest and he felt his anger begin to dissipate. "This has gone on so long that I haven't known how to stop it and I was afraid that a simple apology would no longer suffice."

Suddenly faced with the Cora he knew and loved, he was gladly willing to take an apology, anything that would end this silent war between them.

"I am truly sorry," she said. "Please say you will forgive me." In just two steps he had her in his arms. "I do have an explanation—" she began, but his lips on hers cut off her words.

Her sincere apology was enough for him. He needed to hear nothing else, just having her back where she belonged was pure heaven, and apparently the feeling was mutual. Her arms came around his neck and he cradled her tightly against him while an instant white-hot flame seared him. It had been so long, and he'd missed her terribly. He'd missed the soft feel of her breasts, the sweet scent of her skin but mostly he'd missed the love she now returned. Without concern for control of his passion, he kissed her deeply as he tried to make up for the long absence of her body so close to his. When she pressed against him, meeting his every touch with one of her own, accepting the depth of his kisses and matching his intensity, he scooped her up into his arms and carried her toward the haven of their bedroom. Once inside the room, he kicked the door closed behind him and lowered her to her feet.

Between fevered, hurried kisses he helped her to undress, touching her with his lips wherever her clothing had been. She responded instantly, arching against him so that it took longer to undress than he wanted. With her camisole gone, he admired her breasts, which seemed larger than he'd remembered, touching them and tasting, kissing and laving until at last he could stand no more. He quickly shed his clothes and together they fell across the bed, entangled, entwined, as they strived to quench the fire that burned within them. There could be no more waiting; they'd waited long enough already. She grasped him by the shoulders, pulling him over her, stretching out beneath him, urging him to go on, and he complied. When at last he was within her, he suddenly stilled his movements, wishing the moment could go on, but her urgency tested his ability to wait, and he could not hold out. Together they strained, reaching for that attainment of perfect union that both of them had done without for so long, until at last their souls melted into one unified spirit that soared, giving them the release they sought. Breathless and speechless, they were molded together, bonded by the sweat of their bodies.

"I've missed you," she whispered.

"Not more than I've missed you," he replied hoarsely, then he kissed her forehead and rolled to his side, taking her with him so that they faced each other.

"Not true," she said, smiling.

"We aren't going to argue again, are we?"

She kissed the tip of his nose. "No."

They stared at each other for a few moments, grinning foolishly at each other.

"I have something to tell you," she said, and she traced the line of his jaw, his chin and back to his ear. He trapped her hand, stilling it.

"You'd better be careful doing that," he warned, giving her a devilish look.

"I'm not too afraid," she replied, wriggling closer. "Should I be?"

He laid his hand on her behind, warning her with his eyes to hold still, and she laughed softly in reply.

"You said you have something to tell me," he reminded her, needing to divert her attention for a little while at least.

She smiled but then bit her tongue and chewed at her lip in order to keep her smile hidden, but she failed miserably. "I don't know exactly how to say this." Her eyes sparkled, and suddenly he got a new sensation in the pit of his stomach.

"Tell me. Just say it." His heart pounded, waiting for the words he knew she was going to say.

"A baby," she said, still trying to contain her excitement. "Us. Ours."

"You're serious, aren't you?"

She nodded, making the starched pillow slip beneath their heads crinkle loudly in his ears. He tried to let the idea sink in, but it was too overwhelming to do more than stare dumbfounded at her. So this was the reason for the tears, the abstinence, the hurt feelings, and she had been going through it all alone. Then he became aware of the dimming sparkle that quickly faded to a small light in her eyes.

"You're not angry about it, are you? Oh, Richard, it's such a blessed thing to happen to us. I can't bear it if you're not as happy as I am." She searched his face, watching for some sign of acceptance. "I know now that I was over-reacting to the orphanage. You will forgive me, won't you?"

At last, he understood all of it. Her fear of raising a child in an environment that would be less than perfect, when all along he'd thought she'd become heartless toward the less fortunate children in the world. They had needed to talk it out, discuss their fears as well as their hopes, and they would have found their feelings were the same.

"Richard?" Almost in tears, she said, "Say something. I can't stand this silence any longer."

311

"I'm only thinking."

"About . . ."

"Us. And how grand it will be to have a tiny little girl just like her mother."

She laughed with relief and wrapped her arms around his neck. "Don't ever torture me like that again."

And holding her close, he replied, "I won't. Not ever again."

He should have gotten up and dressed to go back to work, but he didn't. Instead, he stayed where he was, admiring the woman who was his wife and soon to be the mother of his child. He touched the place where the baby was growing and marveled that it could be so. Then he cuddled her to him, protecting her with his embrace and wondered at the change their lives had just taken. Kissing the top of her head, he smiled, feeling as lucky as any man could possibly feel.

Penelope put the last supper dish away and wiped her hands on her apron. Out on the back porch she could hear the slow creak of Jeff's rocker, and somehow it sounded forlorn and sad. They had grown separate in these last few months as she'd stuck stubbornly to having her way over the issue of the orphanage, but if this was winning she didn't much like it. She sighed deeply, but it didn't help. Lately, she'd been doing a lot of that.

She stepped to the screen door and leaned against the door frame, just watching him as he rocked back and forth. The entire situation had gotten out of hand, or perhaps it was blown out of proportion to begin with and she was just now seeing it that way. She sighed again, and his rocker stopped for a brief moment, waiting before resuming the slow pace. He'd heard her; he knew she was there. She ought to go to him and talk about how confused she felt, but her pride still held her back.

"You gonna stand in the doorway all night or are you gonna come on out?" he asked without turning to look at her.

She pushed the door open and stepped onto the back porch. "I guess I might as well sit out here awhile. It's too hot in the house." Not wanting to sit in the other rocker because she hardly had the energy to make it move, she decided on the straight chair against the wall.

"Nice night," she said, sending him a quick glance before staring out toward the abundant growth of morning glories growing on the trellis that he'd put up for her early last spring.

"Yep."

His rocker kept moving, sounding more forlorn than before she'd come outside to sit with him. The house was extra quiet, too, since the children had all gone to play a game of night-tag with the neighbor children down the street. Their shouts of surprise and hoots of laughter could be heard as someone must have been caught or tagged. She would have smiled, but didn't feel much like it under the circumstances.

"I've been thinking, Jeff."

His rocker stopped again, only this time he didn't push it into motion after a short hesitation. Instead, he turned to watch her, waiting for her to go on.

After an interminable silence, she said, "You're not making this easy for me."

"It ain't been too easy for me lately, either," he replied.

"I know." She studied the hem of her apron, lifting it so she could examine it closely but not really seeing it at all. "I've been thinking."

His chair started rocking again. "You already said that."

"Damn it, Jeff. I'm trying to say I'm sorry." She glared at him even though he wasn't looking at her.

"Then just say it and be done with it."

"Be done with it?" she asked, wondering what he meant.

"Yep. Ain't no point in dragging it out more than it's been."

The pride that couldn't quite be subdued, suddenly jumped to the forefront and with an angry spurt of words, she said, "Why are you making this so difficult for me? It's hard enough to say I'm sorry without you being so willing to accept it before it's even said."

"Maybe that's because we're both still hurting."

She leaned her head back against the chair and closed her eyes. "Maybe you're right." Where did she go from here, she wondered? Had anything been solved by her attempt to apologize?

"I guess I could meet you halfway," he said, his rocker coming to a halt.

She opened her eyes and watched him in the lowering twilight. The last thing she wanted was to be at odds with him, but she was. He was a strong man with a will of iron and sometimes she just felt like her thoughts and ideas didn't amount to a hill of beans. She realized now that she'd been exercising a will of her own by taking the opposite path he wanted her to take, and that wasn't fair to either of them.

"I've been thinking, too," he said, not looking at her. "I've been wondering what could make you take such a stand against children who have no home or loving mother and father, and I come to the conclusion that ain't the way it is. You're a good mother. The best. And you'd want the best for all children, especially those who aren't as well taken care of as ours.'' He took a deep breath, then went on. "So that means the orphanage isn't the problem. It's us that's the problem.''

Her heart nearly stopped and she wanted to deny what he'd said, but she couldn't.

"I've been kinda . . . well, sorta . . . well, hard to—''

"No. Don't say it.'' She got up from her chair and went to him. "You are the gentlest man I know.''

He looked up at her and reached out his hand to pull her down on his lap, and she came willingly. How safe and secure it felt to be held in his arms once more. Oh, how she'd missed him! Turning her head, she buried her face in the collar of his shirt. He smelled of smoke, leather and sweat, and all of it was Jeff Chase, the man she cared about more than her need to be independent.

"Sweet, sweet woman,'' he said, cuddling her close. "Gentle in some ways is one thing, but I gotta be careful about being overpowering. You got a right to feel different than me and you got a right to say so. I shouldn't have told you to stay away from Agnes Butterfield.''

"I shouldn't have been so stubborn. If I had been thinking, I'd have seen that she was wrong about the orphanage.''

He set the rocker in motion, pulling her legs up over the arm on the chair and tucking her skirts in around her. "Maybe that's so, but we have to start working from here on, and we've got to find a way to do it together because I can't stand being separated from you.'' He kissed the top of her head.

She sighed, only this time it was contentment that filled her and not despair. With one hand she rubbed the front of his shirt, feeling the texture of the man beneath it. How wonderful it was to be with him again, really with him. Then the rocker slowed as his hand went to the rounded part of her bottom, caressing it, and she smiled against his shirt. It had been a long time, for both of them.

"I believe I'm feeling a little tired kinda early tonight," he said, and she heard the smile in his voice.

"I believe I am, too."

"Then why don't we get an early start on a good night's rest." He helped her into a standing position as he stood up beside her.

"The children aren't home yet," she said, but it was a weak objection and she knew it.

"We'll lock the bedroom door." He opened the screen and tugged on her hand.

"I ought to leave a lamp burning," she said.

"If you want to," he replied.

So they lit a lamp and turned it low, then placed it on the kitchen table. Without looking back, they went into the bedroom together and while the last of the sun's rays dipped out of sight, Jeff closed the door and locked it.

Chapter Twenty-two

Sitting alone at the table, Lydia finished her coffee. Grandma Winnie had gone to visit with Opal Grayling just as she'd been doing each morning. The two had become fast friends after their initial meeting. Having time to herself was important and she relished these few morning hours to think about all that she had to do, and all that had transpired lately.

It had been a week since she'd last seen Nathan on the day she'd taken Daniel to him. Without explanation, he'd simply stopped coming to work on the house or even to see her, so none of her burning questions had ever been answered. She wondered how Daniel was getting along and Nathan, too, as he resumed his natural place as father. Once, she had nearly gone to him, but the idea of repeating their parting scene was too much to contemplate. And the fact that he hadn't stopped by at all told her that he didn't want to see her, but she couldn't understand. Did he feel she had exposed him? Was there more he was hiding? Didn't he know how much she cared? There were so many questions but no one to answer them for her.

With her mind so occupied with the matters of her heart, she'd nearly lost sight of her goals for Spring Meadows. The work had slowed to a crawl since she and Sarah were the only ones left, not including the well-intentioned suggestions given by her grandmother. There were no extra funds coming in since the benefit money had all been used up, and still the house was a long way from being done. She didn't hold out much hope for receiving any funding from any society because they would never approve a house in the condition of hers, and she certainly couldn't blame them. Children needed a solid home that was safe and warm, and this one didn't qualify, yet. Maybe it never would. Giving up wasn't in her nature, but being realistic had suddenly become very important with so many things at stake. If she went blindly forward, what would that achieve? Nothing but heartaches for herself, she concluded.

Brisk footsteps across the front porch and through the parlor told her that Grandma Winnie was back, so she tried to force a bit of cheer onto her face. The last thing she needed was a lecture.

"Well, it certainly is a lovely morning." She stopped in the kitchen doorway. "Have you been sitting there the entire time that I've been gone?"

"I had a cup of coffee."

"Took you a mighty long time to drink it."

"I had two cups." She tried to smile.

"Hmpf. You've been sulking."

Lydia sighed, waiting for the impending, unwanted lecture.

"You are going to have to get over this melancholy, Lydia. It is not doing you one bit of good."

"Yes, Grandmother."

"Just because that man hasn't been around, you seem to think that this house can't be finished. Well, that's plain foolish. He isn't the only man who's handy with a hammer. What about that nice preacher who used to help you? Or why not enlist the help of some of the school boys? Surely, there must be at least a handful of them who would be capable."

"Yes—"

"And don't you 'yes, grandmother' me. I'm only trying to get you moving. It isn't like you to mope around like a sick cow. Perhaps I should have brought my tonic."

Lydia had to laugh. "No, you shouldn't have. That horrible stuff still gives me nightmares."

"Well, it always gave you some energy, if I remember correctly."

"Sure," she replied, nodding and smiling. "It made me run as fast as I could the other direction."

Winnie smiled back. "Was it really that bad?"

"Yes, it was. I never could understand why you liked to torture us with it."

"Torture! I believe you're exaggerating."

"Maybe I am." Just being able to smile seemed to ease her worries.

"I would have a cup of tea with you, but Opal and I must have gone through an entire teapot." She sat down across from Lydia and fidgeted absently with the glass that held a bouquet of wildflowers. "I probably shouldn't tell you this because I know it's going to upset you, but you'll most likely find out from Sarah or someone else anyway."

Lydia sat up straighter. "What is it?"

"Well, it seems that the boy, Daniel, is not living with his father. Sarah says Mr. Stockwell took him back to wherever it was he'd run away from, and Opal didn't dispute it, although Opal is not given to gossip the way her daughter is. Still, I have to put some merit on this since I can't say I've seen the boy in town at anytime.''

"He took Daniel back? Surely, you're mistaken. How could he do such a thing? Daniel wanted to stay with him. He loves his father. I could see it in his eyes.'' She was on her feet, pacing the floor feeling angry, more angry than she'd ever felt.

"Lydia, sit down here. It will do no good to work yourself up this way. Daniel is not your business. He is Mr. Stockwell's son.''

"Not my business! How can you say that? Any child who loses a parent, whether it be by death or abandonment, *is* my business! That's why I wanted Spring Meadows in the first place—to insure that all children have the right to a home, and Daniel's place is with his father. Why can't Nathan see that? Why is he being so pigheaded about this?''

"There must be more to the story than you know. A man doesn't abandon his son for no reason.''

"But what can it be?'' She sat down again, searching her grandmother's face as though she might find the answer there. "Daniel loves his father. And I know Nathan is capable of love. So what is the problem?''

"I can't answer that, child. I really can't.'' Winnie reached out to her, squeezing her hand in solace.

"No. I don't suppose anyone but Nathan can tell me that.'' She rose to her feet again.

"Wait.'' Winnie stood up, too. "I want you to promise me that you will not meddle in this.''

"I can't promise that, Grandma.'' They studied each other for a moment, both of them strong-willed and determined.

"I suppose I can't stop you either. But I want you to wait, to take a little time to think it through before you get yourself in a place that you might regret.'' Winnie's eyes beseeched Lydia to listen. ''Some things cannot be undone, and it's best to leave them alone.''

''I can't leave this alone. There is something wrong here. But I will take your advice and wait a while, although I'm not going to be able to wait for long.''

''Well, so be it. That's all I can hope for.'' She took Lydia's hand and patted it. ''Now, I have some other news that I hope you will like.''

If it didn't have something to do with Nathan and Daniel, she doubted if it would matter much to her, but she nodded for her to go on.

''I ordered new bedroom furniture for you and it's in town at the general store right now waiting to be delivered.'' Her smile was wide and proud.

''You what?'' She couldn't quite fathom the shift in topic, and floundered as she tried to grasp the meaning of what her grandmother had just said.

''Well, dear, the Graylings are going to need their furniture back since the new teacher is due into town within the next few weeks. I understand she is from someplace in the South and very anxious to begin her first year of teaching. And since I'm going to be leaving soon, I thought I would do this for you before I go. I do hope you like it. Consider it my contribution to Spring Meadows.''

''Grandma,'' was all she could say.

''I believe in you, Lydia, and what you're doing here. I know sometimes I can be rather contrary, but that's only because I worry about you. Grandmothers are entitled to do that, you know.''

''I'm speechless.''

''That's quite all right. I can tell by the look on your face that you appreciate my gesture.''

''I do. Really, I do. Thank you.'' She leaned down to

321

hug the older woman, who was so small and frail in spite of her bravado.

"I think we should go upstairs and remove your bedding and clothing in preparation for the new furniture to be moved in. The gentleman at the store said he didn't know when he would get a chance to bring it out, but if he couldn't then he would get someone else to do it."

While they were upstairs unpacking the chiffarobe and dresser, Sarah let herself her in the front door and stood at the bottom of the stairs and called up to them.

"Hello? Lydia, are you up there?"

Lydia looked over the railing and said, "Come on up. We're just packing." Then she went back to the bedroom to help her grandmother.

Within seconds Sarah stood at the doorway. "Are you moving, Lydia?" she asked, clearly upset.

"No. We're getting ready for the new bed grandmother ordered for me." She smiled over her shoulder at Sarah. "Wasn't that sweet of her?"

"That's what grandmothers are for," Winnie said, matter-of-factly while she folded a quilt.

"Now I can give your mother's furniture back to her," Lydia said, pulling the sheet off. "And I really appreciate the loan, but I'll tell her that when we have it delivered back to your house."

"Oh, dear." Sarah made a strange face. "But . . . well. I wasn't supposed to say anything, but I'm going to anyway. Mother wants you to keep it. She says it's her contribution to Spring Meadows. She also says you're going to have plenty of beds to buy as it is."

Lydia and Winnie stopped and stared at her.

"Oh, I can't accept a gift like that," Lydia said, overwhelmed by such generosity. Sarah shrugged. "I think you'll have to. The new furniture came in yesterday. Mr.

Stockwell brought it.'' She said his name softly as though she wasn't sure she ought to say it at all. "Mama was excited about having the new teacher come and she couldn't possibly take this bed away from you. She says it's more yours than hers and she wants you to keep it. I know she will insist on it.'' She shrugged again. "I guess you've got two beds now.''

"Well, I declare,'' Winnie said. "Opal is a mighty charitable woman.''

"So which room are you going to put the second bed in?'' Sarah asked, smiling.

"My goodness, I don't know,'' Lydia replied, dropping the sheet onto the bed and going to the hallway to look at the other doorways. "What do you think, Sarah?''

"Well, if I were a child who was going to live here, I'd be partial to the room over the porch. I know it isn't as big as the others, but it looks out on the street and someday the fence will be painted and have flowers blooming along the bottom, so I think it will have the prettiest view.''

Lydia listened to Sarah's voice the same dreams she'd had earlier, back when she believed that all of this could come true. A part of her wanted to continue dreaming, but another part said she ought to face reality. Even though she felt a measure of excitement over the much needed new additions of furniture to the house, she also wondered if these weren't just false hopes. The deadline loomed ever nearer, and the house was a long way from being finished. She knew she couldn't complete the project even if she had unlimited access to money and full-time help. Time had narrowed the prospects of meeting that deadline and deep in her heart she knew it.

"I'm not sure it matters anymore,'' Lydia said as she leaned against the framing around a window. Earlier, Nathan had rebuilt the beautiful old window with its arched glass.

"I can't believe my ears!" Sarah said. "You are not giving up. I won't allow it."

"Tell that to the council," she replied with a half-smile, half-grimace. "The deadline is bearing down on us as we speak."

"Well, then we'll get an extension. We'll borrow some money. We'll beg."

"We've managed to do one out of those three, and it hasn't been easy doing that."

"You cannot give up, Lydia Jefferson. What about those children who need a home?"

"Children like Daniel?" She had already discussed part of the story with Sarah, but only the part that concerned Daniel.

"Yes, and all the others who don't have any parents." She frowned in disappointment at her friend. "What has come over you?"

"Do you know that Nathan took his son back?"

Sarah nodded. "I know."

"Somehow I feel like, if I can't help Daniel, how can I help any other child? Do you know what I mean?"

"Not exactly. But maybe just a little." Then she softened her words. "Are you giving up on helping Daniel, too?"

Suddenly alert, Lydia felt as though someone had just given her a dose of Grandma Winnie's tonic. "No," she replied. And she realized that she couldn't give up on the boy, or his father. Both of them needed help, whether Nathan knew it or not.

"Good," Sarah said. "Now, why don't we move the furniture from your room into this one? Then your new furniture can go right into your room. Then later we'll put up wallpaper in here and I can sew some curtains with ruffles. After all, this is going to be a little girl's room, I just know it is.''

For the rest of the morning and into the afternoon, they struggled with moving the furniture after the clothing had been unloaded from it. While they positioned the bed Sarah talked nonstop about how they would make the room so sweet for the little girl who would sleep in it.

"There," she said, hands on hips as she surveyed everything. "If your bed doesn't arrive, you can always sleep in here until it does.''

Nathan drove the wagon with the furniture to Lydia's house, wishing he hadn't agreed to do it. But Jeff had asked him as a personal favor so how could he say no? If it had been anyone else, he would have. As it turned out, he'd put it off until the last possible moment, but that had been a mistake, too. He should have hauled the stuff out there immediately and gotten back to work. Instead, he'd thought all afternoon about having to see her again and ruined two perfectly good spokes for a new wagon.

Twilight barely scattered its remaining light while a low fog hung across the meadow behind her house. The air was cool and damp, but the heat from the day still radiated from the ground, giving the feel of an early fall. He smelled the wood smoke from her kitchen chimney and remembered the parlor stove the mayor had told him she could have. He didn't want to think about her freezing in that old house all winter, so he guessed he'd be hauling that, too.

He pulled up to the front gate, which still hadn't been fixed or painted, and felt a tremor of remorse. So much had happened that he'd never intended, beginning with the first day he'd come to work there right on up to the evening they'd spent in her bed. All of it had been a step away from reality. He'd allowed himself to feel things he never thought would be possible again, but he'd known deep in his gut that it couldn't last. He'd been a fool for letting any of it happen. The only thing he could do now was to unload the furniture and be on his way, forgetting all that had transpired between them. In the last couple of years, he'd gotten better at forgetting, so with a little more practice he should become an expert.

After braking the wagon, he jumped down and unloaded the wooden sections of a bed. Without thinking any further about whose bed it might be, he carried the sections to the front porch and leaned them against the house. Then he struggled with the dresser and finally got it on a skid to pull to the porch to unload. By this time, Lydia and her grandmother had arrived at the front door, holding it open but saying nothing while he worked. He was glad for the excuse not to speak since he hadn't come up with a reasonable greeting, so the awkward moment stretched longer as he tugged and shoved on the last piece.

"Good evening, Nathan," she said, but he gave her only a quick glimpse and a nod.

"Lydia," Winnie said, pulling on her granddaughter's arm. "Move aside so he can bring it in."

She continued to stand in the doorway, staring at him. "It looks like you're going to need some help."

"I can manage." He put the skid on the parlor floor and tried to maneuver the dresser over the hump of the threshold, but she stepped forward and got a grip on the end coming into the house.

"I'll help you."

He stopped long enough to stare at her across the top of it. Her eyes were darker than he remembered and something new shined in them that he couldn't quite comprehend so he ignored it.

"No. It's too heavy for you."

"Let me decide that. I'll be the judge of what I can handle."

He met her gaze steadily, and then he knew what that light was shining in her eyes, but he didn't want her sympathy or her understanding or anything else from her. She didn't know how it was with him, and that was the way it was going to stay.

But she went ahead and lifted her end of the dresser just enough to get it over the hump, and he was able to slide it inside. Then he busied himself again, getting it on the skid and letting her help because he couldn't keep her from doing it. After he pulled it to the bottom of the stairs, he wedged it off the skid and tipped it over on its side, and she was there ready to help again.

"You can't do that," he said sternly. "It's too heavy for you."

"When are you going to stop telling me what I can't do? I said I'm going to help so you may as well give in and accept it." She stood on the step, making her the same height as he was, so they were able to study each other eye to eye. He knew she wasn't going to listen, but he hated giving in.

"I have been handling furniture for a long time. I can keep on handling it," he said.

"I said I'm going to help you. Now what would be the most beneficial use of my help?"

He thought for a moment, then said, "Do you have an old quilt?"

"Yes, the one on my bed will do." And that brought a vivid memory to both of them of their night together on that same quilt. "I'll get it." Then she turned and hurried up the stairs and was back almost immediately.

They worked together at getting it under the dresser to protect it from the bumpy ride up the stairs. He instructed her to pull on the edge of the quilt while he shoved and for the most part it went smoothly. At the landing, he took over and she opened the door wide for him to get it inside her nearly empty room. Without lingering longer than was necessary, he set it in the place she indicated then went to bring up the bed sections. She followed him and carried the slats. When he put it together, she stood over him ready to help if he needed, which he didn't. And lastly, he carried up the mattress and flung it on top.

"Thank you," she said, and he nodded.

By now darkness had fallen completely so her grandmother retrieved a lamp. Lighting it, she hurried into another bedroom where she fussed with some linens, then brought them into Lydia's room.

"I guess that's it," Nathan said as a sort of farewell. Then leaving them to their work, he headed back down the stairs, but he heard her on the steps behind him.

"Wait. Wouldn't you like a drink? You must be thirsty after that," she said, pointing in the direction of the top of the stairs.

"I'll just get some water at the pump out here, if that's all right."

"Certainly. I'll bring you a cup."

"I can manage fine without one." And he went out the side door toward the pump with her following. A new moon cast very little light between the clouds, but he had no trouble locating it and began pumping a cool stream. He drank from his hands until his thirst was quenched then prepared to leave.

"Nathan. Please, stay." She stepped closer and he stepped back until he hit the pump handle.

"I'd better be going," he said, but he didn't move.

"I'd like to talk."

"There's nothing to talk about."

She studied his face in the dim light. "Yes, there is," she said softly.

He couldn't answer; he didn't want to answer.

"Why didn't you tell me about Daniel?"

He stiffened, bracing himself against the inevitable, yet still refused to bring up his painful past. "I don't want to talk about Daniel. He's none of your concern."

She reeled slightly from his words, then choked back a strangled half-laugh, half-cough in disbelief. "How can you say that? What do you think this house is all about? Don't you know my greatest desire is to help children?"

"Daniel doesn't need your help. I've seen to his welfare."

"How . . . by abandoning him? You call that looking after his welfare?"

He heard the rising anger in her voice and felt his own anger surface along with the guilt and the remorse. It tasted like bitter gall in his throat, and he tried to swallow it back but it burned a path straight to his heart. She had no idea what pain she was causing him. If she did she surely would let it go, and him, too.

"Nathan. Talk to me!" He saw the flash of fire in her eyes with the sudden appearance of the moonlight. Her hands were clenched at her sides as her body leaned forward in her earnest to drag his secret from him.

"Don't do this, Nathan. Don't do this to yourself. And don't do this to Daniel. He needs you."

Like a dam in disrepair that could no longer hold the force of the trapped water behind it, he felt all hell break loose within himself and was impotent to stop it. He could neither speak nor shout as the pent-up energy of his guilt consumed him, threatening to make him burst. Suddenly he grasped the pump handle beside him and with one violent shove he watched the water spew out. He shoved it again and let it flow. Then using both hands he worked the handle until it gushed, splashing water into the pan set under the spout, spilling over and flooding the area. With each push on the handle he gritted his teeth and the muscles in his arms bunched and knotted with the force, and the air was filled with the sound of *clink-clank, clink-clank, clink-clank*. Water splashed in a wide arc, dampening his shoes and his pant legs, then broadening out farther until he stood in a pond of it, but he didn't quit. He couldn't quit. Down and up and down and up, he worked the handle until sweat beaded his brow, but still he kept on pushing, and pushing. Until finally, he felt numb. Then he let the handle fall against the pump casing with one last *clink*.

Lydia stood by, helplessly watching his torment. With one hand covering her mouth, she held back the need to cry for the anguish he suffered, wishing she could do something to ease his pain. What could have done this to him? she wondered. Her own heart hurt to see him this way, and she reached out to him but he didn't see her. With his anger finally spent and his head hung low, one hand came up to cover his face.

She walked toward him until she stood in the same puddle that he did. Then she reached up to take his hand, pulling it down so she could see him.

"Nathan," she whispered, her voice hoarse with emotion. "Let me help you. Please." Then the tears streamed unheeded down her cheeks. "Please. I only want to help you."

Suddenly, he reached out his arm and pulled her close in stranglehold and she felt a shudder run through him as first one sob then another gripped him. His pain filled her as she wrapped her arms around his waist and held him tight. Whatever it was, he couldn't bear it and neither could she so they clung to each other for comfort and support.

When finally it passed, she felt his hand press against her hair, smoothing it until both of them were calm at last, but still she clutched him tightly to her. They stood like that for a long time, unaware of anything but each other. Then he took her chin and raised it up so that he could look into her eyes.

"There is nothing good in this story," he said, his voice low and almost harsh. "Are you sure you want to hear it?"

She nodded and a fresh flow of tears streaked down her face.

He pulled her close again, smoothing her hair as if she were the one who needed the comforting. Then with his lips so close to her ear that he had only to whisper to be heard, he began to tell his story. With her eyes shut tight, she listened, wishing she could erase the pain from his memory but knowing she couldn't.

Six years ago he was a happy man with a wife and three beautiful children, but one day a part of his life was destroyed. His voice became a monotone as he spoke of the horror he'd been through.

"We lived on the other side of Cincinnati, had a little farm of our own, but Anna never liked being so far from town. She was frightened of almost everything. She missed living in town and she hated it whenever I was gone. Every time a stranger rode through, she would hide the children in the barn in a cubbyhole that nobody but them could find. But I didn't take her fears seriously. I didn't see any reason for it."

He stopped for a moment, then went on.

"That summer I knew the crops weren't doing well, so I took a job with the wheelwright in the little crossroads town about ten miles away. She tried not to be afraid because she knew I didn't understand. I didn't even try to understand. All I could think about was making sure we had enough money so we could get by. And sometimes I was angry with her for being so childish. She wanted to sell and move back to Cincinnati but I refused to listen.''

Lydia felt the tension in his body as his arms gripped her and his hand stilled in her hair.

"Then one day, after I'd gone into town to work, leaving her all alone with the children . . . something happened. A man rode in and she sent the children to the barn out the back door. Exactly what followed I'll never know . . . but when I got home I couldn't find her. I couldn't find anybody. The cookstove was cold but there was food burnt in the pan. I called and called, but nobody answered. Daniel and James and little Annie didn't come out either. I tore the barn apart looking for them, hoping they were just too scared to move. Nothing. So I rode into the countryside, nearly out of my mind. By now I knew that something terrible had happened to all of them. I knew my life was over if I didn't find them. Then after hours of wandering back and forth across the countryside, I found her.''

"Oh, Nathan," Lydia cried. "I'm so sorry." She buried her face against his chest, feeling his pain.

"She'd been badly beaten. And worse. Her clothes were torn. . . .''

"Shhh. Don't say anymore. Don't torture yourself like this.''

"I took her home. Then I fell completely apart. It was all my fault. I should have listened to her. I should have been there to protect her. If I had—''

"Stop it!" Lydia looked up at him. "You cannot blame yourself for what an evil, sick man did to her.''

"You're wrong. I have to blame myself. I'm the only one who could have saved her, if I'd been there.''

"No! You can't carry that kind of guilt. Believe me, I know. The death of someone you love is hard enough without feeling that somehow you could have prevented it. But you couldn't. Nobody can give that kind of protection twenty-four hours a day.'' She had so many arguments to offer him, but hardly knew where to begin. Then clutching the front of his shirt, she said the only thing she could think of: "You have to forgive yourself. You have to."

He placed a hand on each side of her face as though searching for an answer. She wished she could give him that forgiveness, but all she had to offer was love, pure, unconditional love.

"Why are you trying so hard to help me?" he asked.

"Because I love you. And I know you could never be the cause of Anna's death. Never."

He pulled her to him, crushing her in his embrace. While they stood quietly she willed her love to seep into him, hoping now as he'd told her everything, that he could begin to heal and allow himself to be forgiven, to be free of the guilt he should never have accepted. And she sensed a change in his stance, felt him relax in her returning embrace.

"I love you," she said again, and a feeling of calm descended on both of them.

For the first time in years, Nathan experienced the lifting of his burden. His mind seemed clearer, more alert than it had been for so long. She was right: He needed to let go of the past, and he needed to look to the future. He'd lived in the present, not caring about tomorrow, and regretting the past, but no more. Suddenly, he felt drained. He was ready to put the last six years behind him, to forget the year of depression and drinking, to let go of the self-recrimination and despair, and to stop rejecting himself as an unworthy father. It was time to move on; it was time to accept that what was done was done. He could not change it. He could only accept it.

He lifted her face so that he could see her eyes and kissed her lightly. "I love you," he said, and she smiled up at him, making him feel even lighter. "There's more I want to say, but the words just aren't there."

"I'm satisfied," she said. "I can wait."

"I just need a little time to get used to this . . . this feeling of being free."

"I know."

"Tomorrow. I'll bring Daniel back. James and little Annie, too."

Her eyes slid closed in thanksgiving and she sighed. "They're all right, thank goodness. I was afraid to ask about James and little Annie. I didn't want to put you through any more than—"

He touched his lips to hers. "They're fine. Somehow they'd managed to stay hidden until almost dark. And the last sensible thing I did was to take them to my brother's before I completely lost control of my life. But now, I've got that back again and I want them with me. With us."

She smiled broadly as the realization of those last two words sunk in. "Bring them home. We need them."

"Is that a yes?" he asked, smiling at her.

"If that was a proposal, then that was a yes."

"This is to seal it." He touched his lips to hers gently, to seal his vow of love, and she accepted it, returning the kiss with a vow of her own.

Chapter Twenty-three

Mayor Butterfield sat at the table with the usual fried mush in front of him, only this time he pushed it aside. He'd had enough of sneaking around, harboring food in his tiny office and eating in secret like a man without a home. He had a home and he had a kitchen, and he damned well had had enough of mush.

"Agnes, I will not tolerate this slop for one minute more." He rose from the table and marched to the kitchen, leaving a smug Mrs. Butterfield behind. But when he started rebuilding the fire in the cookstove, clanking lids, doors and dampers, she was instantly on her feet.

"What on earth do you think you're doing?" she asked as she stood beside him.

"Cooking."

"You can't cook."

"Watch me." He grabbed a skillet from one those that hung neatly on hooks and it clattered on top of the stove.

"But . . . but you'll ruin my—"

"I won't ruin anything. Now, stand back. A man has to eat and he has the right to do so in his own home." He found the small crock of bacon grease and poured a puddle into the skillet. Then he searched the pantry for a couple of handfuls of potatoes, plopping them into a granite pan.

"You're making a mess!"

He turned to give her a warning stare, saying, "I'll damn well make a mess if I want to."

"You can't talk to me like that!"

"Then get out of the kitchen." He found a peeler and proceeded to make short work of the skins. Then he sliced each potato and tossed the whole pile into the hot skillet, enjoying the sound of sizzling and frying. He would cook them until they were crisp and brown—just thinking about it made his mouth water. Returning to the pantry, he found the onions and selected the largest one, which he sliced into thick pieces and added to the potatoes. The aroma was absolutely, most definitely the best he'd ever inhaled. After adding a sprinkling of salt and a dash of pepper, he quickly flipped them over to begin browning on the other side.

"I didn't know you could do that," she said, her amazement apparent in her voice.

Turning toward her, he replied, "You don't give me credit for very much, do you, Agnes?"

"Why, I don't know what you're talking about."

"Yes, you do."

She stared at him open mouthed.

"You think you can control everything I do. Well, I'm here to tell *that* has come to an end," he said, feeling quite good about putting his foot down and wondering why he hadn't done it sooner. "You've tried to entice the ladies of your club to do your bidding," he went on. "And you think you are the one with the power over the council, but you are wrong.'' He marched into the pantry and retrieved a handful of eggs, which he set in a dish on the counter of the baking cupboard.

''I don't know what you are talking about,'' she repeated.

''Yes, you do,'' he said again. Then he took a loaf of bread from the bread box and sliced three thick sections, which he buttered. He flipped the potatoes over once more and dribbled a little more bacon grease across them.

''How did you learn to cook like that?'' she asked, eyeing him suspiciously.

''By watching you, my dear.'' He cracked the eggs and dumped the contents into another bowl, whipping them with a fork. ''I'm not at all the imbecile you think I am.''

''I never thought you were,'' she said, suddenly looking sorry for having treated him so badly.

He gave her a quick glance and stirred his potatoes. ''I'm glad to see your change of heart, my dear. But I don't believe it will last for very long. So that is why I am taking matters into my own capable hands and cooking my own supper.'' He scraped the potatoes aside, then went to the icebox where he retrieved a hunk of ham, which he laid on the empty space in the skillet.

''That looks more like breakfast to me,'' she replied lamely.

''It's whole lot better to eat breakfast for supper than to eat that unpalatable mush.'' He turned the ham over and scorched the other side then scraped the potatoes on top of it. Finding a trivet, he quickly lifted the skillet onto it away from the heat. Then he selected another skillet, poured bacon grease into it and when it was skittering hot, he added the whipped eggs.

She glanced around at the mess he'd made in her lovely

clean kitchen. "I don't suppose you're going to clean this up."

"Oh, of course, I am. I'm in charge so I'll take care of the details. You have nothing to worry about anymore. Nothing at all."

"Hmpf." And she left the kitchen.

He whistled a tune while he searched for a dish large enough to hold his supper. Sometimes a man had to step beyond the usual duties in order to take control of a situation, and he had taken that first step. Furthermore, he liked the new position. And it wasn't going to stop with just cooking his own meals.

Agnes called another emergency meeting of the M.M.C.C. the next day, but nobody came. She sat in her parlor while the lemon meringue pies cooled in the kitchen, wondering what had gone wrong. Her only intention had been to create a better community and to preserve the well-being of the same. Apparently, she was alone in her endeavor. Sitting with her hands folded in her lap, she stared at the spotless floor and thought about all the things that had changed over the summer. If the truth be told, she'd felt like a harridan as she'd forced the mayor to partake of food she wouldn't wish on herself. There had been no satisfaction at all in trying to gain the upper hand, and she shouldn't be so surprised that she was sitting alone. Her need to control had suddenly left her, so what was she to do now?

She rose from her chair and walked about the lovely room, wiping her finger along the surfaces of tables and the backs of chairs. Clean. But she knew they would be since her entire time was taken up with being spotless. She had enjoyed her moment of glory, but that was all over. There was little she could do other than clean, cook and organize, and all of those things were done. Of course, she had spent a fair amount of time minding other people's business, although she'd never called it that, but she had to admit that was exactly what she'd done.

In the kitchen she cut a wedge of pie and put it on a plate, then tasted it. Well, she was a good cook, she told herself. Actually, she was an excellent cook but nobody seemed to care, not even the mayor. Perhaps if she'd had children, a daughter or two, she could enjoy teaching them the culinary art she'd perfected over her lifetime, but that hadn't happened and it was useless to fantasize about a daughter at her age. She supposed she could offer to teach other girls, but then they all had mothers to do that and she would only be minding someone else's business again.

Then a new thought struck her and she nearly choked on the tart lemon pie. What if . . . what if there were young girls at the orphanage someday who would like to learn? Orphans did not have mothers, and certainly, Miss Jefferson couldn't possibly take on such a task if she did indeed manage to fill up that old house with children. The idea was so startling that she put down her dish and found herself a chair. If she were to do such a thing, why she'd have no trouble at all helping two or even three young girls discover the art of cooking. She had all the necessary equipment, in fact, it was the newest and latest. But it would take swallowing a large dose of pride. She could do that, she told herself. It wouldn't be easy, but it would be necessary.

She said it out loud. "I can do this." And the room echoed it back to her.

She wouldn't act on the idea right away. She'd take her time. After all, there were no young girls in the home yet anyway. Now what was the name of that home going to be? Oh, yes, Spring Meadows. The more she let the idea simmer, the more she knew she wanted to do it—but not yet. She would wait until the right moment came along, and then she would speak to Miss Jefferson. And certainly, her offer wouldn't be turned down. She just knew it wouldn't.

Lydia hummed as she ran the iron over the last dampened skirt in her basket.

"You certainly have been in a good mood for the last two days. Is there something I ought to know about?" Winnie asked as she bent over the torn stocking she was mending.

"Oh, there might be," Lydia replied, then turned the skirt and chose a fresh iron.

"I figured as much. It wouldn't have anything to do with Mr. Stockwell, would it?"

"Could be." And she gave her grandmother a quick glance before ironing more wrinkles out of the black material.

"Lydia, I insist that you tell me what is going on." Winnie laid down her mending to focus on the problem at hand. The torn stockings she'd found in her granddaughter's drawer could wait until this worrisome matter was solved.

"Well, I suppose it isn't fair not to tell you." She turned the skirt and continued to iron.

"Of course it's not fair. Now, put down that iron and come over here so we can talk face-to-face."

"I'm almost finished," she replied, continuing to iron the last section of the skirt. She did want to talk about Nathan, the children and his proposal. As a matter of fact she'd nearly burst with the need to talk to someone. But she had kept it to herself, not wanting to say anything until Nathan arrived back in Peaceful Valley with the children. The last thing the children needed was to have gossip floating around about them, and she wasn't fond of being the topic of conversation either. So with his return imminent, she felt safe telling her grandmother about the events of two nights ago, or at least part of what happened.

"Then I'll come to you." She rose stiffly from her chair, and Lydia noticed the effort.

"Stay there, Grandma Winnie. I'm nearly done and I'll be ready to sit in a minute. How about some tea? We could have a cup while we talk."

"I'm up now," she grumbled. "So I might as well make the tea while you finish. But it seems as though you could talk while you work and enlighten me on this new whatever-it-is."

Lydia smiled at her, feeling more indulgent of her contrariness than usual. When the skirt was finally finished, she left it draped over the board to cool while she sat with her grandmother at the table.

"Are we ready now?" Winnie asked.

"Yes." Lydia leaned forward with her arms folded on the table, excited to share the news at last. "Nathan is bringing the children home today."

"Children? I thought there was only Daniel." Her pot of tea was suddenly forgotten.

"Well, as it turns out, he has three children. Daniel, James and little Annie."

"My word!" For once she was speechless, but Lydia knew it was temporary so she hurried on with the rest of her news.

"Grandma." She placed her hand over her grand-mother's. "He's asked me to marry him. And I said yes."

Winnie studied Lydia's smiling face, the warmth that seemed to flow from her and a serenity that hadn't been there when she'd first arrived. "I don't know what to say," she told her. "I only know that I want you to be happy."

"I am, more than I've ever been. And believe me I've

been quite happy in the past, growing up with such a wonderful family to call my own. I've been very blessed. And I want the same for other children who have been less fortunate. I hope I will be able to be as good a mother for Nathan's children as Irene was for me and Jonathan.''

Winnie returned the gesture of patting Lydia's hand in reassurance. ''There is no doubt in my mind that you'll do just fine.''

''I hope so. But it isn't going to be easy, I know. The children have been through a terrible experience.'' She shuddered when she thought of how they'd hid themselves and being so small, how frightened they must have been.

''You mean being away from their father,'' Winnie said, her voice still disapproving of him.

''No, it's worse than that, Grandma.'' Then she told her the story, leaving out all of Nathan's personal, emotional suffering and only telling the rudimentary facts of Anna's death. By the time she'd finished, Winnie was clearly shaken.

''Oh, my dear, how awful for those children.'' She sat staring at her hands where she rested them on the table. ''It sounds very much like a story I'd heard from our Janie. I don't suppose you remember hearing it, do you?'' Lydia shook her head. ''A very dear friend of Janie's had moved to a small farm with her husband and three children. . . .'' Her voice faded away and she stared up at Lydia. ''Stockwell.''

''Aunt Janie knew Anna?''

''I thought there was something familiar about him, but it was only his name.'' She sat silent for awhile. ''I remember the story now. So tragic. Those poor children.''

''I know.'' Lydia said thoughtfully. ''I hope I can give them the kind of home that will take away some of their pain. At least ease it a little. And of course, they will have their father again and that should make all the difference."

"You'll do fine," Winnie said, smiling encouragingly. "Now, tell me about this wedding."

"Wedding?"

"You said he proposed," she said, looking confused.

"He did, but I don't think either of us want a wedding."

Winnie stared in disbelief at her granddaughter. "I don't even want to hear of anything less than a real wedding."

"Grandma, we haven't talked about it, but I'm sure Nathan feels the same as I do. Just saying our vows before Preacher Ted is all we need."

"The Baptist church? But, dear, we are Presbyterian."

"Ted is our friend."

"Your mother will want a wedding, too, you know."

"Hmm. I distinctly remember a conversation very similar to this one when she married Ross. And they weren't even married in a church."

"You aren't considering the backyard, too, are you? Oh, Lydia! A church wedding is so beautiful and I missed that so much when Irene got married. I know, it all turned out quite nice, but I want you to have a church wedding, dear."

"Grandma, don't get so upset. Nathan and I haven't talked about the details."

Winnie sighed. "You girls will be the death of me yet."

Lydia laughed and patted her grandmother's hand. "It isn't that bad. Cheer up. At least you won't have to worry about me being alone anymore."

"Well, there is consolation in that, I admit."

They talked through two cups of tea, discussing whether she ought to send a telegram immediately to her mother and her aunts in Cincinnati. The final decision was to wait until after Nathan and the children had arrived.

For the rest of the day, Lydia finished up the laundry, and then she and her grandmother baked bread and a few pastries. With the house being nearly bare it was easy to keep clean, so when they finished washing the last dish there was nothing to do but sit down and wait. But they didn't have to wait long.

Nathan's wagon pulled up out front and Lydia heard it first. Hurrying to the door, with Grandma Winnie behind her, she stepped out on the porch to catch her first glimpse of his family all together. Daniel stood up and waved at her, and she waved back as her heart thumped in anticipation of a similar response from the other two. But James only stared while little Annie, beribboned and ruffled, gave her a shy smile. Nathan helped them out, taking Annie's hand, and Daniel led the way with James falling slightly behind.

"Hello," Nathan said to Lydia, and she felt his smile go clear to the depth of her soul.

"Hello." She desperately wanted to wrap her arms around him in welcome, but knew it would not be the right time with the children still unsure of who she was.

"This is Daniel. He's ten," Nathan said.

"We've already met, Pa," Daniel said. "But it's nice to meet you again." He reached out and shook her hand, bowing slightly. He was remarkably cleaner and dressed tidily in a jacket and long pants. His hair looked freshly cut, as did James's and Nathan's, too.

"This is James. He's nine."

James stepped forward with a little help from his father, and the wary look in his eye reminded her so much of her brother Jonathan at that age that her heart went out to him immediately.

"Hello, James."

"I'm very glad to make your acquaintance, ma'am," he said in an obviously rehearsed speech.

"The pleasure is all mine," she replied with heartfelt sincerity.

"And this is little Annie. She's seven."

There was little resemblance between the child and her father since Annie had blond hair and deep blue eyes, so Lydia knew she must favor her mother. She wore a large white bow in the back of her hair, where rows of sausage curls cascaded.

Annie dropped a quick curtsy and said, "Hello, Miss Lydia." Then she smiled, showing a space where two front teeth were missing.

"What a lovely dress that is," Lydia said.

"Thank you. My daddy bought it for me. I like it, too." She sidled a little closer to Nathan and gave him an adoring glance. Not once had she let go of his hand, not even for a second.

"I have some lemonade and pastries, if you would all like to come in," Lydia said, nearly bumping backward into her grandmother. Then she realized she'd forgotten to introduce Winnie in her eagerness to meet Nathan's children. "Oh, where are my manners?" She looped her arm though her grandmother's, holding her close. "This is my grandmother. You can call her Grandma Winnie if you like."

"Welcome, children," Winnie said, and Lydia heard the catch in her voice. "Please, everyone come in." As they all filed past with Nathan coming in last, she smiled at him and said in greeting, "Nathan, it's nice to see you again."

"Thank you, Mrs. Stephens. It's very good to be back."

Letting her grandmother lead the way to the kitchen, Lydia lagged behind while she shared a glance with Nathan, trying to put as much of her feelings into that one look as she could. It was wonderful to see him so light and burden-free, and she'd noticed it immediately when he'd walked down the path to the house. Seeing him like this made her own heart feel light.

"Can you come to my house later?" he whispered. "After the children are in bed. I need to see you."

She nodded and smiled. They had so much to discuss, so much to plan that she could hardly wait to begin.

Lydia walked the distance to Nathan's enjoying the coolness that went along with the end of summer. Around her the locusts blended in an unusual harmony with the whippoorwills and the frogs down at the river, filling the air with a new kind of song. The days had become a little shorter, but the night was perfect for a walk, especially when it took her to Nathan.

She stepped up to the back door and knocked lightly and he opened it immediately.

"I've been waiting," he said, stepping outside and pulling her to him. The light from the kitchen behind him caused his face to be in shadow, but she knew from his voice he was smiling at her. With her in his arms, he side-stepped to stand under a vine that grew alongside the door.

"This is convenient," she said. "Did you plant this?"

"No, but lucky for us that someone did." Then he kissed her softly.

"Mmm. Lucky for us," she replied, her voice as languorous as her muscles.

"Tell me what you did after we left," he said, nibbling on her neck.

"Thought about you." She tipped her head, arching so he had more access.

"I thought about you, too," he replied, between light kisses that were making her dizzy.

"Are the children asleep?"

"Mmm. Almost."

She let him find her lips and press them with his own until she felt seared to her toes. Then she pushed at him until he raised his head. "I'm thinking we ought to go a little slower."

"I'm thinking just the opposite." But she kept a steady pressure on his shoulders until he acquiesced. "All right," he sighed. "It's just that I haven't been able to quit thinking about you."

She smiled. "That's very reassuring."

"And I was hoping you felt the same way."

"You know I do, but if one of the children comes out and finds us . . . well, I don't think that should happen."

He tipped his head forward until it touched hers. "You're right."

"They're beautiful, Nathan."

He smiled. "They are, aren't they?"

She nodded, making his head nod along with hers. "Are they doing fine? I mean, they seemed like they were. Do they know about us yet?" He leaned back against the house, relaxing, then pulled her against him with his arms looped around her waist.

"It's going to take some time, but I think for the most part they're doing pretty well. James is my only concern. He seems so distant, but I guess I can't blame him."

"Give him time, and lots of affection. That will make all the difference, you'll see."

He sighed. "I hope so."

"Did you tell them about us?" she asked again, worrying a little about the answer he might give her.

"Yes. Daniel is all for it, Annie thinks you're pretty, and James . . . well, he just doesn't say much about anything."

She touched a finger to his lips. "Don't worry. We'll win him over together. You'll see."

He kissed her finger, then said, "You have an unbeliev-

347

able amount of love inside of you. I don't know where it comes from, but I'm glad it's there.''

"It comes from my heart." She smiled up at him.

He leaned down and kissed her deeply, stirring her emotions and rekindling the passion she'd felt that night of the storm. When he stopped, she said, "When are we going to say our vows? I have to warn you, I don't know how long I can wait.''

"Is tomorrow too soon?" he asked.

"Not soon enough." She pulled him down to her and returned his kiss until they were both shaken from the intensity of it. Afterward, they stood forehead to forehead, breathing heavily, feeling the heat of their passion.

"I'll talk to Ted tomorrow," he said, his voice low and husky with emotion. "Whenever he can do it.''

"Good."

"Unless you want a wedding—"

"No. Just our vows. With the children present, and Grandma Winnie.''

He nodded, feeling calmer now. She took a deep breath, feeling calmer, too.

"Whose house are we going to live in?" she asked.

"Yours. It's bigger. I'll sell this one and we can use the money to finish yours.''

"Ours." She smiled at the idea and he smiled with her.

"There's something else I have to tell you," he said, and the tone of his voice sobered her instantly.

"What?"

"Before I went after the children, Jeff told me there's going to be another council meeting. About Spring Meadows.''

"What? They can't do that! The time isn't up yet. Nathan, they want to take Spring Meadows away from me. How can I stop them?" She had let the worry over the deadline slip from her mind since she had so many other pressing emotional matters to tend to, but now she had to focus on this problem. She had to fight back!

"I don't know what's going to happen, but I'll do what I can." He lifted her chin and looked into her eyes. "I promise."

"When is the meeting going to be?"

"Tomorrow night."

"Oh, no. That's so soon. I'll never be able to—"

"Shhh. I'll be there with you." He kissed her lightly. "I'll always be there with you, from now on."

She searched his eyes and found only love reflected in them. "Shall we seal that with a kiss?" He smiled, then covered her lips with his, once more melding their souls together.

Chapter Twenty-four

Mayor Butterfield pounded his gavel three times before anyone paid him any heed.

"See here, now! This meeting shall be called to order!" He smacked his gavel once more and everybody quieted. "That's more like it." He cleared his throat and pinched the ends of his waxed moustache.

Lydia sat beside Nathan while her heart thumped loudly in her chest. Daniel, Annie, James and Grandma Winnie squeezed into the row with them. She reached for Nathan's hand, holding it beside her in the folds of her skirt, and tried to feel reassured by the return grip he gave her. Around them, the room was packed to bursting with everyone from inside the town as well as a few outside. They stood two or more deep around the perimeter of the schoolhouse and some had even gone outdoors to listen through the windows. The Graylings were all there, sitting near the front along with Cora Davis, Penelope Chase and of course,

Agnes Butterfield. She saw Hattie Arthur, Lila Petersen, Carrie Marting and Ted. She had come to know more of the townspeople in the last three months than she had in the last three years, but at the moment she couldn't spare them any attention since her focus was solely on the mayor and the council members.

"As you know we are here tonight concerning the old Mercer house, which has been renamed Spring Meadows Children's Home. And as you also know the selling of that property came with stipulations of complete renovation by a specific date or the property reverts back to the town."

Hattie Arthur stood up and interrupted the mayor. "Excuse me, Mayor Butterfield, but isn't this bein' a little hasty? I mean it isn't even September yet. You can't take back the rules after you've already laid them out. That ain't fair."

"If you will let me finish—" he began, but was quickly cut off.

"Mayor, if I might say something." Ted stood up and looked around the room. "I don't know what it is that you're about to say, but if you've decided that Miss Jefferson must forfeit the house, then I have to ask you to reconsider. There has never before been such a united effort in our community toward a charitable institution, and we owe that unity to Lydia. I don't think I have ever seen such devotion to a cause by one woman. There is a lot of good that can come from having Spring Meadows here in Peaceful Valley—as a matter of fact some of that has already happened. Just look at the socials and benefits that have brought more of us together."

Before he could go on, Lila Peterson rose to her feet and took the floor away from him. "I was one of those who was skeptical about having a woman trying to start an orphanage, especially since it was right next door to my

351

house. But I have to say that I've changed my mind. I don't recall seeing any woman work harder toward what she believed in than Miss Jefferson has. If we were taking votes on this, I'd vote that she should stay.''

Lydia could hardly believe what she was hearing. The town that hadn't wanted anything to do with orphans now championed her idea, and their vocal support brought tears to her eyes. She glanced quickly around the room at the people who nodded in agreement with those that stood in her defense, and she said a silent thank you to each of them. Then Nathan let go of her hand and stood up while her heart nearly burst with love for him.

"Mayor," he began. "I'd like to add something. I've worked with Lydia and I know what her goals are, and I also know she's capable of reaching them. I'd also like to say that I'm as committed to those goals as she is, and if it makes any difference, you have my promise that the house will be completed before hard winter sets in." Then he sat down, smiled at Lydia and took her hand and squeezed it. Without caring if anyone was watching, she silently mouthed the words, I love you.

"Well," Mayor Butterfield said, looking over the large crowd. "I might as well listen to more testimonials, although I don't see the need for it."

A heavy silence hung like fog and nobody offered another word.

"All right then. What I was going to say seems to have just been said by all of you, so I will make this short so we can all go home. Miss Jefferson may keep the house. The deadline and other stipulations have been removed."

A stunned silence was quickly replaced by a round of applause and those sitting around her suddenly converged to shake her hand and offer congratulations. She was barely able to get to her feet as the crowd pressed in on her.

Grandma Winnie grabbed her, hugged her tight and said, "I'm so happy for you, Lydia. You have your dream now." Lydia returned the hug, brimming with happiness.

"Thank you, Grandma."

"Oh, Lydia!" Sarah said, giving her shoulders a squeeze. "I'm so happy for you. I knew you could do it."

"Congratulations, dear," Opal said.

Lydia thanked all who wished her success and offered their help. She couldn't stop smiling and laughing, and feeling overwhelmed with the council's decision.

Then she looked up to find Ted and Carrie waiting their turn among the well-wishers. But she spoke to him first.

"Thank you for all that you've done, and for Spring Meadows. You are a dear friend." And she meant it with all her heart.

He smiled and leaned forward to kiss her cheek. Then he said, "I hope my wife won't mind." His smile crinkled his eyes as he took Carrie's arm in his, and his bride blushed a becoming pink that almost matched the deep rose of her dress.

Surprised by the news, Lydia said, "My goodness! Congratulations to you both. Now, tell me, when did this happen?"

"Early last week," he said, still smiling. "We slipped away to Cincinnati."

Nathan shook his hand in congratulations. "We're glad you're back."

Then the crowd crushed in further and Ted and Carrie faded back out of sight as others took their place. It was a long time before Lydia and Nathan could finally leave the schoolhouse. Grandma Winnie had long since gone home. When at last they were outside in the cool night air, there were three very tired children who needed to be taken home.

"I'll walk with you," Lydia said.

"I'd like that," he replied, lifting Annie so that he could carry her.

They took the straightest path from the school to Nathan's house and at one point along the way, Daniel slipped his hand into hers. She turned to look at him as her heart overflowed with happiness.

"Is that the school where we'll be going?" he asked.

"Yes, it is," she replied.

"Are you going to be our teacher?" asked a very sleepy Annie. "Daddy said you're a schoolteacher."

"No, dear. That's not my job anymore."

"Are you going to take care of us now?" Annie asked.

"Would you like me to?"

"We have to have somebody take care of us while Daddy is working. And I like you a whole lot." She yawned and cuddled against her father's neck.

"Me, too," Daniel said. Then he tugged on her arm, pulling Lydia down so he could whisper in her ear. "Don't worry about James. He'll come around. He just thinks he's a tough kid."

"I do not!" James said, taking a stand.

"James and I will get along just fine." Then turning to James, she said, "As a matter of fact, you remind me a lot of my brother Jonathan. He's the best brother in the whole world."

James looked thoughtful then replied, "Not better than Daniel."

"Well, now you might be right. I'll just bet Daniel is as fine a brother as you'll find anywhere."

"He's the best brother anywhere," James said, and having gotten that off his chest, he seemed less defiant.

When they reached Nathan's house, Lydia went inside and waited in the kitchen while the children got ready for bed. She hoped it wouldn't be too long before they accepted her and let her be a part of their nighttime rituals, but she would be patient. Then Nathan came to the doorway, smiling.

"Would you like to say good night to them? Annie asked for you."

"She did?" And she thought maybe her prayer had already been answered. She walked behind Nathan through the little house to the room that should have been a parlor but had become a bunkhouse. Pallets on the floor were strewn in different directions so that she had to step around carefully.

"Good night, Miss Jefferson," said Daniel.

"Good night," James echoed quickly.

But Annie wasn't satisfied with a simple good night. She scrambled from her makeshift bed and threw her arms around Lydia's neck, squeezing her tight. "Good night, Lydia." And she nearly cried when she heard Annie call her by name.

"Good night, dear." Then Annie bounded across the others and slipped inside the sheet.

"Sleep well, all of you." Lydia spoke softly because her throat had constricted with tears and those were the only words she could get out.

Nathan carried the lamp back to the kitchen and set it on the table, then led her by the hand out the back door. Instantly, she went into his arms, unmindful if any neighbors were watching. She needed his strength around her, needed to feel his love for her. So much had happened that she could hardly take it all in, and yet, there was so much to come. She sighed as his arms held her close.

"It looks like you have your house."

"We have *our* house," she corrected, and smiled at the sound of it.

"I suppose you'll be wanting a bathing closet for sure now," he teased.

"And a furnace," she replied, teasing him back.

"I suppose you still want to buy the meadow, too."

"That might be asking too much, so I'll let that one pass."

"Wouldn't you know," he said. "The one thing I can give you and you don't want it."

She raised her head and stared at him through the dim lamplight that came from the kitchen. "It's yours?"

He nodded. "I bought the section of it behind the house. I thought it would be something I could leave to the children someday. I guess they'll get to use it now."

"Nathan. Why didn't you tell me? That's wonderful!" She kissed him then leaned back to study him. "You aren't teasing me, are you?"

"No. The meadow is ours," he said, smiling at her.

She circled his neck with her arms and pulled him close. "You are full of surprises."

"And you haven't seen half of them yet," he said just before putting his lips on hers.

"Mmm." Then breaking away, she said, "That's a nice beginning."

"Come here."

She smiled and met him halfway, promising a few surprises of her own.

Epilogue

Lydia sat in front of the parlor stove, her mending in her lap, enjoying the warmth of the fire on their first really cold November night. So many things had happened since that council meeting in August that she felt especially blessed as she went over them in her mind. They had completed nearly all of the house except for a few of the bedrooms, and come spring those would be finished, too. The outside hadn't yet been painted but she didn't mind. In time they would get it done. At least there was a new picket fence as pristine as the front porch, with a new gate that the children enjoyed swinging on. There was only one thing that made her feel sad and that was when Sarah had gone off to nursing school. She knew it was what Sarah wanted but she missed her just the same. Then she smiled as she thought about the mysterious vegetables that had shown up on her back door until the first killing frost. Nobody had come forward to take the credit, and she'd never gone asking, but then one day she'd caught sight of Lila Peterson slipping away from Spring Meadows' kitchen door and her mystery was solved.

Lydia sighed with contentment and glanced around the parlor.

Nathan sat at a small table playing a board game with Daniel, and both of them had studious frowns on their faces. James was stretched out on the carpet staring up at the ceiling with his hands stacked behind his head. He seemed to be a million miles away. She still had trouble getting him to open up his thoughts to her, but most of the time he was willing to listen and to talk, as long as it wasn't too serious—then he shied away. So she didn't push, but gave him plenty of private thinking time, which he seemed to need more of than the other two.

Annie had her dollies lined up on the settee, pretending they were having a tea party. She was a real joy for Lydia, so free with her hugs and smiles. Her laughter and giggles could be heard all over the house when one of the boys teased and chased her. There seemed to be no end to the love that she had to give. She never tattled or taunted, and always kept loyal silence if one of her brothers got into trouble. They knew they could count on her.

And then there was the new addition to their family, Benjamin. Orphaned at age two, he had come to them after a year of being cared for by an elderly aunt who could barely take care of herself. He immediately took to Nathan, becoming his shadow whenever he was home from work. Even now, he sidled up to his foster father, who picked him up to sit on his lap while waiting for Daniel to make his next move. Nathan tousled Ben's hair and cuddled him close.

Lydia smiled and returned to her mending.

"I saw Ted and Carrie today," she said to Nathan.

"Oh?" he replied absently.

"They would like to adopt a child. Maybe two."

Nathan looked up as he wrapped his arm protectively around Benjamin. "Really?"

"I told them I thought that was a wonderful idea."

"You did?"

"Certainly. There are so many children who need loving homes and I think they would be exceptional parents. Don't you?"

"Yes. Yes, I do, but . . ."

"But not Benjamin, right?" She smiled at him with understanding. "No, not Ben. He belongs to us." And she wondered if they would ever be able to part with any child who came to them.

"Nathan?"

"Hmm?" He had returned to his board game, still holding Ben on his knee.

"Remember when Richard Davis resigned from council?"

"Yes," he replied, his attention still on the game.

"You know, it's never been filled."

"So I've heard." Daniel made a few moves across the board and Nathan groaned in defeat while Ben clapped his hands to cheer the winner.

"I was thinking about running for the position."

"What position?"

"Nathan." She turned to stare at him. "You aren't listening to me."

"I am now," he said, and he swung Benjamin high making him squeal with delight. Then he came to sit in the chair next to her. "What position?"

"On the council." She resumed her stitching.

He frowned, studying her. "You want to be a council member? Why?"

"Well, I just thought it would be nice to have a woman's point of view. That's all."

Without replying, he continued to watch her until at last she looked up from her mending. "What are you staring at?" she asked, tilting her head.

"You."

"And what do you see?" she asked, smiling at him.

"A very unusual woman."

"I am not."

"Yes, you are. But I wouldn't change a thing, even if I could."

"Which you can't."

"So then, why are you asking me about the position on council?" His eyes twinkled at having trapped her into admitting that she had already made up her mind.

"Just to be nice, I guess," she replied, and threw a sock at him.

He caught it and grinned. She knew that look in his eye and started putting her mending away, keeping her gaze locked with his.

"I guess it's getting late," he said, making silent promises to her.

"Past time for a school night," she replied, making a few promises of her own.

Nathan banked the fires while Lydia readied the children for bed. Then both of them made the rounds to say good night. When they reached their own bedroom, the one that had been Lydia's before they were married, he closed the door and she stepped into the circle of his arms.

"When are we going to get that furnace?" she asked.

"I don't think we'll need one tonight." He carefully backed her toward the bed.

"But it's so cold in here with the door closed."

"Then we'll build a fire of our own."

She let him undress her and hardly noticed the temperature of the room. Then he pulled back the covers for her to crawl in, and he followed as soon as he shed his clothes. Snuggled together, bare skin to bare skin, he teased and tempted, until she flung the covers away.

"Too hot," she said, but he was relentless as he kissed and caressed her, and finally in their ultimate embrace they lay together, dripping with sweat.

"Forget the furnace," she said, and he grinned into the moist heat of her neck.

"I thought you'd see it my way."

"You are unfair," she replied, biting his ear.

"Ow!"

"Shhh. The children will hear you."

"All right, but stop biting or else I'll . . ." He reached around to pinch her bottom.

"Uh-uh. I wouldn't do that," she warned.

"Okay, truce."

"Truce."

They lay quietly together, their damp bodies exposed to the chilling air.

"I'm getting cold," he said.

"I win." And she pulled the covers over them, smiling as he pinned her to the mattress.

MELODY MORGAN

Defiant Hearts

By the Bestselling Author of *Abiding Love*

To Katie O'Rourke, a pioneer of the daguerreotype, capturing the lives of everyday people on film while wagonning west is going to be the adventure of her life. But having to share that dream with a bossy, arrogant, and ruggedly handsome man infuriates the young photographer.

Since Spence McCord owes Tim O'Rourke a favor for saving his life, he promises to deposit Katie on her brother's Colorado doorstep. But Spence never imagines that repaying his debt of gratitude will lead to battling harsh prairie fires, fiendish outlaws, and the irresistible beauty of the independent redhead.

From New York to Colorado, Katie and Spence's passion mounts beneath the prairie skies. But it will take more than Spence's warm embrace to convince Katie's defiant heart that his picture of blissful love is worth more than a thousand words.

_4053-0 $4.99 US/$5.99 CAN

Dorchester Publishing Co., Inc.
P.O. Box 6640
Wayne, PA 19087-8640

Please add $1.75 for shipping and handling for the first book and $.50 for each book thereafter. NY, NYC, and PA residents, please add appropriate sales tax. No cash, stamps, or C.O.D.s. All orders shipped within 6 weeks via postal service book rate. Canadian orders require $2.00 extra postage and must be paid in U.S. dollars through a U.S. banking facility.

Name_____
Address_____
City_____ State_____ Zip_____
I have enclosed $_____ in payment for the checked book(s).
Payment <u>must</u> accompany all orders. ☐ Please send a free catalog.

SONYA BIRMINGHAM

Song of the Lark

When the beautiful wisp of a mountain girl walks through his front door, Stephen Wentworth knows there is some kind of mistake. The flame-haired beauty in trousers is not the nanny he envisions for his mute son Tad. But one glance from Jubilee Jones's emerald eyes, and the widower's icy heart melts and his blood warms. Can her mountain magic soften Stephen's hardened heart, or will their love be lost in the breeze, like the song of the lark?

___4393-9 $5.50 US/$6.50 CAN

Dorchester Publishing Co., Inc.
P.O. Box 6640
Wayne, PA 19087-8640

Please add $1.75 for shipping and handling for the first book and $.50 for each book thereafter. NY, NYC, and PA residents, please add appropriate sales tax. No cash, stamps, or C.O.D.s. All orders shipped within 6 weeks via postal service book rate. Canadian orders require $2.00 extra postage and must be paid in U.S. dollars through a U.S. banking facility.

Name_____
Address_____
City_____State_____Zip_____
I have enclosed $_____ in payment for the checked book(s).
Payment <u>must</u> accompany all orders. ❑ Please send a free catalog.
        CHECK OUT OUR WEBSITE! www.dorchesterpub.com

ELIZABETH CRANE

Time Remembered. Fed up with the boring wimps she dates, Jody Farnell puts all her energy into restoring a decaying antebellum mansion. And among the ruins of Whitefriars, the young architect discovers the diary of a man from another century who fascinates her like no other and a voodoo doll that whisks her back one hundred years to his time.

___52223-3 $5.50 US/$6.50 CAN

Reflections in Time. When practical-minded Renata O'Neal submits to hypnosis to cure her insomnia, she never expects to wake up in 1880s Louisiana—or fall in love with fiery Nathan Blue. But vicious secrets and Victorian sensibilities threaten to keep Renata and Nathan apart...until Renata vows that nothing will separate her from the most deliciously alluring man of any century.

___52089-3 $4.99 US/$6.99 CAN

Elaine Fox
Untamed Angel

Bestselling Author of *Hand & Heart of a Soldier*

With a name that belies his true nature, Joshua Angell was born for deception. So when sophisticated and proper Ava Moreland first sees the sexy drifter in a desolate Missouri jail, she knows he is the one to save her sister from a ruined reputation and a fatherless child. But she will need Angell to fool New York society into thinking he is the ideal husband—and only Ava can teach him how. But what start as simple lessons in etiquette and speech soon become smoldering lessons in love. And as the beautiful socialite's feelings for Angell deepen, so does her passion—and finally she knows she will never be satisfied until she, and no other, claims him as her very own...untamed angel.

___4274-6 $4.99 US/$5.99 CAN

Dorchester Publishing Co., Inc.
P.O. Box 6640
Wayne, PA 19087-8640

Please add $1.75 for shipping and handling for the first book and $.50 for each book thereafter. NY, NYC, and PA residents, please add appropriate sales tax. No cash, stamps, or C.O.D.s. All orders shipped within 6 weeks via postal service book rate. Canadian orders require $2.00 extra postage and must be paid in U.S. dollars through a U.S. banking facility.

Name_____

Address_____

City_____ State_____ Zip_____

I have enclosed $_____ in payment for the checked book(s).

Payment <u>must</u> accompany all orders. ❑ Please send a free catalog.

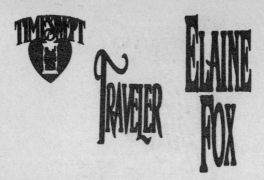

With a thriving business and a stalled personal life, Shelby Manning never figures her life is any worse—or better—than the norm. Then a late-night stroll through a Civil War battlefield park leads her to a most intriguing stranger. Bloody, confused, and dressed in Union blue, he insists he has just come from the Battle of Fredericksburg—more than one hundred years in the past.

Maybe Shelby should dismiss Carter Lindsey as crazy—just another history reenactor taking his game a little too seriously. But there is something compelling in the pull of his eyes, something special in his tender touch. And before she knows it, Shelby finds herself swept into a passion like none she's ever known—and willing to defy time itself to keep Carter at her side.

_52074-5 $4.99 US/$6.99 CAN

Dorchester Publishing Co., Inc.
P.O. Box 6640
Wayne, PA 19087-8640

Please add $1.75 for shipping and handling for the first book and $.50 for each book thereafter. NY, NYC, and PA residents, please add appropriate sales tax. No cash, stamps, or C.O.D.s. All orders shipped within 6 weeks via postal service book rate. Canadian orders require $2.00 extra postage and must be paid in U.S. dollars through a U.S. banking facility.

Name_____
Address_____
City_____State_____Zip_____
I have enclosed $_____ in payment for the checked book(s).
Payment <u>must</u> accompany all orders. ☐ Please send a free catalog.

A WANTED MAN.
AN INNOCENT WOMAN.
A WANTON LOVE!

Renegade Heart
Madeline Baker

When beautiful Rachel Halloran took Logan Tyree into her home, he was unconscious. A renegade Indian with a bullet wound in his side and a price on his head, he needed her help. But to Rachel he was nothing but trouble, a man whose dark sensuality made her long for forbidden pleasures; to her father he was the answer to a prayer, a gunslinger whose legendary skill could rid the ranch of a powerful enemy.

But Logan Tyree would answer to no man—and to no woman. If John Halloran wanted his services, he would have to pay dearly for them. And if Rachel wanted his loving, she would have to give up her innocence, her reputation, her very heart and soul.

_4085-9 $5.99 US/$6.99 CAN